The Fiery

"Don't leave me, Fian," Aileen whispered. "Three times now you've saved my life. Superstition has it that after the third time I owe you a favor."

"I don't need any favors." Tyson's voice was hoarse.

"Is sharing warmth too much to take? As you said the night we slept in the haystack, we had to keep warm, and after all, we almost died together, then as now. . . ."

Her eyes were like the Irish sky pulling him down, and so he knelt there still.

The blood raced in his head, and he watched the light of a single candle near the bed throw shadows off her face. He wanted very badly to lay his head between her breasts.

She reached out and shyly began to unbutton the shirt he wore. "Why should other women have the Fian and not me?"

Innocent girl. He lay down beside her. "What if I told you no woman has ever had the Fian?"

FIRES OF MIDNIGHT

KAREN FINNIGAN

DIAMOND BOOKS, NEW YORK

FIRES OF MIDNIGHT

A Diamond Book / published by arrangement with
the author

PRINTING HISTORY
Diamond edition / February 1991

ISBN: 1-55773-458-5

Diamond Books are published by The Berkley Publishing Group,
200 Madison Avenue, New York, New York 10016.
The name "DIAMOND" and its logo
are trademarks belonging to Charter Communications, Inc.

PRINTED IN THE UNITED STATES OF AMERICA

10 9 8 7 6 5 4 3 2 1

To my father,
Olaf Wattum,
who was my *first* hero

Acknowledgments

For invaluable critiques, as well as generous advice and encouragement, I wish to thank Charlou Dolan, Pat Tracy, and Sherry Roseberry. My deepest appreciation goes also to the members of Southern Idaho Romance Writers of America.

Author's Note

Among Irish folklore some of the most frequently anthologized stories are those of Finn MacCumhal or the Fian (pronounced *Fee-áhn,* accent on the last syllable). Stories place the Fian in the second or third century, when he served Cormac, legendary king of Ireland, whose palace was known as Tara and whose royal militia bore the name Fianna.

Chief of the Fianna—until his death in a great battle—had been the Fian's father. From that tragic day forward young Fian lived to pursue the Fianna's enemies and avenge his father's death. This younger Fian knew so many brave and heroic adventures that eventually he came to follow in his father's footsteps as leader of the Fianna himself.

And after him, now and then through the centuries, whenever Ireland was most in need of a hero, other men came taking the name Fian. . . .

Ah Love! could thou and I with Fate conspire
To grasp this sorry Scheme of Things entire,
Would not we shatter it to bits—and then
Remould it nearer to the Heart's Desire!

—The *Rubáiyát of Omar Khayyám*
Edward Fitzgerald, trans., First edition

FIRES OF MIDNIGHT

Prologue

Ireland, 1824

FROM SOMEWHERE IN the distant darkness Tyson Winslow could hear the pounding of horses' hooves and the rumble of wheels. Bystanders on the quay scattered. Suddenly alarmed, Tyson stood up from the boat deck and watched in growing horror as horses appeared, whipped into a wild frenzy, a carriage careening behind them. In their deadly path stood his mother, and before he could even think the word *danger,* he saw her tangle with the hooves. The scene blurred into a scream that trailed off . . . the sudden screech of carriage brakes . . . people running. Terror wreaked havoc on the docks.

"Ma . . ." With thirteen-year-old agility Tyson jumped off the plank leading from the boat and raced toward the accident, fighting panic as everywhere people blocked his way, big people with shoulders and arms and legs that wouldn't move. "Let me through," he demanded in a choked voice. All the while his disbelieving mind tried to say, *It's a trick—a trick of the banshee.*

No sooner had he squeezed past the last elbow when a

man reached out and held him back. "Stay, lad. 'Tis not a pleasant scene."

"But she's my mother. . . . She's come to meet me. . . ." Desperate, he flailed against the burly long-shoreman, whose strong grasp prevented him from going closer, and he strained to see through the curious people. Wharf buildings loomed like giant sentinels. Gulls dipped from the sky, and the pungent salt smell of the docks and the Irish Sea imprinted itself in his memory. In the center of the thickening crowd stood an elegant phaeton, its skittish horses held in check by a dockhand. Directly behind the carriage's path, just yards away, lay his mother, dressed in the black shawl of Ireland and her own blood.

The high-strung team pulling the phaeton had felled her on the dock as if she were no more than a tender sapling, and this in full view of passengers disembarking from the boat. "Poor colleen," women murmured. Men spoke in hushed Gaelic. A priest moved to his mother to administer last rites. And still big hands held Tyson back. No one seemed to understand. "That's my mother. . . . I have to get to her," he pleaded, struggling.

The dandy who'd commanded the reins of the phaeton—an inebriated rake dressed in a bottle-green coat—staggered over to the woman. Obviously, not of majority, his face showed not a trace of remorse, and Tyson felt cold suddenly.

The dandy made a fastidious brush at the sleeve of his coat. "I say now, that was jolly rude of us, wasn't it?"

"Terribly," came his companion's reply. "I wish I'd as much c-claret left to drink as she's spilled blood." A hiccup punctuated this young man's words, and as Tyson watched, the fellow lurched against the open side of the stylish phaeton.

With a sneer the green-coated dandy stood looking down

at Tyson's mother. Relief apparent in his gaze, he turned away from the broken woman.

"It's only an Irish," he spat out in a voice loud enough to carry not just to his companion, but to Tyson as well. The driver's accent gave him away as English. He staggered back to the carriage and with the ebony handle of the whip tapped his companion on the shoulder. "Father says you're not a man until you've killed one Irish pig. Did you know that?"

"I daresay I do n-now," his friend replied with a hiccup.

At the callous words the murmurs of the crowd suddenly took on a hostile tone. Instantly sober, the pair of dandies looked up, as if the idea of being hemmed in by a mob became a distasteful possibility. They climbed back up into their carriage. "Stand away from those horses, my good man." The dandy's imperious tone matched the cut of his coat.

At the same time the numbing fog lifted from Tyson's mind. With one last desperate effort he broke loose from the arms that held him back and ran to the phaeton.

"You conceited English dogs!" Screaming curses, he tried to climb up after the young men, but the whip came down on his hand, once, twice, three times, and Tyson fell back to the ground, doubled over from the excruciating pain. At once the carriage and horses drove off, scattering bystanders.

Rising, Tyson let his grief-numbed gaze follow the carriage. "Don't think I won't find out who you are!" he screamed, his voice hoarsening. Swiping at his tears, he made quieter vows. "Someday I'll find you both, and I'll bring you to ruin. No, I'll kill you. . . ." His words trailed off into sobs.

His mother moaned, and Tyson ran to her. She still lived. She needed him.

Numb with shock, he dropped to his knees and bent over her. "Mother . . ." Words caught in his throat, and he swallowed hard.

"Ty . . ." Her faint voice wavered.

"Ma, don't leave me." Whispering, he began to talk to her, encouraging her, reminding her of their plans, touching her face gently. "You're taking me home tonight for Whitsuntide, and you'll tell me the legends about the Irish warrior—the Fian. Remember, the last time we said good-bye, you told me there was one more tale yet to be told? You were saving it for me. Mother"—his voice rose in anxiety—"you'll mend. I'll help you." He'd lived his mother's stories a million times in his imagination while sitting bored at his uncle's English estate, plotting a way to escape, if only through thoughts, counting the months till his next holiday in Ireland. She *had* to live.

With obvious effort, Bridget O'Ryan Winslow opened her eyes to gaze with love upon her son's handsome face, now streaked with his tears and her blood.

"Sure"—she coughed, then continued—"and you can tell the story yourself, son. . . ." Slow and labored her words came, obviously at cost of great pain. She coughed again, then her hand went limp.

Overcome, Tyson wasn't aware of what he did next until he felt his face touch the cold ground. At first he couldn't breathe for the lump in his throat, then jerky sobs shook him.

After a few moments he raised up, tears still burning down his face. Ignoring the bite of cold, he removed his woolen coat and folded it to cushion his mother's head from the dirt. Her black hair spread over the makeshift pillow. He touched her hands, hands that had cradled him, held him with affection. With a trembling arm he made the sign of the cross over her.

Tyson felt the priest patting his shoulder, a signal that it was time to move the body, and the finality of this cruel twist of fate swept over him.

Checking his sobs, he took a deep breath, kissed his mother's cheek, then stood up tall, staring off across the sea, his shoulders straight as his mother had taught him.

If he'd thought of himself as half English, after this night both heart and soul disowned that allegiance. He was henceforth all Irish.

And he would have an Irishman's revenge.

One

MIST HUNG IN the sky from an impending shower, and in the distance shadows draped the Wicklow Hills in lavender.

Mary Aileen Connolly had lingered far too long. Still she couldn't leave, not yet. She spoke in a whispered voice that men who tried to woo her called dulcet—sweet and soft. Except today her tone expressed pain as well.

"I will lift up mine eyes unto the hills . . ." she began. Never had she felt so alone or longed so for strong arms to comfort her. A good man she'd never known, except her father, and she'd have given anything to have his arms about her now.

But perhaps that wish was a bargain with the Devil, she worried, putting the thought away. She concentrated on reciting the psalm and cast her eyes downward to where her hands were clasped at the waist of her black dress. She should leave. Grieving should not keep her any longer from those God had spared.

God had not spared many. Only two brothers. Three counting the one already in America. Typhoid fever had raged through this little village, ignoring some families, devastating others. And now before her, amongst the headstones and Celtic crosses, lay the graves of her father and mother and two baby sisters.

As she stood there, the rain began, and she pulled her shawl close over her hair. With head bowed she watched the rivulets of water pour off the four fresh mounds of sod. A single raindrop angled its way down her face. She felt so miserably lonely that nothing could disturb her vigil—until the sound of a whip cracked through the distance like a thunderclap. Still reciting the psalm, she looked up to the hills at the road from Dublin and the words ". . . shall preserve thee from evil . . ." died in her throat. A too familiar dark coach was outlined against the beautiful lavender shadows of the distant hills. Black it was, like a spider crawling along on those vermilion wheels. The landlord, who some said broke bread with the Devil, was coming.

At the farm bordering the churchyard Aileen saw the O'Hurleys pause in the digging of potatoes and look up at the hills. Mrs. O'Hurley crossed herself, and Aileen could well imagine her thoughts and those of everyone in the village—wondering whose farm the landlord would visit, each family hoping it wouldn't be theirs. Aileen could have reassured them. It was her farm he'd come for. Ever since he'd seen her spying on him at his whiskey still, she'd known someday he'd come.

Again Aileen regretted wishing for anything, particularly the feel of manly arms in comfort, for Lord Fitzwilliam had a way of turning wishes into nightmares. Too often she'd heard stories in the village of how the master was more concerned with his profits than with a tenant's health and well being. And then, with her own eyes she'd seen his evil ways.

With the flat of her palm Aileen wiped the mixture of
tears and rain from her face, then, picking up the hem of her
black skirt, she ran away from the churchyard and across
the fields. She headed straight for the thin plume of smoke
that rose above the thatched roof of the two-hundred-
year-old Connolly cottage.

By the time she reached the stoop, she was winded, and
her shoulders rose and fell while she caught her breath.
Scarcely noticing her cold chapped hands, she reached for
the door latch, and when she flung open the door to the
small kitchen, she was just in time to see one of her brothers
knock over the last geranium pot with the broom. The cat
took advantage of Aileen's entrance to jump behind her
skirts and hide from such a wicked instrument of destruc-
tion.

Her brothers were quarreling again, with Patrick getting
the worst of it. For a precious minute Aileen stood there
watching them. They were all she had left, and argue
though they would, love for them overflowed from her
heart.

Seamus was the spitting image of Aileen, even to his
heart-shaped face and the dusting of freckles on the bridge
of his nose. His eyes were a less vivid blue, and his hair
closer to brown than black. But the features had been made
from God's same mold. The younger lad's hair, on the other
hand, was nearly as red as the geranium petals that lay
scattered on the floor.

"It's no fair, Seamus," he complained loudly to his
brother, "you always get to play the Fian and make me be
the English. I want to be the Fian."

His big brother remained crouched behind the butter
churn and, with the tip of a knife handle, expertly flipped a
gooseberry across the room, where it landed on the hearth
next to a griddle of soda bread. With his withered right hand

close to his side, he reached with his left hand into his pocket for more berries. His brother continued to complain.

"You're too little to be the Fian." Seamus looked over at Aileen in the doorway, but if he noticed his sister had been crying, he did not let on. "Isn't Patrick too little, Aileen?"

As soon as she hung her shawl on a hook, she rescued the broom from Patrick. "Don't take advantage of your brother, Seamus. And don't be forgetting I've told you, one more gooseberry fight and it's to your bed with no supper."

But her heart wasn't in her threat. Seamus was right. Patrick *was* too little—too little for everything that had happened—certainly too little to be left with no one to protect him but an eighteen-year-old sister.

And now that dreaded coach was coming, the master's coach, the landlord of their farm. Aileen shivered. They said bad things happened in threes. A failed crop. Death. And now the landlord. She was only surprised it had taken him this long to hear the news and come.

"I'm not little," Patrick was arguing with a fire in his voice to match his red hair. "Da says I'm big. Ma says I can—" He stopped abruptly, swallowing hard. Below his red curls his eyes shone with tears. He'd had such a hard time these last days remembering he could no longer speak of his parents in the present tense.

With an anguished look the eight-year-old followed his sister around the room while she swept up the spilled dirt and pieces of geranium.

"Aileen, I want to be the Fian. Make Seamus play fair." His words conveyed a larger loss than the role in a game.

Aileen set the broom beside the hearth, then swung a kettle of water over the peat fire. Potatoes boiled in their jackets it would be for supper, and she dropped the vegetables into the water. When Patrick didn't let up, she turned and gave him a gentle look. "Fair, Patrick? No.

There may be leprechauns for certain, but in this life there's no such thing as fair."

When she leaned over to stir up the fire, her dark hair—hair the black of a moonless night—fell about her shoulders. If her shoulders bent a bit more than usual, it was from larger than ordinary cares. Only half a sack of flour, some leavening, and one tin of tea remained. And as for potatoes, the crop had not been good. Turning her head, she listened again for the sound of the coach.

When she heard it coming down the village lane, worries about food fled before greater troubles. If only the landlord hadn't heard about the deaths. If only her big brother would reply to her letter.

"Hush, now, boys. The landlord's coming. Be good and he may let us stay till Roddy sends the rent from America." The sound of horses' hooves and lumbering wheels grew steadily louder.

"Don't worry, Aileen," Seamus said. "If Roddy doesn't answer in time, then you must write a letter to the Fian. Tell him what happened to Ma and Da and Kathleen and baby Kerry. Sure and he'll help us pay the landlord."

Suddenly concerned at her brother's abundance of fantasy, Aileen walked over and laid a hand on the older boy's shoulder, the only gesture of affection he'd allowed lately. "Seamus," she explained gently, a little frown creasing her brow, "this Fian in your game was a legend from the old days."

"No, Aileen, he's not."

She tried to smile but couldn't. In the background she kept hearing the sound of the coach coming ever closer, and she felt like a moth about to be drawn into an evil web. The man approaching in that spidery coach, her landlord, was operating illegal whiskey stills, competing with the villagers' own attempts to augment their paltry incomes. Worse, some weeks ago she'd made the mistake of letting him see her spy on him.

Sighing, she tried to temper her brother's imagination. "The Fian's only a story. It's important to remember such stories. Now that Da's gone, you're the keeper of the tales and old ways for the family. But remember they are just that—stories that can't come true." Her stomach knotted in apprehension.

Seamus had stubbornness written all over his face. "I know . . . and I'll keep Da's stories. But, still," he argued, his voice rising with emotion, "the Fian *is* more than a tale. He's real, and I know he'll help us."

"The Fian can't help us," she said firmly. Seamus was so fanciful that no amount of reasoning would ever change him.

True to form, her brother continued to argue. "The Fian *is* a real person. Roddy said so before he left for America." While he spoke, he reached out moodily with his foot and squashed a single gooseberry left from his earlier play.

Aileen removed another kettle from the hearth and poured boiling water into the teapot, then turned to her brother, wishing she had a storybook answer. "Seamus, no one, not the Fian, not even King Cormac, can help us if Lord Fitzwilliam decides to take our land."

The carriage sounded ominously close to the cottage. Both young boys—Patrick with the cat in his arms—elbowed each other for a spot in the narrow recess of the window. After a quick look through the rain-splashed glass, they flanked their sister and tugged for her attention.

"Lord Fitzwilliam is here," Seamus whispered.

"No!" little Patrick shouted, and dumped the cat from his arms. Like a young master protecting his home, he moved to block the door with his sturdy body. "Da didn't like the landlord, and I do na either."

"Nor I, Patrick," his sister agreed, "but keep your tongue and try to show your manners." Her voice trembled. Because her father had always dealt with this man, she wasn't sure what to say. On impulse she grabbed a wooden-handled knife from the hearth and slid it down the high top of her boot.

Outside, the sounds were unmistakable. A coachman's voice calling, "Whoa," was followed by the rattle of a heavy harness. The pound of horses' hooves suddenly quieted. Coach springs creaked and a door slammed, followed by footsteps on the gravel.

Aileen stood stock-still waiting for a knock on the door.

Seamus watched his sister. "Sure and he'll let us stay here?" Some of the earlier bravado had left his voice.

"I hope so." Aileen felt utterly alone.

A moment later the door burst open, and Aileen gestured for her brothers to stay close by her.

Lord Fitzwilliam, Aileen noted, did not trouble himself to knock, but with a proprietary air strode right in, the mud from his boots dirtying the hard earthen floor. Standing six feet and then some, he looked like a castle turret and smelled as though surrounded by a moat of whiskey. From his fleshy face narrowed eyes gleamed at Aileen, who'd positioned herself and her brothers behind a table.

"You look comely in that black dress," Lord Fitzwilliam observed with no preamble of sympathies whatsoever. "You've grown up since I've been here last."

Except for the slight flush that stole over her face, Aileen made no response. This was no time for compliments. To wish away the typhoid, she would be ugly and wear sackcloth, she thought to herself. Struggling to bite her tongue and mind her own manners, she looked uneasily at the muscled steward who walked in the landlord's wake, raindrops dripping from his coat.

Aileen drew her brothers close to her in the suddenly cramped room. A hand on each of their shoulders warned them to remain quiet while the two men strolled around the little room, as if inspecting the place. Lord Fitzwilliam raised an amused eyebrow and fingered the fine crochet work bordering the linen tablecloth.

Irritated, Aileen watched in silence, hating the way he touched her grandmother's treasured handiwork.

She swallowed hard, wishing he'd get it over with and state his business. Maybe he'd forgotten about her accidental appearance at his secret whiskey stills. Then, too suddenly to suit her taste, his features hardened and he spoke to her.

"You're all alone now. You can't work this farm yourself."

"I'm not alone. Seamus can do a man's work on the farm, and Patrick's a good worker, too." Her voice wavered, and she paused to draw a steadying breath before saying the words she'd heard her father say many a time. "By spring we'll have the rent."

"Aye, you might, but then again you might not. Seamus isn't yet fourteen and hasn't the strength of a man. . . ." Lord Fitzwilliam's gaze swept over the boy in a dismissive way. He walked to the hearth, where he poked the wall and peered up at the ceiling. When he glanced suddenly over at Aileen, she had the uncomfortable feeling of being inspected herself.

"It's better if I oversee the place from now on," he said.

Momentarily at a loss for words, Aileen tried to imagine what her father would say. Da would reason clearly and logically, but with respect. "Sure and your lordship has more pressing matters than wanting to worry over a little farm like ours. You'll grant us time to hear from our brother, won't you? Roddy will send us money from America."

"I cannot wait for the ship from America. Forty days it takes in good weather. No, I'm taking back what's mine. You mustn't fear, though. You'll be provided for." Lord Fitzwilliam took a step toward her.

Aileen put up a hand of protest and moved to keep the table between them. "No. Stay back. I'm the oldest in the family left now, and I won't let you near us. If you touch any of us, I'll—I'll tell in confession and then God will punish you."

His face split in a lascivious grin. "Punish me for what?"

"For your greed."

Lord Fitzwilliam placed his hands on the other side of the table and confronted Aileen. "I'm not greedy, colleen. On the contrary, I'm most generous. I've allowed you to stay on here a week and do your grieving. Yes, I'd call that most generous on my part . . . considering how you've spied on me."

Her throat dry with fear, Aileen could only hope her face didn't reflect that emotion. When she spoke, her words came out in a rush. "We've lived here in this village all our lives. We've nowhere else to go."

Horrified at her outburst, she stopped. This wasn't at all how her father would have talked to the landlord. She picked up the teapot to still her shaking hands. "This is home," she said.

"As to that," he began, looking at her as if to gauge her reaction, "you three are evicted, but . . ." He looked at their shocked faces then continued. "To prove I'm a benevolent landlord, I'm not turning you out on the road. I've arranged a more suitable future for you."

Aileen slammed the teapot down onto the table so hard

the handle cracked. "You've no say in what happens to me and my brothers. My brothers stay with me."

Lord Fitzwilliam displayed a crafty smile, but said nothing.

Patrick moved forward to tug at his big sister's sleeve. "Aileen, I don't want to go with him."

With a quick hug she reassured him. "It's all right, Patrick. I'll take care of you."

Seamus sauntered bravely to the middle of the room, shaking back a lock of dark hair from his forehead. Then, with his withered hand hidden in his pocket, he took up the defense. "The Fian is coming to Ireland soon. I heard it from Roddy's best friend, whose brother works in the underground and goes on midnight raids. The Fian doesn't like English landlords. He'll help us get rid of you English, then we'll have our own Parliament here in Ireland some-day. Roddy said so. The Fian's coming to help us."

"No, Seamus." Aileen took a step in the direction of her brother. "Mind your tongue."

But Lord Fitzwilliam held up a dismissive hand to Aileen and gave the thirteen-year-old his undivided attention. "Well, said, lad, though you've got it quite backwards. It's your sister here who'll go to the Fian."

"What do you mean?" Aileen felt her blood turn cold.

Lord Fitzwilliam merely smiled at her question as he did at the bravado of little Patrick, who declared with eight-year-old decisiveness, "I don't want Aileen to go anywhere."

"Hush, Patrick, I'll make it right," soothed Aileen, who assumed Lord Fitzwilliam's words were merely a threat. After all, he wouldn't really take them away from each other. "You'll stay safe with me. I'll never leave you." With both hands she tenderly cupped the little redhead's face. "I promise. Please believe me, Patrick."

Patrick looked up with a worried version of his sister's own blue eyes, listening intently to her promise, and she decided then and there to take them all to the O'Hurleys' house. Let Lord Fitzwilliam have the cottage if it had to be, but Thomas and Annie would find room for them until Roddy could send money. Yes, then they would all go to America. With a quick kiss for her brother's cheek, she ruffled his hair.

Lord Fitzwilliam growled in impatience. "Enough of this female chattering. Now be tending to your supper, Aileen Connolly, and let me discuss this matter with the boys. They're the men in the family now, and it's more fitting to talk business with them."

Feeling a surge of hope that the landlord might even yet have a change of heart, Aileen watched him motion her brothers and the steward outside, then shut the door of the cottage behind them.

Wary of provoking the landlord with another humiliating outburst, she didn't attempt to interfere, but listened to the sounds of her brothers' voices, knowing Seamus would try his best to fill the role of man of the house. She turned back to the hearth where the potatoes boiled and the pan of soda bread warmed.

After testing the potatoes with a fork, she cut up the soda bread into small pieces. It was only gradually she realized the talking had ceased. Outside it was too quiet. Even the cat seemed to have vanished. On an impulse she set down the fork and moved to the single window, where she peered out into the deepening twilight.

Alarm sliced through her heart. Her stomach knotted. She couldn't see anyone. Where had the landlord taken her brothers?

She rushed to the door and flung it open. "Seamus. Patrick. Come here—now!"

"Aileen. He's taking us away." She barely heard the muted voice of Patrick, but she'd comforted his cries in the night so often these past days, she could recognize his slightest sound. What she saw made her heart catch in her throat.

Her brother struggled to get out of the landlord's ugly coach. But more men than simply the steward had accompanied Lord Fitzwilliam. In fact, he'd hidden them with the same cleverness with which he'd concealed his illegal whiskey operation. Now the steward himself pushed Patrick back inside the coach and slammed the door. Immediately a small face topped by a thatch of red hair pressed itself to the glass, fingers spread wide on either side. Someone—a thug dressed as a footman—jerked the boy away.

Panic welling inside her, Aileen darted from the doorway and ran smack into Lord Fitzwilliam, who had moved with surprising speed to intercept her, grabbing her elbows and immobilizing her effortlessly. But only for a moment. Fear gave her unexpected strength, and she struggled to get loose. Her heart pounded from the effort, as she tried to jerk away, but he merely tightened his grip.

The coach began to roll away, the two boys at the window, one beating at the glass, the other crying. Aileen died a little inside, then recoiled and swiftly kicked the landlord in the shin.

His calf-high boots had been fashioned of the hardest leather, she discovered. Her kick stung her own toes but provoked no more from him than mocking laughter.

"Bring them back, you bloody bastard!" She tugged away from his grip. "Let me go. May the Devil see you in hell, and may the road rise up to take you there faster."

For an indolent landlord Lord Fitzwilliam had the surprising strength of a country farmhand, Aileen discovered.

"Why? Why are you doing this?" she begged.

"You had best learn, colleen," he said, "that my wishes are all that count. No one interferes with my plans. You asked for this when you spied on my private business. Now that your father's gone, I'll do what I need to keep it private."

"I won't tell."

"Ah, but I can't take that chance. I've a lot at stake."

With raw desperation she sank her teeth into his hand.

He flinched but held her still. "Tie her," he said in a rough voice to an invisible accomplice. "And gag her."

From out of the twilight stepped two more liveried men. Aileen felt rope bind her wrists, and suddenly too numb to struggle, she scarcely cared what they did to her. Heartsick, stomach turning, she watched the coach fade into the horizon. Her gaze didn't waver until the coach was a wee thing down the road. Guilt washed over her. She should never have left her brothers alone with this greedy Englishman.

"Where have you sent them?" she asked. Her words were unnaturally calm, like the air before thunder.

"To London," he said with emphasis on the second word. Lord Fitzwilliam's voice sounded too close to her ear. "I've sent them to London, where strong Irish lads learn what real work is."

"No-o, no-o." London. She'd heard tales of its size, its wickedness. How would she ever find them? When she flailed out at him, her fury matched her words. "A curse on you! May all your crops fail from now till the resurrection of Saint Patrick."

"I told you to shut her up!" he yelled at his men, grabbing a rag himself and stuffing it in her mouth until she gagged and her eyes teared from the pain of it.

And then the landlord addressed her as if they were sharing a cup of tea. "Be proud of them, Aileen. They've become working lads," he commented, then added calmly, "and you . . . you've grown passionate as well as beautiful. I always fancied blue eyes myself. What a waste having to send you off like this." He flicked away a tear from her cheek.

She averted her face from his touch, and he slapped her. "Don't turn fey on us now, Aileen. You've an important task ahead with this man who calls himself Fian—you're to be mistress to him—a great honor that no ordinary street girl could provide. No, indeed, only a special Irish colleen could be chosen. You'll be perfect in the role."

She felt her eyes grow wide with confusion, knew the landlord saw tears shimmering in them.

"Oh, yes," the landlord said slyly. "I've heard all the taproom gossip and the scoffers who doubt his existence. In Ireland he may be a legend, but in England he's flesh and blood. In all the clubs and coffee houses, wagers are placed on his real identity. He'll no doubt fancy a spirited Irish girl like yourself. Who knows? You might even distract him from those bothersome riots he stirs up in London."

Again she came to life and kicked out at him, causing him to yell at his minions, his voice thunderous. "Do I need to help you get her on the horse?"

"She's a handful, milord."

"That's why I hired *two* of you. Now get her to Edmund Leedes at the Kingstown dock. He's a tough enough bloke to handle this spitfire—and even deliver her to the Fian safe and sound." As if privately amused, he burst out laughing. "Yes, safe and sound."

His laughter reverberated off Aileen's taut nerves. This man no doubt enjoyed caging wild birds and tossing the keys away while he laughed at their brave songs.

That could be the only reason for his laughter. As strong arms lifted her, the last words she heard spoke of greed.

"Make certain you bring back the amount of coins Leedes agreed to—not one shilling less."

Someone shoved her onto a wet horse, then pushed her skirt up and forced her leg over so that she rode like a man. Beyond humiliation, she grieved more than tears could show.

Lord Fitzwilliam's laughter echoed in her ears long after the cottage disappeared from sight. She'd sooner die than be a kept woman to any man, but she had two reasons to calm herself and pretend to stop fighting Lord Fitzwilliam's plan—Seamus and Patrick, who'd begged her, after all, to ask for the Fian's help.

Two

England

As soon as Tyson Winslow spotted the Romany camp in the meadow, he slowed his horse. Riding straight through to Liverpool would have been best, but for his horse's sake he decided to stop soon.

With quiet words he soothed the animal. "Take care, boy. Slower, Cormac, we're almost there."

Normally, the journey between London and Liverpool demanded twenty-three hours by mail coach and that with several changes of horses. For him—a lone rider with no change of horse—it took much longer, especially because the backroads he used to avoid people were rutted and rough. Now, on top of that, for the last few miles Cormac had been favoring his left foreleg. A brief stop awhile ago had verified the reason—as Tyson had suspected, the shoe was coming loose.

If he didn't see to it, Cormac would end up lame, and Tyson would miss the smuggling rendezvous at the Irish Sea. Months of planning would come to naught, and the fight for Irish independence would suffer a severe setback.

Tyson knew the Romany men frequently earned money as nomadic blacksmiths. If he approached these gypsies in a spirit of friendliness, they would not bother with his London identity like a village farrier might. Of course there'd be caution—on both their parts. But in addition, he hoped this particular band of gypsies would be hospitable, not simply for his horse's sake, but because some anonymous companionship with gypsies would ease the solitude of the long journey. With luck, they might know of the Fian from other friendly bands who had helped him in the past, willingly exchanging English silver for discreet silence.

After dismounting, he tethered Cormac to a tree near a meadow strewn with autumn golds, then walked undisguised toward the Romany camp. The haunting lilt of a violin led the way, but it wasn't long before the music ceased, and he knew the nomadic band had seen him approach.

Though he shared none of their blood, Tyson was as bronzed and dark-haired as any Romany, but in height taller. He'd been told by bolder London ladies that his features mirrored with an uncanny precision the strong-lined aristocratic likeness of his father that hung in the hallway of his uncle's estate. His uncle said much the same, though he never failed to point out the two chief differences—the hazel eyes and cleft chin of his Irish mother.

Nothing about his clothing, Tyson felt sure, revealed his identity. In black trousers and billowy white shirt open at the neck, he could probably pass for a villager strolling across the meadow. Only his aristocratic bearing might suggest a prominent Londoner.

Whoever had been playing the violin had vanished inside one of the vardos in the caravan, but dogs barked, and dark-skinned children stared in open curiosity. Gaily colored skirts swayed about the ankles of barefoot women who looked up only briefly before turning their attention back to the campfire and the task of cooking the evening meal. The pungent scent of herbs and cooking meat wove through the air. A young girl cast covert glances at him, then blushed and bent to her work.

So far these Romanies gave no sign of recognizing him, nor did he see any familiar face. The chief, an old man distinguished by his red embroidered vest, rose from his haunches and walked forward to meet him.

After a handshake and words of greeting in English, the chief said, "Other bands tell us of a gorgio who rides alone and resembles a Romany, except for his green eyes." His gaze locked with that of Tyson. "They say he is fighting the English." After he'd looked his visitor up and down, he asked, "Are you this gorgio the English call the Fian?"

Only for these gypsies would Tyson acknowledge his secret identity. He nodded.

"Is it our hospitality you seek?" the man asked.

"My horse threw a shoe."

The old chief nodded. "We will fix your horse's shoe, and you may share our food, but beyond that we will not go. If any English come seeking you, we will not help. We live apart from the gorgio and its conquering ways."

"You honor me with your hospitality," Tyson replied, accepting the chief's conditions and the offer of a meal.

Rabbit stew, gently herbed, and wild blackberries rich with autumn's nectar infinitely surpassed the hardtack and jerky he carried in his saddlebags.

He spent the evening in small talk, and the sun rode low, an orange ball in a sooty sky. No one asked his real name, nor did they ask of his past.

They conversed briefly of horses, and eventually the talk turned to storytelling. Mellower after the meal, Tyson's nomadic hosts told several tales. As a gesture of gratitude for his food, Tyson told one tale, an Irish legend of how the Fian came to lead Ireland's royal militia, and the Romanies nodded and smiled in appreciation.

At last, before the light faded completely, Tyson expressed his thanks and began walking toward his solitary camp where a newly shod Cormac awaited him.

Near the last vardo before the open stretch of meadow, a pretty girl with snapping black eyes intercepted him. With a wide smile, she held out for him a selection of scarves.

"Would the gorgio buy a scarf for his sweetheart?"

"I have no sweetheart." His statement echoed fact more than regret. The terse tone hid any feelings on the matter.

She smiled at him saucily. "But many women would *like* to be your love, would they not?"

"No," he said gently, "but I'll buy a scarf for myself." Taking the only dark-colored scarf in the girl's display, he flipped her a coin.

She deftly caught it in her palm and with a bold sashay and glint in her eye moved closer. "You would perhaps like me to read in your palm to see your future, to see if someone will be dear to your heart? You have a roguish smile, and I wager you know how to please a woman. Let me see the lines to prove it."

"No, just the scarf." She was pretty, and he regretted the Romany code that made gorgio men taboo to their women. "You must have a young man of your own waiting, don't you?" he asked, flashing a sudden grin.

With a coquettish laugh, the girl retorted, "My marriage will be arranged when the time comes. We are different from you English." Before he could reply, she moved away and vanished into the dusk.

Ah, but I'm not English, he thought as he continued the walk across the meadow to his camp.

Briefly he considered the women who awaited him in London, but the thought of them failed to stir in him anything much beyond physical memories and a certain cynicism. No, none of them were what he would call "sweethearts." He was, he realized, heartily bored with the feminine side of the beau monde—the marriage-minded mothers, the vapid daughters, and the petulant mistresses. A need far beyond a physical one shadowed him. The meal had filled him, but the conversation reminded him of how empty he was of companionship. These gypsies were companions for one night only, and loneliness was an ache as severe as a hunger pang.

Settling down on the ground in front of a small fire, Tyson stared across the meadow, listening to a haunting violin while darkness stole down on the landscape. Yes, he envied the vagabonds' freedom, their tight-knit families. Not for the first time, he wondered what his life might have held if he'd grown up in Ireland. Would he have a family of his own now?

As he slid the silken scarf between his thumb and forefinger, memories came unbidden like the stars of the night. His mother, crushed and broken by an Englishman's carriage. A boy's tears crystallizing into a man's revenge.

He reflected upon his uncle, the English uncle who'd been determined that only school in England would befit the sole heir to a peerage. To that end his uncle had not only taken custody of him but, after the tragic death of Tyson's mother, had sold the Irish farm as well. As if selling a square of sod and a stable of horses could cut out memories and love of all that was Irish. Someone would have to cut out his heart to do that.

Through the remainder of his boyhood, he'd suffered the persecution and taunts from other boys and engaged in daily fisticuffs. Even as he matured he'd endured the snide remarks and subtle innuendoes from proper gentlemen and learned the fine art of verbal debate. And all this as penalty for his father's audacity in marrying an Irish lass. Small wonder he counted the memories of his early years in Ireland as the best.

Most of all, he'd never forgotten his promise of revenge against his mother's murderer, a promise now tied in with Ireland's cause. And to that end, dozens of weapons on the west coast of England now waited to be smuggled across the Irish sea; waited for the arrival of him—the Fian.

Stuffing the scarf into his pocket, he pulled out the great cape he used as part of his Fian disguise, but which at night served as his blanket. In moments he'd arranged Cormac's saddle for a pillow and lay down for the night—alone.

As the sounds of crying filtered through her dream, Aileen awoke from a nap, pins and needles in her arms because of the awkward position in which she'd fallen asleep. The close space of the gently rocking ferryboat allowed little freedom of movement. People of all ages filled the lower boat deck, most with their life's possessions clutched tightly. Heartsick, Aileen stretched her arms up to relieve the stiffness.

Close by she heard weeping, tiny jerky sobs that took her mind off her own misery. She reached out for the hand of the slight girl who sat beside her on the swaying floor of the boat. At the touch of Aileen's hand, the girl sat up, her face blotched red from her tears.

Aileen swallowed back a lump in her throat, wondering if her brothers, especially Patrick, were crying. If so, she prayed someone would be there to comfort them, to feed them when they cried in hunger.

"Hello," she said softly to the girl, who looked no more

than fifteen. "It's going to be all right. We're only going to England, a few hours' journey. Are you seasick?"

With a shake of her head, the girl wept anew until Aileen had to reach over and take her in her arms. "I d-don't know anybody in England." Her tears dampened Aileen's bodice.

"Shh," Aileen said in a comforting voice. "Of course you know somebody in England."

"Who?" the girl hiccuped and wiped her eyes. A brown coil of hair bobbed above each ear.

"Why, me of course. Because you see, we've the rest of the boat ride to become friends, and by the time we get to England—in just a little while—you'll feel better because we'll know each other. Are you going to London after we dock in Liverpool? Do you have any family to send for?" she asked as she patted and stroked in an attempt to comfort her.

The girl shook her head miserably. "I'm an orphan. My ma was a seamstress, and that's all I know how to do, too. I don't even know which road goes to London. But it's no matter because I spent my last coins for passage to Liverpool."

"What's your name?" Aileen spoke quickly but reassuringly.

With naked gratitude in her eyes, the girl moved closer to Aileen, almost as if she'd never known a kind person in her life. " 'Tain't nobody asked me name since me ma died. It's Maeve. Maeve O'Brien."

"And I'm Aileen." She smiled encouragingly until finally she coaxed a smile from the poor girl and eventually a conversation that distracted Maeve from her homesickness and Aileen from her own sorrow. Somehow, telling Maeve about her brothers made it seem possible that she really would find them, and she felt grateful that Edmund Leedes, her escort, rode above deck with the other English, no doubt in more comfort, but Aileen would rather endure the discomfort of this lower deck than the company of Mr. Leedes.

When Aileen explained about Leedes to Maeve, she described him as a toad. "Yes, it's true," she declared to Maeve's shocked look. That was the kindest possible description of the man to whom Lord Fitzwilliam's minions had handed her over. "They did it in the shadows of the Kingstown ferry dock. If they'd taken the gag off sooner, I'd have screamed."

"Is he truly your chaperon all the way to London?"

"I'm going to the Fian, wherever he is, and if he's not in London, I'll find my own way there."

Maeve's eyes widened. "Truly? And leave the Fian himself? Wouldn't he help you?"

"I hope so." Aileen didn't have the heart to explain that she'd been sold as the Fian's mistress.

Not long after, near the end of the short sea crossing, Edmund Leedes finally ventured down to claim his charge. Holding a handkerchief to his nose to mask the smells of the closely confined lower deck, he walked carefully so his dandified clothes wouldn't touch the passengers. He was a big man, almost as big as Lord Fitzwilliam, and no doubt as strong, thought Aileen, but with no neck and with jowls that spoke of too many rich meals. She watched him make his way toward her and merely tossed her hair again, contemptuous of the contrast he made, a toadish man in prissy clothing.

Never in her life had she seen such rich colors and fine fabrics on one man. A yellow and black tartan vest under a top coat of black velvet. The latest collar on his shirt and a cravat of blue silk. Trousers of real wool. Affectations from an earlier era—snuff and a lace-trimmed handkerchief, and an elaborate pocket watch. Why, she could have fed her brothers for a year on the price of his one costume. And because of his toadish appearance, it was a waste, she thought, eyeing with disgust the silver flask that bulged from his coat pocket.

"You're to come up on deck now and try to behave like a proper lady," he said.

Aileen took Maeve's trembling hand in hers, and they climbed the narrow stairs to the deck, where they huddled together at the railing, their shawls pulled close over their shoulders and hair both as protection from the biting wind.

Through blurred eyes Aileen stared at the coast of England. All she saw was wild open land and the occasional smokestack of a factory as the ferry made its way across the tide of the Irish Sea and into the current of the Mersey estuary. Sea gulls swooped in front of her, cawing for attention. She saw other passengers pointing to the Pier Head, and then the boat bumped into the floating stage dock, and the crew secured it with ropes.

When she focused her attention on the bustling wharf off in the distance, she felt panic anew. Assembled were relatives come to meet the boat and passengers waiting to embark, not to mention brazen painted ladies. More intimidating were the rough-looking dockhands, the multitude of cartmen and peddlers. More people stood on this wharf than she'd seen at one time in her entire village of Devintown. Carriages and wagons mingled with enormous coils of rope and stacks of barrels bound for great ships. Dogs barked, and the stench of the city surrounded all until she felt dizzy at the thought of setting foot on English soil.

She held back, waiting while other passengers disembarked, and shy Maeve, after a glance at Leedes, suddenly hid behind Aileen. Aileen didn't blame the girl. Leedes's gaze was too bold entirely, Aileen thought with a flush and looked away. This loathsome Leedes looked at her as if she were a body only, devoid of mind.

But it wasn't so. She had a good mind. Seamus was the storyteller and Patrick the daydreamer, but Aileen was the practical one. Clever with book learning, so they had said in the village and had made her feel her cleverness was wasted because she was a girl. Well, she needed every bit of cleverness now. Her mind began to weave plans, discarding first one idea, then another.

She could see no way out other than to meet this Fian and hope she could convince him to help her rather than to use her. Certainly when he heard her sad tale, an Irish hero would agree to help.

Gradually the crowd of immigrants thinned, and Aileen could not avoid walking down the ramp, her legs shaking, unable to give Maeve any more support because she was too disoriented herself. People and trunks and dockhands jostled her until Leedes caught her arm and tugged her over against the brick wall of a warehouse, where a dog barked near her feet. She felt closed in and nearly panicked at the overwhelming number of English accents, as if she'd been surrounded by a thousand people all like Leedes. Be strong, she told herself, momentarily closing her eyes to shut out the confusion of everything English.

Taking a deep breath, she opened her eyes and faced Leedes, who seemed to have absolutely no plan of action. "Well, where is this Fian?" she demanded in her bravest voice.

Leedes smirked. "Now, then, if I knew exactly where he was, I'd not need to be waiting for the coach, would I, luv? Ireland's hero is a difficult man to find. We're waiting for a friend of mind, then we'll know."

And so they waited and waited some more, until time dragged on chains. After several coaches and wagons left for London, the peddlers thinned out as well, and the dock seemed more open. Aileen leaned tiredly against the stone wall, tentatively taking in the English sights and sounds. Maeve was quietly weeping again, some feet from the intimidating Leedes. When Aileen started to walk over to her, Leedes placed a detaining hand on her, and she sighed in impatience.

Finally at dusk it came, a rich dark coach with vermilion wheels like the landlord's and much more ornate than the public conveyances.

"That's my friend," crowed Leedes, and grabbing Aileen's arm, he shoved her roughly into the coach. With a whimper, Maeve slipped past Leedes and insinuated herself in also.

When Leedes tried to pull Maeve out, Aileen clung to her friend. "No, I promised I'd help her get to London."

"It's quite all right, Edmund," said a stranger's voice from the shadows. "I'll handle the ladies."

Aileen swung around in the coach in the direction of the voice. Feminine. Cultured. Through the dim light she made out the figure of a woman sitting across from her, a woman wearing a gown of silver-gray silk, face concealed by a veil.

Leedes heaved his bulk into the vehicle, pulled the door shut, and sat next to the mysterious woman. "Did the Albino verify the Fian's location?"

A gloved hand shot out and slapped Leedes so hard his jowls shook. Aileen flinched and reached out to hold Maeve's hand.

The voice of the veiled woman was curiously muffled. "Mind your tongue. Have you no concept of discretion?" With careful movements the woman tucked her veil in about her dress collar.

Aileen sat perfectly still, clutching Maeve's hand, and hid her shock at the woman's violence, so at odds with the

beauty of her clothing. Gradually she became conscious of
an unusually lovely scent. Orrisroot. Lord Fitzwilliam's
wife had frequently worn that fragrance.

The mysterious woman chose this moment to examine
Aileen from behind the secrecy of her veil. "So this is the
one? Pity. What a waste just for *him*. I could use her myself
to better purpose."

Leedes fidgeted with his lace-trimmed hankie.

"Her complexion's terribly pale. Have you fed her?" the
woman asked.

"No. Wouldn't that be rather a waste of shillings?"

"If she faints from hunger before she gets to her
destination, you'll perhaps regret your economy. . . ."
The veiled woman turned to Maeve and studied her.

Obviously uncomfortable with the scrutiny, Maeve shrank
back against the seat.

"Perhaps we should use that plain one instead and take
this one on to London . . . though on second thought he'd
probably not accept her."

Aileen stared after the woman, disliking her imperious
manner. With a hand pressed to her momentarily queasy
stomach, she drew a steadying breath, and the coach started
forward.

They rode in silence through the streets of Liverpool, past
the grand Town House and enormous churches and more
factories than she could count. Gradually buildings gave
way to countryside, though they were never far from the
sea.

They were well out of Liverpool in some lonely spot
when the coach slowed down, and Aileen readied herself to
get out. Frankly, she was anxious to get away from the
cloying scent of orrisroot, but took time to press Maeve's
hand one last time for luck. When the coach stopped,
Leedes and the woman climbed out, and soon came the

sounds of luggage being removed from the boot. Momentarily left alone, Aileen found the chance to whisper to Maeve.

"Meet me at London Bridge. Look for me every evening just before sundown. I'll come to find you there. That I can promise. We'll make our way together. I shall find my brothers, and we'll find you a safe place to be a seamstress. Agreed?"

Maeve's nod was enough.

"Get out now and be quick about it," Leedes barked, and Aileen complied.

Stepping down, she looked around in the quickening darkness. The road on which she stood appeared to lead nowhere. The land was barren and wild, covered with nothing but marsh grass and heath and dotted sparsely with pines and yews. A harsh wind blew Aileen's hair about her.

Without warning, Leedes placed into Aileen's hands a heavy satchel.

"You must take this with you to the Fian," Leedes said smoothly.

"Why?" Aileen balked.

"Lower your voice or you'll run him off, and that won't help you find your brothers, now, will it? . . . It's a gift. A gift from an admirer of the Fian's cause. A box of dueling pistols. Irish in origin, and the box itself would fetch a fortune. Now, then, all you have to do is hand this to him, though I daresay when he gets a look at you the gift will pale in comparison."

Aileen looked away from his too easy flattery.

"Don't open it," the veiled woman instructed from the carriage door. "And walk carefully. Your hero won't want his new love to arrive with a turned ankle."

Aileen was tired and cold, and the satchel dragged on her arms. Clutching it tightly with both hands, she set off with

Leedes to a narrow road that headed out across the eve
more remote moors. Only the occasional tree afforded a
break from the wind. Beneath her feet the ground was rocky
now, and Leedes annoyed her with his fussy admonitions
about the satchel.

Behind her a coach horse whinnied. Frightened, Aileen
wished she could drop the satchel and run back to Maeve
and proceed directly to London, but Leedes had a pistol
pointed at her. On the other hand, she was on her way to
meet the Fian, the man who helped Ireland. Hope soared.

"The Fian's a passionate fellow," Leedes said by way of
conversation, though he had to puff to catch his breath. "He
may frighten you at first. But that won't last." When the
track narrowed to a mere footpath along the water's edge,
he stopped. A patch of scraggly pines half hid the way, as
if they'd been planted for that very purpose.

"There you go. Follow this path. It will open out at an
unexpected cove. Don't be scared, luv. If you talk to him
with the spirit you've given me, all will turn out fine." His
last words were uncharacteristically kind considering the
pistol at her back.

Aileen continued on alone to find this man people called
the Fian. The low-growing heather caught at the hem of her
skirt, and pine branches brushed her arms. Picking her way
carefully along the path, she moved on, feeling with the
toes of her boots for rocks along the way.

Bracing his foot on a rock, the Fian grabbed one end of
the burlap bag and with Digby Trigg's help heaved it into
the rowboat that bobbed at the edge of the sea, then moved
aside to make way for the accomplices.

Colin Grey and his brother Thomas grunted under the
weight of another gunnysack. Thomas momentarily lost his

footing on a slippery rock and nearly dropped his end of the sack. Both the Fian and Digby Trigg moved to lend support, and the four of them finally hefted the bulky burlap into the rowboat. Digby and Colin moved toward another sack of weapons, while Thomas and the Fian secured the rowboat more tightly. Cold waves sloshed up against their boots.

Far down the coast a boat whistle sounded, and the Fian moved away from the others to listen.

A cloud skidded across the half-moon and poured black ink over the night. The Fian's gaze narrowed on the work at the cove that he supervised. This secret transfer of weapons had no reason to fail. Before he'd left London, he'd started a rumor that the Fian might riot this night, so his men had perfect cover. Yet he couldn't shake the feeling that a banshee hovered behind him, ready to wail with the warning of death.

After all, should anyone stumble into this cove, particularly Scotland Yard, questions would be difficult to answer. It was never easy to explain away activities involving high treason.

At the edge of the cove Colin and Thomas strained under the weight of yet another sack of weapons. With quiet strides the Fian was there a moment later to assist in sliding the awkward sack down to the rowboat. As they dragged it toward the water, the burlap tore, and they were forced to load the pistols one at a time. When they were nearly done, the Fian moved away from the water, the better to keep watch, and he studied his men from a distance. Their movements were as quiet as a pantomime. With the price on all their heads, especially the Fian's, stealth counted heaviest.

Pensive, he stared out at the dark water. In a short while the ferry from Liverpool would return on its night run to

Kingstown, Ireland, and the fishing vessel for which this rowboat was being loaded would make its way to a dark rendezvous farther up the Irish coast. There sympathetic rebels would help transfer the contraband to men of the underground. The timing of the smuggling and the coordination of so many men's actions had to be precise, as precise as the schedule of the ferry. So far, so good.

Then, without warning, a lone sea gull cawed in the night. The stems of the marsh grass swayed as if the breeze had suddenly grabbed them by their throats. From far up on the shore, confirming his feeling of uneasiness, a bird took wing. While Colin and Thomas worked, he signaled Digby aside.

"What's the matter, Fian? Is someone coming?"

"Digby, have you ever felt a banshee grab your shoulder?"

"Humph. Now, what would an old Englishman like me be knowin' about banshees for? Just because you call yourself the Fian don't mean I'm goin' to start believin' all those other tales. I don't even know what a banshee is, man."

"It's a female spirit," the Fian said quietly. "Her wail signals that someone will die."

"That wail you heard, man, was your horse neighin', not any banshees. I think we'd best lie low after this."

"*You* will lie low. You've risked your life once too often lately."

"Hell and damnation," said the older man with gruff affection. "We both lie low. If I die, ye can find another old sea captain as replacement, but where d'ye think I'll find another hero for Ireland, eh?"

Despite his uneasiness, the Fian smiled. Ever since he'd rescued Digby from a shipwreck several years ago the Fian had the impression the old man thought he owed someone his life and loyalty, never mind the linen cargo that had floated away and cost Digby any future as a captain. Fatherly to a fault, Digby was thoroughly English—except in one way—he carried no Irish prejudices. He was rather keenly sympathetic and, most important, above suspicion. The perfect accomplice for the Fian's complicated life.

Still, the Fian had to give his accomplice occasional reminders. "Hero means nothing if Scotland Yard finds me. It's those damn police spies in disguise now that make our work more dangerous."

"Well, whatever it be's got you so skittish, you're givin' me a cravin' for gin."

"Turning soft?" It was a jest from one friend to another.

"Nay. 'Tain't me standin' here talkin' about banshees and fairy spirits. I'm workin' fast as I can."

The Fian moved away to stand next to a rocky slope near where an open spot revealed the downward path to this cove. If he listened carefully he could almost hear the crunch of footsteps.

He cocked his pistol.

At the quiet click of the pistol Digby stopped in his tracks, listening closer, then whistled as a prearranged signal for Colin and Thomas to take the rowboat far out in the water to the fishing vessel.

"Mother of Lucifer, if we live through this night, we'll stay in London and hide out in fashionable drawing rooms awhile," the Fian promised himself. Then he was silent, listening.

It was the sound of the waves lapping at the shore, the breeze slapping the marsh grasses, not footsteps. It couldn't be. Still, to be safe, he aimed his pistol directly up the slope.

When a cloud moved away from the half-moon, he saw a figure emerge from that path—a woman. His heart picked up tempo. Cursing himself for not bringing a mask tonight, he reached into his pocket for the gypsy scarf to tie around his face. Then with stealthy footsteps he moved out from behind the rocks to confront the intruder.

Three

CAUTIOUS, AILEEN MOVED more slowly now, picking her way along the marsh grass and rocks of the primitive path, which was descending steadily to meet the waves of the Irish Sea. To her right, above the path, up on the moor, stood a little stone church, its steeple outlined in the half-moon, the windblown silhouettes of yews circling it.

As the wind whipped at her thin dress and shawl, she shivered and again debated running away. Surely she could find a farmer's wagon to take her to London. But the autumn night was cold, her choices lonely.

And somewhere out in the darkness of the moors, Leedes waited to intercept her if she didn't go on to this Fian.

Seconds later the figure of a man emerged on the shadowy path. Just like that he appeared silently out of nowhere, pushing aside a swaying pine branch to stand before her.

She stopped in her tracks, set down the satchel, and stood looking up at the stranger. As dark as the very rocks he was, with a black hooded cape carelessly tossed over a peasant smock. With the breeze whipping the fabric, the cape billowed like a dark storm cloud on the horizon.

Aileen held her breath, unable to see much of his face. A scarf covered all but his eyes, and in the dark she could not even tell their color, let alone gauge the depth of their friendliness.

"Hello," she ventured with a half smile, hoping to ply him with an innocent look. "Would you be the Fian?"

"What makes you think I'd claim a name like that?" His voice held an unexpected intensity.

"From the man who brought me to you," she said as if he ought to know. "If you're the Fian, then this is for you." With an outstretched hand, she gestured to the satchel at her feet.

Briefly he studied the bag, then looked back at her. To her utter stupefaction, he turned and with bold strides vanished down the path. Above the wail of the wind she heard him call out down the incline to the cove. "Trigg, get out of here." His return was so sudden it startled her, and she reached down for the satchel. But the dark stranger caught her wrist as if to stop her. Just as quickly he let go, and she pulled back her arm and gathered her shawl to her, mystified.

"That satchel contains a gift for you," she explained.

"Who sent you?"

Who sent her? Aileen didn't understand the question. How many men did this Fian employ to buy him paramours? And as to that, it was time to make her position clear now, before he assumed she'd agreed to the bargain. "Before we go any further, I want you to know I can never be your mistress, and you'll have to obtain your money back. I only came to get help for my brothers so . . ." Her voice trailed off because he didn't seem to be paying a bit of attention. Instead he bent down in the heather to peer at the satchel. Even when he stood up, he didn't remove his gaze from the gift.

"Don't move." The command was fierce.

A strand of hair blew across her face, and out of habit she naturally reached up to brush it away. As the moments passed, she was becoming colder than ever and impatient with his strange behavior. "You've not told me if you're the Fian. If you're him, why don't you say so? I've only come because—"

"I said don't move, that is, if you want to see dawn rise again." His voice was more than deep. It was harsh and shaded dark with a quiet fury she couldn't understand. With a frown he put out a hand to touch the satchel, picking it up with the care one might use to handle a fragile vase.

"Pretend you're a statue," he said through gritted teeth. "And stop talking."

"What's wrong?" she blurted out, then pressed her lips shut. Her stomach twisted into a knot of unexplained fear, and she had the most awful premonition that the worst was yet to come.

What happened next was all a stunning blur. Horror shot through Aileen at the unexpected ferocity of the man's movements. He flung the heavy satchel out to sea, his aim sending it low, barely above the waves.

A second after it hit the water, a violent explosion of fire, smoke, and debris from the sea rent the night. Water rose up like a maelstrom where the sea shattered, and pieces of driftwood and seaweed blew inland from the force of the explosion.

When Aileen could think again, she found she'd been knocked to the ground, thrown down among the scratchy heather. The scent of sulphur hung heavy in the air, and one frightened sea gull cawed as it flew up through the smoke.

Aileen tried to sit up. Her eyes teared from the acrid fumes, and a wave of dizziness washed over her. After a moment she dragged herself to her knees, but had to lean against a nearby rock for support.

How had it come to this? A boat ride. A woman in a veil who smelled of orrisroot saying she was too lovely for the Fian. Edmund Leedes telling her she must take a gift to the Fian. A walk along a dark and narrow path.

A box. A gift.

The admonition not to open it—to walk carefully.

And then a man with a scarf over his face telling her in a voice full of dark danger not to move.

Don't move. Don't move. Over and over she heard the words.

The scent of sulphur permeated her lungs still, and she wanted, dearly wanted, to believe she was dreaming, prayed she'd awaken and find this was only a nightmare.

A bomb. Oh, yes, she'd heard of such things. Roddy had told her of exploding devices made from sulphur powder used against the Irish rebels, but she'd never imagined such a thing could be this powerful.

Then other words came back to her like pieces of a puzzle that was growing clearer in her mind.

She's too lovely for him. Why don't I send the plain one instead?

Wouldn't feeding her be a waste of good shillings?

With a stroke of stunning clarity, she realized she was a . . . she forced her mind to fold around the dreaded word . . . a murderess. No, worse. An assassin.

Sent to kill a man.

Sent not only to kill, but also . . . to die. Lord Fitzwilliam had planned her fate well. Was he that worried about his whiskey stills that only her death would satisfy him? And what a cowardly weapon.

Clutching at the rocks, her mind began to play tricks on her. Try as she might, she couldn't remember exactly where she was or how to get back to her cottage in Ireland. Somehow, she had to go home to the cottage, where the cat would be waiting on the hearth, and her brothers running in for supper any minute. She had to get home. . . .

Vaguely she was aware of the touch of a hand on her shoulder, but when she gasped and drew back, the touch went away. Gradually shock receded and with clarity of thought came the awful memory of the past moments, the reality of the night and the sea and the explosion. . . .

Slowly she lifted up her hands and with just her fingertips touched her face. Yes, she was alive. And awake.

She took a shuddering breath but choked on the acrid air. After a few smaller breaths she reached down and felt for her shawl. Looping the coarse fabric over her arms, she pulled herself to her feet. Immediately her legs buckled beneath her, and the dark stranger gathered her up. She fought to keep her mind clear, feeling the strong arms of the man tighten around her then, and she clung to her shawl as if it were her sole belonging in the world.

And the man—he held her in a way she'd never been held before. Not gently like her father had embraced her, but with restrained strength. Rough fabric from his cloak scratched her face, and her hair fell in a loose black banner except where, at the back of her neck, his hand tangled in it.

Too clearly she remembered standing at her father's grave wishing for the strong arms of a man to hold her. So it seemed her wish had come true. But not quite as she'd imagined it, for the embrace that now captured her could only be taking her to some perilous destination.

But that didn't stop her senses from coming alive in his arms. As he carried her, she heard the ebb and flow of his heartbeat, sensed the deepening of his breathing, and most of all felt the tension in his muscles as he moved with her.

Her blood raced fast and her body tingled strangely. Briefly she shut her eyes as if that would stop the direction of her thoughts.

More and more a strong sense of worse danger to come filled her. Whoever this stranger was, he'd blame her for the exploding box, she knew that. And soon, too.

With precious little ceremony he deposited her on her feet. They stood high up on the moor, outside the little stone church. For a few moments she didn't move, but tried to still her beating heart while she gathered her wits and took stock of these new surroundings.

A black Arabian that had been standing nearby came up to nuzzle the hand of the man she'd nearly killed. With surprising efficiency the man tied the reins of the horse more tightly to a yew tree. He absently stroked the animal's muzzle in a calming gesture before suddenly turning to Aileen.

"Who the devil are you? Are any others with you?" His voice held barely restrained anger. His accent sounded more English than Irish, the tone of voice dark with a passion she couldn't explain any more than she could explain the way it made her pulse race.

"Answer me." His gaze narrowed with suspicion.

In a stubborn gesture she lifted her chin. "Why should I?"

"Because I'd like to know who nearly killed me," he said.

Oh, yes, she would have to defend herself from his worst suspicions. On shaky legs she backed away from the angry man and his horse, but to her consternation he quickly closed the space between them and placed his hands on her shoulders. She shook, not because he was rough, but because his touch was gentle, restrained.

No, she chastised herself, it wasn't the touch of his hands

that caused these strange sensations within. It was simply her near brush with death that left her still weak-limbed, and she had to dig her fingernails into her palms to stop herself from shaking all over.

In front of her she could see one dark cape and a pair of strong arms in which she longed to wrap herself as a source of comfort, but the man to whom they belonged was presently tightening his grip on her. Perhaps, after all, he was going to shake her to pieces. And why shouldn't he? Hadn't she nearly killed them both?

But strangely, this angry man, this Fian—for she'd decided it could be no other—he acted as if narrowly escaping death were as natural a part of his day as waking.

With a few muttered oaths he slid his hand through her arm and guided her through a creaking door and into the church, after which he let go of her and moved into action.

She stood still watching while the Fian flung off his cape and rid himself of the peasant smock to reveal the full-sleeved shirt and dark trousers of an ordinary Englishman.

As she watched him, she felt her strength return, and she glanced around the church. An open coffin stood at the back of the single aisle, illuminated by the light of a lantern swinging from a nail directly above.

Curious about both the contents of the coffin and the ability of her legs to function, she walked over to the wooden box and peered inside. The light fell in a pool on dozens of pistols and muskets—flintlocks, matchlocks, blunderbusses and Brown Besses.

She was still staring at them in mute astonishment when the Fian came up behind her and swung her around so fast that the lid of the coffin slammed down with an echo that reverberated off the church walls. In the Fian's hands gleamed the blade of a dagger.

Aileen felt her uncooperative pulse hammer wildly at the

sight of him, so tall and strong. He had not removed the dark scarf hiding his face, and it muffled his voice.

"Tell me who you are and who you work for. Your name."

The knife blade teased at the waistline of her dress.

"I—I was sent here against my will," she said. Her throat felt dry and hollow, but she found her voice, choppy though her thoughts were. "They told me you'd bought me as a—a mistress." Her voice trembled, but she was sure he didn't notice.

Indeed, a look of disbelief flashed in his eyes. After a moment of absolute silence he sheathed his knife. "I have never in my life had to buy a mistress."

The scorn in his voice was unendurable, so she stiffened and answered him with every bit as much pride. "And I will never be any man's mistress." Instinctively she backed away from him, feeling her way around the shape of the coffin until she stood on the other side of it. "In any case, I believe they lied to me. Someone wanted me dead, too."

For a long time he stared at her, as if weighing her answer. "Who sent you to me?" His voice rose impatiently. "Damn gift of death." Obviously, he saw the stricken look on her face, for his next words softened. "Why would anyone want you dead?"

"My landlord would. But he failed, and I'm far away from him now," she said with an attempt at bravery. She met the gaze of the Fian and saw there a new expression— part disbelief, part speculation.

"Who brought you here?" he repeated.

"A woman in a veil. That's all I know of her. And Mr. Leedes. Lord Fitzwilliam sold me to Edmund Leedes."

"Leedes." A fist came down on the lid of the coffin. "I should have guessed. . . . Always it's Leedes. I can't believe they've resorted to using an innocent woman. . . .

If you're indeed innocent. Why did you go along with them? You could have escaped without much effort. You came down that path alone with that satchel." His outburst ended with a harsh last word. "Why?"

"Because I wanted to meet the legendary Fian." Her voice shook with emotion and a hint of sarcasm. "I thought you could help me find my poor kidnapped brothers, but it appears I was wrong."

His gaze narrowed on her. She didn't know what to expect until she heard his voice again.

"What's your name?" His words softened, but with no loss of authority. A knife blade to her emotions, his voice was. "Your name?" he demanded again.

"Aileen. Aileen Connolly, and I'll have you know you're no hero. You may call yourself Fian, but you're not deserving of the name. You're an indecent cur, bullying me this way. I thought the Fian was a fine Irish legend, but now I find he's a madman who fills coffins with pistols and takes a knife to a girl after almost causing her death." Her voice rose and choked with emotion. "A week ago I had—" Her voice broke. "I had parents—a home. My brothers used to play at being the Fian, who, in case you're curious, was their hero." She stopped to check the tears that suddenly threatened. Above all, she would not let him see her cry.

To prevent that happening, she started to walk out of the church, but when she tried to walk by him, he captured her wrist, and again she was aware of restrained strength, his touch slicing through her emotional defenses the same way his voice did. Surely his fingers felt the way her pulse betrayed her.

His words were calmer now, almost gentle. "You can't simply leave now. They'll be checking to be sure if that explosion killed us."

"You're just wanting to be saving your own skin." Gently she extricated herself from his grasp.

With a nod he acknowledged the truth of her accusation, and his reply contained a wry irony. "Always I'm thinking of saving my skin."

The lantern light shone directly on her face, but except for his eyes, his features were hidden, not only by his scarf but also by the shadows. She supposed she must look a fright, what with tangles in her hair and mud on her face.

Dear Mother of God, what was wrong with her? She'd never been given to vanity. Just minutes ago she'd nearly died. Who cared how she looked? Strangers at her wake?

The Fian interrupted her thoughts. "Where's Leedes now?"

"He walked back to—" Shivers ran up her spine, and it wasn't from the way this Fian cut her emotions into shreds. Suddenly cold, Aileen felt as if the door of the church had blown shut in an autumn gust, trapping her inside. She turned briefly to be certain no one was in the doorway. It was empty. For the moment she was safe still from Leedes. But she felt encircled by danger. They shouldn't linger in this church.

"Walked where?" the Fian prompted, his voice again darkly passionate.

She made herself look at him, despite the risk that he might see written on her face her unwilling reaction to him. "Mr. Leedes walked back to the coach," she began again in a less certain voice. From above, the lantern light glared hot and white and pale, hurting her eyes. "The woman was going to wait for Leedes where the path joins the road."

At this revelation the Fian's words became even more intense. "Didn't the woman mention anyone else?"

"I—I can't remember." A name, a description, floated in her subconscious, but she couldn't pull it out.

"Tell me more about the woman," he demanded. "You must know something more. You can't have walked off a boat from Ireland and simply had something as primitive and obvious as that bomb handed to you."

In his eyes she could almost see reflected the abashed expression on her face. She had done exactly as he'd accused. As improbable as it sounded, she'd been utterly duped, and she took out her anger on the Fian. "It isn't every day I concoct sulphur mixtures in my kitchen so that I'd be recognizing such a thing as an exploding box."

Then Aileen shrugged, helpless to argue anymore. The intensity of his questioning had become almost too much to bear. She tried to dredge up what she could from her memory so the Fian would believe her innocence. At the same time she was curious how Ireland's hero behaved when he wasn't angry. She wanted him to—to have met her under other circumstances. . . . But that was a foolish thought, and so she forced herself to say something sensible.

"The woman dressed in silver-gray silk and smelled of—of orrisroot and—"

Scoffing, he demanded more. "Anyone can dress in silk and splash on scent. Who was she?"

"I don't know. Truly I don't." She thought of her new little friend Maeve riding alone in a coach full of assassins and almost choked on the rest of the sentence, but suddenly the word she'd been searching for came to her. "Albino. That was it. Do you know of an albino?"

He let go and looked straight ahead. Taking a deep breath, he replied, "Perhaps," and demanded in a ragged voice, "Tell me more."

Her words tumbled out. "When she first came, Leedes asked something about the Albino, and she slapped him for it. . . . Viciously. Do you believe me now?"

With a tired sigh he nodded. "I'll have to keep you hidden somewhere, I suppose, until they show themselves again." For the first time he actually looked at her as if she were a woman.

His gaze traveled up and down, from her face to the hem of her dress and back, and she died a little at his bold look.

His voice became mocking and sounded not at all displeased. "I should keep you anyway, since they gave you to me."

"No, you won't." She hated his mocking. Didn't he have a gentle side? If so, she supposed she'd never know it, not after tonight, nor should she even want to.

She backed up a step or two until she was out of his reach. If he nicked her emotions with passionate words and burning touches, it was involuntary. Remember, she told herself, this man is dangerous. Her heart raced even while she reached under her skirt and down her boot for the knife she'd carried all the way from Ireland. Suddenly she brandished the knife at the Fian, catching him off guard as she guessed few men did.

She watched him pause and tense. It wasn't every day of the week she fell in with assassins and smugglers, but she'd show them. Even though she could be duped, she still had the courage to fight her way to safety. Besides, she had to get to London.

"I've told you what I know. Leedes is an evil man, just like my landlord. And that woman—whoever she is—she's bad too. May the devil see them to their due reward. And you too if you won't help me." Without taking her eyes off him, Aileen backed toward the door.

It took the Fian only an instant to cross the tiles of the church floor and pin the Irish girl against the wall next to the door with his body. Even though she struggled against him, he easily removed the common kitchen knife from her fingers and kept it himself. He'd relaxed his guard, been tempted into thinking of her as a vulnerable woman whose story he could believe—until she pulled that knife. Now he was once more on guard against her.

With an easy motion he gathered both her arms behind her back, which in turn arched her against him. Feeling her light body next to his reinforced his impression of her as someone young. He liked the feel of her breasts pressed against his chest, and he liked the look of that wild black hair falling over her shoulders, teasing his hands. He felt the delicate bones in her back and measured her vulnerability while all the time she wriggled and half turned against him.

His body warmed, and the blood stirred a bit hotter in his veins. Almost for a moment he forgot the cause that drove the Fian. That bothered him. After all, he certainly never bedded potential assassins. No. He wouldn't let his body distract him from his duty. This newest plot of assassins and accomplices was thickening too fast. Taking her hand in his grasp, he pulled her away and drew her up the side aisle till they stopped in front of the darkened altar. He allowed her hand to slide away.

"As you honor truth, lass, talk. Think hard and remember the names you claim to have forgotten. Who works with Leedes?" He'd been shaken more than he cared to admit by the mention of the Albino, who was a notorious highwayman. "I want names."

Before Aileen could answer, someone else spoke for her.

"What's in a name?" Leedes's too familiar posturing voice—rough with anger held in check—came quietly out of the shadows near the door. "Tut, tut, indeed, a traitor by any name will still die eventually. . . . Do I interrupt your—uh—assignation?" Footsteps clicked against the flagstones. "I'd hoped to attend a funeral here, but it seems I'm premature."

Beside him the Fian felt Aileen go utterly still, and when he reached for her she shook like a leaf in the wind. Quickly he drew her back against the side of the church. Oh, Leedes knew they were here, all right, but he couldn't yet see them. All the Fian could think of was protecting himself and now of necessity this girl. As he jammed her kitchen knife into the waist of his trousers, he thanked God for dark shadows.

The only sound in the church was angry footsteps echoing on the flagstones, louder and louder, until suddenly they stopped, and now Leedes's voice echoed off the stone walls.

"Damn you, Fian," Leedes called out. "You might as well show yourself. There's no way out except through that door."

A long silence followed. The Fian held the girl—Aileen Connolly, she'd called herself—and covered her mouth to prevent her panicking and crying out. At the moment he was inclined at last to think this Aileen was on his side. With an arm through hers he pulled her along, moving down the rows of darkened pews faster, he hoped, than Leedes could follow in the dark.

"Where's the Irish lass?" Leedes demanded to the darkness, his words creating eery echoes. "I want her back. There's no need in you interrogating her. She knows nothing you care about. She was simply a lovelier means of delivery than a common doxy would have been. And her death would have pleased her landlord."

Without warning, the Fian stopped and pulled Aileen closer to him. As he did so, he felt her body tighten at the callous words of Leedes. He'd heard and seen a lot, but using this innocent girl in an assassination plot sickened even him.

With easy strength the Fian carefully eased her down to

the floor. They were, he realized regretfully, on the opposite side of the church from the door.

In the darkness she turned, so close to his face he could smell the lavender scent of her hair, and he felt a fleeting relief that she was, after all, his ally and not his enemy.

For the first time he acknowledged to himself that she was a most provocative creature and felt regret that he'd met her under circumstances where he was forced to fight rather than pay court. But then, as he reminded himself, the Fian never had time to dawdle over a woman, not even one as apparently innocent and lovely as this one. He'd be doing well to rescue her from Leedes and send her on her way.

"Lie low and hide here," he spoke against her hair.

"It was your idea to trap us in this church," she whispered back. "How will we get out? Say our prayers and hope he'll go away?"

"I've gotten out of worse fixes," he whispered in turn, "and it'll be easier if you stay put."

"I hear you!" Leedes suddenly shouted. "You're not going to escape."

The Fian stood up. It was easy to determine Leedes's position by the staccato click of the man's boots, and he guessed that Leedes faced the direction of the coffin, for it contained the only source of light and would attract Leedes like a moth to the flame.

Crouched low, the Fian moved down the side of the church, then slid through a pew and headed for the sound of those boots. What damnable irony, he thought. A coffin full of pistols just yards away, and all he held was a paltry knife from an Irish waif's kitchen. Suddenly the click of the boots ceased, and the Fian stopped in his own tracks, listening.

Leedes lunged at him, attempting to pull off the scarf. The Fian dodged Leedes but fell against the wooden back of a pew, his ribs stinging from the impact. With a sudden fist to Leedes's gullet, the Fian regained the offensive, and with a fierce shove pushed the portly man down into the hard seat of the pew behind them. Then he backed out into the open space of the aisle.

Leedes staggered up, following, then suddenly straightened and drew from his coat pocket a pistol, which he held mere inches from the Fian's heart. As the Fian stole quick breaths of air, he felt beads of perspiration dampen his own forehead. If he was going to act, it had to be fast.

Before Leedes's finger could move to cock the pistol, the Fian moved with lightening speed and slammed the palm of his hand and all his weight against Leedes's inner wrist.

The pistol went off, the shot lodging somewhere in a wall of the church, and Leedes dropped the weapon, his hand helplessly outstretched. He was still staring at his wrist when the Fian smashed a left upper cut to Leedes's jaw, and when the portly man swayed toward the right, the Fian's right knee was already coming up to kick his ribs.

Leedes fell to the floor, winded, and the Fian stood, legs spread, staring down at him. In his career as the Fian he'd been involved in so many fights like this, he'd lost count. All he knew was that swift action had always kept him alive, and every time he finished cracking the ribs of some fat weasel like Leedes, he was grateful for the years in English boarding schools where he'd perfected his fighting skills.

Now Leedes gasped for air and crawled toward his pistol, but with the toe of his boot the Fian kicked it out of reach. As he did so he spotted Aileen from the corner of his eye. She wasn't where he'd left her. Instead, she was at the coffin, reaching in for a weapon. Damn females. Never did what you told them to.

He only turned a second to look at her, but when he

turned back, Leedes had used the support of a pew to struggle to his feet.

The Fian reached for his knife, but Leedes surprised him first, pulling a tiny dueling pistol from inside his coat. Obviously Leedes had no idea the girl had found another store of weapons, but not even she could save the Fian if Leedes decided to shoot now.

The fat man backed away just far enough so the Fian couldn't grab him again. Without even cocking the tiny second pistol, he smiled and began to talk.

Behind his scarf the Fian smiled, too, for talking would be a fatal waste of time for Leedes. Out of the corner of his eye he could see Aileen, flintlock in hand, advancing stealthily toward Leedes's back, but he was careful to keep looking at Leedes and not give her away.

Leedes's voice gloated. "You're going to die, you realize. I'm going to be the hero. I'll collect the reward on your head and my bet on your identity as well. I could take you in alive and let everyone see you themselves, but I've decided to kill you instead."

From the corner of his eye the Fian saw Aileen moving closer behind Leedes, and he forgave her for not staying put. Then he watched her hand come up with a pistol in it, and with the suddenness of a fairy shadow, she bashed Leedes over the head. Once again the big man slumped to his knees, not knocked out, but definitely dazed.

Without moving yet the Fian eyed the flintlock held by this feisty girl and then the girl herself. Looking at the fire in her face, he was of the opinion that she'd recovered well from the fright of the bomb. "Is that mine?" he asked with a nod in the direction of the flintlock, knowing full well she'd picked it up out of the coffin.

"No longer." Without giving him a chance to reply, she

turned on Leedes. "Have you said your prayers you—you Englishman?"

Leedes put a hand to the lump forming on his skull and turned on the Fian. "Well, you're the hero of Londontown's poor. Can't you do something about her before she kills a pair of good Englishmen?"

Despite himself, the Fian half-smiled at Leedes's sudden patriotic gesture of friendship.

"Actually she's only got one shot, Leedes. She can't kill us both." In fact, he knew the pistol she held was not loaded at all, though Leedes couldn't know that for certain.

With both hands on the pistol Aileen waved it between the men, and it wobbled in her hands.

Leedes was visibly shaking, while the Fian stood quiet, watching. It was to him she spoke, and her words surprised him.

"You'll take me to London, Fian. I have to find my brothers."

The Fian gave her a narrowed look, but said nothing. Surely she couldn't be serious, for she had no idea of the danger he could put her in. Certainly she was no simpering, ringletted Englishwoman given to vapors and flirting and gossip, but was she daft on top of beautiful?

Leedes was laughing. He tried to stand up but immediately dropped down again into a pew, holding his head for a second. Then he pulled his silver flask from his coat pocket and, after uncapping it, raised it to his lips and tilted his head back for a quick swallow. With an extravagant gesture of his handkerchief, he wiped the excess whisky from his tartan vest. "Yes, take her to London, Fian. Scotland Yard would be delighted to have you drop in at teatime."

"Shut up, you fool." The Fian moved closer to Leedes. Actually, he was tempted to plunge Aileen's knife into the blackguard's heart. But he'd managed so far to ply his cause without resorting to cold-blooded murder and wanted to keep it that way.

Swiftly he chanced a look at the girl. Hell and damnation, women could be a nuisance and a bother, even ones who weren't afraid to get mud on their dresses and hold a gun to a man. Why was it the banshees in his soul warned him of danger and death threats, but never of women's fickle moods? The flintlock still wavered in her hands.

"You put your life at risk, lass," he warned her at last.

"And so do you if you refuse," she replied. "Besides, I can't imagine being at worse risk than I was awhile ago when we came near to being blown up."

Leedes blustered at Aileen, his jowls shaking. "See here, you're mine. I paid for you, and as long as you're alive, you're not going off with someone else, especially not with the most-wanted traitor in England."

His whining resembled that of a petulant child, and Aileen spared him a contemptuous glance. "Your misfortune, sir, that you missed your chance to do away with the Fian, and as for me, I'm not yours. One way or another I'm going to London."

Intrigued, the Fian listened to her, weighing his own choices. She could, in a matter of seconds, take his horse—Cormac, his pride and joy—and ride off.

On the other hand, if he wanted to, he could easily overpower her. He hadn't stayed alive this long without some skill at gaining the upper hand, over men bigger and more cunning than this girl.

"Would you dally and lose your horse to me? I said you're to escort me to London."

She moved outside, where she picked up Cormac's reins and looked back at him, chin high, the wind whipping at her dark hair, her stance straight and proud. He'd never seen any female quite like her.

With quick, practiced motions the Fian undid Leedes's cravat and, jerking the blustering man's hands behind his back, tied him tightly, then walked outside to Aileen. Before she could open her mouth to give him one more order, he tossed her up on Cormac's back.

Smiling suddenly at her look of consternation, he decided to surprise her further and gave her the formal bow of a London aristocrat. "I was brought up to be a gentleman. I believe, lass, you've convinced me to help you." He mounted the horse himself, and reaching around Aileen's waist for Cormac's reins, he lightly touched his heels to the animal's flank.

Only once did he look back, regretting the weapons he had to leave behind, but knowing loyal Digby would take care of them as soon as he came out of hiding. At least there was no danger Leedes could get to them. In the door of the church the fat man stood as still as a churchmouse in front of a trap, his face as angry as if the devil himself had caught him.

The Fian turned away from the scene and tightened his grip about Aileen's waist. For a while they rode in silence.

"You might have been better off taking your chances with him, you realize," he said finally.

She tossed her head in a defiant way but kept her thoughts to herself.

He wished he could help her, but if her brothers had been sold, it wasn't to any open factory. It was to a slave factory, and those were well hidden. When she didn't say anything more, he was bolder, a bit more truthful. "You shouldn't have come with me. If you're found in my company, you'll hang for treason."

"I told you—I have to get to London any way I can. You provided the quickest means."

"How convenient of me—and brave of you," he said, struggling to hide the wry humor he felt at her naive words. He didn't want to disillusion her too quickly, yet he needed to talk of anything that would distract him from the scented hair teasing his throat, the dulcet voice taunting his ear.

"London's a vast city," he added softly.

"I'm not afraid of you or London," she declared.

"Then I envy you, lass," he said, and he did. For he lived in constant fear. Fear of betrayal. Fear of assassination. And now he'd discovered a new fear—the fear that he might pull this little banshee off his horse and into his arms.

But that could only lead them both to a fate worse than a homemade bomb. Far worse . . .

Forcing his thoughts away from the girl, he concentrated on the road ahead.

Four

STEERING CLEAR OF the main roads to London, the Fian guided his horse into more pastoral country. He had to get as far away from the bomb site as possible. With every breath he took, he wondered if Leedes had hedged his bets and laid an ambush ahead. Alert to unnatural sounds in the woods, he scanned the trees on each side, wary, watchful for strangers.

But after they'd traveled far enough, his thoughts turned back to the cove. He was reasonably certain Digby had gotten away, and he could only assume the smuggling shipment had fared well.

Holding tight to the girl, he reminded himself over and over she'd nearly assassinated him—as if the plot had been hers. A banshee she was, delivering death, and he tried—but failed—to ignore the subtle seduction of womanly curves so near his hands.

"I can't take you all the way to London," he announced at last. "I'm going to put you on a train sometime tomorrow. I'm not sure where—at some quiet village stop—I'll give you your fare to London." He waited for her reaction.

Her reply sounded small and quiet, as if betrayed. "But why? Everyone in Ireland says you help the Irish. Why won't you help me find my brothers?"

His throat tightened as he searched for the right words. It wasn't that he wanted to turn an innocent young girl loose in London. No decent man did.

"Those people who tried to assassinate me know your face. If they were to see you with me, they'd know who I am."

"Then you'd die," she said with easy perception. Her voice sounded flat, emotionless.

"And you'd die, too. I'd not be much of a hero if I led you to the gallows."

Impatience laced her voice. "I've done no smuggling."

"Guilt comes by association with Ireland's hero. Do you hear me?"

"Yes, and my ears tell me that you're English, not Irish. How does an Englishman dare to take on the name of the Fian?"

"My mother was Irish—that makes me as Irish as you—as Irish as it's possible to be."

"Who's your family, then?" she asked next.

"All Ireland," he said lightly.

"Pshaw. You will lose your ears telling such tales." Then, after a pause, "How did you know that was a bomb?"

"Sulphur. The smell of the box. That's not the first bomb I've seen. Do you take me for a naive lad?"

"Are all Englishmen so daring?"

"All those with a price on their head. I'm probably the least desirable traveling companion in England at the moment, you realize," he added dryly and was relieved when at last she had no further retort.

They rode on in silence, listening to the steady clip of the horse's hooves and the wind blowing through the hedgerows. For half an hour raindrops fell. Dark clouds raced with them in the direction of London. But clouds could travel in hours. London was days away by horseback, and his would-be assassins might still be hunting for them. Soon they'd have to stop and rest—and hide as well.

When his horse faltered on a rut, the sudden movement jolted him out of his dark thoughts. "Easy, Cormac," he said, slowing the horse from a trot back to a walk.

"Did you name your horse after Ireland's own king?" Aileen's voice came again unexpectedly, with a hint of mockery, as if she were still questioning his right to call himself Irish.

"Oh, so now you don't think my horse is Irish enough?" he said with a half laugh. "He was born and bred in Ireland, same as you."

"I only asked," she said with a toss of her head.

He tried to ignore the tangle of hair that sent his senses racing. As soon as he spotted a haystack at the edge of a field, and beyond it a thickly wooded copse, he decided this would be a safe place to stop.

The Fian walked Cormac through an opening in the roadside hedge and on across a field. In the night sky the moon shone pale, and beneath it newly scythed hay was mounded up like browned bread. Each rick of hay wore a little thatched roof to protect it from rain.

They stopped near the stone wall that divided open meadow from copse, and he scanned the area, checking for suitability. The haystack nearest the wall would provide a comfortable bed, and should they be spotted by searchers, the copse afforded easy hiding.

After letting Aileen down at the haystack, he moved Cormac closer to the trees before unsaddling and feeding him. He took his time, wondering how best to broach the subject of sleep to such an innocent girl. The arrangements were bound to be more intimate than any she'd known.

Finally he strode toward the haystack, where the girl waited. She hadn't moved, but stood watching for him, looking utterly vulnerable. He felt like a bow pulled taut.

"If it doesn't rain again, this haystack will do as a bed for us."

He saw her hesitation, and her voice reminded him of a mother superior he'd once known. "Sleep together?" The tremble in her voice threatened to spill over.

"We almost died together, lass," he reminded her.

"That's not at all the same."

"It's not just sleep," he said. "We've got to hide here." With the light of the half-moon he could see her looking up at him.

"We're still in danger?"

"I'm always in danger."

The ride had only temporarily relaxed him. Now he felt wary, nervous again, all the more because he had this girl to protect. At the same time, though, she intrigued him with her saucy questions, and she didn't let up, not even when he knelt down and busied himself pulling dry hay out of the rick for them to lie on.

"Why have you become the Fian?" she asked unexpectedly.

Caught off guard, he stopped making their bed and knelt back on his haunches. Her question wrenched him, and he couldn't say why. "No one's ever asked me that before."

"Not even Scotland Yard?"

"Especially not them. They'd hang me before they'd ask reasons why."

"Then you'd best tell me, so if they do hang you, I can tell my brothers and your legend will be complete."

He pulled out another handful of hay and crushed it flat, and the sweet scent filled the darkness. Aileen Connolly had a way of knocking him down with words. This girl would know reasons why, but he'd give her careful answers.

"It was long ago that I became the Fian, long before I ever grew up or wore a disguise."

As he talked, he went back to work pulling out hay, and she began to help him.

"Please tell me," she said softly. "I won't tell anyone else except Seamus, and he'd save it as a secret."

He swallowed thickly, trying to form words. It had been so long, so many years, that he wasn't certain he could state it in a few easy sentences.

"My mother, who taught me the legend of the Fian, was killed when I was very young. I saw it happen. It was Englishmen who murdered her." Lost in thought, he stared out at the lonely pasture a moment before rearranging more hay. "Young, careless Englishmen . . ."

"Were they hanged?"

"No . . ." Suddenly he stood up, needing to distance himself from her. Standing was less personal somehow, and he turned the conversation to the less personal as well. Again he had the sensation he was a too tightly strung bow.

"Through the years it's become more than avenging my mother. All of Ireland needs help. I ride as the Fian because of all the wrongs that have been done to Ireland. The cause needs me." Abruptly he stopped, wondering what had given him a tongue as loose as a woman's.

Aileen sat on the hay looking up at him, asking cheekily, "Is that all?"

"That's all I can tell you. All you must know of me is why I'm fighting for the Irish cause—for home rule and an independent Ireland."

"Then a pox on you and your cohorts," she said, and that simple threat almost unstrung him.

Voice rising with emotion, she continued. "The cause, the cause, always this talk of the cause. Talk to me of food and home and finding my brothers. Then I will listen to talk about Ireland needing her own government. Causes don't feed Irishmen's bellies when potatoes are scarce." She sounded as if she wanted to pummel him. "You're so wrapped up in saving everyone that you save no one, least of all little boys like my brothers—"

Suddenly the bow inside him snapped. Reaching down, he grabbed her by the elbows and yanked her to her feet. "You're talking about a cause as if it were a paragraph in a schoolboy's book. I'm talking about the Bible for my life—the reason I've given up all else I care about, and you stand there, fresh from a kitchen kettle, and tell me I don't care?"

He almost flung her aside, but instead released her and stalked off the few yards to the stone wall where Cormac stood.

Damn her, but he ought to ride off and leave her here. He called over to her. "You can stay there safely enough. There'll be a wagon by in the morning."

As he reached for Cormac's saddle, he gave her a backward glance. Her shoulders slumped, and the moonlight slanting across her face allowed him to see she was crumpling, tears filling her eyes. It was the way women always reacted to his rejection, and he didn't have to guess what would happen next.

In a moment she was beside him, her hand touching his sleeve. "I'm sorry," she said. Suddenly she looked up so that he had to watch the tears welling in her eyes. "If you don't help me, no one will." Her voice broke on a sob.

He stiffened, feeling guilty now that he'd been so harsh

with her. Women didn't understand politics the way men did. How could he explain to her that she aroused feelings in him he didn't want to deal with?

"There are limits to my help. I can't look for your brothers."

"I understand. Truly, I won't ask again." She started to cry openly then and pressed herself to him, arms about his back, tears dampening his shirt, as between sobs, she said, "You're the only Irishman I've met here in England. . . . Please don't leave me here alone."

He'd known many women in his time who'd suddenly thrown themselves at his chest and pressed their cheek to him while they wept hot tears and pleaded for another chance in his life. He'd made it a rule never to embrace them back, but merely let them cry themselves dry.

But this woman had called him an Irishman, and even while she wept on his shirt, she made him feel less lonely somehow, and without being aware of it till it was too late, his arms came up around her, too, and he touched his face to her hair, which smelled of raindrops and lavender. He'd been hoping she wouldn't feel this soft. . . .

Gradually she stopped crying, but not trembling. Nevertheless, he disengaged himself and took a step back from her.

As soon as he moved she looked up at him. "You'll not stay with me, then?" She was wiping her eyes with the back of her hand.

"I never planned on leaving."

"You were going to saddle Cormac."

"I use his saddle as a pillow when I'm not welcomed in local haystacks."

She glanced back over her shoulder at the haystack, glistening in the light of the half-moon, and he took her by the arm and steered her back to it.

"I've never done this before, you know," she said.

"Slept in a haystack?" he asked, secretly smiling.

"You know very well I mean with a man so—so nearby."

"Actually, it's been awhile since I've slept in a haystack myself, but I believe I recall the correct behavior. I promise to shut my eyes."

His attempt at humor didn't work. When she sat down, looking forlorn, she hugged her arms to her bodice. She shivered all the more, and he realized she was clad in less than he.

With wide eyes she looked up at him and in a grave voice asked, "What are the precise sleeping arrangements?"

He sighed. "It depends. If I thought you might uncover my disguise, I'd sleep on the far side of the hay. On the other hand, if you continue to cry and shiver, we risk the chance of a farmer hearing us or you freezing all night."

"Then you would sleep—"

"Close to you, but only if you promise not to touch this scarf."

She nodded solemnly, her mouth quivering as she said, "I won't touch it. I promise."

With a curse he sat down and took her in his arms and wrapped his cloak about them both. When she stiffened slightly, he ordered, "Put your arms around me also. You'll be warmer."

As soon as she obeyed, he felt her body relax against his. "Now, don't cry or else I'll have to kiss you to prevent your being heard."

She immediately caught her breath and took little gasps until she stilled.

"You're very warm," she said at last.

"I'm gratified to know that," he said dryly. It was the first time he'd held a woman in his arms and been rewarded with that particular compliment.

Meanwhile, in a soft voice she began to talk. "My big brother Roddy knew all the stories about the Fian. . . . He's gone to America now . . . but he taught my younger brothers all the old legends. For a long time I wouldn't believe in such fairy tales. I was much too sensible. . . . Now Ireland seems so far away."

"Everything seems far away when you're on the run from an assassin. Even the years seem long."

She made a sympathetic sound and began to talk about her home in Ireland. Her voice fascinated him, especially the way she talked so softly. The way lovers did before they fell asleep, he realized, except he guessed she had no idea of *that*.

With a guileless motion, she curled herself closer to his warmth. "Now tell me," she whispered, "what happened to the men who killed your mother?" She might have been requesting a bedtime story.

His voice felt huskier than normal. "The inquest returned a verdict of death by accident. The English don't think it such a terrible crime to kill an Irish. Do you understand now, lass?"

He felt her nod against his chest. "I do now . . . and what of you? Will the Fian bring these men to justice?"

"As God is my witness . . ." Their clothing provided a scanty barrier between them. He felt her breasts, the slender outline of one hip, and swallowed hard before continuing.

"One's a very important man in London, and it won't be easy, especially since his main goal is to capture the Fian—me."

"And what of the other?" She moved and, when she did, unwittingly brushed closer.

"The other?"

"The other murderer."

"Dead. Long dead of too much drink."

Her voice vibrated through his skin. "And now tell me about your English father—"

"I can't, lass." Voice husky, for a moment he struggled with his baser needs. "I can't tell you anything about my English family any more than I can let you see my face. Let me tell you of London instead. . . ." For a few minutes he described it, then stopped, close to shaking from the physical self-restraint necessitated by these close arrangements. At last she lay still and calm in his arms, her breathing even.

He pulled the cloak tighter about her and tried to control his taut body. Her arms clung to him, and even in sleep she hid her head in his chest for protection. As for himself, all he could feel was his pulse throbbing with a deeper need than merely warmth.

A lone horse and rider trotted by on the road below the meadow, and he put his hand gently over her lips in case she awoke and cried out. His arms stayed around her. Far away, down in the valley where a village nestled, a train whistled.

Sleep eluded him. This girl had asked about his English family. What would he tell her if he could?

What a tangled web his father and mother had spun. Though only eight at the time, he still had only to see winter's snow to recall his father's death. The sod had scarcely settled on his father's grave when his uncle had arrived and taken him back to England to be raised "properly" in English schools. Years of endless loneliness. On the outside he was frozen into the mold of the proper English schoolboy his uncle wanted as his heir. But on the inside . . . what longings.

Then the long-awaited holiday to his mother—an annual visit which he lived for. Without warning, the best part of boyhood ended—the camaraderie with other Irish boys, the romps through Irish hills, the hunts, the fishing under carefree Irish skies.

With no effort at all he could call to mind his mother's still face after the coach struck her down, and feel again his own grief and rage, taste the blood in his hatred. As clearly as if seeing the icebound Thames caught in a rare freeze, he could recall the last rites in the little parish church, but the interminable years at his uncle's estate rushed by in his mind like water through his hands.

Though replete with luxury, never again had he been completely happy. When they thought he wasn't listening, the servants had gossiped, particularly about Tyson's father, Lord Weston's younger brother, who it seemed had been a most rebellious second son. Apparently, no one was surprised at the eccentricity of Tyson's father in eloping with an Irish beauty. Scandalized, yes. But not surprised, not even when his father had died young.

Secretly Tyson had read the tales of the Fian and other Irish heroes. He also memorized the names of his mother's murderers from the records of the assize court and, through unobtrusive questioning, learned the details of the life of Nicholas Seymour, the drunken driver. Their paths had crossed repeatedly through the years, at first accidentally, and then deliberately as he followed Nicholas Seymour into politics, the better to keep watch over him.

Oh, yes, he could have killed his mother's murderer years ago, but there were some punishments worse than dying, and that's what Tyson meant for Nicholas Seymour to have—and part of that punishment was the constant turmoil the Fian created with the Irish.

Always, too, beneath the carefully contrived facade, like a second heart, beat his dream of Ireland. Irish he was, and no amount of English schooling and English uncles could change that. And as for his English father—rest his soul—

the Fian felt certain he of all men would have understood his double life. But his father would not understand about his plans for this girl lying in his arms, because, unlike him, his father had been free to follow where his emotions led.

As the too familiar empty feelings enveloped him like the very darkness, he closed his eyes. He might hold Aileen Connolly of Ireland for this night, but his double life prevented him from feeling anything for her, and he'd be wise to remember that. On that stern thought he finally let himself fall asleep.

Unaccustomed to lying so near a man, Aileen woke up once during the night, remembered where she was, and scarcely dared breathe. She'd never realized how infinitely safe and warm a man's arms could be.

And how good his whole body could make her feel.

An ache began deep within, a trembling not caused by the danger of the bomb or Leedes's threats or even by the dampness of the night.

His hold tightened, and she shivered, only now the shivers were deep within—like waves of unbidden sensation Aileen couldn't explain. She felt as if she were unfolding in the warmth of his body like a flower might unfold to the sun—and this in the dark of night.

Still she lay unmoving, until the lying together seemed natural. Aileen fit into all the angular places of this man's body, into the very maleness of him as he made a natural refuge for all that was feminine in her.

The crown of Aileen's head brushed the tip of his chin where she nestled against his throat. With his pulse beating a soft tattoo, she fell asleep again.

When she awoke again at dawn, she lay thinking over the events of yesterday. In sleep the Fian's arms had fallen away from her, but she had only to look at him to remember his embrace.

She felt ashamed for throwing herself at him, for giving in to tears. But when he'd threatened to leave her, she'd felt it was the last straw. For a split second last night, just before she ran to him, she'd felt that she couldn't go on alone.

But now in the early hours of the morning, rested, she could think with a clearer head. Of course she could continue on alone. From the way the Fian talked last night, apparently she'd have to because she had a feeling he meant exactly what he said.

Carefully she turned to stare at him in sleep. Such a strong-lined profile and . . . more. A tempting discovery, in fact. In sleep, not only had he flung his arms from her, but his scarf had slipped, and, oh, how she wanted to look at his face once before they parted.

Purple streaked the sky, and soon there'd be enough light to see him clearly, but she felt guilty. After all, she'd promised him not to touch the scarf that hid his face, and a promise was a promise.

For a few moments she lay there very still, battling with her conscience, asking and answering questions that seemed to go in circles. Would he know she'd seen him? Of course not. Would anyone else know she'd seen him out of disguise? Only Cormac. A tiny smile teased at her mouth.

Then suddenly she sobered, knowing she had precious little time before he would surely waken. Finally she asked herself the question she'd been tiptoeing around. Could she live the rest of her life wondering what the legendary Fian looked like when she'd been this close?

Her lips moved with the silent answer. No . . . No.

Very slowly, so as not to wake him, she raised up on one elbow, holding her breath while she peered at his face. She had to stop herself from taking a quick catch of breath. Oh, but he was handsome. Her gaze took in the bold profile of his face, the strong mouth, the straight fine nose, the brown sleep-tousled hair, the shadow of a dark beard, and right in the middle of his chin, a cleft. Her finger yearned to touch his chin, just for a second. But she refrained.

She looked at his eyes, still shut in sleep, and wondered at their color. His lashes lay long and dark against his strong cheekbones.

A bird flew up suddenly, and he stirred.

With a soft motion she dropped to the hay and shut her eyes, pretending to be asleep. She could tell when he sat up and when he turned to look down at her, and she had to be careful to keep her breathing even. Finally he moved away, and she heard him talking to Cormac.

Immediately she missed his warmth, but for a few minutes longer pretended to be still asleep. Delicious sensations enveloped her.

Is that what lying together did to you? Was it supposed to give this ache to a body, a longing to touch forever like trees that have grown accustomed to being intertwined?

Finally, when a reasonable interval had passed, she stretched, opened her eyes, and sat up. She looked in the direction of Cormac. The Fian was there, saddling the horse.

He looked like a stranger, yet she couldn't shake the feeling that something fateful had linked them together last night, and she tried to shake off such self-delusion. It sounded too much like the stuff of fancy.

He came toward her then, disguise in place, but his gaze was on her, intent, almost angry.

When he walked up close, she looked into his eyes. They were hazel-colored, very nearly green, and she could have lingered in their depths. Worried he'd read the guilt in her own eyes and guess what she'd done, she looked down.

She ran her hands over the folds of her skirt, and her fingers caught in a ragged piece of the damp serge.

"Are you all right?" he asked.

"My dress is torn," she said, not knowing how to express her inner turmoil.

"Kate Reilly will have another gown for you, something warmer. You'll have to memorize your way to her. Do you remember what I told you last night about London? It won't be easy in a city that big. Can you do it?"

Aileen nodded. "I'm not afraid."

Bits of hay and tinier bits of heather clung to her dress, and she made a try at sweeping them off.

"We have to leave soon," he said.

"I'm ready." She stood and looked at him, her chin high and proud, silently daring him to mention their intimacy.

Abruptly, as if he'd forgotten something, he moved away and rummaged in Cormac's saddlebags. In a moment he returned.

"You'll be ready after you've got train fare. Hold out your hands," and when she did so, he poured into them coins from a sack—coins in a variety of sizes, too many for just train fare.

"You don't have a place to hide these, I suppose?" and at her wide-eyed look of surprise, added, "You can't show this around London, or you'll be robbed straight away."

After a moment of thought she suggested, "The hem of my skirt?"

He shook his head. "They'd be too heavy. . . . Lift your skirt and show me your petticoat," he said matter-of-factly.

Color rushed to her face, but she complied, lifting her skirt ⌐ inches.

"Don't blush," he said, kneeling down to feel the fabric. "I'm going to make the cloth into a sack. I saw a maid do this once, a clever girl who used to say, 'Better lose a petticoat than your last coin.' "

With quick movements he tore a long strip from the hem of the garment and knotted the coins inside, forming a money belt. Then he instructed her to tie the long ends about her waist, under her dress, keeping handy only the few coins she'd need for a hackney cab and for one stop at a pie cart. She went behind the haystack and put on the strip of cloth, and when she came out from around it, he was waiting with Cormac, watching her.

After he helped her up on the horse, he reached out and brushed a last bit of purple heather from the hem of her skirt.

They rode in silence, and he tried to think of the future instead of the past, but the immediate past—last night spent in a simple haystack with this girl in his arms—kept intruding. To put that out of his head, he planned details of his next London riot, but his concentration was disturbed by worries of Aileen on her own in London. Finally, with a silent curse, he realized that, like Cormac facing an enormous cliff, he was shying away from the gaping reality of never seeing her again.

Too long, he told himself. Last night had been too long to be so close to a woman and not fulfill needs. Even now, as he tried to concentrate on the reins, Aileen's dark hair blew about his cape, whispering at his grip, distracting him. This journey as an escort had to end, because this girl was in danger of more than Scotland Yard and all of London's anti-Irish factions. She was in danger of his desire. And desire was a dangerous passion, he reminded himself—one that needed to be properly channeled. *His* needed to be reserved for the cause.

That thought carried him as far as the outskirts of the village, where he handed her two apples to tide her over till London, then helped her off the horse. Pausing with his hands on her waist, his voice close to her tangle of black hair, he asked, "Have you memorized the address to the Reilly house? Let me hear it again."

When Aileen verified the address, he nodded and released her. His guilt was eased by the spirit in her voice. "You'll likely get there before I can ride back, but Kate Reilly will give you shelter. Above all, be careful. Not everyone you meet's to be trusted. Do you understand me?"

At last she nodded and with a little smile said, "Sure and I think I found that out the moment I met you."

His banshee. His messenger of death. "Yes, I suppose you must have." He could still feel the softness of her body against his, and now he saw unshed tears darkening the blue of her eyes.

"You have to leave now," he said, surprising himself with the sharpness in his own voice. He understood the enormity of what lay ahead of her. Still, he surprised himself again when he pulled her close, for reassurance. "Good-bye, Aileen," he whispered against her hair.

"Good-bye."

When he heard the quaver in her voice, he nearly reached for her to pull her back into his arms, but she'd turned and started walking down into the valley, her gaze steady on the tiny train station. He watched her and felt his throat tighten.

He sat alone in the secluded copse until he heard the whistle of the departing train, and for a long time after she'd gone, conflicting passions dueled. The Fian yearned only for Irish freedom, but the man behind the disguise ached for this girl, for one more night with her in his arms. He'd not be so gallant a second time, he thought.

"Damn you, Leedes," he cursed his enemy.

Five

IN LONDON A little creature scurried across the rafters of the workhouse garret. Patrick rolled over on his straw pallet and whispered to his big brother. "Did you hear that?"

"Yes."

"Was it a ghosty, Seamus?" His voice quavered.

Seamus imagined rats and spiders crawling through the night and pretended a confidence he didn't feel. "It's a fairy, come to see if you're still being brave."

"It's too hard to be brave, Seamus. I'm hungry." Patrick's voice broke on a sob.

"Pretend you're eating Aileen's soda bread. Remember the gooseberry jam we used to eat with it?"

A pause. "Where's Aileen?"

Seamus sighed and swallowed thickly. Somewhere a mouse gnawed at a widening hole in the attic walls. They'd been here only a few days, and already it was getting hard to invent new answers. He pulled the thin blanket they shared up over his brother. "She's coming," he said with assurance.

"When?" Patrick's voice shook.

*Seamus had given the same answer night after night.
"Soon."*

*"How will she find us when we don't even know where we
are?"*

"We're in London, Patrick."

"But it's such a big place. How will she find us?"

*"Well, she needs help, I expect. Remember, the landlord
said she was being sent to the Fian. She may have to go a
long way to find him before she can come for us."*

"Is he as hard to find as us?"

*Seamus sighed, reliving the treacherous way they had
been parted from their sister. "More. Now go to sleep." He
ached from long hours of hard labor and longed to rest
himself.*

"What if the Fian won't help Aileen?"

"Do you think even the Fian could say no to Aileen?"

*Patrick shook his head, his face still hidden in the straw
ticking. "Will you tell me a story, Seamus?"*

*Seamus stretched his one good arm behind his neck.
"Very well," he said on a sigh, aware that every other little
boy in the attic was also listening intently.*

*"Once upon a time in the Kingdom of Tara there lived a
king named Cormac and a great warrior named the Fian.
Now, one day the Fian, who journeyed far and wide in his
adventures, chanced to meet a princess, a princess named
Aileen. . . ."*

*Seamus's voice blocked out all the night noises, until one
by one he was certain all the younger boys had forgotten
their rumbling bellies and fallen asleep.*

"London! Euston Station!" called a voice from another
arriving train, and the words forced Aileen back to the here
and now. The journey was over. She was in London, and
she couldn't stand in one place forever.

She stepped off the platform and followed the crowd through the gate, then stopped. Immediately all her optimism vanished like the pigeons that scattered up into the air, and she stood there pirouetting, staring after them, wishing she could travel with that much ease to her brothers.

Crowds of people and carts made their way around her, buffeting her. And all of these people seemed to know exactly where they were going.

Nothing could have prepared Aileen for the enormity of the place, not even the Fian. Euston Station was new, that was obvious, and except for a canopy of storm clouds in Devintown and maybe—just maybe—a Dublin cathedral when she was a child, never had she stood beneath such an enormous ceiling. She turned in place on the station platform, trying to get her bearings.

Afloat on an uncharted sea she was, her only compass the memory of *his* words. She drifted with the tide of people, looking for a hackney cab as the Fian had instructed, but when she found a vacant one, the driver refused her. "Ain't never known an Irish yet what could fork over the coins."

"But I have the fare," she insisted.

"Show me yer money then."

When she held up a pair of coins, the driver's eyes grew wide with surprise, but he snatched them from her and with a grunt told her sourly, "Get in but mind ye, don't touch nothin'."

The hackney was dirty inside, more ragged in fact than Aileen's own dress. But when she repeated the address the Fian had given her, the driver didn't argue anymore, just flicked the reins and set off.

Aileen pressed close to the window of the cab and stared in fascination as they made their way. If the home she'd left behind in Ireland had been a soft petal, then London was an unpruned climber. Her optimism peeked out, just a bit, as if she'd scrubbed just one cheek of its face.

As the journey continued, narrow lanes twisted through rows of houses in varying stages of decay, and on the streets hundreds of people made their living. Optimism hid its face again.

Nevertheless, she found the narrow redbrick house, slightly sooty, looking exactly as the Fian had described, like a grand old lady in need of rouge and powder. On the porch sat a scrawny cat, a poor imitation of the one she'd left in Ireland.

A little soot-covered chimney sweep walked by, a boy not more than eight—about Patrick's age—and just imagining that might be her little brother's fate caused her to shiver. She hurried up the stairs.

After a short wait the door opened, revealing a plump woman of rosy cheeks and twinkling eyes.

Aileen introduced herself. "You probably weren't expecting me, but—"

"As sure as I'm Kate Reilly, I'm always expectin' another Irish lass or lad. Fresh off the boat then, aren't you?" With a smile she pulled Aileen into a quick embrace. "There's always a pot of soup ready for a newcomer."

Moments later, after climbing up several floors past private flats let to Irish working families, Aileen arrived in a simple kitchen fragrant with the familiar smell of leek and oatmeal soup. On a plank table sat a single candle in a bottle, surrounded by a line of mismatched soup bowls.

"Kit, fetch coal for the fire!" Kate bellowed, and all at once there emerged from a hidden alcove a handsome little boy of about twelve years—about the same age as Seamus—but with a streetwise look about him. While Aileen slipped off her torn shawl, she drank in the sight of the boy.

Affecting a swashbuckling stance, the boy shook back a shock of blond hair from his forehead. "Don't you have a family neither?" he asked.

Sitting down, Aileen explained briefly what had happened to her brothers. Kate set a bowl of hot soup on the table in front of her. Suddenly ravenous, Aileen ate a few spoonfuls before a more pressing question occurred to her. "Where are the factories? Near here?"

"Everywhere, dear," Kate replied. "You'd best pray it's not a slave workhouse that's got those brothers of yours, because those places can swallow little boys."

"Factories are going to have a riot, too," chimed in Kit. "There's rumors on the street the Fian will riot again and that means—"

"No dawdlin', lad," Kate interrupted, "and don't be spreadin' tales of the Fian. Our house is watched close enough because of him." With a wooden spoon she good-naturedly chased Kit in the direction of the coal scuttle.

Remembering her brief time with the Fian, Aileen felt unaccountably uneasy. Maybe the Fian had not been telling tales from the mouths of leprechauns. Maybe he was indeed a dangerous man to know. She wanted to ask, but Kate's warning look at the boy held her back.

Aileen had no idea where to begin searching on her own for her brothers. "This Parliament," she asked. "Would it help me?"

Kate glanced over at Aileen as if amused by the girl's naive spirit and shook her head. "Parliament? Full of self-important men. Mr. Melbourne and Mr. Peel and maybe the Honorable Nicholas Seymour are probably the most powerful. Tyson Winslow is the most sympathetic. . . . But forget about important men—they have no time for the likes of us. If it's brothers you're wantin' to find, you'd best use

Kit there. He knows London like the back of his hand—better than any hoity-toity English gentlemen. . . . And before you worry on this any longer, you need a new dress."

Kate Reilly led Aileen up yet one more flight of stairs to the attic, which was filled with rows of cots, neatly made up with plain mended counterpanes. By the only window stood an antique wardrobe out of which Kate drew an assortment of gowns.

Distracted from her troubles, Aileen reached out to touch one gown and marveled at the finery. "It's more beautiful than what the landlord's wife wore."

Obviously pleased, Kate nodded, explaining, "When the original owners moved, it was sure enough hasty. Why, they didn't even bother with what was in this attic. . . . Go on now. Choose."

Aileen ran a tentative hand against the fine skirt of one dress after another. Green, blue, and rose danced in front of her eyes like an Irish field on a summer day.

Kate turned a shrewd look on Aileen. "You're such a pretty thing, but you look like you were rolled here in a barrel. That black piece, if you'll pardon my bluntness, belongs in my scrap bag. What happened? You didn't meet some of those aristocratic ruffians on the way, did you?"

Uncertain how to reply, Aileen fingered the rip in her skirt. This was her chance to ask. "I met a horrible Englishman who tried to use me to capture the Fian . . . Of course, I have no idea who the Fian is," Aileen hastened to add because, after all, she'd promised him she'd never give him away. "I don't know why, but someone wants him dead."

"Someone?" Kate Reilly had been heading out, but now paused by the attic door. "Mercy, but that's puttin' it mildly, lass. Many wealthy Londoners want his death. Just see him lead one riot, and you'd understand. . . ." She watched Aileen.

"Be careful, dear. Don't mention the Fian outside of this attic bedroom. He's Irish like us, but he's too dangerous to know." At Aileen's nod, she was gone.

Kate was right of course. Aileen mustn't mention him— or think about him. From the way he'd sent her off, Aileen doubted she'd ever see the Fian again. Nevertheless, she hugged her arms about her, remembering how it felt to lie with him.

No. Fanciful thoughts . . . Wee people in her soul . . . She simply wasn't going to listen to them anymore. Or mention his name. Without further hesitation, she selected the dress that would be warmest—velvet, in a shade of rose not unlike the wild roses of home. That done and a cot selected, she looked around her temporary home. The lone window drew her.

Curious, she leaned over the wardrobe and peered out. As if it were a fortuitous omen, the fog had burned off, though the autumn sun had not yet set. Down below, the courtyard of the narrow house may once have sheltered a secret garden, but now grew tangled weeds. Lines of drying clothes crisscrossed from the windows of the house and its neighbors. Beyond the house stretched rows and rows of London rooftops with their endless chimney pots and spiraling smoke columns.

Aileen said a silent prayer. In one of those rows of buildings, in one of those smoke-spewing factories, please, God, let her brothers be waiting safe.

Lady Pamela was not looking forward to the interview with her husband. For all his political expertise, Nicholas Seymour was deep down a weak man given to excess drinking, and, consequently, did not tolerate failure with any degree of patience.

Seething with frustration, she stood in her room while Agnes—the housemaid, who was filling in for Nesbitt, her regular maid—helped her change. Both a fire and a lamp burned away, brightening the dusk.

It had been a long journey back to London, and Lady Pamela was fighting a headache, yet her mind spun with details. She'd covered all her tracks, she was sure, the last detail having been to drop the little seamstress off at Lady Grenville's. And Leedes could be counted on for discretion as always.

Sighing, she rubbed her temples, then with a resigned air allowed Agnes to fasten her into a day dress. She didn't need to look in the mirror to know that her eyes were red-rimmed from lack of sleep. Moreover, to her everlasting regret, she'd never been beautiful, and there was no use looking to see if the mirror now told a different story. She'd simply had Agnes freshen the center part of her hair, then brush it out before tucking it up into a cap. Pity having to hide her auburn hair. It was her best feature while her face couldn't have won her a lowly baron, let alone a prince.

"Hurry up, Agnes," she said, irritated, as the clumsy girl fastened the back of the dress. Lady Pamela had no time for slowness. Ever since she'd been the plain, impoverished daughter of an earl—ever since she'd endured the contempt of the richer, prettier girls—she'd possessed a dreadful rush of ambition to improve her lot.

Adulation. That was what she'd always craved. The kind that prissy little Queen Victoria received, the squat little frump. If Victoria had not been the heir to the throne, she'd never have married her prince, nor would people comment on her beauty now.

Yes, it really was a shame the assassination plot had

failed. That rabble-rousing Fian appeared in more places, incited more trouble, than a criminal in one of those newfangled Edward Bulwer novels that her husband dragged home.

"Ouch," she snapped crossly when Agnes pinched her. "Do you have to do up a dress as if you're shaking out a rug?" Annoyed, she finally pushed the girl's pudgy fingers away. "Get out of here. I'll finish it myself." Agnes scurried out of the room, leaving it in disarray.

Lady Pamela stood up, smoothing the skirt of her dress. Her husband, the Honorable Nicholas Seymour, awaited her. She'd best get the interview over with, she thought, patting back one last strand of auburn behind the lace frill of her Babet cap.

Downstairs, she stepped into the drawing room and observed her husband taking his leisure in a wing chair. As soon as he spied her, he leapt to his feet, nearly splashing the brandy in his glass onto the embroidery of his silk vest.

With quick steps she moved toward the fireplace, and he followed her. When she turned so that her back was to the fire, he was already standing practically on top of her, his breath heavy with liquor, the finely cut features of his face more flaccid than usual.

"What took so long?" he asked.

She'd been gone only a sennight and smiled briefly as if at an impatient boy.

"You know what I'm waiting to hear," he demanded. "Tell me it worked. He's dead, isn't he?"

"Not unless his horse threw him when he escaped." She watched the angle at which her husband tipped his brandy glass, wary lest he spill it on her gown.

Obviously disappointed, her husband backed into the wing chair by the fireplace and slumped down into it.

"What went wrong? It should have been a foolproof plan. Did the girl open the box and destroy herself first?"

"No. They're both alive." She ran a finger along the mantel checking for dust and feigned a casual voice. "The Fian apparently hasn't stayed alive this long without scenting a rat."

"What happened?"

"I'm not certain. I wasn't there. Leedes says the girl complicated things, but what's done is done," she said in her airiest voice. "I'll think of another plan. Think of this as no more than an inconvenience—a temporary setback."

"How can I? I have duties at Parliament—and now this."

Pity, her husband never could see the silver lining in anything. "Let me know if our chief suspect—Tyson Winslow—shows up at Parliament. Then we'll know he's returned to London. That would be valuable information for me. I really shouldn't have to rely on Leedes to provide everything."

"I provide well for you—very well indeed." Nicholas Seymour scowled at the expensive ribbons dangling from his wife's cap, then tossed off his brandy.

Uneasy with both his sarcasm and his drinking, Lady Pamela feigned a light laugh. "You know what I mean. We're talking about the Fian, not finances."

"Enlighten me. Did he fight? Wasn't he at least injured?"

"I didn't stay to watch . . . but according to Leedes, the girl turned out to be a fighter."

Nicholas Seymour's fingers tightened on the stem of his brandy snifter. "Leedes is incompetent when it comes to choosing women."

"I suggested he use the plainer girl, that sparrow Maeve, but—"

"Maeve?"

"The seamstress friend of the other girl's. A mere detail.

Is there anything else you want to know?" She watched the flames consume her fine crystal.

"Yes," her husband whined. "Is it absolutely necessary to kill this Fian in order for me to be prime minister? I'd be just as happy merely revealing his identity."

His tone of voice grated on Lady Pamela's nerves. She turned a tired gaze on him. "You need some kind of proof to reveal who the Fian is. Besides, the point, my dear, is not what happens to the Fian, but that you need to do something quite spectacular—something that will show up Melbourne, who's obviously getting too old, especially to be making cow eyes at the queen. And as for Peel, well, all you need do there is show up his fancy Scotland Yard by capturing the Fian yourself and then—"

"Enough." He stood up as if he'd been unleashed. "I didn't request a speech. I can't abide it when you try to discuss politics. It's unladylike. I'm going out," he stated bluntly, stalking from the room.

Stinging from her husband's sudden dismissal, Lady Pamela stalked past the butler, who stood poker-faced near the door, and regally made her way back upstairs. She slammed the door to her room so hard it startled the maid. "Well, don't just stand there, Agnes. Get me some sherry. I'm exhausted."

Inside, she felt both humiliated and angry. She knew where her husband would be going—to that mistress he kept. Once, in an awkward moment, she'd caught a glimpse of the hussy, wearing a gaudy gown and hanging on her husband's arm. . . . Lady Pamela's thoughts suddenly halted.

Gown. All the loose ends weren't tied up—she'd forgotten about the gown. The girl from Ireland and her seamstress friend had both seen the silver-gray dress. Obviously, she'd need to dispose of it—especially since the seamstress, Maeve, would likely come here in a few days as a dressmaker for the Seymours' daughter. Lady Pamela crossed to her bed where Agnes had left the gown, picked it up, and traded it for the tray of sherry Agnes set down on Lady Pamela's dressing table."

"Burn this dress. Do you understand? Burn it. Tear it into shreds if you need to, but destroy it."

The sullen-eyed maid bobbed a curtsy. "Yes, ma'am," and reached for the gown, her eyes brightening suddenly.

Lady Pamela saw the look and immediately chastised the girl. "Don't get any notions of keeping this dress, do you hear me? I want it burned."

"Yes, ma'am."

"Now leave me awhile. I want to rest." Agnes might be worthless as a lady's maid, but at least Lady Pamela could count on the ninny to be obedient—to follow orders.

"Curious, isn't it, that the Fian didn't stir up one single riot in London while Parliament was in recess? Do you suppose he could have been out of town?" Standing in a lobby of the crowded Parliament buildings, Nicholas Seymour spoke in a voice loud enough for just one man alone.

Tyson Ryan Winslow never flinched. Not even a blink gave away his thoughts to Nicholas Seymour, who as usual appeared to be nursing a hangover. "Actually, I was so occupied with my own pursuits that I never noticed," Tyson replied.

"The bets are running heavy at the club that he'll riot again soon."

"Are they?" Tyson said. "Myself, I prefer to place my money on faro. You ought to try it. The odds are better. At least in that game you can see what cards you hold." And with that he turned, knowing he'd left Seymour the way he liked to—flushed and at a loss for words.

Damn Seymour. Impatiently Tyson prowled through the Parliamentary construction, unable to abide one more debate on either social reforms or on the gothic architecture planned for the rebuilding of the Parliament buildings. All he could think about was the girl. Had she arrived safely? Had Kate Reilly taken her in? Certainly, he could go see for himself, but he didn't want to take the chance she might recognize him.

To clear his head, he stepped outside the buildings and drew in some breaths of fresh air . . . and then he saw her—at least, someone resembling Aileen. Across the courtyard, staring up at the burnt shell of St. Stephen's Chapel, stood a slim young girl with wild black hair flowing down around a black dress.

With an involuntary movement he took a step toward her, then checked himself. A strange man came and joined the girl. Together the pair stood arm in arm on the cobblestones staring up at the Parliament buildings. They looked as if they were having a tour of London and had paused to gaze and comment on the coming reconstruction. Damnation, thought Tyson, but he'd been almost positive that was Aileen.

This obsession with her had to be caused by guilt—guilt that he'd sent her off alone. Perhaps if he went and saw for himself that she had indeed arrived safely, then he could relax and put her out of his mind. . . . Still, he fought against the impulse to find her. Hadn't he been the one to tell her that association with him was dangerous?

Yes, but that was when he'd been acting and thinking like the Fian. Today, attired in the trappings of a gentleman from cravat to topcoat, he was merely Tyson Winslow, heir to Lord Weston and a member of the Commons. No one had proof of his double identity, least of all Nicholas Seymour.

As Tyson Winslow, he could see Aileen Connolly—once—and not risk her safety.

No.

As undecided as a schoolboy, he paced back and forth in full view of passing carriages and coaches. Again, he glanced over at the strangers across the courtyard. When they stared back, noticing his obvious curiosity, he felt foolish.

That settled it. With uncharacteristic irritation, he turned and barked at the doorman to fetch his coach and driver. After all, he did have to visit Mrs. Reilly's neighborhood today to collect information on the Irish situation. If in the process he found out Aileen had arrived in the building, then that would be sufficient to reassure him.

By the time the coach arrived for him, the other girl and her escort were gone, and he'd calmed down. "Drive to the Irish district," he told his ever-patient driver. "To the Reilly house. Park across the street."

Since Tyson Winslow frequently did eccentric things like drive around the Irish district for hours at a time researching conditions or studying for a debate, he knew his driver took sudden excursions as routine. When they arrived outside the house Kate Reilly occupied, Tyson walked inside and knocked on a private door.

Martin Kelly, who occupied the front flat on the first floor, drove a delivery wagon and was one of Tyson's best sources of news. Bridget Kelly, baby on hip, invited Tyson inside, informing her landlord that Martin should be home anytime for the noon meal.

"Would you care to sit down, sir?" she asked, not completely at ease with her important visitor.

"No, thank you kindly, Mrs. Kelly. I'll just wait here and watch for your husband by the window. I don't want to disturb you, but I need to speak with Martin as soon as he returns."

After only a few minutes Tyson's vigil was partially rewarded. Martin had not arrived yet, but Kit ran down the steps of the building, immediately followed by Aileen. Tyson stepped back slightly and partially concealed himself behind the curtain.

At first sight of her, Tyson silently caught his breath. Even in the gray light of a dull autumn day, her hair shone rich and black about her shoulders. She talked animatedly with Kit and stared around the street as if wondering about the elegant coach.

Now that he knew she'd arrived safely, he could turn back and visit with Bridget Kelly and fuss over her baby, but he didn't. He remained where he was, staring out the window, hoping perversely that Martin Kelly's wagon might get caught in a rut and be delayed five or ten minutes.

As Tyson watched, Kit tugged Aileen over to a peddler's cart, and in fascination of choosing a treat, the pair lost interest in an empty coach. But Tyson's interest in them only heightened—especially in Aileen, who was wearing a new gown the color of roses. An Irish rose, he mused with rare whimsy.

She handed over a coin, one of his coins, to the man for a ginger cake, which she broke and with a smile shared with the boy.

If she hadn't smiled he might have been able to forget her. But when her face lit up like that, he saw her again, vulnerable and alone—depending on him. He could still remember holding her and again cursed the foolish gallantry that had kept him a gentleman.

He wished he could hear her voice, her laughter. Light and soft it was, and at the memory desire rammed into his gut hard and tight. His hands were balled into fists from the longing to touch her again, and for the first time in his life he knew a desire stronger than revenge.

In the back of his mind Tyson's duties as the Fian reared up and fought with his emotions. Now was not the time to let a woman into his life, particularly not this Irish girl.

Behind him, the Kellys' baby gurgled and laughed, breaking the silent spell. A moment later he saw Kit hail a passing wagon, and he and Aileen were gone—searching for those brothers, no doubt. Martin Kelly returning in his wagon passed them, and Tyson saw him wave at Kit.

"Is there some excitement going on outside?" Bridget Kelly asked shyly.

Tyson turned from the window to where she sat, simultaneously rocking her baby and stirring a stew. "Only a great fuss over my coach, I'm afraid . . . and Martin's come home," he added with a kind smile, walking over to stroke a lock of the baby's hair. Bridget Kelly dimpled, flattered by the attention.

As soon as Martin Kelly came in, they all sat down to eat, and Tyson immediately asked for news of the neighborhood. The Kellys' faces sobered. "It's the O'Flaherty lad. Donal. He was killed last week—eleven years old," Martin told him.

"Where? How?"

Martin kept his voice low. "At Percy's Whip Factory. The foreman took one of the whips to him. Left a widowed mother, poor woman, with five young 'uns to feed, and Donal was her eldest."

As he watched Bridget's eyes fill with tears, Tyson felt as if a rock had hit him. He knew the O'Flahertys. In fact, he'd known the widow O'Flaherty's husband before the man had died of consumption. "Do they have any help, then?"

"Aye, a bit. We've done what we can, but we're all

barely making ends meet. . . . Creditors are threatening to throw poor widow O'Flaherty in debtor's prison. I was hoping you'd come soon."

"Parliament's been on recess—not that it's any help, but I'll see what I can do privately." His own voice was grave, his mind already racing with plans to avenge this latest murder.

The Dog's Paw Tavern crouched low on the dark bank of the Thames. A banner sign swung over the mullioned window, through which could be seen a motley crew of beached seamen swilling ale. In the wee hours of the morning, after a long night of Parliamentary debate, Tyson made his way through the door of the place. He wore old clothes as well as a hat pulled low over his forehead. Changed as he was into common clothes, Tyson went unrecognized.

He welcomed the easy anonymity of the place and casually made his way to the back, where the windows looked out on the murky Thames. A staircase there led him to the upper floor.

Upstairs he rapped on the door to Digby's room, all the while hoping Digby had the good sense to be here at the inn tonight rather than on his barge.

"Wake up, Trigg, you no-good old sea dog."

Moments later he heard the sounds of a lock being turned; the door opened, and he slid inside.

A disheveled Digby Trigg rubbed the sleep from his eyes and clapped Tyson on the back in greeting. Reaching over to light the single candle on the washstand, he talked low.

"Ah, lad . . . lad. You gave us a devil of a fright when you disappeared after that bomb at the cove. Captured we thought you were. I was about ready to drink to your swift release from prison."

Instead, the older man celebrated their reunion by splashing some gin into a pewter tankard as well as a tin mug. He handed the tankard to Tyson and toasted their recent close escape.

"To the Fian," Digby said, relief in his gravelly voice.

"To Ireland," Tyson returned and took a second swallow before pulling out the single wooden chair and sitting. "I've had to lay low, then return directly to Parliament. And what about you? You weren't at your barge. No one followed you?"

"Me? I keep trying to get that through your head. You may have rescued me from a sinking ship and given me welcome work, but don't think anyone else cares a lick what happens to me. . . ." With a sheepish look, he left off reminiscing and addressed Tyson's query. "No, I had no trouble. The pistols that were left behind I buried in a grave at the church and rode straight back. Just an old man making his way to Londontown. I stayed low in the barge for a few days, and now you see for yourself."

Haunted by the memory of his own journey to London, Tyson had been only half listening. He stared into the tankard, seeing in his mind's eye Aileen's vulnerable face. . . .

Digby Trigg cleared his throat. "The last I saw or heard of you, lad, you were telling me about banshees. I feared when that girl came down to the cove you might actually 'ave met one."

Tyson knew the words were an invitation for details.

"If it had been a real banshee, then I'd likely be dead by now. The lass was just off the boat from Ireland and lost. She was a pawn as well." Tense suddenly, Tyson took another swallow of gin. He needed to forget seductive black hair and guileless blue eyes and think on more pressing matters, like his cause.

Digby Trigg watched and commented. "Am I to wait all night to hear about this lass then, or do we plan what the Fian will do next? Or," he asked with head tilted, "is the answer to those questions somehow one and the same?"

For a moment, except for the flicker of the lone candle, not even the long shadows on the walls moved, then Tyson shot Digby an impatient look. "I helped her find her way to London. Now, are you going to yammer about females all night? If so, I may as well leave and let you go back to sleep." Bolting up, he slammed down his tankard and headed for the door, then stopped with his hand on the latch. Digby's voice pulled him back.

"In case you're wonderin', the gun shipment is safely in Ireland. And as for London, the men are ready to act. You've only to say the word. . . . Did you bring news from Irishtown?"

With a nod, Tyson moved to the window and looked out at the Thames, staring at its blackness, lost in thought.

Defying the command not to chatter over females, Digby asked with wry bemusement, "Where's the lass now?"

"Swallowed up in London, I expect," came Tyson's dry response, almost as if he were talking to himself. He continued to stare out the window.

"Then she won't affect our plans, will she?"

"Has any woman . . .?" After a moment Tyson turned back to his cohort, his expression now hard-set. "And as for our plans . . . they've changed." In a voice that held only deadly calm he elaborated. "We need to get organized—as soon as possible. There's been another killing at Percy's."

Six

SEVERAL DAYS PASSED, and Aileen still hadn't found her brothers *or* Maeve. Nor had the rumored Fian riot come off. Yet tension in the Irish section of London was almost palpable.

"Kit Burtenshaw, you mind me now," Kate ordered. "None of this bringin' Aileen back here with blisters and too tired to move. You're startin' out late, and the days are short so don't try to check too many factories." Lowering her voice she spoke to Kit alone. "The word is out. The Fian may strike tonight."

"The word's been out for days now," Kit replied. "Aileen won't believe it's true anymore."

"Never mind that. She doesn't know London." Kate tied an apron about her old dress and cast a stern look at Kit. "Mind me now about staying clear of Percy's Whip Factory."

"Aye, mum, I'm not lookin' to walk into a riot."

Aileen finished tying her cape and joined them, bonnet in hand. She pretended not to have overheard Kate's warning. "You know, Kit, if we have time I'd like to go back to that button factory. Those little ones look like they need a hug."

She tied on the bonnet which Kate had loaned her, a simple brimmed affair of green velvet and white roses. As she tied the ribbons beneath her chin, Aileen debated what to really do. Kate Reilly meant well, but Aileen knew she could take care of herself.

Besides, it still hurt to see all the poor children in every factory—all the wee faces, the ones who wept openly, the others who pleaded mutely for help. Somewhere out there were Seamus and Patrick. Aileen couldn't give up.

She gave the bonnet ribbons a last tug and followed Kit.

But as soon as she had him outside on the street, Aileen whispered to him. "Kit, do you truly know the way to Percy's Whip Factory?"

Kit gulped and flushed. "Aye, miss, but I promised not to lead you there. It won't be safe tonight."

"It's still daytime."

"But not for long. Aileen," stammered Kit, "ye've never seen one of the Fian's riots."

"Whisht. All this riot talk is obviously nothing more than fearful worry." Aileen's voice held only confidence. "I've not seen one riot yet. Besides, I'm not afraid of the Fian. I'd ask him to help me." And she would. Maybe if she found the Fian, he'd reconsider his earlier refusal to help her find her brothers.

She started off into the crowded street. No, she wasn't afraid of meeting the Fian again. Hadn't she known the gentleness of his arms after all? She'd decided if she had anything to fear it might be the touch of his arms about her again. . . .

"But . . . but, Aileen . . ." Kit blustered and finally found his tongue. "It's not the Fian you've got to be afeared of. It's the rioters. . . ." He was distracted by an approaching wagon. "Ho, here's Smythe."

Aileen gathered this was their transportation.

"Hurry up, lad," barked Smythe. "The gentlemen at White's won't have their supper if I don't get there soon."

Kit and Aileen climbed aboard amidst crates of squawking chickens. "Do you pass by Percy's Whip Factory?" Aileen asked in a casual voice.

"At a fast clip, miss," replied an obviously besotted Smythe, who stared at Aileen until she blushed.

As Kit climbed over a couple of chicken crates to try and object, Aileen turned over her shoulder and had the last word. "Listen, Kit, you only promised not to take me there, but if I find it on my own, that's another matter entirely and one for which Mrs. Reilly can't take away your supper." Turning back, she buried her hands in the pockets of her cloak and stared ahead with determination.

When, a short ride later, Smythe stopped to let them off, Aileen had her first glimpse of the immense Percy's Whip Factory, and she very nearly called Mr. Smythe and his wagon back. A multiheaded dragon the factory was, spewing out smoke from great chimneys like so many blackened mouths.

Standing with Kit on the lane, Aileen sensed a different mood on this block. Danger scented the air, and for the first time she regretted the late start they'd gotten.

Aileen watched as a vendor closed his bread stall and moved away for the night. Nearby, one lone member of the London police force and a private watchman stood conversing on a street corner. As Aileen walked past, she overheard talk of the killing done inside this factory and shivered. Stopping, she studied the two doors that led into the factory, each up a short flight of stairs, each flanking the place like guard towers. Both appeared impregnable. And in the shadow of the stairs leading up to one of the doors, a man crouched down hiding.

With a tug at Aileen's sleeve, Kit's eyes shifted in the

direction of the ruffian. "I know him," he whispered. "He's like trouble standing guard, announcing danger here. We shouldn't go inside, Aileen," pleaded Kit.

"I have to, Kit. Imagine my brothers locked inside and a riot breaking out! The Fian's got no reason to harm us, Kit. If anything too dangerous happens, we'll simply leave."

Choosing the nearest door, she and Kit climbed the stairs, knocked, and waited. Presently a shriveled old woman opened the heavy old door a crack.

Even though she had become as accustomed as one probably ever becomes to calling on strange factories, Aileen felt the tension in this one as if a thunderstorm were about to break. She glanced at Kit, at the sweat breaking out on his forehead, and felt an overwhelming urge simply to leave and run.

Instead, she clasped her hands tightly together for courage and inquired of Mr. Richard Percy, the owner. The old woman pointed to a shadowy alcove underneath the staircase leading up to the first floor. With determined footsteps Aileen made her way there, Kit following. She stopped by a wooden desk lit only by a single candle and in a trembling voice said, "Good afternoon, sir."

Mr. Richard Percy, a pock-faced man of gaunt build and cold demeanor, lit up at first sight of Aileen's velvet gown. He stood up. "How may I help you, dear?"

"Sure and I'm not your dear. But if it's two boys like my brothers you'd be knowing of, I'd be grateful for help."

As soon as he heard her soft Irish brogue, the light in his eyes dimmed. "I don't need any Irish snooping around here." Sarcasm replaced the earlier warmth in his voice.

Aileen was standing there, deciding whether to try and talk to the man or listen to the tugging of Kit at her sleeve, a tugging that begged her to leave, when a crash sounded from the front of the factory. Like a thousand voices shattering the night, glass shards fell to the floor, indicating the path of the rock that broke through the window. Mr. Percy immediately pushed past Aileen and Kit.

Pressing Kit against a wall, Aileen hung back in the shadows, waiting to see what was happening.

"It's the riot," Kit said under his breath. "Oh, Lordy, I knew we shouldn't never 'ave come here. . . ."

Outside the factory, at the sound of the first brick crashing through the window, the Fian pulled back on the reins. Cormac reared, screaming his defiance, jerking his head around.

The crowd split apart as if a bolt of lightning had rent the sky, and Cormac charged out of the shadows. Men who had been in hiding revealed themselves and their weapons. Torches lit the night, and from the street rose up the cry, "The Fian! The Fian! He's come! Follow the Fian!"

As the Fian well knew, no other man in London, or indeed, in all of England, could have exercised the slightest control over the crowd, and even his control was barely maintained. "Go after Percy, but leave the other establishments intact," he called to them. "And no pillaging."

The factory watchman took one look at the dark-caped Fian riding on Cormac's back, looked next at the mob behind him, and took off running in the opposite direction, screeching for Scotland Yard. A rock struck him in the back, giving added speed to his flight.

"Free Ireland!" The chant was started by one of the Fian's loyal men and picked up by others in the crowd. As an exclamation point, another larger rock crashed through a ground-floor window of the factory.

"Repeal the Act of Union!" More and more men took up the chant. "Free Ireland."

Angry words spiraled into the night like a battle cry, and with an upraised fist, the Fian gave the signal, a cue to

begin a performance of violence. As if a match had been
struck to dry powder, the crowd exploded into a mob. They
threw small stones, rocks, garbage. Even precious eggs and
coal struck the outer walls of the factory.

The Fian stayed on horseback so he'd be visible to the
people, in particular the owner of this factory, who'd
flogged to death young Donal O'Flaherty. To extract
revenge, the Fian hoped to lure Richard Percy outside the
factory. He looked back once to be certain his chief
accomplice was in position.

Digby Trigg was astride another horse near the rear of the
mob watching for the arrival of Scotland Yard men. It was
Digby's task to waylay or slow down the progress of law
enforcement.

"Freedom for Ireland!"

"Power to the Fian!"

"English murderers. You've killed one too many!"

The crowd's chant echoed through the dusk in a litany of
anger. The Fian knew the noise could be heard blocks away
and smiled to himself, imagining that as far away as the
Dog's Paw Tavern, Londoners would be lowering their
drinks a moment to listen.

Many a smile would be hidden behind a mug of gin or
ale, and that night more drunks than usual would be thrown
out on the streets. Barmaids told him it was always that way
when the Fian rode.

Inside the factory Aileen's own heart beat faster, so she
could well imagine the emotions of the workers. Yet,
watched over as they were by burly foremen carrying
whips, they continued to bend over their thongs of leather.
Except for the occasional flinch or furtive glance, no one
reacted.

Kit ran to a window, rubbing away the grime with a fist
so he could see out into the darkness. Another rock crashed

through nearby, and rushing to him, Aileen jerked the boy back, examining his face for cuts.

She chanced a quick look at Richard Percy. His eyes had grown colder. "I don't deserve this," he muttered. He shoved the old woman at the door aside to steal a glance outside. Aileen hoped he would forget about her and Kit. Gazing beyond him, she looked for a rear door that might provide escape. Seemingly oblivious, Richard Percy rushed back to his desk and, pulling open a drawer, retrieved a pistol.

Aileen could hear the battering of a log crash again and again against an outside door. Men's voices called out now and then through the confusion, cursing and grunting with their efforts to break in. Aileen flinched with each blow.

When Mr. Percy's foremen left their stations to grab pistols, she backed Kit into a secluded corner, and from there the two of them watched in breathless terror as Percy called for his strongest men to counter the rioters by pushing their weight against the inside of the doors. The explosive mood inside the factory was palpable, but still the more timid workers didn't leave their tables, not even when one man slipped in through the door just ahead of the log.

Like a pirate having broken into the inner sanctum, he straddled the floor and crowed. "I'm for tannin' Percy's hide and turnin' him into a whip. Are the rest of you goin' to sit there like mewlin' cowards? I'm for the Fian." And when the crack of a Percy whip hit the brick wall, Mr. Richard Percy's workers flinched.

The front door still separated the mob from them, and gingerly Aileen pushed Kit out of the corner and edged along a rear wall of the factory. The battering ram broke through, ending her hopes of escape. Where the door had once sat on squeaky, albeit sturdy hinges, now stood a gaping hole. And through that hole rioters spilled inside.

Pulling Kit behind her, Aileen now ran for the place where she'd spotted a quiet back door. Together they pushed against it, but it was locked—with a stout padlock.

There was no time to feel disappointment, even fear. Immediately Richard Percy came up from behind and grabbed her by the elbow. More and more rioters spilled into the front of the factory, and the workers huddled together.

Aileen trembled from the pain of Richard Percy's grasp. Kit had been right. She could never have imagined this.

With Richard Percy's vicious hold, Aileen had no choice but to drop the brick she'd picked up and abandon any hopes of smashing the formidable padlock. Tightening his grip on her arm, he twisted it behind her back so hard she feared he might break it. With crude movements he marched her through the factory, quickly steering her past the part of the mob that had entered and toward another door at the far end of the factory. Shoving her outside, he stopped on the front stoop. Immediately the crowd scrambled toward Richard Percy.

The ribbons untied, her bonnet swept off in the confusion, Aileen tossed back her head so that her hair spilled in an inky ribbon down her back. It seemed to her that she was caught between a dragon and a mad dog. She wasn't sure which would eat her first. Her head felt light, and perspiration dampened her palms. With her one free hand she quickly crossed herself. Richard Percy rudely yanked her hand down.

For a moment it actually seemed as if the crowd paused and caught its breath, taking in the unexpected presence of Aileen. All at once the mob surged forward and thrust torches and abusive words at Richard Percy. One lump of coal hit Richard Percy on the arm holding Aileen. A small rock struck Aileen's skirt, bruising her leg. Unable to fight back, she could only flinch, and she bit the inside of her lip until she tasted blood.

The Fian sat astride his horse some yards away, but he immediately spotted Percy and the girl. He stared, motionless, as if he'd seen a ghost. Black tresses, scented like lavender they would be—the piquant nose, dusted with freckles—cheeks of rose and that stubborn chin—eyes that blazed with anger, blue they would be if it were daylight—and soft she would be if he held her in his arms.

Aileen. His breath cut in so sharply it hurt.

Percy yelled at him, barely able to make himself heard above the sounds of the mob. "This lady . . . visiting . . . Talk sense . . . mob stops this vandalism . . . she'll die . . . I'll say . . . mob did it."

The Fian only wavered a second. Taut with shock, he could think only of the danger to Aileen, and he cursed the grapevine that had spread news of this riot. An unwilling banshee she was—still.

He held up a hand to the crowd, but he had done his nighttime work too well. They were, as he had planned, a wild thing out of even his control. The Fian mustered his men, incited riots. He didn't control them. For the first time in his dubious career, he cursed his well-laid plans, his talent for inspiring the mob. Edging his horse through the furious crowd, he only knew that somehow, he had to get Aileen from Percy.

Yet another rock hit the door only inches from where Percy and Aileen stood. Time for thinking had become a luxury. With rare force, the Fian pushed Cormac through the mob, all the while scarcely daring to take his eyes off the black-headed girl in Percy's grip. She looked so little.

Though she stared at him, chin held high, eyes blazing, she gave no sign she recognized him. And for that bit of common sense he praised God and Aileen. It had him hoping he might by some miracle get her out of Percy's clutches and away from the pelting of the mob.

The Fian again held up a hand trying to signal the crowd to back off, but as he well knew, only time and maybe Scotland Yard could cool their emotions. As soon as he got close enough to Percy, the Fian called out above the din, "Why should I trade a factory for a girl I don't even know?"

"Because she's Irish like you," snarled Percy. He ducked to avoid a rock, and the full force of it hit Aileen on the shoulder. For the first time she cried out and looked ready to collapse were it not for Percy's arm holding her upright.

The Fian was almost within reach of her when Percy, for no apparent reason, let out a yelp and loosened his grip on Aileen. From where he sat on Cormac, the Fian had to crane his neck, but then he smiled to himself at what he saw. Kit, on his hands and knees, had his teeth fastened on Richard Percy's ankle.

Face pained, Percy reached down and grabbed Kit by the hair. Kit squealed, and Percy raised his hand, triumphant, to show off the fistful of blond hair he'd yanked out. When he raised his foot to kick the boy, he forgot his hostage and nearly lost Aileen. In the confusion Kit scurried off.

Hand to her shoulder, Aileen staggered and caught the cement banister of the stairs. The Fian urged his horse forward the last few feet, reached down, and grasped her around the waist. As he swept her into the saddle with him, for the second time in his life, he knew the vulnerable weight of her. Hiding the relief he felt, he forced his voice to be angry, growling in her ear, "What the deuce are you doing here?"

"Looking for my brothers. What might you be doing here?"

"Nothing, it seems, has blunted your sharp tongue, banshee."

For the benefit of the crowd he flashed a broad smile of triumph and held her just under her breasts in a possessive embrace as if she were the Fian's loot. But, privately, he wished he didn't feel the earth move while he held her. He moved his mouth close to her hair and whispered, "For God's sake, believe what I said. We don't know each other. Should anyone ask, I'll lie and pretend I don't even know where you live."

He had a fleeting glimpse of Digby Trigg, coat collar pulled up high, firing two pistols in quick succession straight up into the air before riding off—their prearranged signal that Scotland Yard men had been spotted. Grim-faced, the Fian knew Digby would be wanting another explanation later about why the Fian had for a second time abandoned carefully laid plans to go off with a woman.

And on that thought, he swung his horse through the rioters, who parted for him only because he was the Fian. Behind them, bricks, rocks, and garbage continued to fly, and the screams of Mr. Percy could be heard as someone took one of his own whips to him.

The Fian and Aileen rode without speaking through the noisy London streets. Assuming she still resided at Kate Reilly's, he rode straight there. There was no further opportunity to talk, even if he'd wanted to. As soon as they arrived, the Fian reined in his horse in the mews behind Mrs. Reilly's house. He didn't move to dismount, but instead held Aileen captured in his arms, listening to the rise and fall of her breathing. He didn't speak, nor did she, not immediately. The contrast between the surly mob and her quiet innocence was like night and day, and he savored the transition.

"You picked the wrong factory to search in," he said in a low voice, for once glad to be away from the violent place where people expected him to play the role of Fian.

Her reply came swift, but in a velvet-soft voice. "Sure and maybe it's you who picked the wrong factory to lead a mob of mad dogs against."

Leaning his head back, he laughed briefly at the truth of her viewpoint. Suddenly sobering, he slid off Cormac. Standing close by Aileen's ankle, he stared up at her, looking at the proud way she sat up high on his horse. The night was very dark, chosen for the riot because of the waning moon and the clouds.

But where the darkness had always been his welcome cover, now it was his frustration. Never yet had he been able to look his fill of her in broad daylight—always, even the day he'd sent her away on the train and the day he'd spied on her from the cover of the Kelly's flat—always they'd been furtive. Not even by modest candlelight had he been able to simply stare into her eyes. He felt as if a gravity stronger than the cloud-covered moon were tugging at him, pulling him toward this woman.

"Come down from there, Aileen Connolly, and explain yourself to the Fian." At the first touch of his hands on her waist, he felt her tremble and knew he should release her.

"Not so long ago you defied me to see you," she said, resting her hands above his on her waist.

"Time has passed and long ago is gone," he said with quiet fierceness, pulling her off the horse. He slid her down the length of him, and it was like a blade of soft grass against the strength of bark. Yes, the feel of her in his arms came back to him along with a thousand other sensual memories, and he added to them this new sensation of her vulnerable curves wrapped in velvet.

He had never trembled—not in his adult life—not till now.

"We will never see each other again," he said, as if to explain why he gave himself permission to yank the mask from his face. The passion of the mob was overruled now by the passion hardening his body.

Aileen touched a hand to his cheek. "It is too dark to see your face clearly," she said, as if reassuring him. "And I don't know your name," she reminded him.

His hand covered hers. "I don't know where you will be a month from now, a year from now." If he never saw her again, would a kiss be wise? Or would it be a torturing memory? He felt she was destined never to see him by the light of a candle or sun, but only by disguise and darkness.

"Nor do I know where you call home," she said softly.

"I don't know where you will take your brothers if you find them." His voice was a husky whisper, and his head moved down to her lips, touching them softly, then retreating a few inches to drown his face in the rich blackness of her hair.

"And I don't know what you do to earn your supper, sir." Her voice was like a caress.

"I lead an extremely boring life in the daytime, my lass," he replied.

"And I—I lead an extremely unsettled life in the daytime. If I find my brothers tomorrow, I will leave London and only hear of you in legend."

"So if I kiss you now, it is for luck and good-bye," he explained more to himself than to her.

"And if I kiss you, it is in thanks for twice saving me."

"Only twice was it?" he whispered, lowering his head to her again.

She nodded, and when she spoke her voice was the barest of whispers. "Do you believe that things happen in threes? If so, then you will have to rescue me once more."

Even though he tightened his arms around her, his words tried to push her away. "I told you, we will never see each other again. This is for good-bye." The last syllable was a whisper against her lips. Lord, she was sweet.

All he meant was to give her a gentle kiss. But her arms stole up around his neck, and she was kissing him back. As he crushed her to him, his lips hardened on hers and his cape blew around her, embracing them both.

He'd forgotten his riot. Somewhere in Londontown, far away, human passions clashed in a roar as the riot went on into the night. But nowhere did passions blend as much as on this square foot of earth where he held Aileen in his arms once again, and not so gallantly this time.

The sound of Kit calling Aileen's name came from far away like the wind. . . . Quickly she broke away from the Fian, her hand in his, then just fingertips touching, until finally contact between them broke.

Closing the space between them just long enough to take her hand, he kissed the inside of her wrist at its pulse point. He wanted to prolong his time with her, but knew he couldn't.

"Will you help me?" she asked.

He let go of her and looked up at her face, shadowed by darkness. He felt anguished at refusing such a simple request. "You know why I can't." He saw her nod. Swallowing back his misery, he turned from her, then mounted Cormac, and rode off. He forced himself not to look back, for fear he'd reconsider his decision and sweep her away with him.

"I can't, banshee. I can't help you." The Fian muttered a dark oath as he rode away. She could make him forget why he'd ever needed to be the Fian. He'd not help her. Yet his mind was so full of her that he looked neither to the right nor left.

Edmund Leedes had been in a tavern within a short distance of the riot. Ever since the aborted assassination on the west coast, he'd felt a stronger compulsion than ever to catch the traitor. Tonight he arrived at the riot close on the heels of Scotland Yard—just in time to see the Fian ride off into the night with a black-haired girl in the saddle with him.

Leedes would never forget the girl he'd escorted across the Irish Sea, the same female who'd pulled a gun on him and outwitted him. No, even in the dark he'd recognize her. Oh, yes, that was Aileen Connolly. He'd stake his new silver timepiece on it.

With a swift order to his driver to follow, he climbed back into his coach. Immediately the horses became hopelessly bogged down in the confusion. Mere seconds before the mob tipped the carriage over, Leedes managed to jump out.

Now he pursued on foot, only to be slowed when he walked into a group of rioters who'd begun fighting one another and considered him fair game. From his coat pocket he drew a small pistol and shot into the mob, which dispersed in bloody disarray, allowing him to move more freely.

At the fringes of the mob he found an unattended horse and appropriated it, rapidly leaving the riot far behind. The law had its work cut out for it this night, and Leedes was glad to be out of the melee. He followed at a discreet distance, not wanting the Fian to remotely suspect he was being watched. With acute interest Leedes noted the exact house where the Fian stopped with the girl.

He knew the house. A common Irish refuge run by a tyrant of an Irishwoman named Kate Reilly. Edmund Leedes smiled in satisfaction. The Seymours, particularly Lady Pamela, would pay well for tonight's information. Discarding his horse, he moved closer on foot, hiding in a shadowy doorway across the narrow alley. No one else was about, and most of the houses were shuttered tight against the sounds of the riot. Still, he took no chances and knelt down on his haunches to watch under cover of darkness.

Of course, he knew Seymour would ask why he hadn't killed the traitor, but truthfully Leedes didn't feel he could capture the Fian single-handedly even with a pistol. Hadn't the Fian proved he could escape the most foolproof trap?

Watching with eyes like a cat's, Leedes excitedly fingered the flask in his pocket. Oh, yes, he was certain that the black-haired Irish girl would become their best weapon for capturing the Fian. He had a clear view of the alley next to the Irish shelter, and as he watched the exceedingly tender scene between the Fian and Aileen Connolly unfold in silhouette, he smiled again in anticipation.

This time the Fian had made his own trap, of that Leedes was certain.

Seven

LADY PAMELA STOOD up and pulled the cord to summon the butler. "You've been most helpful, indeed, Mr. Leedes. Good day and thank you," she said coolly, nodding to the butler to escort the man out.

A maid entered, carrying a tray containing fresh pots of tea and hot water and milk. A footman followed, on his tray crumpets and marmalade.

As soon as she and her husband were alone, Lady Pamela picked up her teacup. "Come here, my dear, and pour a fingerful of that brandy in my teacup. Don't look so innocent. I know that isn't tea you're drinking."

With a sly smile Nicholas Seymour did as she asked and watched while she sipped from her teacup. She knew he waited for her reaction to Leedes's news with more anticipation than he did the queen's opening of Parliament. Taking her time, she set her cup down into its saucer and spread marmalade onto a buttered crumpet.

"Leedes is right," Lady Pamela said at last. "This Irish girl—this Aileen—could be a most effective lure . . . once again. She is quite beautiful, as Mr. Leedes says. But naturally what is most to our advantage is the—apparent personal interest the Fian has in her." She looked up to see her husband nodding in agreement. If she'd never captivated him with her looks, she knew at least her imagination and cunning fascinated him—and of course the title she brought to the marriage.

Lady Pamela narrowed her eyes and continued. "I'm going to let Lucy's maid go. She's not at all right for a sixteen-year-old. I shall replace her with this Irish girl."

"Oh . . . how do you mean to use her? From the determined set of your mouth and the calculating hardness behind those eyes, I know you've got something in mind." Nicholas Seymour leaned back in his chair, waiting to hear the details. "I want to know exactly what you're thinking."

She looked up at him quite suddenly and gave him her most beguiling smile. "I was thinking of the emerald pendant—the one I've been admiring at the jeweler's."

Her husband's face hardened. "Perhaps when the Fian is captured, an emerald will be an appropriate means to celebrate. First tell me your plan."

She felt her smile fade. "We need to force a confrontation between Tyson Winslow and the girl . . . to see how they react toward each other in public," she said thoughtfully. "Perhaps a dinner party or a soiree for the ton is in order. A Christmas party. With select members of Parliament invited, of course. You are that certain Tyson Winslow is the Fian, aren't you?"

"Not certain—else I'd have collected on my bets . . . but I've a strong suspicion. Tell me—how will you lure that Irish girl into our house after almost killing her with your bomb?"

"Don't be a ninny, my dear. I have my ways."

"You're bringing a virtual eyewitness into our house? How can you take that chance?" He leapt to his feet and began to pace the drawing room in agitation.

"Calm yourself." Lady Pamela picked up her needlework and gave her husband a disparaging look. "The chit would have no idea what complications she's walking into and never will, unless you tell her. Don't ever doubt how well I cover my tracks."

He turned and looked at his wife with mild disbelief. "Why should I be calm? You're taking too big a risk," he objected, slumping down in his chair again and eyeing his wife with frank skepticism. "How can you pull it off?"

"Really, dear, you don't want to know the petty details of how one hires a maid, do you? That's women's work." She picked up her embroidery from the settee.

"I could bear a few details. Enough to know you and Leedes will succeed better than you did on your last venture."

"Please, don't badger me." She threaded her needle and began stitching before revealing a few tidbits of her plan— just enough to pacify her husband. "Really, it's terribly involved. You've simply got to trust me—me and my contacts."

Uneasy with her audacity, Nicholas Seymour stood up yet again and positioned himself in front of the fireplace, hands behind his back. He waited while a parlor maid scurried in with a dish of lemon slices, then when he was alone again with his wife, he voiced his doubts. "Are you saying you want an Irish girl serving our daughter breakfast in bed and helping her dress?"

Lady Pamela looked her husband in the eye. "You have a Scotsman for your valet."

"That's entirely different," he said.

"I know. But, dear, think. It wouldn't hurt your reputation in Parliament to let others know you're not as small and prejudiced as they."

He sat down with a heavy sigh. "Yes, it may work. If this

Fian does indeed have feelings for—what was her name?"

"Aileen."

"Yes, that girl. The queen would be impressed if I could solve the problem of the Fian, wouldn't she?"

Lady Pamela nodded, her attention on the embroidery and the skeins of thread beside her on the settee.

He thought of a last objection. "What if the girl refuses to serve as your maid? What if she scents another trap?"

"A girl in her place will hardly have many choices, I expect. Don't worry so. Aileen Connolly is a total innocent. When I spread the word that a position is open, I'll be most particular, terribly choosy in who I hire." Lady Pamela snapped off a strand of green embroidery thread before she looked up with a cool smile and added, "Now, then, I know how to get the Irish girl here. But can you get Tyson Winslow here? You know he'll refuse a dinner invitation."

Nicholas Seymour mused on the problem. "I think we can make the guest list so enticing, particularly for someone of Irish sympathies, that he'll come out of curiosity."

"Quite." Lady Pamela bent her head over her embroidery, unraveling an unwanted knot. She flashed a dismissive smile, rethreaded her needle, and began to create a tiny green leaf in her design. She never looked up at him, not even when he strolled over and stood staring down at her needlework.

"Find the Fian," Lady Pamela commanded, then added in a soft voice, "else it doesn't matter whether I hire the girl or not, does it? And stop worrying. Exposing the Fian here in London is child's play compared to the bomb."

Aileen stood with Kit in the middle of London Bridge, staring through the light fog at all the boats. She hugged her arms about herself for warmth and unbidden came the feel of the Fian's arms about her. He was somewhere in this vast

city, but, she scolded herself, thinking about him would do
no good. Hadn't he refused her plea for help—twice
yet—and ridden off without a backward glance? A man like
the Fian had no time for the likes of her.

All at once she heard her name called. From far down on
the bridge, a feminine voice called her name.

Turning, staring through the last light of dusk, she saw
the unmistakable figure of Maeve standing alone against the
granite outline of London Bridge, the girl's skirts half-
enshrouded in fog. Yes, it was Maeve, her friend from the
ferryboat—the brown coils of hair still bobbed above each
ear.

With Kit following, Aileen picked up her skirts and ran
along the bridge to greet her friend. It seemed so long ago
they'd said good-bye on a windswept moor. "Maeve. Oh,
Maeve, you've come." She hugged her friend. "You'll
never imagine all that's happened."

"You've found your brothers?" Maeve pulled out of the
embrace and indicated Kit. "Is this one of them?"

Briefly Aileen explained who Kit was and a little about
their adventures on the London streets. She carefully left
out any mention of the Fian and shot Kit a warning look
when he would have said something.

"You're so different, somehow, Maeve." She was no
longer the weepy, frightened girl from the boat. Gone too
was the black dress. In its place was a tartan gown and a
pretty shawl. "You look grown up," Aileen added.

"But of course, I'm in London now, and I've had to grow
up fast, I expect."

"Yes, that's true." Impulsively she hugged Maeve again,
as if she couldn't believe she'd actually found her. How she
wanted to tell Maeve about that woman in the coach,
wanted to tell her about the assassination plot, but couldn't,
absolutely couldn't mention a word, else she'd be breaking

her promise to the Fian, and what's more, putting innocent Maeve in danger, too. She pulled away and told her friend instead about Kate Reilly's shelter.

"I have a position already," Maeve announced proudly, twirling to show off her new dress.

"As a seamstress?" Aileen guessed.

"For a real lord and lady. Sure and they own the grandest house, Aileen, except it's very far from London Bridge. And I only have one afternoon off a week, so I couldn't simply walk over here to meet you when it pleased *me*. I had to please my new mistress."

"But of course, Maeve."

"I tried once before and got lost almost. But today one of the Grenville grooms showed me the way. A handsome groom who works where I do, too," She blushed.

"How kind of him and your new employer."

"Lady Grenville is kind—and—and witty, but very demanding. She has me stitch the most beautiful gowns of real velvet, like the one you're wearing."

"Aren't you a clever one, finding work so fast—and such grand work." Aileen's voice held a hint of wistfulness. "And here I'm still wandering around to factories." She wiped her sudden tears. "I'm so happy to see you. I'm behaving quite silly."

Maeve took Aileen's hand in hers. "I understand, Aileen. You won't be happy till you find your brothers." She frowned, then suddenly brightened. "I've some good news for you—I know of a position you can try for."

When Aileen didn't immediately answer, but stood staring at Maeve, the girl added, "You're needin' a position then, aren't you?"

"Work? Yes, of course. I can't stay on much longer at Mrs. Reilly's . . . but . . ."

"There's a—a position open in a grand house," Maeve

stammered, as if fearful Aileen wouldn't like her idea. "It's just come available. The servants hear of these things first, you see."

"Sure and that's fine of you, Maeve, but without a letter of recommendation, they'd shut the door right in my face." She turned back to Kit.

Maeve darted around to face Aileen. Now she was the encouraging one. "But of course you can apply," she argued gently. "I've talked with other maids at other houses. They all started out knowin' little if nothin'. They told me how to put on a good interview."

"Even if you're Irish?"

"Why, being Irish doesn't hurt. The rich ladies don't care where you're from, just so the work gets done."

"Yes, I see. I need to think. . . ."

"You could do it. There are days off. I could help you look for your brothers." Maeve continued to encourage, even while she slipped her arm through Aileen's. "And here I thought you were the brave one," Maeve teased. "Promise you'll at least think on it? The position won't last long."

Nodding, Aileen walked off the bridge with Maeve and Kit. Maeve was right and a true friend. Other immigrants had come and gone from Kate Reilly's shelter while Aileen lingered on there. She did have to find a post so she wouldn't be a burden.

Ever since she'd arrived in London, she'd been curious what life would be like in a grand house . . . and so she really wasn't too surprised when curiosity won out.

Eight

LIFE IN A grand house, Aileen considered, as she made her way along the upstairs hall toward the back staircase, was not as fine as she'd imagined. Indeed, the more she thought about it, the more this grand house bothered her, as if the shadows cast by its fine draperies and statuary hid darker secrets—or a curse, even. A Druid curse. Certainly, this was the finest place she'd ever been inside, yet a happiness was missing that she'd known from her own cottage in Ireland.

As for her position—she found it not difficult at all. Once upon a time she might have considered that doing nothing all day except reading novels, eating comfits, and complaining that the maid had shrunk the waistline of her gowns to be a desirable life. Not so any more, she thought, as she made her way downstairs to the basement with a pile of Miss Lucy's laundry. After less than a month here in the Seymour house, she decided she much preferred physical activity to indolence.

Later that night, her chores completed, Aileen sat at the simple table in the spare attic room she shared with two other maids. By candlelight she wrote a long overdue letter to her brother Roddy. Her life in London was temporary, she explained, describing the humble attic shelter, giving him the spare details of her position, and asking him to write her in care of Kate Reilly. She wasn't certain she liked this Seymour house enough to stay on, but for now it paid well, and soon she'd help serve at a real soirée. With enthusiasm for the coming party, she was able to gloss over the more mundane part of the position, and she gave not a hint of the way the servants sniped at her Irishness.

More difficult were explanations about Seamus and Patrick. She described what had happened with as much delicacy as possible, trying to maintain an optimistic tone. The village school in Devintown had taught her to write adequately, but no schoolmistress had ever given her such a difficult assignment as this.

She paused, quill poised over the bottle of ink, hesitant to overcrowd her precious paper with too many words. Just one more line wouldn't hurt, she decided. Just one line about the Fian. Roddy would be so surprised. She turned the paper sideways and wrote up the margin, all the while trying not to squint in the faint light.

"You'll never imagine who I've seen here in London, Roddy. Now don't show this letter to anyone. Promise. It was the Fian himself. At a real London riot. You mustn't worry. I wasn't in the riot—only in the vicinity, and I'm very careful. The Fian believes in Ireland more than anyone, more than anything . . . you were right about him, dear brother. . . ."

She paused again, nibbling on the quill until it stained her lips faintly blue. She was not thinking of Roddy at all. Instead she was remembering the Fian and things she could never write to her brother—the Fian's kiss, his arms about her, a shared night in a haystack.

Sighing with impatience, she flung down the quill. She

was allowing her thoughts to turn fanciful. She sealed the letter and slid it under her mattress until she could post it on her next afternoon off. The mattress, she'd discovered, was the only safe place to hide her few possessions.

She'd no sooner straightened up than the door squeaked open. Like a hungry rat on the prowl, Agnes shuffled in, ready to change for her afternoon off. Agnes shared the double bed with Sally, the kitchen maid, and it was to that mattress that the sullen upstairs maid now headed. She threw her apron onto the bed as if disposing of a long gray tail.

"You aren't using my candle, are you?" Her accusation followed a glare at Aileen.

"No, it's mine. I bought it on my day off."

"Don't you have work to do?"

"Miss Lucy is having her violin lesson."

"I'm going to tell Mrs. Pembley that you're being lazy. She'll need your help polishing the silver."

"Mrs. Pembley knows where I am."

Aileen paused at the table, watching Agnes pull out a dress from under her mattress. She'd been about to pinch off her candle and leave the sullen maid in darkness—but hesitated. The flame shone brightly, reflecting off the dress Agnes had been hiding—a dress woven with silver threads—a most luxurious and rare color.

A memory of a woman in a silvery-gray dress illuminated the recesses of her memory. The woman who'd sent Aileen to the Fian—to assassinate him—had been wearing silver, a luxurious silver gown. Moving quickly around the table, Aileen stared at the dress in shock. Eyes narrowing, Agnes clutched the dress to her like a prize and backed away to the washstand.

"Agnes, wait," said Aileen, urgency in her voice. "Let me see the dress, please."

Agnes clutched it tightly to her bosom. "No, it's mine. Her ladyship gave it to me. I'm going to sell it now, and the money will be mine. You can't have it."

Heart thumping in her ears, Aileen advanced on Agnes. "I don't want the dress," she reassured Agnes. "You can sell it. Only let me see it closer. To smell the perfume on it. Please." She reached out for the hem of the gown, but Agnes drew back.

"It's mine, do you hear? It's mine, and I'll do what I want with it."

With a sudden thrust Agnes pushed her away so suddenly, she shoved Aileen to the hard floor. In a final insulting gesture she reached out and pulled Aileen's hair—and lost her grip on the gown.

Aileen tugged away and fell directly on top of the contraband gown, her face pressed to its bodice. The aroma of orrisroot, cloying and sweet, filled her nostrils.

Agnes began to pummel her back. "Get away, you Irish witch. I hate sharing my bedroom with you, hate having your clothes near mine on the peg, hate sharing the same wash pitcher with you, and I won't share the dress."

Aileen rolled away and flung the dress at Agnes. "Keep your dress, only quit your whining at me, else I'll tell her ladyship you're hiding it under your mattress."

"You wouldn't dare," Agnes spat out, eyes narrowed like a cat's when its fur rose in fury.

"She'd sack you if she knew you'd hid that dress. I wager you were supposed to burn it." Oh, yes, thought Aileen, if any dress was meant to be destroyed, it would be that one.

"How do you know?"

"We Irish have banshees and Druids who tell us secrets like that." Aileen couldn't help the taunt in her voice.

With a sniff Agnes bundled up the dress and wrapped her cloak around it and headed back out. "Her ladyship'd never believe you. She trusts me. Besides, I'll have it sold before she'd come up here looking."

"Say what you will, but lay a hand on me again, and I will tell what I saw, and the devil take my position here."

"Witch," hissed Agnes before scurrying away ratlike with her precious bundle.

Numb, Aileen sank down onto her cot, thinking back to her interview with Lady Pamela. Her employer had been so kind, the house so elegant. Aileen recalled the assault on her senses—the scent of beeswax, the glow of myriad candles, and the gloss of ceramics—a place that begged for fine ladies to make grand entrances and exits. In the midst of all this had sat Lady Pamela, the epitome of graciousness. Aileen's first impression had been of a woman of too much nose and forehead, not enough mouth. If it hadn't been for her stylish clothes, the lady might have been considered plain, except for the thick curls of auburn hair. And her questions couldn't have been easier—except for one.

"Are you engaged or likely to be married?"

To Aileen's mortification, she had blushed. "No, ma'am," she'd managed at last. "I've barely arrived from Ireland."

"You're a very pretty girl." The words were not said as a compliment. "I'll take a chance you'll not leave my employ too soon." Lady Pamela's voice had held an odd expression, and she had stared off at the rain falling against the windowpane.

Yes, the interview had been so easy—too easy. Aileen saw that now. And her growing feeling that this house held dark secrets had not been fancy.

Standing up, pushing her hair back into the knot she was required to wear, nervously brushing down the skirt of her black maid's dress, Aileen finally squared her shoulders and headed back downstairs. She felt wooden, numb with the implications of that silver gown.

Unexpectedly, the warning of the Fian returned. Remember, no one is to be trusted. *No one*.

So Lady Pamela was not to be trusted. Poor Maeve. Aileen couldn't bear to think of telling her friend this wonderful position had turned out to be a trap. But Maeve and all the other maids who'd known of the job had obviously been duped, also, and now all Aileen's suspicions pointed in only one possible direction—the woman in silver wasn't done using Aileen for her own purposes. But what Lady Pamela had planned next, Aileen couldn't fathom. For sure, Aileen wasn't here merely to tend to her daughter's dresses.

Her first instinct was to pack her few belongings and head straight back to Kate Reilly's, and yet . . . the Fian had saved her life. If there was another plot afoot to capture him, didn't she owe him a return favor? There was an immense problem with warning him, however. She had no idea who he really was or how to find him.

The voice of the housekeeper, starchy Mrs. Pembley, broke into her reverie. "Mary Aileen, where have you been?"

Aileen looked up and saw the woman standing in Miss Lucy's doorway. Beyond her, inspecting Lucy's room, was Lady Pamela herself.

Aileen felt herself go cold. Instead of lowering her gaze diffidently, she looked at the housekeeper.

"Took your time, then, didn't you?" Mrs. Pembley hissed. "You wouldn't be knowing anything about missing linens in this house, would you?"

"Mrs. Pembley, that will be enough," Lady Pamela said, appearing in the door and looking Aileen up and down.

"Are you finding everything satisfactory here, Mary

Aileen?" she asked. "I'm very pleased with the fine job you're doing caring for Lucy."

"Yes, quite, thank you, ma'am," Aileen said woodenly. Shy Lucy might have been a changeling, so different was she from her mother. What made it even more difficult with the other servants was Lady Pamela's obvious deference to Aileen. Now Aileen saw through the sugared words—saw the hidden manipulation as clearly as she saw her own face in the mirror.

"You may await me in the servant's hall, Mary Aileen." Black, starched, and jangling with keys, Mrs. Pembley's sole mood seemed to be somber and annoyed—especially at having to train an Irish maid.

Anxious to be alone and lose her thoughts in some mindless task, Aileen bobbed a curtsy and retreated to the back stairway. Holding the door slightly ajar, she stood on the first step, listening just for a moment. The voices of the housekeeper and Lady Pamela carried clearly down the hall.

"Now, then, Mrs. Pembley, what's this about pilfered linen in my house?"

"From my closet. The count is off."

"Then talk to the washerwoman. I shouldn't have to deal with such matters."

"The washerwoman is as honest as the day is long. I'd look under the mattress of that Irish maid," suggested Mrs. Pembley.

"Listen to me, Mrs. Pembley," said Lady Pamela clearly. "I don't want any trouble with the Irish maid. She's not a thief. I need Mary Aileen Connolly in this house, and you're to accord her the status of the other servants. Nothing more, but nothing less. That your brother was injured in an Irish riot is no fault of this girl. I want no trouble, and I have my reasons."

Moving soundlessly downstairs, Aileen's mind shouted,

Go ahead and hope I'll lead you to the Fian for whatever insane reasons you've got, you evil woman. As sure as I'm Irish, as sure as I know I'll find my brothers, I know you'll fail. She felt so shaken that she had to stop a moment at the bottom of the stairs to compose herself.

Mrs. Pembley put her to work polishing every piece of silver in the house—punishment no doubt because Lady Pamela had sided with Aileen. Long after the other servants went to bed, Aileen worked at the long table in front of the hearth in the servants' hall. Three times she polished the silver tea service, until by candlelight it shimmered with the same luster as the silvery gown that belonged without a doubt to Lady Pamela.

Hours later, an exhausted Aileen sank to her knees in front of the dying embers in the fire. After dipping her fingers into the still-warm ash, she spread a cross upon the breast of her dress. "Preserve me from evil," she mouthed silently.

With shoes in hand she tiptoed in stocking feet up to her room and retrieved the letter to Roddy from under her mattress. If Mrs. Pembley did search her room, Aileen had no doubt the housekeeper would read it, with all its incriminating words about the Fian. Next Mrs. Pembley would destroy the letter, but that couldn't happen. Roddy *had* to receive it.

Tomorrow Aileen would give it to Tim—the footman Tim—whose sister had married an Irishman. Earlier this evening he'd agreed to post her letter the next day while delivering invitations to the soiree. Grateful that she had one friend in the household, Aileen had promised to pay him a coin for the stamp, and he'd cheerfully told her to slip her letter to Boston into the pile of invitations. *Invitations.* Of course . . .

The rest of the plot fell naturally into place as easily as if she'd read Lady Pamela's mind. In the deserted hallway she flipped through the envelopes, reading. One of these guests—one of these names—was very likely the London identity of the Fian.

With ill-concealed impatience Tyson Winslow glanced at the handwriting on the envelope and broke the seal. Frowning, he scanned the contents. In spidery black ink on the finest parchment, an elegantly worded message invited him to a soiree given by the Seymours. They couldn't be serious about his attending, could they?

A second more personal note from Nicholas Seymour promised to invite a wide array of personalities across government and society lines. That new author Dickens. The architect of the new Parliament buildings, Sir Charles Barry. The newspaperman Marcus Owen. Lord and Lady Grenville. The former Prime Minister Melbourne. A selection of Irish and Radicals from Parliament, not to mention all the most important Tories and Whigs. An evening of conciliation and entertainment, the note said. But Tyson wasn't swayed by the guest list. He penned a note of regret, blotted it, and set it aside.

Feeling restless, he decided to visit the Irish district and feel out Martin Kelly on the latest news from Irishtown. He directed his coachman to Brushfield Street and stoppe opposite the fading brick dwelling that he owned. He stare up at the windows of the two upper floors—Kate Reill shelter—Aileen's home. He should have sent Aileen som where else, to a place where he had no connections. T he wouldn't have to fight this temptation to come and c a glance of her under the guise of checking with Marti Kate.

"Hello, Mr. Winslow."

Tyson turned and saw young Kit abandon a gar

marbles to run in his direction. "Hello, Kit." He glanced around in case Aileen should be nearby. She wasn't, and he felt profound disappointment.

"What are you doing here? Come to see Kate? She's out at the market."

"No, I had business in this neighborhood. . . . How is Kate Reilly's shelter doing? Full up?"

"Not right now. It's half full. Most everyone's found factory work."

"And you—what have you been up to?"

"Well, Aileen and I spent a lot of time searching the factories, so we knew where there were openings, and that helped people."

"Aileen?" He frowned, pretending not to know her.

"The girl who lost her brothers. Don't you know her, sir?"

"Ah, I think I know which girl you mean. Are you two—uh—going out today?"

Kit was shaking his head. "I'm going by myself now. It was a promise I made Aileen when she found a position."

Kit's words jerked Tyson's attention back to the boy, who was shuffling one worn shoe on the dirt pavement. "A position? Aileen's working in a factory?"

"Oh, no. Aileen was luckier than the rest. She's in service at the Seymours' townhouse. . . ."

Tyson moved a step closer to Kit, aware he must have a menacing expression, but he quite suddenly felt as if he might explode with rage. "A girl went from Kate Reilly's to the Seymours'? Why wasn't I told?"

Kit's eyes widened at the sudden severity of Tyson's tone. "She's only a maid. We've never told you where the others go. You've never asked before."

Tyson's features tightened. He was aware of his heart hammering in his ears.

"I say, sir, did we do something wrong?"

"What?" Tyson had to force himself to focus on the boy. "What? No. No, lad, you did right." With a gentle hand on Kit's shoulder he forced himself to speak in a normal voice. "I was only a bit surprised that the Seymours hired on an Irish."

"Mrs. Reilly says it doesn't matter as long as Aileen pleases them. Jobs like that are hard to come by."

"Yes, quite right." He gave Kit a half crown for his trouble and watched the boy run happily back to the marble game.

Tyson told his coachman to return home immediately. As he sat in his coach, aristocratic features set in anger, he was barely aware that the rain had begun outside. Nor did he pay heed to the raindrops that drenched his frock coat when he walked into his townhouse.

He didn't have to guess why he'd been invited to a soiree at the Seymours'. Nor did he imagine Aileen's new position there and his invitation posed a coincidence. Far from it. Someone suspected him of being the Fian and had seen him with Aileen. As simple as that. He'd stake his life on it.

Hands behind his back, he paced the floor of his study. He could handle himself, but he feared for Aileen. She doubtless had no idea of the danger she could be in once again. And all because of him. He owed it to her to warn her. To warn her that she was once again intended to play the pawn while someone tried to lure him out of disguise.

He tore his note of refusal up into little pieces, which he tossed onto the cold grate of his fireplace.

What to do? He stared out the window at the moon, hands clasped behind his back so tightly the knuckles ached. As the Fian, he ought to stay away. But as Tyson, he felt a deeper pull.

Aileen. The memory of her touch, her kiss, her embrace, had tortured him for weeks. It was with the utmost effort he had kept himself from seeking her out more blatantly and hauling her into his arms, and saying the devil take the Fian and the cause. He thought over the situation until he knew only one compelling emotion. He had to see her again, once more, if only to warn her and then watch the candlelight play across her face.

With sudden resolve, he sat down, and penned an acceptance to the Seymour soiree.

Nine

GRIMACING, TYSON GAVE his cravat a last tug and headed down the stairs of his townhouse to join his uncle in a waiting coach.

"Well, for a man who hates dandified costumes, you certainly took your time dressing," was his uncle's acerbic comment when Tyson had settled himself in the coach. "But if it attracts a marriageable lady, I count it worthwhile."

Knowing his uncle had been a rake in his own day, Tyson couldn't hide his smile. "You seem determined to see me bedded."

"Wedded would be more apropos. "I've seen your thirtieth birthday come and go, and I see no sign of you settling down. You're my heir. If I fell on a sword tomorrow and went to join Charlotte and my unborn babe in heaven, you know what you'd inherit."

Tyson sighed. "Rosmere Estate. Your townhouse. Coaches, horses, family jewels . . ."

"The title," his uncle said impatiently. "You'd inherit my title and become Lord Weston." He sounded as if he'd just bagged a fox. "And then you'd be forced to quit the House

of Commons and all this debating over causes and enter the
House of Lords, where decorum reigns."

"Uncle James, you needn't bury yourself to give me a
title. It won't work. I'll never change. My mother was Irish
and I honor that, even if you don't."

While his uncle droned on about responsibilities, Tyson's
thoughts drifted. He was in a particularly ill humor,
impatient, and he didn't know why. Some vague feeling
gnawed at his insides, as if he stood at a point of no return
or some crossroads. If he had a shilling's worth of sense,
he'd stay on the road he traveled as the Fian—single-
mindedly fighting for the Irish cause.

Instead, what was he doing?—taking the road that led to
Seymour's soiree . . . and to that Irish girl. . . . It
wasn't like him, but a man was allowed to stray from his
ideals once in a while, he supposed. He thought of Aileen
waving that pistol at him, ordering him to take her to
London to find a pair of lost boys. Stubborn. Practical. Too
comely . . . Ever since he'd met her, she'd affected his
concentration, which wasn't like him a bit. Tyson was
staring at the raindrops chasing one another down the
window of the coach. He was remembering how Aileen's
face looked with those tears on it.

Lord Weston rapped him on the knee. "If you're going to
be such poor company, then tell me why you accepted this
invitation. The Seymour family has never invited us inside
the door since you—since you pushed young Nicholas
Seymour's face into the bowl of rack punch at the house
party at Rosmere—the one celebrating your twenty-first
birthday."

"That was a long time ago. I was young."

"You were old enough to know better. Your grandfather
and great-grandfather undoubtedly turned over in their

graves that a Weston could do such a thing to a guest in Rosmere Manor."

Tyson clenched his jaw. Damn the old man for bringing up that black mark on his public behavior. On the other hand, maybe it was time he set his uncle straight about a fact or two. With no preamble whatsoever, he announced, "Considering Nicholas Seymour killed my mother, pushing his face into a bowl of punch seems tame retribution, although a waste of good punch."

He could almost hear the breath leave his uncle's body. Lord Weston thumped on the roof with his cane, and the coach lurched to a stop.

"Say that again."

"You heard me, Uncle James. I saw Seymour's name in the court records."

"It was an accident and probably a different Seymour. . . . Besides, you were a mere boy. You weren't even present at the inquest."

"I may not have been at the inquest, but I saw the 'accident,' as you call it. And it was the same Seymour."

Lord Weston gripped his cane tightly, as if nervous. "Well, it's water under the bridge. There's nothing you can do, except throw away your career arguing for the Irish cause." His uncle looked up sharply, and a slight tremor shook his voice. "Good God! You're not planning some stupid revenge tonight, are you? You'd be risking political suicide. Exile certainly."

"Have faith in my common sense and judgment, Uncle James. I'm not planning anything rash. But perhaps you understand why having Seymour as my rival in the Commons quite gratifies me."

"Humph. Forget all that. Be grateful for all you've got, for all the advantages I've given you that you wouldn't have if you'd stayed in Ireland with your m—"

"If you're looking for gratitude, you've got it. Thank you, Uncle James," Tyson cut in with mounting sarcasm.

At Tyson's sharp look Lord Weston cleared his throat and toned down his acerbic attitude. "All right, all right. I won't deny your mother. But if that's your feeling toward Seymour, then tell me why you've accepted this invitation."

"Perhaps I just want to be entertained."

His uncle visibly relaxed. "Ah, is there a special lady, then?"

"Let's just say I have my reason for attending. Don't worry, Uncle James. I shan't embarrass you." He grabbed his uncle's walking stick and, thumping the roof, gave the driver the signal to continue.

Aileen stirred the punch the way Mrs. Pembley had shown her—slowly so that the ladle would not clang against the cut-glass punch bowl. Elegant little slices of lemon floated along behind her ladle in the ruby current she created. She practiced filling one silver punch cup without spilling.

The trick as Mrs. Pembley had demonstrated was to hold the punch cup over the bowl so that if the ladle were so gauche as to drip, the offending ruby punch would land back in the cut glass and not on the pristine white tablecloth. Aileen practiced with two cups without a mishap. Continuing to stir slowly, she dared look up again—to glance in the direction of the door through which the guests would arrive. The holly and ivy were hung. All was in readiness for the Christmas soiree—even Lady Pamela.

But sure and the devil had a hand in Lady Pamela's claret-colored costume, though. Never had Aileen seen such a low décolletage, nor so many rows of black lace as were sewn on the skirt. At Lady Pamela's throat there clung a necklace of garnets as plump as a cluster of grapes, and to one side of her ringletted hair a spray of pink roses nestled. As Lady Pamela idly waved her fan and inspected the last-minute preparations, Aileen never forgot for a minute that the hostess was as talented in arranging an assassination as she was in overseeing an elegant soiree.

Aileen remained calm only by constantly reminding herself why she was here now. Not for the work, but for the Fian. And one slip on her part could mean death for him and for herself. He'd told her so. He'd gone so far as to conceal his London identity from her. Fleetingly, she wondered . . . what would his reaction be when he saw her? Would he be terribly shocked? Afraid for their lives? A tiny bit pleased?

Lady Pamela's voice cut into her thoughts. "As no doubt Mrs. Pembley made clear, you'll be attending full time at the punch bowl, and never forget servants do not speak to the guests—unless there are unusual circumstances. Is that clear?"

"Perfectly. Mrs. Pembley explained the need for discretion." Aileen's answer was rewarded with a faint smile from Lady Pamela. Oh, but Aileen didn't want to be discreet. She wanted to run through that soiree like a banshee, shouting to everyone about her employer's evil ways.

In a steady stream the guests began arriving, and the empty spaces between candle sconces and mirrors gradually filled with men in white cravats and evening frock coats and with women in glittering gowns and jewels. Again and again Aileen had to keep from putting down the ladle and pinching herself. Sure as she was Irish and a Connolly daughter, Aileen had never expected to see anything as fine as this.

One by one, Pembley the butler announced the guests' names. Each time he spoke, Aileen felt her hand shake for the wondering. Would this be the Fian?

Eventually Pembley called the name of Lord and Lady Grenville, and Aileen knew a moment of relaxation. She recognized this name as that of Maeve's employer. Aileen looked up from her task long enough to examine the woman—an inimitable blond matron with pursed mouth and beringed fingers who cut a swathe through the room toward the refreshment table and looked with frank curiosity at Aileen. When Mrs. Pembley asked Aileen how many cups of punch she'd ladled, a nervous Aileen felt her brogue magnified a thousandfold, and knew Lady Grenville found it curious.

Lady Pamela was at the table in an instant, and the ladies made no effort to conceal the subject of their gossip— Aileen herself.

"An Irish serving girl, Lady Pamela? Really, you're trying to outdo me in outrageousness." Lady Grenville smiled maliciously. "You can't accuse me of being the only eccentric in London anymore, can you? Tell me, can she do anything besides pour punch?"

Lady Pamela's voice held a mild reproof. "Now, Cornelia . . ." Aileen had heard the servants talk about how Lady Pamela deliberately used Lady Grenville's Christian name out of spite because Lady Pamela was to her title born while Cornelia had only married hers, and Lady Pamela was never going to let her forget the difference. . . . But right now they were still talking about Aileen, who had no title at all.

"Cornelia, I'm merely being practical. She can fetch more than your cocker spaniels, and she even reads to Lucy."

Cornelia, the Lady Grenville, affected a look of surprise. "No! But I'd have thought it would have taken forever to train her to wear shoes."

"You're teasing now. I know you've an Irish seamstress."

"Yes, but not nearly as lovely. I wouldn't dream of putting her on display like this serving girl." With fan fluttering, Lady Grenville swirled away.

"Lord Weston and the Honorable Tyson Winslow." The butler's voice startled Aileen. These guests were late arrivals, and in the crush of people she couldn't see them at all. Worse, Mrs. Pembley was standing there watching how Aileen ladled the punch.

"You're pouring too quickly. Slow down. I can't imagine what her ladyship had in mind giving you this task," the housekeeper whispered, obviously irritated.

Blushing at the criticism, Aileen set down a cup and made a great show of stirring. Oh, but she didn't think she could get through this evening. Was the Fian coming or not?

"If you need anything, ask a footman to get it for you. Don't leave," Mrs. Pembley ordered.

"Of course, ma'am." Aileen bit her lip to resist the urge to scream.

Just then a man moved toward her, blocking the light of the candles. Aileen looked up, alarm coursing through her, but at first sight of his features she relaxed. It wasn't the Fian—not yet. No, it was a young blond man in spectacles, and he smiled down at her. Aileen felt unaccountably uneasy. According to Mrs. Pembley, no one should be smiling down at her, a mere servant.

"Hello," the friendly guest said.

"Good evening," Aileen managed, blushing again. She glanced up quickly.

"You're Irish," he said in a low voice. "What city?"

"Devintown," said Aileen with a note of surprise. It had been so long since anyone had expressed any interest in her except to call her an Irish witch. "A village, actually," she added in a whisper, then pressed her lips shut.

She'd been told point blank that for guests and servants to act familiar was improper. Didn't this gentleman know that? Already the butler was scowling and Lady Pamela impatiently tapping her fan on her arm. Aileen filled a cup with punch and extended it. He gave his name as Marcus Owen, as if a serving girl needed to know.

He asked her name and upon hearing it smiled. "You're the first Mary Aileen I've known to be employed at Seymour's."

"Begging your pardon?" There was a desperate note to her voice. She feared Mrs. Pembley would descend upon her at any moment and reprimand her.

"They've never to my knowledge had Irish servants before."

"Indeed. You're most observant."

"As a *Times* reporter, you might say that's my job—to be nosy."

"I understand, sir, but I'm not allowed to talk, only hand you refreshments." Oh, let this evening end. She'd been wrong. The Fian wasn't among the guests after all.

Marcus Owen murmured some sympathetic words about the lot of the servants, and his conversation became more hurried. "It's never easy here for the Irish. Don't worry," he said softly while reaching for a serviette for himself. "I'll not get you in trouble. Not all the guests here tonight are society sorts, so I imagine the butler will have to be tolerant if some of us don't know all the correct social rules."

Aileen smiled at that.

"And should you ever need direction or help, call on me, please. It's good to have a friend or two when you're new to a big city like this." Marcus Owen drew a card out of his vest pocket. He set down his empty punch cup, then discreetly laid the card on top of a serviette close to Aileen's hand. She read the name and address, but didn't pick up the card—not yet. Marcus Owen backed away a step or two, as if surveying the guests.

She was stirring the punch, staring at the finely engraved card, wondering where to put it, not daring to slip it down her bodice. At that moment another gentleman walked up, and she heard a distinctly familiar voice, "Marcus, are you overly fond of the punch tonight, or are you avoiding the other guests? My uncle's arrived, and I believe our hostess is in need of one more player for whist. I suggested you."

Aileen felt as if she were riding on a horse to London, wrapped in a dark cape, and being threatened at knifepoint. Her quickened heartbeat told her that. She swallowed hard. Without looking up, she knew the exact color of this second man's eyes and what his hands would feel like on hers. And what it felt like to lie in his embrace. She'd never dared hope to see him again—yet she couldn't summon the courage to look up into his face yet.

A quick glance across the crowded room confirmed her every suspicion. Lady Pamela stood behind the piano, staring from behind the cover of her fan. On the other side of the room Nicholas Seymour stood before a full-length portrait of his wife, watching the refreshment table with more eagerness than if he were merely deciding whether or not to eat. Like sentinels they were, watching for her reaction. With shaking hands she reached for a cup.

"Hello, Tyson," Marcus replied equably. "I didn't expect to have competition from the Winslows here tonight."

"It's a night of surprises, then, Marcus."

Oh, yes, this was the Fian, but she dared not look up, not yet. Instead, she busied herself with filling punch cups, not counting, only thinking. Tyson Winslow was his name?

Suddenly Aileen found herself ladling the punch too

quickly, spilling tiny scarlet droplets on the white linen. The
fruity scent combined with the warmth of the room rose up
and made her dizzy. Out of the corner of her eye, Aileen
saw Lady Pamela frown and move toward the butler, as if
to press him on to harass her about her shoddy serving. To
Aileen's everlasting gratitude, Cornelia, the Lady Grenville, intercepted Lady Pamela, and the butler was intercepted by a footman.

Scarcely daring to breathe, she still stirred the punch—
but more slowly—and counted to ten while she memorized
the Fian's real name, the identity he'd tried to conceal from
her—Tyson Winslow, aristocrat.

Guests came and went from the refreshment table. But
the two gentlemen lingered on. Aileen slowly exhaled,
though that did nothing to still her wildly beating heart.
Fortunately, the men made casual conversation as if she
were merely a wall ornament. Unable to bear the suspense,
she glanced up.

There stood Marcus Owen, friendly-looking blue eyes
smiling at her from behind his spectacles . . . and beside
him—stood the Fian. No, Tyson Winslow, nephew of Lord
Weston.

Her glance was brief but telling. Oh, yes, except for his
fine clothes, this Tyson Winslow looked exactly like the
man whose profile she'd studied in a haystack by dawn. The
same cleft chin and bold aristocratic features. The same
hazel eyes burning with intensity. Yet, she also knew that
now was the moment of most danger for them, and looked
down. She had no idea if he even remembered her.

Ten

WHILE MARCUS OWEN and Tyson Winslow talked politics, Aileen stirred the punch into a scarlet whirlpool, and somehow managed to repeat a silent litany over and over: The Fian is not one of your people. He's an aristocrat. An English aristocrat. Banish the memory of his arms about yours. Her mind spun more dizzily than did the punch. Aristocrat or not, she and the Fian had nearly died together. She'd once felt a kind of bond between them.

"How did Parliament manage to adjourn so early this evening?" Marcus asked.

"Luck, I suppose," Tyson replied, only taking his gaze from Marcus once—when he swung a cautionary glance at the punch bowl.

Aileen kept stirring but looked up once to gauge Tyson Winslow's expression. There was not a flicker of recognition.

Relieved, she glanced in the direction of Lady Pamela, who quickly snapped her fan shut and turned her head away. The Fian—that is, Tyson Winslow—briefly followed her glance, and his gaze narrowed on the sight of his hostess. When he turned back to Aileen, his expression was carefully neutral. Only the invisible sparks that leapt between them gave away the situation.

With the most casual of gestures, Tyson Winslow picked up a glass of punch and, with no more than a perfunctory nod for Aileen, made his way through the crowd. Aileen had to fight to keep hot tears from filling her eyes.

She'd failed. Not only had she not warned him, but he'd merely smiled at her as if he found her country gaucherie amusing. But what had she expected? That he act as if he knew her and give himself away? And now he'd walked off to some sophisticated London lady. Even the good-natured Marcus Owen followed.

As Aileen watched, Tyson Winslow leaned close to Marcus and spoke low in his ear. Marcus shot a careful glance Aileen's way, almost as if they were talking about her. Marcus smiled and nodded, then in a casual gesture took off his spectacles and polished them on his sleeve.

Miraculously, before her own tripping heart could slow down and let her think, Marcus Owen returned to the punch table. "Excuse me," he said in a low voice. "I'm so sorry."

Aileen looked up, baffled at his unnecessary apology. A split second later Marcus Owen spilled his full glass of punch directly onto her apron. Jumping back, she stood there watching the punch drip in conspicuous red blotches down her formerly pristine apron and puddle onto the floor. She knew at once the action had been deliberate.

Almost at once the butler appeared and with a snap of his fingers summoned a footman and maid. The next thing Aileen knew, Sally was there, rag in hand, on her hands and knees mopping up the mess, while an obsequious Marcus apologized profusely to the oh-so-proper but stony-faced butler.

"Most unfortunate. I tripped on the table leg. There's the blame, you see. So sorry," he said to a silent Pembley, who seemed to issue orders to the bustling servants without saying a word.

Except, naturally, to Aileen. "You're dismissed while you rearrange yourself." Pembley's voice was low and carefully controlled. "See Mrs. Pembley about the apron and—and whatever needs changing."

Aileen's face went pink. Did he have to speak loud enough for the entire room to hear? Why couldn't he issue orders to her in the same silent way he did the others? And Marcus Owen, why had he been so deliberately gauche?

The guests, if they looked up at all, appeared vaguely amused at the situation, shrugging as if to say, "What else could you expect from an Irish?" Aileen heard their comments behind her back on her way out.

Cornelia, the Lady Grenville, sounded as if she'd come out to see a fire. "I knew *Lady Pamela* was going too far. Just because she's born a lady she thinks she's omnipotent. Really . . ."

In a huff Lady Pamela flounced back to her guests and announced partners were still needed for a whist game.

Aileen hurried toward the servants' hall, where, like a frantic insect, Sally scurried by carrying a fresh tablecloth. "Silly witch," she hissed to Aileen in passing. Sally would get even, Aileen knew that. But for now she had other worries.

As quickly as she could, she changed her apron in the servants' quarters, taking but a moment to blot dry the skirt of her dress. She walked up the servants' staircase toward the drawing room, so busy tying on a fresh white apron that at the sound, "Psst," she jumped. Marcus Owen appeared from behind the door.

With a steady hand on her elbow, he pulled her back through the doorway into the servants' hall and quickly, under cover of darkness, propelled her away from the servants' quarters and from the rooms occupied by soiree guests. All the way down a dim corridor he took her, to a place where no guests were wandering. What did she expect? Lady Pamela waiting to sack her? That was a distinct possibility. But when Marcus stopped outside the closed door to the breakfast room, another hope suddenly soared in her.

"I'll stand guard, but don't take too long." Without another word Marcus opened the door and stepped aside for her.

Instinctively she knew why she was there and slipped in, her heart fluttering madly. She stood still, her back against the door, letting her eyes grow accustomed to the dimness. A trestle table filled the small room. The single candelabra sitting on it barely illuminated the place, and it took her a moment to spot the other occupant in the shadows. Tyson Winslow stood as perfectly still as herself.

In the soft light he appeared once again to be the dangerous man in the black cape and mask—the man in whose arms she'd been carried away from an assassin's plot and a London mob.

The Fian.

"You told me we'd never meet again," she whispered, looking through the shadows at him.

"Circumstances change." He paused, finally asking, "How did you recognize me?"

"Your voice." She remembered the way his voice vibrated against her the night in the haystack. He was looking at her, as if lost in memories of his own. "I didn't give you away, did I?"

"No, if anyone wonders about me, they've only their suspicions to keep them company."

"Your friend spilled punch on my apron."

Tyson moved to the table and stopped. "I asked him to."

Slowly Aileen walked toward the table, too, but paused at the opposite end, her fingertips resting ever so lightly on it. She felt torn between running from the room and running into his arms. The candelabra glowed brightly between them, throwing shadows off his face. Above them could be heard the sounds of music and murmured voices, the occasional high-pitched laugh.

"You're in some danger here, you know," she said.

"You little fool. I arranged this meeting to tell *you* about the danger you're in, not the other way around," he explained dryly.

Before she could move again, he'd closed the space between them and reached for her. Gently holding her wrists, he pulled her toward him. He held her then in his arms, the way he had at the haystack when she'd been trembling.

Her heart soared at his touch. She took a deep breath so that she might talk and not give away her longing for him. She wanted to tell him everything she knew, but was afraid he'd scoff at her. Never had she imagined the social gap between them to be this wide. She was a mere serving girl and he an elegant aristocrat—so changed from the man in the simple white shirt and dark trousers who'd held her in his arms on the way to London, who'd kissed her after the riot. The silence stretched between them.

"We're *both* in danger meeting like this," she said, striving to sound matter-of-fact, trying to pull away, to resist the velvet prison of his touch, the touch that still did wild things to her.

"Aileen, Aileen, calm down and listen to me." His husky voice vibrated against her hair.

"I can't. If we're seen together—" Her voice broke.

He tightened his hold. "Aileen, I plan subterfuge involving dozens of men. Don't you think I know how to safely plan myself into a room with one woman? . . . Besides, tonight you needn't worry. The Fian is going to riot—wait and see. Let the Seymours suspect all they want. I'll have an alibi."

She let herself savor the feel of his arms about her. There was no longer an elegant society party upstairs, and the night belonged only to him and to her.

But the stitching outlining the brocade of his vest scratched her cheek, reminding her this was an aristocrat who held her, a man desired by the eligible society ladies upstairs and no doubt by some who weren't so eligible. She pulled back and looked up at his bold features, conscious all the time of his hands on her waist. She might be fresh off the boat from Ireland herself, but this she knew—no serving maid allowed a well-born gentleman to dally with her. Even now she sensed the dangerous attraction sparking between them. But she couldn't bring herself to walk out of this small room and never see him again.

"I—your uncle's a lord, isn't he? I don't even know what name to call you," she said.

"It depends where you meet me," was his sensible answer.

"Yes, of course."

"We need to discuss matters."

"Not here. Lady Pamela is going to notice we're both away, I'm sure." She tried again to pull away from him. "Besides, you said it could mean your death if we were seen together alone, and so—well, I only wanted to warn you, and that's done."

She was free, but not for long. He caught her again by one wrist and pulled her back close against him, so close she could see the candlelight glittering like tiny stars in his eyes.

He was smiling at her. "You don't think Lady Pamela is

going to stop her midnight supper to send out a search party for a serving maid, do you? At worst, you'll be dismissed tomorrow."

"I shall resign before they can dismiss me."

She felt him reach up and push a strand of her hair back behind her ear, and she wanted to melt against him.

"What do you want from me?" she asked in a tiny voice, trying her best to conceal her longings. She tilted back her head and with a woman's instinct saw the answer in his eyes.

"Secrets," he said lightly. "All I ever want is information that helps the cause." His voice belied the sensuality of his gaze. He paused, looking at her strangely, as if Ireland were the farthest thing from his mind.

As if a wee person were speaking to her, the temptation formed full-blown in her mind. . . . "If it's secrets you want, then I have one," she whispered, looking him straight in the eye, daring his glittering gaze with a taunt of her own. What did she have to lose? This man was too fine for the likes of her. At best her information might interest him enough to give her a few more moments with him. "Lady Pamela is one of the assassins," she rushed on.

Immediately tensing, he dropped his hold on her, backed away a step, as if she'd truly startled him. "How do you know?"

Despite his fancy clothes, she felt as if Tyson Winslow had suddenly vanished and the Fian stepped into his place.

"How?" he repeated.

"I—I found her dress, the exact silver-gray dress she was wearing that night when we met. That's the only secret I know." She pulled away. "Now I have to go back—unless you want us caught." She turned to leave.

He only paused a beat, before moving up behind her.

"Why did you stay here after you found out Lady Pamela was one of the assassins?"

Slowly she turned and looked at him, the candlelight shimmering in her blue eyes.

There was only one answer that would undo him completely, and somehow he knew those would be her next words.

"I had to warn you. You helped me when I was in danger, and I felt I owed you the same." She sounded utterly vulnerable, and the dulcet voice pulled at him like a magnet.

He reached out and pulled her back into his embrace, and her slim body melted against him and filled something in him that had been empty. He swallowed hard. This was not the place to lose control, yet he hadn't realized how much he'd yearned to hold her like this. He felt a strand of her hair move when he breathed close to her cheek. That wild black hair that so intrigued him.

"It's obvious you were brought here to lure the Fian out of disguise."

"I know," she said calmly.

He never ceased to be surprised by her courage. "If you want me to find you another position—"

"Where? Your uncle's place? Thank you, no."

He let her go then, dropping his arms to his side. "Lass, I warned you I'm a dangerous man. You're one of only two people in the world who know my double identity." The touch of her fingers to his face felt reassuring. "And I told you I'm not afraid of you or London. And see—here I am safely in one piece."

He felt no reassurance at all from himself that he could continue this conversation much longer—not as long as she touched him like this. Gently he removed her hand.

"Brave words. And a remarkable piece of spy work on

Lady Pamela. If you were a man, I'd give you a position as one of my accomplices. A reward," he said, half jesting, recalling her holding the pistol on both him and Leedes.

She lifted her chin and gave him one of those haughty looks that spoke of quiet strength. "I would gladly become your accomplice, but I'd not do it for the glory of your cause, you know. I'd want payment."

He smiled. "But of course, you've a practical bent to you. And what would that payment be?" he said, still jesting, using light words because he was too close to saying serious words.

"I made a promise to you that I'd never ask it of you again."

He felt the smile on his face vanish, replaced by the astonishment he felt. She was serious. "Your brothers," he said, his voice flat, strangely deflated at the single-mindedness of her thoughts. "You want me to search for your brothers."

She nodded. "That's my price for being your accomplice. Now, what is it I have to do for you?"

"I wasn't serious."

"I am. I'm inside the Seymour house already—a house that holds secrets. Surely no one in your cause has my connections, my knowledge of Lady Pamela's comings and goings, of her visitors—such as Mr. Leedes—"

"Aileen, it's a dangerous life I lead."

"I mean it, I'm going to find my brothers no matter what. Besides, living here can't be near as bad as whatever Seamus and Patrick are enduring."

For a moment he was too stunned to react. She offered both information and the promise of future meetings with her. It was a temptation sent directly from heaven or hell. "You realize I may not find them, that possibly no one will ever find them?" He hated the blunt words, the way she shut her eyes at the harshness of what he said.

Worse, when she opened them and looked at him, tears welled.

"What's your day off?"

"Thursday," she said in a strained whisper. "Afternoons only."

"If I meet you to obtain information, there's no point in it being secret, nor is it wise." His gaze roved up and down her, clearly saying what he meant. "If I as Tyson Winslow meet you with my coach on your afternoons off, society will merely think I'm making advances toward you—improper advances. Society will brand you as my mistress."

He stopped because the sudden image of her in his arms, fulfilling that role, tempted him beyond words, and he felt his body tightening with desire. "To put on such an act would simplify our meetings," he added in a husky voice.

She turned away from him and nodded. "I don't care what society thinks of me—except, of course, we won't really dally, will we?" She turned back.

There was such utter trust in her face, looking up at him, vulnerable and brave, that he couldn't immediately answer.

"No, I won't seduce you," he said bluntly.

She looked back at him, her eyes shimmering with tears, and he immediately regretted his promise. Speaking low and fast, he outlined plans. He heard Marcus tap softly on the door, a prearranged signal that too much time had elapsed.

"Are you certain you want to do this?" he asked again, his words more hurried now.

"Only if you promise to look for Seamus and Patrick."

"You still drive a harder bargain than most men, lass."

"But you'll try?"

His pause was scarcely noticeable. "I'll try and that's all

I can promise." And it was no hollow promise. He had enough spies throughout the city factories that he could set a few to this task. "You love them very much, I can tell," he said.

He saw her nod and then a smile, a tremulous smile. He drew her back into his arms and held her close a moment. Tenderly, he kissed the crown of her head before releasing her. "We have a bargain then."

When she slipped through the door and retreated down the corridor, a small figure in black, he stared after her until all he could see was the dark of the empty hall. Even blacker was the thought of returning upstairs to the shallow women and pompous men at the party. After this, all talk would be meaningless, all women shadows of the one he wanted.

He gave Aileen a few minutes' head start and then sauntered up another way to the drawing room. He made a mental note to handle his emotions with better care. A man could too easily become emotionally involved with such a girl. Still, he calculated the days until her afternoon off.

Indeed, the rest of the party dragged. But just before midnight, he gained a reprieve from his torment. The festivities were interrupted by the butler, who came into the room with a message that someone was at the door. As soon as Pembley whispered the message, Nicholas Seymour's face went white, and, dropping his drink, he rushed out into the hallway. Several men, including Tyson, followed him. A messenger stood in the hallway, new snowflakes melting off his shoulders. It was a man from Scotland Yard, come to find members of Parliament.

"What is it?" demanded Tyson.

"It's a riot. The Fian and his men. He's leading another mob over on Whitechapel Street."

Nicholas Seymour tossed a coin in the messenger's hand

and questioned the man further. "Are you certain it's the Fian?" He looked directly at Tyson as he asked the question.

"Absolutely. He's in the robe and riding the black horse. There's some terrible rioting and—"

Lady Pamela waved the boy to silence. "Yes, enough. We'll hear more in the morning."

Turning the fellow over to the butler's care, Nicholas Seymour looked at the surprised face of first his wife and then a few of the guests, including Tyson Winslow.

Unable to conceal all of his amusement, Tyson stared at the mottled confusion on his host's face. "What's wrong, man? I told a few people where to find me if any Irish matters needed attention. Did he inconvenience you? Ruin the evening?"

"No, not at all. It's the Fian. Your hero." He looked at Tyson and then back at the door as if he could see through it to the riot.

Tyson secretly smiled. He knew what Nicholas Seymour was thinking. How could the Fian be rioting when Tyson Winslow was right here? Digby Trigg had performed well. Perfectly, in fact. Now, besides acquiring a spy in the very house of his mother's murderer, he even had suspicion averted from himself—for a while.

Tyson put just the proper tone of ironic sympathy into his voice. "Damnable nuisance interrupting your party." He accepted his top hat and cape from the waiting butler and added, "The Fian has a way of being unpredictable. You've got to give him that."

Late that night Aileen lay awake in her bed, remembering how she'd felt when she'd first learned the identity of the Fian. Tyson Winslow. Silently she mouthed the syllables, the pieces of his name, and marveled. An English aristocrat. Unexpectedly, with the memories of his name, came the feel of Tyson Winslow's arms about her. Though she might know him by two identities, only one dizzying sensation could describe how she felt in his embrace.

Pulling her thoughts up short, she frowned in the dark, her gaze focusing on a tiny shaft of moonlight on the ceiling. She imagined he embraced all women like that, even the aristocratic ones when it got him what he wanted. Tears pricked.

Across the tiny attic room in the larger bed, Agnes and Sally made no secret of their talk. It was petty, spiteful.

"The Irish witch is a wanton baggage," Sally said. "I 'ad to mop up the puddle of punch she spilled, and then she takes 'alf an hour just to change 'er apron."

"While I 'ad to sit with Miss Lucy and didn't get to see the grand people," added Agnes. "That witch needs a lesson taught."

Aileen kept her head close to the pillow to block out the rest of their cruel words. Perhaps she did need a lesson taught. About what happened to maids who became enamored of society gentlemen—handsome gentlemen such as Tyson Winslow.

"Seamus, are you asleep?"

"Shh, you'll get us whipped."

"You won't die like that other chap?" Patrick persisted.

"No, I won't die. What's the matter? Are you still sick?"

In a wobbly voice Patrick answered, "I don't like working here. The smell of the glue pots makes me ill."

Seamus pulled a precious crust of bread from his shirt and tore off a bite for Patrick. "Eat this much. Remember what Aileen would say."

"Where's Aileen now, Seamus? Finish the story."

Seamus was bone weary, but he summoned up the energy to whisper.

"I can't finish it, not till she finds us."

Patrick lay close to his brother on the smelly straw ticking and nibbled the bread. "When will she find us, then?"

Seamus swallowed his own hunger. "First she has to get out of the cave."

"Why's she in a cave?"

"Well, because the evil Druid almost captured the Fian, but Aileen killed him with a stone, and they're hiding away in a cave so no other evil spells are put on them. Now that the Fian owes his life to Aileen, he says he has to give her his life in return. Besides, of course, Aileen is the most beautiful lady in all of Erin, more beautiful than the wild heather. But she doesn't want his life, of course. She only wants to come and find us."

"And so the Fian decided to help her after all?" Patrick's voice rose hopefully.

"Of course, and together they'll find a secret passageway out of the cave, then ride his great horse searching far and wide till—"

"Quiet in there," a night watchman barked, and with the suddenness of an angry snake a whip crashed against the door.

Trembling, Patrick reached out for his brother's hand.

Eleven

WITH EAGER STEPS Aileen hurried along the snowy street, not stopping until she reached the bookshop. Behind her on the street a rare February snow muffled the sounds of horses' hooves and coach wheels, but as far as Aileen was concerned, warmth reigned. This was Thursday, and she'd come here to meet Tyson, as she'd been doing for weeks, and that was enough to put heaven in its place.

She slid inside the shop and stood there stamping snow off her boots. Shivering, she clutched tighter to her cape. The bell rang again over the door, signaling another customer, and with a longing she couldn't begin to disguise, her gaze went to the door. But Tyson wasn't there.

She worried. For weeks they'd maintained a kind of friendship or camaraderie during their meetings. At least, neither of them had spoken of feelings . . . until last week when she'd blushed at a particularly funny remark of his, and Tyson had looked at her curiously, saying, "You remind me just now of the night I met you when I took you to the haystack."

"Oh . . . why?" she'd made the mistake of asking.

"For a brave lass, you're terribly naive."

"I'm not. It's only that you promised not to—"

"Seduce the lass all London assumes is my mistress? A most regrettable promise, I'm afraid."

"But I admire your sense of honor," she'd said, and both had let the subject drop. As a topic of conversation.

And Aileen, who'd long known she was falling in love, fell a little deeper because he honored that promise.

"Looking for a particular title, miss?" the clerk asked from the other side of the counter. With a start Aileen came out of her reverie.

"Would you have the latest penny romances in stock?" She named the title that Lady Pamela had suggested for her daughter.

With quiet efficiency the clerk extracted the volume for Aileen's inspection. She longed to buy one of the heirloom books her family had pored over back in Ireland—legends of Finn MacCumhal, for example. But her post depended on her ability to read fashionable novels out loud to Miss Lucy. Sighing, Aileen scanned the first page.

Not long after the bell over the door of the little shop trilled again, the winter air blew in, and once again Aileen glanced up only to be disappointed. Had Tyson finally had second thoughts about this arrangement?

And then the door opened again, and she heard his voice, deep and resonant, the sound of it vibrating straight through to the core of her. "Good afternoon," he said to a departing customer. Her heart leapt into her throat, yet she managed not to move. She knew exactly when he came to stand beside her at the counter.

"Good day, sir," he said to the clerk. Even with underlying silken tones, Tyson's voice commanded respect. "I'm looking for a particular book—a special book." Aileen caught the wry amusement in his voice before he paused for effect. No matter the shop Aileen went to, Tyson always was looking for something impossible—an out-of-print book, an exotic tobacco, pineapples out of season, a rare tartan.

"An American book?" the clerk was asking, having struck a blind alley with Tyson's first few requests.

"*Davy Crockett's Autobiography*. Surely, you've stocked it before, young man? It was, after all, a best-seller in Boston." He tapped a pair of leather gloves against the counter, while the clerk mumbled something about being new.

"Never mind, then," Tyson said. "I'll take that other book instead," and he pointed to a volume slightly above their heads on the shelf.

"Yes, sir." Spectacles falling to the end of his nose, the clerk clambered up the ladder, retrieved the slim volume, and handed it down.

At the same instant Tyson turned to look at Aileen. Even in the weak winter light of the shop his eyes glinted a startling shade of green. As always, Aileen drank in his elegance—the frock coat, cravat, and vest, and trousers like all the fashionable men in London wore. She looked up into his eyes. Their gazes met and held, and she wished she knew what he was thinking. He looked away first.

He made his purchase and had it wrapped before the clerk approached Aileen again. "Have you decided then, miss?"

"Yes, this will do nicely." She counted out the required shillings onto the counter and looked up. Tyson stood there in the little bookstore staring at her as if he'd forgotten who she was, and she had a glimpse of the haughty aristocrat, a man who would look disdainful when a lowly servant girl approached him and boldly laid her hand on his arm.

But when he looked into her eyes, the haughty expression melted. "Miss Connolly," he said, feigning surprise, taking her hand and brushing it with his lips. "Allow me to give you a carriage ride."

The world turned rightside up again. Together, so close she felt his coat brush her sleeve, they walked outside the shop and he handed her into his waiting coach. She sat opposite him, waiting. Always, on these days, she brought him some tidbit about Nicholas Seymour's comings and goings. Always, he told her about the latest workhouses where his men had looked for her brothers. Always, they were together.

She looked into his eyes—those hazel eyes that today were unyielding. Nor was there a smile for her. No gentle look. Instead . . . Discouragement? "Shall I give you my news?" she asked softly, hoping last week's conversation was finished for good. She could never really be his mistress. He knew that.

Taking a deep breath, she began.

"It's only gossip. I didn't get it firsthand—"

"Tell me," he said in a low voice, not taking his eyes off her, lingering especially long on her lips.

Despite his candid inspection, she complied. "Nicholas Seymour entertained a visitor from Scotland Yard, and they discussed new ways to capture the Fian."

"They're always discussing ways to capture the Fian. . . ." He sounded unimpressed, curt. "That's all?"

She nodded. When he was silent, staring at the passing white landscape, she prompted him. "Is there news about my brothers?"

He clenched his jaw and said between gritted teeth, "I haven't found your brothers. At least—" He shot an anguished look her way then, and she felt her throat knot, panic form in the back of her mind, but no matter what bad news he might tell her, she would be brave. Only not yet. So she tiptoed around his news, asking an oblique question.

"Did your spies find any new factories?"

He turned toward her and sighed. "Aileen." the word echoed the pain in his eyes.

She frowned and felt panic welling up. "Please tell me, Tyson. Now isn't the time to play gallant. As you honor the Fian, tell me." She hadn't realized until the last two words how her voice was gradually rising. Never had she known this man to be anything but in total control—too much control. "Please, Tyson, I'll have the carriage stopped in the middle of the street if you don't tell." She reached up to signal the driver.

"Aileen, look at me," he said softly, with command.

She sat down. One telltale tear welled over. Please God, don't let him tell her that her brothers were dead. She reached up to flick it away, but before she could, he leaned forward and caught her hands. Still leaning forward, he held her hands so close to his knees she could almost feel the warmth of his trousers. Her fingers tightened around his. Silently his gaze searched her eyes.

After a long moment he spoke huskily. "Do you realize that someday I might actually be captured and unable to help you? Or worse, that someday you might have to give up searching for your brothers and admit they're lost for—"

"No." She pulled her hands away. "I'll never admit it." She turned her face to the side of the carriage to hide her tears, tears caused as much by the thought of his capture as over her brothers. Without a word he reached for her and in one strong motion pulled her over to sit beside him. Staring out at the passing carriages, he dispensed an elegant handkerchief from his pocket. "For such a brave girl, you shed tears easily," he commented.

"There's not a thing wrong with shedding tears," she sniffled. "They're like rain—God weeps. So, too, our souls weep. Haven't you ever shed a tear—just once in your life?"

He looked away, out the window of the coach. "Possibly once, I believe, but I was very young."

"It's perfectly all right to cry." Nevertheless, she took the handkerchief and pressed the fine linen to her eyes. After moments of silence punctuated by her sniffles, she dropped the handkerchief and slanted a glance his way. "I thought you might be tired of meeting and not come today. . . . If my spying hasn't been useful enough to you, I can still look for Seamus and Patrick alone," she offered.

He almost smiled. "I never break my promises." Then he handed her the wrapped parcel from the bookstore. "For you."

Hesitantly she opened it and found a book of poems. Andrew Marvell poems.

"To be worthy of calling oneself the Fian, a man must prove himself a poet as well as a warrior."

She glanced up, charmed by his romantic gesture. "Ah, you slay your ladies with words and save riots for the men." In fact, she felt so surprised that the light response was all she could think of. Tyson and poetry. She'd discovered a whole new dimension to him and busily turned the pages. This was such an improvement on Miss Lucy's tastes in reading.

"There's a poem in there I consider appropriate for you," he said. "I memorized it back in school."

She let the book fall open where a marker lay and read. " 'Had we but world enough and time, this coyness lady were no crime . . .' " She stopped, touched. "Thank you," she said softly. "I never thought to have a gift from an aristocrat such as yourself."

He leaned toward her. "You weren't listening. Poetry is the gift of the Fian—not aristocrats."

"I see."

He recited another line of the poem. " 'The grave's a fine and private place, but none I think do there embrace.' "

The word *embrace* hung in the air like the memory of their hands touching. She still felt the imprint of his finger where he'd traced away her lone tear, and she swallowed hard. If this was bribery, Tyson played the game of seduction without rules.

Abruptly she wrapped up the book and tried to change the subject. "You've heard all the gossip about us, haven't you? Is your uncle very angry?"

Tyson sighed again, a long-suffering sound. "No—I mean, yes. Actually, my uncle's opinion is of scant consequence to me, nor do I much care what society thinks when it comes to you and me."

She stiffened. "We covered this subject last week."

The corners of his mouth threatened to turn up. "On the contrary, my blue-eyed banshee, except for a night in a haystack with you, I've barely scratched the surface of the subject with you." At last there was a smile lurking in his eyes for her.

And the subject was once again in the open, longing to be taken seriously. She had to talk sense into him. "Have you forgotten that you're an aristocrat and I'm but an Irish maid?" she asked as though saying one and one made two and everyone in the world knew that. "It's a mistake for a maid to dally with a man of the upper class—I tried to explain that last week. . . . And while we're on the subject of kisses and . . . and such things, are you so bold with aristocratic ladies?"

He laughed. "I believe I've lost count of the number of times you've reminded me that I'm not good enough for you—" He held up a hand to stop her protest. "And as for the second question, boldness keeps me alive. You may slap me once for being overly bold. Be gentle though, banshee. The cause wants me returned alive."

"Slapping's too common."

With a sudden arch of his eyebrows he pinned an enigmatic gaze on her. "My, my, the Irish lasses have much loftier notions than the aristocratic ladies I've encountered."

"Perhaps because every serving maid lives by her wits, not her title. I won't find myself sent out of the country in disgrace because an aristocrat took a momentary fancy to me and left me alone to bear his—"

"Stop. You overestimate my conceit." He turned away momentarily. Actually there'd been one false alarm a long time ago during which his uncle had proposed the young lady retire to Italy. At the memory now Tyson felt color rise in his face, and he took control of the discussion. "We were discussing the dangers of kissing, I believe," he reminded her. "Some misbegotten notion that servant girls must never kiss men of my lofty station in life."

"I haven't forgotten." Her heart pounded in her ears, her skin still burned from his touch, and her mouth ached to know his lips on hers again.

"And—?"

With a sigh she gave in. "All right then, I'd not be so hasty as to sever a business arrangement with the Fian—not over a mere kiss," she said gravely. "But I believe it's a mistake and will adversely affect our—our business arrangement."

"You do?"

She nodded and sat there primly waiting for him to place his lips on hers. He gave her a sidelong look, hopeful, amusement lurking behind his eyes. "It wasn't a *mere* kiss that I had in mind. Perhaps the first kiss we shared might be described as a *mere* touch of the lips, but starting with this second one, I'd change adjectives, toss out *mere* for more intense words like *passionate, heated*—"

"Don't jest. A kiss is a kiss."

"Ah, I see. As with London, you're not afraid of kisses, either? Scare them away with pistols if they feel dangerous?" Tyson asked lazily. It was a gauntlet thrown down, a challenge to her statement of expertise about men's kisses.

"No, but—"

"But what?"

"We're in a coach in full daylight. And even though we're pretending, it seems to me there's enough scandal about us. The Seymours—"

"Devil take the Seymours and daylight." He reached for her and began placing tiny kisses on her skin while pushing his hands through her hair. The book slid to the floor with a thud, she moved her hands onto his frock coat, which was almost as warm as she was beginning to feel . . . but not nearly so warm as when he moved his mouth to hers.

At first a light kiss, simple and straightforward, the kind of kiss she'd known from the night of the riot, and then his kiss deepened and became something more than the simple dallying of lips. No, this was different from before. In the first moment he'd managed to reduce her to something tingly, and now . . . now she was quivering in his arms.

His mouth slanted across hers, as if he were reaching into her soul. She trembled at the dangerous mingling of their tongues. Never had she known such thrust and caress as what his tongue wrought against her lips, then unexpectedly inside her mouth. Her arms came up to his shoulders and around his neck. He tasted salty and smelled slightly smoky and all things masculine. Her heart beat so fast she was certain he must hear it. She certainly could feel his heartbeat, strong and fast, and his hands tangled in her hair, stroking her the same way his tongue stroked inside her mouth.

It took a bump when the coach went round a corner to get him to stop kissing her, that and the fact that she nearly fell off his lap. He pulled back and seemed to be breathing much more deeply, as if he were winded. Aileen regained her balance and, moving to sit beside him, rearranged her skirts. Her lips felt deliciously numb, and she licked off the taste of him, as if searching with her tongue for a last drop of honey.

He leaned back, eyes closed, looking quite pained.

"Don't you like how I kiss?" she asked.

"It wasn't long enough," he said tautly.

No, she agreed. It wasn't long enough at all. She could have spent the rest of her life wrapped in his arms like that, but she wasn't about to tell him. "That's the fault of the coach then," she said smartly. "You're quite right, you know. Not all kisses are alike. The night of the riot was definitely a good-bye kiss. This wasn't a good-bye kiss at all."

"Oh, what was it, then?" Eyebrows raised, amused hazel eyes scanned her, smiling.

"An invitation to dally, I suppose. How should I know? I've never been kissed the way you did it. Is that the way you kiss the aristocratic ladies, or is that how a man kisses his mis—?"

"Must we analyze it?" he asked. "It's painful enough having it end abruptly." He retrieved the book of poems and handed it to her. The coach had nearly brought them back to the bookshop across the way from St. James Park. From there she would catch an omnibus to the Seymours' house.

"Thank you," she said quietly. She retrieved the paper and took her time wrapping it around the book of Marvell poems. Actually she didn't want to talk about the kiss, either. She wanted him to still be kissing her. Most of all, she longed to know if he kissed the London ladies on all the long lonely days she wasn't with him.

The coach stopped. "I'm not being coy."

"Nor am I."

Pursuing that statement would be asking to step into a bottomless chasm, so she ignored it and stepped out. With a lump in her throat she realized this bargain to spy in exchange for her brothers couldn't last much longer. She'd give into more dallying, he'd hurt her, simply because aristocrats had duties to provide heirs, and heirs came from ladies, not from maids. She walked away.

When she turned back once to wave, he stood outside the coach, watching her walk off across the snowy park toward the pond where the ducks swam in the sunshine.

At that moment his driver leaned down. "Sir, I do believe another coach is following us."

"For how long?"

"For the last half hour, sir. Wasn't sure until we stopped."

Casually Tyson stepped around back as if checking the wheels of the vehicle, then moved about to converse with the driver.

"Do you have any idea who it is?" he asked under his breath.

"Couldn't say for sure, sir. Scotland Yard perhaps. Sometimes they use unmarked coaches. Or it might be a Seymour coach."

"Most likely." Tyson tried to sound nonchalant, but he also looked off in the direction Aileen had gone, watching until she was safely on an omnibus. While he'd been kissing her, they'd been followed, and he'd completely forgotten the danger to her.

He remembered then that he had a cause to lead, and its

intrigues followed him everywhere. He held the last sight of
Aileen close to him, carefully considering the danger he'd
involved her in all because he lusted for her. He shut his
eyes and saw her still as he'd left her.

The sun had glinted off her black hair, and her breath had
come out in frosty clouds. Ducks had followed her across
St. James Park, web feet wading right beside her through
the occasional purple crocus peeking out of the snow.
Dressed in her everlasting black, like a banshee she was,
bearing secrets that if overheard by Scotland Yard could
hang them both.

No, there was more reason for her practical concerns than
she knew. Dallying with the pretty maid was nothing
compared to what could happen to her if Scotland Yard got
their hands on her.

He told his driver to set off to the Seymours' and to
hasten the pace. His coach was parked discreetly down the
block from their townhouse when Aileen returned, oblivious to Tyson's guardian gaze. Only when he was reassured
of her safe arrival did he really let himself breathe freely.

Twelve

ALL PRETENSE OF calm gone, Lady Pamela flung aside her embroidery. "Imbeciles! Scotland Yard followed them while they drove aimlessly around London engaged in dallying?"

Nicholas Seymour sat calmly by the fire sipping a drink. Edmund Leedes, on the other hand, sat timorously in the drawing room, looking as if he were ready to topple off the delicate chair. He opened his mouth to say something, but never got the words out.

"There must be more." Lady Pamela stalked over to Leedes. "Where did they meet?"

Leedes's teacup rattled in its saucer. "In a small bookshop. As usual, they began quite discreetly, your ladyship."

"Discreet! Everyone in London is talking about them. Do you call that discreet? Listen to this—" Snatching up a newspaper from the sofa, she read out loud.

"'Traitor though he be, the mysterious Fian at least attempts social reform, but the scandalous goings-on between a certain Lord's nephew and an Irish maid can't help the Irish cause at all. It can only exacerbate the threatening crisis and serve as a poor example to the high moral conduct set by Her Majesty. When dealing with the Irish, or indeed any servants, decorum is the responsibility of the employer.' Discreet! Bah!"

With an angry motion, Lady Pamela crumpled the paper and tossed it into the fire. "I'm being maligned in public. This should have been resolved weeks ago, Mr. Leedes. I'm falling in society's estimation. This can't go on."

"You could hold another soiree," suggested her husband sarcastically from his place by the fire, where he swirled the brandy in his snifter.

"I could put hot coals down your pockets, too," she said with disdain. "Even after you're prime minister, you'll still need to come to me for any original ideas."

He raised his glass in a mock toast to her, then tossed the drink off and poured himself another. Lady Pamela glared at him. Except for his money and the scandal of divorce, she'd throw him out. But he kept her too well provided for. Only occasionally did she wonder how a second son managed to get his hands on such great sums—enough not only to run a large household, but to keep a mistress.

She wouldn't be surprised to find out he owned a slave ship or some such. She put nothing past him, for his ambitions were second only to hers. But at least when it came to mistresses, unlike Tyson Winslow, her husband knew how to be discreet.

But dawdling over such thoughts was as much a waste of time as examining a tray of stale petits fours. Meanwhile, the trail of the Fian, like her tea, was growing cold. "Now, then, Mr. Leedes," said Lady Pamela. "Get someone else following that girl. Hire some thugs. The more intense her relationship with Tyson Winslow, the more likely she is to make an error." She turned quickly to her husband. "And you, my dear sir, use your influence to call off Scotland

Yard. If *they* unmask the Fian, then you've lost your chance at glory."

"My influence is dwindling since the last critical essay in the *Times*," he commented. "I say you should dismiss the girl. She's no longer useful."

"I'm not dismissing her, my dear, despite all else. In fact, I'm going to increase her hours off, allow her an evening or two free after Lucy is asleep. The other servants will be resentful, but that's a mere detail."

Her husband rose from his chair. "Like a fig it's a detail. I've a reputation at stake, also, my wife. I do not want this household in disarray, and the servant gossip is already at fever pitch."

Lady Pamela cast an impatient look his way. "How would you know?"

"From the servants out in the mews, my dear."

Lady Pamela shrugged. "Servant gossip has its uses. From what Agnes and Sally tell Mrs. Pembley, if our Irish maid found her missing brothers, she'd throw caution to the wind and immediately enlist the aid of her beloved Fian—in or out of disguise—to rescue them."

Leedes's chins waggled as he shook his head. "Yes, but we don't know where her brothers are."

Lady Pamela felt her temper rising. With a sudden swirl of taffeta she turned back to Leedes. Such a dense man.

"We don't need her brothers. All we need is a description of them." She waited, her look expectant. "Well?" she prompted when Leedes simply sat there.

"Don't ask me," he blustered. "I never saw them. She was alone when I took her from Ireland."

"I suggest you do better than that, Mr. Leedes."

Fear flicked across the man's face. "Lord Fitzwilliam— he knows them," he amended. "I do believe he's in London

now. I could inquire." He pulled at his collar as if too
warm.

"Excellent answer, Mr. Leedes. You earn high marks for
the day." Quickly she gave Leedes his final instructions.
"Find out more details from this Lord Fitzwilliam, and I'll
ask a few discreetly concerned questions of Aileen. Be
certain to ask for distinguishing marks, anything to make
these brothers stand out in a crowd."

"What have you concocted now?" her husband asked as
soon as Leedes left. Vague curiosity edged his voice.

Lady Pamela graced him with a smile that on another
woman might be termed saintly. "It's very simple really. On
the one hand, we know the Fian makes a habit of leading
riots against the most vile factories. On the other hand,
we know Mary Aileen goes out looking—with Tyson
Winslow—for her brothers, who, it would seem, are lost in
a factory somewhere. The rest is obvious." Her husband's
blank stare annoyed her. "Well, don't you see? We simply
start a rumor that those brothers have been located at a
factory—one of your factories."

Suddenly his face went quite white. "Which factory?" he
asked, eyes uncharacteristically panicked.

"I had in mind the one by Vauxhall Gardens."

He visibly relaxed his grip on his glass. "Oh, yes, that
one. Yes, then, a good plan."

Lady Pamela advanced on her husband until she stood
close over him. "A brilliant plan. She'll lead us straight to
the Fian. . . . I suggest you place a deposit on that
emerald pendant."

In another swirl of petticoats and taffeta she left the room.

Aileen counted out her change and paid for the single
candle—a purchase to replace the one someone had pilfered. There was no chance to linger in this shop, and it

didn't matter, for Tyson hadn't come. Disheartened, she walked outside.

Yet when she stepped out into a late winter sun, there he stood, arms folded, ankles crossed as he leaned in seeming nonchalance against the door of his coach. Her heart flew to her throat at the silly way his cravat—a green one this Thursday—sat askew against his white collar. He wore black trousers and topcoat.

Self-consciously, she reached up to tuck a strand of hair back into her bonnet. Only when she glanced up into his face and saw the dangerous look in his eyes did she sense that today something was wrong, even more wrong than last week. The slight growth of whiskers shadowing his face gave him a haunted look. Everything about him spoke of danger—the same danger she'd felt the night she'd met him.

"Is anything the matter? You didn't come into the shop."

"And you didn't tell me what the servants have been doing to you. Lady Grenville enjoys passing on household gossip. They torment you, she says, because of your freedoms with me."

Was there nothing he didn't know eventually? What baffled her was the pain in his gaze—an expression completely at odds with his angry words.

"I can handle myself with the servants," she offered in a tremulous voice. "Sticks and stones. If they lash out occasionally, it's only with words. That can't hurt as much as a real whip, which may be Seamus and Patrick's daily lot."

He winced. "Get in the coach," he said a bit hoarsely. In a whisper he added, "I have news to tell you."

She felt her heart fly to her throat. "What is it? My brothers?" He looked so—so wildly dangerous today—like a panther ready to tear out of confinement. Immediately she assumed the worst. His news was not good. She climbed into his coach ahead of him, and as soon as they were both settled, she looked over at him. "Tell me."

"First your news," he demanded.

"This week the Seymours have talked about moving to the country come summer, and Lady Pamela's offered me more time to look for my brothers." She looked over hopefully. "What news do you have for me?"

"I'm not done hearing your news." He reached over and, with easy movements, felled the pins that held her hair in back. The black locks tumbled down. "What happened to your bonnet? The one with the roses?"

"It disappeared."

"And your hair. Who cut it?" He lifted one lock that was shorn above her neckline and lay in an errant curl against the longer hair.

The lump in her throat that had been threatening all week grabbed her. "It's only one lock that got cut. It doesn't matter. Agnes is . . . flighty. Even Sally came to my defense and removed the knife before Agnes did more damage." Wary of this intense Tyson, she scooted over into the corner of the coach and positioned herself so she could watch him.

"I can imagine how much defense a kitchen maid provided against a knife," he said. "All winter I've asked you how you've been treated in that house, and you've told me it was quite acceptable. Why?"

"You'd have stopped meeting me," she said painfully.

He was silent, then said, "I'd have sent my men to accost the Seymour butler."

She knew what was different about him then. This was the Fian talking, not Tyson the aristocrat. The dangerous Fain.

"Please, it's all right. They're but poor servant girls with no future, and they can't help but be jealous. Any revenge would only make it harder for me. It's a small price to pay for what I do, for the afternoons I spend with . . . with you."

He looked away, a muscle working in his jaw, as if he were controlling some inner turmoil, then looked back, expression soft. He handed her yet another package. "To keep you warm."

"But your news—"

"In due time. Please open my gift."

With a sigh she undid the string, then folded back the paper, aware without looking that he watched every movement of her hands. It was a muff. Sapphire-blue wool, trimmed in black fur. She felt herself smile and looked up in gratitude.

"It's beautiful," she said.

"Yes, I thought so," he said, never once taking his eyes off her.

To calm his mood, she thrust both her hands into her new muff, testing its warmth. "You're very generous."

"A man generally is with his mistress," he said, his tone more biting than ever before. At last he leaned back in the corner of the seat and looked at her. His gaze settled on her lips.

She felt herself blush and was glad when the coach pulled to a stop. A glance out the window told her they were in Hyde Park, where pale green buds showed against the trees—formed but not yet ready to unfurl.

"No more coyness," he said.

Aileen swallowed, suddenly afraid of this Tyson. Oh, no, this wasn't the urbane aristocrat with whom she rode. This was the Fian, the wild and dangerous idealist, disguised in the clothes of an aristocrat.

The coach stopped, but Tyson made no move to push

open the door. Aileen held her breath. She concentrated on her new muff, stroking the nap of it. On a whim she raised it to her cheek to feel its softness. At that moment Tyson reached for her, and without even giving her time to put down the muff, he tugged her outside, where, without any of last week's verbal preliminaries, he pulled her into his arms.

She meant to remove the muff from her hand, but he was kissing her, backing her into the door of the coach until she couldn't move and didn't want to. She felt the muff slip off her hand and drop to the ground, but didn't care. This was a far different kiss than the calculated experiment in his carriage or the impulsive good-bye after the riot. His lips seemed to skim over hers, and yet reach into her, taking from her. She reached up to wrap her arms around his neck.

She kissed him back, her lips moving under his to taste him, to steal some of the Fian into herself. She stood there, fighting a kind of longing she'd never known existed. This longing rose up from some unknown part of her and threatened to carry her off into the heavens. A heavenly whirlwind, wet and warm and wonderful.

Holding her breath, she let him kiss her until she wanted to plead with him to stop, that she was drowning. He was pulling her into a vortex, deeper and deeper. Finally, as if rescuing her to some solid shore, he pulled her to him, and they stood there like that for the longest time while his hands gradually relaxed and his kiss became just a whisper against her lips. The Fian—that was who had just kissed her, not Tyson.

When her breathing calmed down, she placed a hand against each of his shoulders and pushed. He was an immovable force. "The coachman—" she protested.

"—is paid to be discreet when gentlemen kiss their ladies." Catching her hands in hers, he moved his lips to her hair and whispered close to her ear. "It's part of his job." He kissed her hair.

A stab of jealousy shot through her that she wasn't the first one he'd kissed like this. If she looked down, she could see the way the hem of her dress hid the toes of his boots. They were that close.

Aileen felt a lonely gulf where he'd been. And turbulent thoughts as well. Didn't he know how it felt to have one's breath stolen away, to nearly drown? Wide-eyed, she watched as he picked up the muff she'd dropped, dusted it off, and handed it back to her. With a quick thrust he pushed shut the door of the coach, then reached for her hand.

"You said you had news for me," she said, her own voice competing with the pound of her pulse.

"About your brothers," he confirmed.

Immediately her eyes flew to his, searching. "Why didn't you tell me at once?"

There was no guilt in his face, only a profound sadness. "Because," he said, devouring her again with his eyes, "I guessed quite rightly, I'm certain, that once you heard news about your brothers, you'd choose them over a kiss with me."

She caught her breath at the tone of his voice—like that of a condemned man. She felt quick tears start in her eyes and stared away at the branches of a young elm. For a second the color of the buds ran into that of the sky, then she blinked, and green and blue marched to their places. "Have you found them?" She was surprised at the guilt in her voice and pulled herself away. She had no reason to feel guilt. If anyone owed guilt, it was Tyson, an urbane aristocrat dallying with her when he knew she was an innocent Irish girl who'd want nothing more than to hear immediate news about Patrick and Seamus. "What have you found out?" she demanded.

Silent, he tightened the pressure of his hand about hers and strolled with her across the grass toward a solitary patch of daffodils. "Digby's heard a rumor," he said at last, the reluctance clear in his voice.

Slightly dizzy from the shock, Aileen bent down, pretending to admire one yellow flower. Caressing the petals, she listened in silence.

"Two boys matching the description of your brothers have been spotted in a factory. We don't know if—"

"You found them!" she cried. Unexpectedly, she threw herself, muff and all, against him and felt his arms come up around her. "You've found them," she repeated over and over. "Sure and I knew they were alive. I knew it. Oh, Fian, thank you." She repeated the words over and over. Pure unadulterated joy laced her voice, and she totally ignored the shorn lock of hair, which blew against his face. "How soon can we go get them?" she asked at last.

She felt his pulse jump where her lips touched his neck, but he said nothing.

"Tyson?" With a self-conscious gesture she reached up to touch his face. "Tell me," she pleaded.

He caught her hands and pulled them down to her sides. "Let me explain in more detail. It's not as simple as it sounds."

Breathless, she waited.

"Digby and I feel the rumor's a trap."

Aileen didn't take in his meaning, not at once. "Oh, but I'm not afraid of—"

"I know. Of London, or of me, or of anything. But I've learned when to be afraid, and I'm afraid for both of us."

She felt dizzy. "It doesn't matter. We have to look." Even from a distance she felt him tense up, and he said nothing, just looked at her with those fathomless green eyes. She realized then what she'd implied. The Fian was expendable. Her brothers were not.

With a sad smile she reached over and took his hands in hers and pleaded, not to the nephew of Lord Weston, but to the famous Fian of Ireland. "I didn't mean that. It *does* matter if anything happened to the Fian, but you're so very clever. Surely we can look for them and not get hurt. I'll—I'll go with you. I have to be there when they're found. . . ."

"And back me up with an unloaded pistol, no doubt," he said musingly. He smiled now, too, but there was worry in his eyes. He gazed off somewhere in the distance.

"I knew you'd want to look," he added immediately, "but you're right. We're going to be extremely careful. If anyone is watching us, it will look as if we're instead going to a ball. The factory involved is near Vauxhall, and seven days from now Vauxhall is having a masquerade."

"But—"

At the shake of her head he said, "Humor me. I could go alone," he warned.

"But a ball? Why?"

His gaze suddenly captured her, held her, the way she imagined a dragon would capture a bird about to take wing. "I've seen you in nothing but that banshee black every week. I want to see you in the beautiful gown of a lady, a gown the color of your eyes. I want to—to dance with you just once before you take your brothers and leave. I want a few hours without coyness, lass. Is that so large a price for your brothers?"

Chastened, she shook her head. She looked up at him, oblivious to where they were, and was startled by a sudden realization. Before he kissed her, he'd had this planned out. "Where are Seamus and Patrick?" she asked in a quiet voice.

"Sure, lass, and you don't think I'm going to tell you and let you go alone, do you?"

When she looked up at the whimsical tone of his voice, he was staring down at her. The haunted look she'd seen earlier had been replaced by a look resembling defeat.

Thirteen

IN HIS HIDING place behind the ornately carved piece of shrubbery, Edmund Leedes crouched down, eye level with a convenient hole in the foliage. From there he kept a discreet and unflagging watch on the gate to Vauxhall. This first costume ball of the season was drawing a large crowd, especially considering Vauxhall's mixed reputation these days, a fact which made his vigil long and by now uncomfortable, given the mass of his girth.

An aging strumpet walked by and smiled provocatively at Leedes before sauntering on, her gaudy dress swaying in time to the music. Rich merchants mingled with the poor. Society members in boxes ogled everyone. From ball gowns to court jesters to milkmaids to pirates to Grecian ladies, Leedes studied them all, watching and waiting.

Suddenly, behind his painted face, he smiled at the sight of Tyson Winslow arriving at the gate. Lady Pamela had posted men around the factory, but it had been Leedes's own hunch that Tyson Winslow might come here to Vauxhall. The vigil had paid off. Winslow might be paying admission to the park like all the rest, but Leedes knew he'd come to check out that rumor about the Irish girl's brothers. He had nibbled on the bait.

Curious, Leedes looked at the woman accompanying Winslow. Costumed all in blue and gold, like a princess from some medieval century she was, bewigged and wearing a black theatrical mask. Leedes found himself intrigued. Tyson Winslow accompanied endless women around London—or, at least, he used to. Leedes couldn't help speculating on the identity of this one—and, judging from the looks of all the tongue waggers, all gossip centered on the same female.

Who could she be? Intriguing question indeed. Thoughtful, Leedes looked more closely at the woman's shape and height, and his eyes narrowed, as if closing in on a memory. Of course. The Irish girl. It stood to reason the chit would come searching for her own brothers. It also stood to reason she would come here heavily disguised. The girl, Leedes had learned only too well, did not lack for spunk and intelligence. He rubbed his head where she'd thumped him with a pistol so long ago. The bruise might have healed, but the memory lingered on.

While he watched them enter the gates, Leedes had a sudden intuition that Tyson Winslow had not been completely taken in with the latest trap. He looked on his guard, tense. And audacious. Who else would have the nerve to come to a costume dance in the garb of the Fian himself, the red robe of the medieval Fian of legend? In his opinion, Lady Pamela continued to underestimate the man.

But now that the Irish girl was here as well, Leedes all at once thought of a plan of his own—a plan that would succeed where Lady Pamela's would fail. Smiling, he wandered off to the Vauxhall eatery, where he would fill his rumbling stomach and bide his time before showing himself to either of them.

Unaccountably, Tyson felt uneasy about Vauxhall and wished he hadn't suggested it. But Digby Trigg was waiting somewhere in the shadows, and there would be no going back. Not since the night at the cove, the night he'd met Aileen, had Tyson felt the banshees poised, as if about to strangle him.

Threading his way through the crowd, Tyson guided Aileen down the path that led to the pavilion. Up to that point they'd not been noticed. But now, as he'd expected, sentences broke off in midair and conversation ceased for at least ten seconds while the curious stared. In their wake followed a gossipy buzz.

Tyson led Aileen toward the box he had reserved, his face set in stormy lines. He looked terribly angry and said nothing until she was seated. "Are you ready?"

"To find my brothers?"

"To face the people here. If we stay, you'll be scrutinized as furiously by the gossips as you ever were by society." He sounded doubtful about taking her any farther.

"Let them gossip," she said. All that mattered was the chance to find her brothers, and she told him so. "I don't care what they think of me."

He felt unaccountably disappointed at that, which surprised him. Lady Grenville had told him point blank that he was damaging the girl's reputation, but he'd pretended feminine cattiness had motivated Lady Grenville. Now he'd heard and seen the truth of it for himself. But Aileen cared nothing about the glittering world in which he moved.

She laid her hand on his arm. "You mustn't worry about me. I've heard it all before, and I'll hear it again," she whispered. "They're only noticing my outrageous dress. I heard someone call me the Lady in Blue."

Studying the way the blue gown revealed her figure, unable to hide his admiration, he felt lost in her allure. "Tell

me, my Lady in Blue, what do you suppose the Irish maid
Aileen thinks of me?"

Without hesitation she replied. "That you're gallant to
help her at risk of your own safety." She leaned over to
whisper in his ear. "And that your kisses are even more
scandalous than the gossips give you credit for."

"Banshee," he whispered, leaning close to her, tempted
for a moment to throw all caution to the wind and kiss her
then and there. Just as suddenly he regained control and
pulled away, taking care that their bodies no longer
touched. Oblivious now to staring passersby, he perused her
costume, his gaze lingering on her waist, her breasts, her
lips, struggling against the need to kiss her again.

"I realize it was my idea to see you out of servant black,
to see you compete with the other ladies. Now I'm sorely
tempted to take you back to Digby's boat and live up to my
reputation," he said.

"I never know if I'm with Tyson or the Fian, it seems . . .
or which one is kissing me."

"It's been Tyson Winslow." His clipped voice surprised
even himself. "Remember that for both our sakes. The Fian
doesn't dally with women."

Didn't he? Tyson recalled the last dangerous kiss in the
coach. Yes, it was true he'd nearly lost control there, nearly
forgotten that the Fian did not get involved with women.
His pulse was beating heavily in his ears, making rational
thought difficult, and this night of all nights required him to
have his wits about him.

Aileen was looking up at him, sparks in her own voice as
well as in her lovely blue eyes, sparks so brilliant they set
him on fire. "The gossip shall be quite outrageous if you
continue to stare at me like that, Tyson Winslow." They'd
reached the box and she sank down into a chair.

"Ah, put her in the costume of a princess, and now she

tells me the decorous rules of society." He turned and gave a hovering waiter instructions about food and drink.

"Rules mean nothing. I came to find my brothers."

He felt an inexplicable frustration. She seemed impervious to romance or his gallant overtures. All she could think of was those brothers.

"But promises count with me," he said, taking her hand to lead her to the dance floor. "I'll have my promised dance."

She and Tyson were inching their way toward the dance floor when suddenly someone leaned over the low railing of another box. "Winslow, old chap, who do you think you are? The legendary Fian come to life?"

Obviously eschewing costume, Marcus Owen was dressed in a simple cutaway coat and trousers. At once Tyson saw Marcus's gaze on Aileen, clearly speculating on her identity. When Tyson introduced her as the "Lady in Blue," Marcus nodded politely enough, but clearly curiosity piqued him.

"Come, come, you can tell me," he cajoled. "Who is this fair charmer? Give me a clue."

"If the lady had wanted her identity bandied about in your newspaper, she'd not have come disguised," Tyson retorted. Tyson could almost see Marcus Owen reach for his notebook to jot down details in shorthand. He prayed to God Marcus was not astute enough to associate the Lady in Blue with the Seymours.

Aileen wisely said nothing to give away her Irish accent. She inclined her head and murmured in a perfect imitation of Lady Pamela. "Good evening, sir."

There may have been a slight tremble to her voice, but no hint of her Irish brogue. Tyson smiled at her cleverness, thinking briefly how different she and the aristocratic ladies were—the latter a shallow pond given to no other purpose than gilding itself with lilies, Aileen as deep as the fathomless sea.

"You still haven't told me what you're doing here tonight?" asked the persistent Marcus Owen of Tyson.

"Dancing, perhaps, Owen, if we can ever get to the floor. And you?" With easy skill Tyson turned the questions to the other man. "Confess, now. What are you doing here?"

"The same as I do up in the balcony of Parliament. Reporting on the domestic debates."

"Domestic debates? Here?" Tyson raised a mocking eyebrow.

"Lord Eversham is here with Lady Saxeville, who they say has left her husband. Lord Darby is here with Lady Heath, who's divorced, you know. All the ones who aren't welcomed at court because their morals have sunk below reproach are here, it seems, and you know how that sort of thing sells newspapers. . . ."

"You work too hard, Owen," Tyson said and moved on toward the dancing.

"I don't think I want to dance," Aileen said with maddening timing. "Take me to look for my brothers." She tugged out of his grip.

Tyson closed the space between them and smiling down at her reminded her, "Ah, but remember our bargain. You promised me one dance in exchange for them."

"I thought you jested."

Seeing her tears of frustration, he covered her hand with his. He felt a spark pull them closer, as invisible as if a star had just burst inside him. "I've arranged to meet Digby Trigg at a specified hour," he explained softly.

"Does the Fian live his whole life by plans?" she asked.

"Perhaps, but Tyson Winslow lives by promises, and you

promised me a dance." Reaching for her hand, he led her out onto the dance floor.

Gathering her close into the position of the waltz, he felt the quick catch of her breath before she melted into his arms. She rested her head for a moment against the great golden pin that tied the red cape of his costume, and when her fingers folded down over his hand, he held his breath.

It only took one set of steps, moving her backward in a slow whirl around the floor before she was able to match his rhythm, and he waltzed her in time to the beat of his heart. Silently, around and around the dance floor they whirled.

"If I find my brothers and never see you again, I will remember this night forever," she said softly.

Her voice intruded on the invisible melody he was hearing. He only missed a beat, but she looked up, her alluring blue eyes worried. The pin from his Fian cape had left an imprint on her cheek, as if branding her his.

"And so, too, I," he replied, looking down into her eyes, resisting the insane impulse to kiss her right there while they danced. If he was losing himself in her eyes, he didn't care.

Nor did Aileen care when she drowned in his gaze, pulled into the rhythm of his heartbeat, his steps, locked there, the key thrown deep into some private hideaway. And if the key were never found, she'd have gladly stayed locked like this forever. From the moment she'd looked up into his eyes, it seemed a fairy net had come down around them, capturing her and him as well, she imagined, seeing the way he looked at her.

Despite the dozens of people around them, she'd become caught up in a world of her own. She'd been decreed a princess and this her private ball. She'd have followed him anywhere, not merely around the dance floor, but into passionate battle.

He held her scandalously close and didn't take his eyes

off her, his green-eyed gaze glittering and dangerous.
Mesmerized, she knew with whom she danced, and it
wasn't Tyson Winslow, the aristocrat. This was the Fian.
Her head spun until she fair forgot what it was she wanted
most from London. Brothers? No, this moment, and this
man's embrace.

All the voices and colors and sounds blurred into one
indistinct hum, and she was lost in a world of her own, a
world in which she could scarcely remember time before
this man.

Suddenly the music stopped, and she looked over at a
pair of elegant ladies glaring at her, petulant, willful ladies
costumed like some tattered Marie Antoinettes. Aileen
heard the whispers about herself threaten to crescendo. She
whirled away and began to walk across the dance floor to
their box. Tyson was right beside her, his Fian cape flowing
out behind him. "Ignore them all. No one knows who you
are. They'll pretend to cut you dead out of jealousy. You've
fooled them all."

"It's not that. . . . I—I almost forgot about my brothers."

Tyson's jaw tensed, and he looked away into the distance. "It's nearly time to meet Digby." His words suddenly
sounded remote. He walked her away from the dance area
and headed for the walkways that stretched under a canopy
of lantern-lit trees. He seemed in no hurry, and there was an
easy companionship between them. She wanted her time
with him to never end.

And for the first time she realized what it would mean if
she did indeed find Seamus and Patrick. This association
would end. She'd go to Roddy in America, and Tyson
Winslow would stay here in England and marry someone
like—like those snide Marie Antoinettes. At the thought of
an ocean between them, her chest tightened again, as if

someone had pulled a knot tight. She didn't, she realized with a guilty pang, want to say good-bye to this man.

They turned a corner, and he led her down a more secluded, less well-lighted promenade, past a couple kissing in the shadows. But now that they'd had their dance, Tyson seemed oblivious to thoughts of ardor.

He didn't slow down, in fact, until the path itself stopped, dead-ending in a low-growing hedge, beyond which another gate opened into Vauxhall. Dark it was, and in its shadows she saw a man waiting, a short man, built a bit like a barrel and dressed in a seaman's jacket much like Kit's. At first sight of Tyson he tucked a pistol into the waistband of his trousers. This had to be the man called Digby.

She crossed herself for luck and, looking up, saw Tyson watching her. This was not the lover she'd been dancing with. This was the Fian, as deadly and dangerous as raw lightning. And for the Fian she held no allure—only danger. When was she going to get that through her head?

Digby was watching her, as if wanting to see behind the disguise. His look was frankly curious, yet friendly, but when he turned to Tyson, his words were terse. "Do we talk alone or with the girl?"

"Get on with it. Tell us both."

Digby looked nervously at her, as if worried how she might react. "It's as we feared."

Tyson nodded and cast a quick glance her way. She hadn't felt such quick despair since the night Lord Fitzwilliam had wrenched her brothers from her. "It can't be a trap," she said in a little voice, fighting tears. "Who'd be so cruel?" She saw a quick muscle move in Tyson's jaw. Immediately she regretted her words. He'd tried after all to warn her.

"I should have believed you when you first told me." Her

voice sounded small and far away. And weak. She mustn't be weak, not when he was so strong.

"It was worth checking," he said, staring off into the night, past her and Digby. "It sounded too easy, but still one never knows, and I never go back on my promises—"

"Mr. Winslow," another voice came softly out of the darkness. "A word with you, sir?"

They both glanced over their shoulders, and Aileen at once saw it was that Irish fellow from the downstairs flat at Kate Reilly's—Martin Kelly. Martin stood with a couple of other Irishmen from the neighborhood, and it was clear they waited anxiously to talk to Tyson. More Irish news, no doubt, she thought, dazed. It seemed the Irish had news about everyone except her brothers.

Tyson was looking down at her, worried. "I can talk to them later," he offered.

Aileen shook her head. "No, I'm fine."

"Go ahead and see what they want. If it's the girl you're worried about, she's safe with me," Digby offered in an avuncular fashion.

Tyson shot Digby a wry look, then moved away a few feet to hear the whispered news of Martin Kelly.

Aileen shivered as the chill night air closed around her. Immediately she missed Tyson and worried. No doubt after hearing whatever Martin had to say, the Fian would lead another riot, risk his life. . . .

"He cares for you, you know."

She swung round to find Digby's knowing gaze on her, more curious than ever. Nostalgic, as if she reminded him of someone.

"He's very kind to everyone Irish," she said, a bit sadly, hugging her arms about herself for warmth.

"Aye," agreed Digby, who seemed to chew on his thoughts a moment before adding, "I've known him many years. At first this cause was a pastime with him. Now it's more. Now it's consuming his whole life."

Digby nodded his head in the direction of Tyson standing in animated talk with Martin Kelly. "You see there."

While Aileen watched Tyson, Digby's voice continued on. "The danger of the Irish cause is like a second skin to him. He'll be the Fian till Ireland's free, which won't be before his death, and with all the chances he takes, death walks closer and closer behind him."

Aileen trembled and, holding her arms closer to herself, looked back at Digby. "What are you saying? That I'm making things more dangerous for him?"

"Nay, he makes his own danger. But you're a young girl, with a girl's tender heart, that's clear, and no one to look out for you, I'd wager."

"If I have to, I can look out for myself," Aileen said. "I'd never do anything to put him in danger—not deliberately."

"I know that, colleen," he said with a crusty smile. "You may have to remember it for both him and yourself, that's all I'm saying. Do ye understand?"

Through misty eyes Aileen nodded. She fought to hide her reaction to his words. "Thank you for risking your own safety, Digby, to check on my brothers," she said in as normal a voice as possible.

"Me? I'm an old man, and if something happens to me, it's no great loss, but you're young, colleen."

"The Fian's young as well."

"Aye, but it's no use telling him that. . . ."

Aileen nodded and, not waiting for Tyson, headed back down one of the darkened walkways.

Tyson returned to find Digby alone and immediately his temper flared. Everything was going wrong tonight. "You said you were going to watch her," he accused. "Where is she?"

"Just down that path. Use your eyes and you'll see her."

He started down the path, but turned back, red cape swirling about him. "Warning her away, were you, Trigg?"

"Nay. Giving her some fatherly advice, but I'm done."

"Your version of fatherly advice was never known to cheer a person." Tyson glared at Digby and stalked off.

That everything had gone wrong that evening was an understatement, Tyson thought. Actually, except for some sweet moments dancing with Aileen, the evening could better be described as wretched. Everything had turned out badly, and as he strode down the path, hunting for Aileen, he found himself cataloging the little disasters.

The gossips annoyed him. The members of the haute monde glaring at Aileen bothered him. Then there was the disappointment he'd given Aileen. Even though he'd been almost certain this was a trap, he'd had his hopes up for *her* sake. He felt as if he'd let her down somehow. Now Martin had news of more unrest in the Irish district. And on top of all that, Digby had let Aileen wander off. Didn't the old man know that Vauxhall was no longer the exclusive place it once was, that unsavory sorts mingled here?

Tyson found her sitting alone on a stone bench under a dark tree, silent sobs shaking her. He didn't say a word, but knelt in front of her and used his handkerchief to wipe her tears dry. He retied her mask and straightened her wig. Helping her up, he brushed the grass and bits of gravel from her skirt. Her sniffling gradually ceased.

He spoke to her in a matter-of-fact voice, as if nothing were amiss. "Shall we return to dance? Or would you like to go back to Kate Reilly's?"

She thought about it briefly. What would *he* want? To dance with her some more—or be rid of her? All at once she didn't care what he wanted. She wanted to recapture the magic she'd felt in his arms. "I want to stay here—and dance."

She memorized the expression on his face, the way he smiled, the way his eyes softened. They danced for ever so long, and he held her gently, moving with the rhythm of the sea meeting sand, smiling at her with the tender look of a gallant courting his lady. Yet, no matter how long she danced with him the rest of that evening, the warning words of Digby hung over her, like a wall between them and the earlier magical spell.

She smiled on the outside, but inside Aileen felt saddened because she realized never would she have more than a part of this man's life. A dance. A ride in a coach. A stolen moment in a breakfast room. And always he would be leaving, riding away to his cause—to his death, Digby had predicted. She shut her eyes and let Tyson whirl her around. But the mood was gone. One more dance, then another and another, until finally she slipped her arm through his and with the dignity of a medieval princess led the way back to their box.

Marcus Owen had fished out his glasses and was boldly taking notes on her. And from the same direction came a waiter with a note. "An invitation to join Marcus," Tyson said, tossing the piece of paper down by his glass. "He seems determined to make news of you—or of us. I'll need to go over there, or he'll make it worse."

Nodding her agreement, Aileen watched him make his way across the crowded dance floor, the light from the lanterns gleaming off the scarlet of the great Fian's cape. He crossed paths with pirates, court jesters, men in elegant cutaway coats, a rotund, gaudily dressed clown. The entire dance floor seemed to part for the great Fian.

Pretending nonchalance, Aileen glanced around the place. The spring night was clear, though slightly cool, and Vauxhall, well, it took her breath away. A fairyland it was, every tree lit up with lanterns. In all directions from the open-air dance floor stretched graveled promenades—many more than the one they'd entered by. Hedges divided everything. Gazebos sat here and there amongst the trees, many occupied by couples. From the amphitheater came sweet music.

Unable to hide her curiosity, she glanced back at Tyson. The crowd shifted constantly, now blocking her view of him. A man dressed as a Shakespearean clown planted himself directly in front of her. Impatiently she waited for him to move on. When he didn't, she looked up into his face, blinked once in recognition, and felt herself go white.

Fourteen

"LORD FITZWILLIAM IS most unhappy you're still alive, you know."

"Lord Fitzwilliam doesn't know where I am," Aileen replied quickly, frightened at the mention of her landlord—the landlord who'd sent her to her death.

The Shakespearean clown smiled and his jowls sagged over his neck flounce. "I thought as much—it *is* the Irish lass, isn't it?" His voice dripped with cruel sarcasm.

"Mr. Leedes." Aileen pressed a hand to her mouth in horrified recognition. She backed out of the box, casting one frantic glance in the direction of Tyson, but conversation with aristocratic acquaintances engrossed him.

Aileen ran along the rows of boxes, followed by Edmund Leedes. She'd escaped Leedes once before. She could do it again, especially the way he teetered in his ridiculous high-heeled shoes. But she couldn't see well in the crowd and took a blind alley. The hedge-lined promenade dead-ended at a trysting place, and Leedes caught up.

"You're very good at seeing through disguises—almost as good as I am." His voice was a low hiss at her back. "The others have never seen you and wouldn't know the

Irish maid from a Lady in Blue, though he was clever to
disguise you. But I traveled with you all the way across the
Irish Sea, my dear. I remember how you walk. I remember
your height and shape. You can't disguise that. All it took
was one mention of Lord Fitzwilliam, and you verified my
suspicions for me."

His words echoed in her mind. Aileen stood there near a
bench taking Leedes's measure. His vileness, she decided,
matched his waistline. Overhead, fireworks burst like so
many shooting stars.

How easily she'd fallen into Leedes's trap and revealed
herself. She'd been in low spirits after the disappointment
over her brothers. When the clown had popped up at the low
wall of her box and spoken, she had been off guard. But
now that she'd gathered her breath and her wits, the time
had come to talk. "I've done nothing wrong. In fact," she
hastened to add, moving around to keep the bench between
them, "I'm employed by Lady Pamela Seymour, and she
gave me the night off."

"I know all that." Leedes moved so close she could smell
the reek of whiskey on his breath. Even in costume, she
decided, Leedes had atrocious taste. His clown suit was
fashioned of purple and green pantaloons under a ballooned
tunic the color of wine.

"What do you want?" Aileen demanded, voice shaken. If
she thought anyone in this noisy crowd would hear her,
she'd have screamed.

When Leedes smiled, his face took on a grotesque leer.
"I have a proposition, my dear. . . . Your friend, Tyson
Winslow, is under heavy surveillance, but perhaps on your
jaunts about London, you've taken note of that.

"Scotland Yard," he continued, "may not wait for—shall
we say—private citizens like Nicholas Seymour to take

action against the Irish riots. They're about to arrest Tyson Winslow for questioning in the Fian riots."

"Liar."

"Oh, no, I'm not, my little spitfire. He's long been suspected as the Fian. Dressing up tonight showed cleverness. Who, after all, would imagine the real Fian to be so audacious as to dress up as his legendary self? But it won't forestall the arrest. Being seen so often with an Irish maid hasn't helped, either, you know. You're liable to be questioned as well."

"We've done nothing but dance."

"Maybe. Maybe not. But you were seen not just with Tyson Winslow, but with the Fian himself—with my own eyes. How do I know what you and he did on that ride to London? Or later? You could be an accomplice to England's most wanted traitor."

"No." Shaken, Aileen began working her way backward from the man, but she was hemmed in by the hedges, which presented an impenetrable barrier. And Leedes was blocking the path that led back. People who noticed them leered as if they thought she were merely resisting Leedes's lusty advances.

Leedes moved toward her. A drunken reveler bumped against him, and Leedes brushed off his clown costume. Turning his attention back to Aileen, he added, "All you have to do is agree to testify against him as the Fian, and I'll make certain you're provided for nicely. You wouldn't need to work for Lady Pamela anymore. You could have a little place of your own. I'd give you my protection, which is worth more than the protection of a traitor. I'd even forgive you for that nasty bash on the head you gave me in the church. And . . . not even Lord Fitzwilliam would care to bother you further." He lifted his flask and took greedy swallows.

Around Aileen the music tinkled crazily, and above her
the sky continued to crash with the flash of fireworks. All
the warnings came together with explosive clarity. Digby.
Kate Reilly. The factories. The Seymour servants. All of
them one way or another telling her that the Fian held only
danger for her.

"Mr. Leedes, I believe I'm going to be ill." Aileen sat
down on the bench and tried to look faint, but a moment
later, when Leedes looked off his guard, she jumped up and
darted around him back down the path.

Leedes panicked. He couldn't lose the girl this easily.
Through the crowd, he caught a glimpse of her blue dress
and black mask, and he stumbled after her, cursing the high
heels of his costume. One heel wobbled, and he twisted his
ankle, staggering and falling against a nearby dandy, who
shoved him angrily away.

Straightening, Leedes limped on, scanning the crowd.
The girl would have to head back to Tyson Winslow, he told
himself. Where else could she go? He started to push his
way toward the dance floor when he caught a brief glimpse
of the blue dress. She wasn't headed for the dance floor at
all. She was headed for the main gate, and if she got that
far, he would lose her for good. With crude impatience he
pushed aside a woman in a milkmaid costume and hurried
on, looking for the familiar blue dress.

When Aileen lifted up the skirt of her dress to her thighs,
she found she could move much faster. When, by some
miracle, she found a gate, she fled out onto the road and,
dodging horses and dogs and people, pushed her way back
around the long queue of carriages and coaches that waited
for their owners.

Not certain yet where to go, she headed for the river, only
knowing she had to elude Leedes . . . and Tyson. Neither
one must find her. Each one held his own kind of danger.

She'd have to hide—certainly until the Scotland Yard threats died down. As she moved, she tore off and discarded her mask and her wig and ran until her side ached with the effort. She stopped to catch her breath, praying Leedes's ridiculous high heels might slow him down. Behind her the way leading back to Vauxhall looked long and dark. Ahead of her at the embankment of the Thames, the steps leading down to boats for hire promised even less light.

A coach and four horses trotted down the street, and she ran toward a grove of trees near the embankment to wait in seclusion for it to pass. Instead it stopped, and she moved farther away, finally crouching low by the stone wall of the embankment. When someone touched her shoulder, she jumped, her heart in her throat. She'd heard no footsteps. Swinging round, terrified, she stared through the darkness and suddenly relaxed.

In the moonlight she could make out familiar light-colored hair and spectacles. "Marcus," she breathed, relief evident in her voice. Good, kindly Marcus was frowning, looking at her with concern, his notebook open, pencil poised, ever the efficient reporter.

"Lady in Blue," he said, peering at her through the night. "I was sorely disappointed Tyson came to my box without you. May I be of assistance? My coach is waiting."

Her heart pounded. She was literally unmasked now, and the last thing she desired was for Marcus to write in the newspaper the gossipy details of her flight from Vauxhall. On the other hand Marcus was Tyson's friend . . . perhaps he could be confided in. Perhaps. He moved closer to her, and it seemed she'd have no choice.

"Hallo. Come now, don't be afraid. I saw you run out of there as if the hounds were at your heels. Is anything the matter, and where may I ask is that bounder, Winslow?"

Bereft of wig and mask, Aileen moved out of the shadows and into a pool of moonlight.

Marcus gasped. "Why, you're—you're the Irish lass from Seymour's." He stood mesmerized, as if trying to put a puzzle together.

"Shh." Aileen put her finger to her lips. "Is anyone with you?"

"No, I'm quite alone." He sounded abashed, admitting, "I don't dance." With a quizzical expression on his face, he put away his reporter's notebook in the breast pocket of his coat. "I can't help but be curious as to why Tyson disguised you tonight. I'm guessing to protect you from further scandal. If so, the ruse worked beautifully. But everyone back there is hoping I write an exposé of the Lady in Blue."

"I hope you won't—at least not all the truth, not if you recall your promise once to help me."

Marcus Owen considered this a moment. At last he nodded. "Agreed then. What's wrong?"

"I'm running away."

"So I deduced. May I ask from whom?"

"From Tyson Winslow." Aileen rushed on. "It's not at all what you think. It's got to do with my brothers. Because I'm Irish, I'm being used to hurt Tyson's reputation in the Commons . . . but I won't let that happen." She elaborated a bit more without giving away Tyson as the Fian. "So you see, for his sake, I have to vanish. I'd be obliged if you'd take me into the heart of London and let me out in some deserted street."

"To be set upon by thieves? That's not my idea of helping a lady."

"Then tell me where I can hide out."

Marcus Owen stood there looking as if he'd been struck by a thunderbolt. "My dear girl, you and I both remember the lengths Tyson Winslow went to get you alone at

Seymour's. You don't think you can simply run away from
a man like that, do you? He'll look for you. I ought to
know. I took his slingshot once when we were chaps at
school, and he hunted a week for it. . . . That's neither
here nor there now, but the point is, I know the man, and I
believe he'll look for you."

"Then he mustn't find me," Aileen pointed out with
agonized logic. "Ever since he met me, I've brought him
danger. He calls me a banshee, you know, and it's true. I'll
destroy his life here in London. Others are involved who
will use any treachery to pull him down."

Marcus let out a low whistle. "Is it all as bad as that?"

"Worse. . . . Please, Mr. Owen, are you going to help
me?"

With mounting fear that Tyson would come out of the
park and find her, she turned and began walking toward the
embankment. She knew suddenly what she could do. Over
her shoulder she called. "He won't look for me if he thinks
me dead, will he?"

Marcus ran after her and caught her by the arm. "Here
then, you're not going to drown yourself?"

"Of course not. I'm just going to make it look that way."
He sounded so concerned, quite like a big brother, like
Roddy, except for his unexpected attack of bashfulness. The
man had a streak of modesty as wide as the Thames. As
Tyson had said, hand Marcus a wench and he'd turn to
blushing.

"Will you help me?" she asked again, conscious of his
unease. She began unfastening the drawstring front of her
costume's girdle.

Even in the darkness she was certain Marcus did indeed
blush. He took off his spectacles and made a great project of
stuffing them in a pocket.

"Are you going to help? Yes or no? I need to know by the time I remove this dress," she said.

Befuddled, he finally stammered, "Yes. Yes, for heaven's sake, yes."

"Then lend me your cloak, sir. You do have one with you?"

His eyes grew large with consternation at her own sudden lack of modesty, but he acted without hesitation. He rushed back to his coach, retrieved the required garment, and shoved it at her.

"Turn your back to me, if you would, kind sir."

"Here? Now?" With the abruptness of a soldier obeying a military command, Marcus Owen swung around and stood at attention.

Aileen stripped off the blue gown. Standing in nothing but a chemise and pantalettes, she shivered in the night air and quickly wrapped herself in the dark cloak. Blue gown balled up in her hands, she hurried past Marcus to his coach. Clutching the cloak tightly she climbed in and looked out at him. "Please do open your eyes now, Mr. Owen. I'm quite decent. Can you find a rather large rock or some weight?"

He was blinking at her, as if she and his entire coach were about to turn into a banshee-filled pumpkin. Aileen had had only a glimpse of the driver, and his head had been discreetly down.

"A rock? A piece of stone perhaps from the embankment."

"Yes, the very thing. Then it might look as if I really did fall over."

After a slight pause, Marcus went off in search of a stone, and when he returned, short of breath from the weight of his burden, he laid a hefty chunk of the embankment at her feet. She promptly wrapped the dress around it.

Watching her, he climbed in, declaring under his breath that his sister Beatrice would never believe this—not if he signed his name to the story. "You're quite sure you know what you're doing?"

"Positive. I've never been more sure. Just don't tell anyone."

She asked him one more favor that night—to stop in the middle of London Bridge. He did. A prostitute scurried away in the night, and when Aileen felt reasonable privacy on the public bridge, she stepped out of the coach and dropped the stone-weighted dress down into the Thames.

With cloak drawn tightly about her, she watched through mist-filled eyes as the water exploded up out of the river, the wake from the impact white under the moonlight. The shapeless form of the Lady in Blue's dress floated free, and the current carried it away.

Rain pelted the window of the Dog's Paw, as if competing with the candles for the gloom. Inside, oblivious of all else, Tyson sat getting steadily and thoroughly drunk. He drained his tankard of ale and called for more. Spread out before him on the table lay the latest edition of a London newspaper. Containing one gossipy editorial after another about the mysterious Lady in Blue, the things were selling as quickly as if a Dickens serial were currently running, much faster even than when editorials lambasted the Fian.

Staring into a fresh glass of ale, he relived for the thousandth time the night Aileen vanished. That had been a nightmare, but not as bad as the day her dress washed up on the bank of the Thames, found by a simple mudlark who counted the muddy garment a prize and promptly sold it, whence it made its way to a newspaperman. The Lady in Blue—her dazzling debut at Vauxhall and her mysteriously tragic disappearance—haunted him.

Over and over that awful night came back to him. When
he'd discovered her gone, he'd circled round the entire ring
of boxes, asking first one person, then another, if they'd
seen the Lady in Blue. By now everyone there had seen the
woman in question, but no one had noticed her leave.
Crisscrossing all the promenades, Tyson had wondered if
she'd been waylaid along some path. Again he'd come up
empty-handed.

Finally he'd simply left the park and made his way along
the queue of coaches. Horses neighed nervously at his lack
of patience in moving through them. If a driver slept Tyson
had rudely jostled him awake, snatching whips away and
throwing them to the ground, pulling a cap off here and
pulling one down over a face there. One driver had stood
kissing a maid, and Tyson had boldly pulled them apart to
ask about the Lady in Blue. His reward—curses. At long
last he had stood alone on the mossy steps leading down to
the Thames, despair settling down on his shoulders as
surely as had the nighttime fog.

He slammed down his fist on the newspaper. Enough
thoughts of Aileen. But thoughts, he discovered, had
become as impertinent as his black-haired banshee. They
refused to obey. He downed his ale, then loudly called for
yet another. He missed Aileen . . . missed her more than
he could have imagined, and he blamed himself for her loss.
He should never have involved her with the dangerous
people who stalked him.

How could Lady Pamela have sacrificed an innocent girl?
That was his worst suspicion—that her apparent drowning
in the Thames was the work of Leedes and Lady Pamela.
His jaw worked, and his eyes involuntarily misted. The
wench who brought him a fresh ale propped herself on the
corner of the plank table, smiling flirtatiously. "What do
you want?" Tyson heard himself mumble ungraciously.

"I was hoping it might be you with the wants tonight, my lord," she said in a seductive voice. "Something besides ale to warm yourself?" She touched Tyson's arm.

Through bloodshot eyes Tyson looked up at her, a dark-haired wench of comely face, but all he saw was Aileen—holding a pistol to him, demanding he take her to London, crying against him, begging him not to leave her alone, serving punch and blushing, arguing the merits of kissing, feeding ducks, dancing as the Lady in Blue. And always threaded through the pictures of her was the feel of her, turning pliant beneath his kiss. . . .

"Kind sir?" said the wench, her smile more hesitant.

Tyson reached into his trouser pocket and pulled out a handful of shillings. "Is that enough?"

The girl scooped them up, grinning slyly. "You can meet me upstairs for this sum."

"Nay," he said in a slurred voice, "for that sum, you can leave me with my thoughts." With a shocked exclamation the wench flounced off, and Tyson took a long swallow of ale.

Eventually Digby returned from his barge and sat down opposite Tyson, who was ill-humoredly waving away yet another serving wench.

"What'sa matter? You've found another paper for me?"

"Newspapers be damned. You haven't moved since I went out this morning."

"Haven't I? I've been engrossed in reading the papers."

"That much is clear." Digby pulled off his wet coat and hat and hung them up at a row of pegs near the door. Returning, he stood over Tyson. "You need talkin' to."

"I didn't appoint you to be my mentor all of a sudden," Tyson muttered into his drink, "so don't turn judge and philosopher on me."

"Unless you can get up and walk away from me, you'll

have me for company." Digby pulled out a chair and
straddled it. "Now, then, what are you planning next? The
Irish haven't heard a word from the Fian in weeks."

"What's the Fian plannin'?" Tyson asked rhetorically.
His voice held an exaggerated slur, his sarcasm magnified.
"He's plannin' to call on Lady Pamela, and when he goes to
her drawing room, he's going to demand to know what
happened to her Irish maid. But Lady Pamela, being
worldly, will no doubt feign insult and say she's not in the
habit of discussing her servants with gentlemen callers. No,
she's only in the habit of murdering them." His knuckles
grew white about his tankard.

"Winslow . . ." Digby said,

"And then I'll put my hands around her bare neck and
even the score with her and her murderous husband by—"
Ale spilled over his hands.

"For god's sake, man, you're drunk. I don't blame you,
lad. I got drunk too when I lost me Mary. . . ." Digby
pulled away the tankard and called for a serving girl. In a
low voice, he said, "Listen to me, Tyson Winslow, you're
not going to visit the Seymour house. You'll blow the entire
cause *and* your life to smithereens. Oh, I know, it would
feel good to blame someone for the loss you feel, but you
can't shove your guilt onto Lady Pamela. You have to face
it."

For a moment Tyson stared off into space. "I'd give—I'd
give anything to have a second chance with her."

"You had at least two chances with her," observed
Digby.

Tyson looked up angrily. "Did I ever tell you you've got
too much Druid in you, Trigg?"

"Not five minutes ago, and don't be changin' the subject
now."

"I'm not—I'm commentin' on yer love of preachin'. You

talk too much!" he yelled and again slammed a fist on the table. "Leave me alone, you old sea dog. I don't want to be responsible for your fate, either. Go back and ply your trade by barge," he growled.

"I'll leave," Digby said grimly, standing up, "but only to let you sleep it off. When you recover from drownin' yourself in the bottle, I'll be back with the latest news from Irishtown." He slung an arm about Tyson and helped him upstairs to a bed.

"The cause be damned," mumbled Tyson. Distraught, he sat on the edge of the bed holding his head in his hands.

Digby paused at the door. "If the girl were alive to warm your bed and your life, then you'd have the right to say that, but she's gone, and the cause still needs you."

"She might be alive," he mumbled.

"Slim chance."

"Her brothers are alive."

"Aye, somewhere. So's the cause."

"The cause can rot," Tyson said when Digby headed out the door.

Digby sighed. "And so it will while you're sleepin' off a drunk. But when you wake up, it'll be needin' you, just like before."

When the door slammed, the sound reverberated through Tyson's already aching head and he counted it a mercy when sleep claimed him.

When he awoke, he felt as if a thousand blacksmiths were at work inside his head. Digby was waiting and together they went for a long walk around the London streets, stopping for coffee and beefsteaks, and gradually Tyson became clearer-headed. Eventually they walked to London Bridge. Tyson walked a ways out on it, followed by a reluctant-looking Digby. Carts and horses, coaches and people jostled by in a noisy stream, and below flowed the

eternal Thames, calm depths concealing the secrets of the
centuries. Tyson stared down over the bridge, wind whipping at his hair and shirt, his thoughts now as cold sober as
the water. Over and over, he kept seeing Aileen's innocent
face the night he'd met her—confused and vulnerable. He'd
brought her to London, and he felt responsible for her. Still.

"I'm going to keep looking for her brothers, Trigg. I
should never have refused her—that's why she left—"

"Fian—" Digby put a restraining hand to Tyson's shoulder. "You're wanted in Irishtown."

Tyson looked back up, over at Digby, and then at the
opposite shore of London and its crowded brick buildings.
"I know. There'll be a riot in the works by tonight. Meet me
back at the Dog's Paw."

It seemed as if all he did was sleep anymore. Drinking
only made matters worse. He'd be better off throwing
himself into his work—better yet, the cause. Rioting would
not only help the cause, but occupy his thoughts at night.
Taking leave of Digby, he strode back off the bridge and
hailed a coach for Irishtown.

Lady Pamela stared at Edmund Leedes, hating the way
the man made her settee sink so. On top of that, he fidgeted,
constantly tapping his hat against his knee. She stared at the
Gainsborough painting on the wall behind him. "You
realize how inconvenient it's been for me that we lost the
Irish girl."

"But you know that she was the Lady in Blue. Surely,
ma'am, that's worth something to you in gossip?"

"If you're hoping for a few extra pounds, you're mis-
taken. All the gossip in the papers is of little consequence to
me—unless it concerns the capture of the Fian. Alive, the
girl was useful—dead, she's nothing."

Leedes cleared his throat nervously. "Begging your

pardon, your ladyship, but it's possible the Irish girl isn't dead, after all. She could be in hiding. After all, no body was found, only the blue dress. . . ."

Lady Pamela suddenly looked at him, mind calculating. "Are you suggesting she could have faked her own death?"

"Well, 'tain't me that threw her in the Thames. And I can't picture her killing herself. Those Irish Catholics think it's a mortal sin."

Lady Pamela looked thoughtful. "It could have been a maniacal thug or an accident. No, the girl had her merits, but she's not smart enough to fake her own death. . . ." Pursing her lips, she looked over at Leedes and his incessantly tapping top hat. At her stare he held the hat still. "I suppose it wouldn't hurt to watch the house where she used to live before I brought her here."

"You mean the house that Tyson Winslow owns?" he asked with a gloating smile.

Lady Pamela gasped and leaned forward in her chair. "What did you say? Tyson Winslow owns that house? How do you know?"

"You pay me well to keep you informed, your ladyship," he said.

Her eyes narrowed. "Very well, you've earned an extra amount." Quickly she strode to her writing desk and wrote out a bank draft and handed it to Leedes.

As he rose to leave, draft in hand and a self-satisfied smile on his face, Lady Pamela gave him his instructions. "In exchange for that money I want that place watched constantly—just in case, as you suggested—the Irish girl should return from the dead—or the Fian comes looking for her. Constantly. Do you understand, Mr. Leedes?"

"I'll not fail you."

"See that you don't. Anything regarding Mary Aileen or the Lady in Blue I want reported immediately."

Leedes bowed and took his leave. Left alone, Lady
Pamela toured the room, straightening the Gainsborough,
then moving on to stare at her own portrait on the wall,
admiring, if not the beauty, the cunning catlike eyes of the
woman staring back. Leedes might well be chasing a wild
goose. Most likely the girl was dead. Still, Lady Pamela
never left anything to chance, and if indeed the girl had met
her Maker, that meant no more than an opportunity lost.
She'd had plans before the girl walked into the intrigue, and
she had full confidence in her ability to capture the Fian
without the girl. A sorry day it would be when Lady
Pamela, daughter of an earl, had to rely on an Irish chit to
accomplish her goals.

*Seamus held his hands over Patrick's ears, pretending it
was a game they were playing. On the straw pallet next to
them a little boy younger than Patrick lay dead—stiff
dead—and the overseer was carrying him out. As far as
Seamus knew, this was the first boy who'd ever left the attic.
But he was dead. He swallowed back the lump in his throat.*

*At last he let go of Patrick. "You can listen now. The
English soldiers are gone, Patrick."*

"But where's the Fian?"

"He and Aileen might have gotten lost."

*"They're never coming, are they? There isn't even any
such thing as the Fian. You just made it all up."*

*"No, Roddy wouldn't lie. Roddy knew all the secrets, and
he'd not tell me false."*

"Do you still believe in the Fian?" Patrick asked.

*Seamus sighed and got up off the bunk. With the night
watchman downstairs this was a rare opportunity to look
out the tiny attic window, to gaze at the sky, to see the birds
flying free.*

He took Patrick's hand and led him over to the window,

*mindful for footsteps that warned the watchman was return-
ing.*

*A pigeon flew up from the attic sill and took wing up into
the wide sky, soon hidden in the dark and the clouds. "Did
you see that bird, Patrick? He's there somewhere. Just
because he's lost in the clouds doesn't mean he's not real.
I believe in the Fian, Patrick."*

*Patrick leaned his tousled head against Seamus's shoul-
der and followed the direction in which his brother pointed.*

Fifteen

AILEEN COULDN'T FACE another story about herself in the London newspapers. Marcus kept her too well supplied. Ignoring the latest one he had brought home, Aileen sat down at the table which his sister Beatrice had set with high tea. Aileen had been in hiding for days, and both Marcus and Beatrice, to Aileen's objections, tried to treat her like a pampered houseguest instead of the fugitive she was.

"Actually, today's papers have all followed my lead, and the latest editorials are finally letting go of the Lady in Blue scandal. How fleeting fame is," Marcus said with a smile for Aileen. "How does it feel to know society has already turned its attention back to the Fian? He's led a riot every night this week, and Scotland Yard is doubling its forces—"

"Marcus, let's not discuss politics over tea," suggested Beatrice in her quiet way. Her perceptive glance took in Aileen's suddenly white face.

The three of them had gathered around a snowy-white tablecloth and ate by candlelight. Outside a spring rain pattered at the windows, batting the daffodils in the window box against the pane. Aileen felt restless. Perhaps she could begin sneaking out looking for her brothers. But there was no job, no money. . . .

"Won't you have a tart? Gooseberry," Beatrice asked encouragingly.

Aileen shook her head. Gooseberry. Seamus and Patrick used to have gooseberry fights.

"A scone then?" Beatrice gently urged.

Dear Beatrice. Where Kate Reilly had been hand-me-down dresses and hearty soup, Beatrice Owen was a lover of crumpets on china plates and lace cloths. An impoverished dreamer, she and Marcus were the children of a country rector, now deceased. Beatrice jokingly called herself a spinster, though as far as Aileen could tell, nothing more than shyness held her back from a husband. Quite comely Beatrice was, with brown hair neatly coiled and clear gray eyes, soft skin. Yet, instead of encouraging suitors, she seemed to prefer the life of housekeeper to Marcus and in her spare time, unsung poet. Marcus in his turn appeared quite devoted to his sister, chastising her frequently for her not-quite-robust health.

Hiding away here couldn't have been more pleasant, yet Aileen had had her fill of reading from the book-lined shelves in the study. Her worries marched before her, demanding a frown.

Beatrice saw the frown and easily guessed Aileen's mood. "You're fretting again."

"It's hard not to."

"You mustn't. We're only too glad to have you, especially me. You've quite inspired a sonnet in me, I think, and I know you'll find your brothers. Trust in the Lord." She was gone in a gentle rustle of muslin to the pantry.

Aileen smiled after her, bit into a crumpet, which was much too hot, and dropped it right onto the newspaper Marcus had brought home. Butter melted and ran onto the front page. While rescuing the crumpet, Aileen couldn't resist reading the buttered words. She could feel the smile fade from her face. The article contained an account of the latest riot and the details of the Fian's near capture. Aileen felt quick tears start in her eyes.

Marcus stood by the fireplace, rearranging a wet umbrella while simultaneously toasting another crumpet. He turned the brass toasting fork and said noncommittally, "Perhaps I shouldn't bring home so many newspapers. Habit you know, being in the business. But you're reading far too many unsettling editorials, I fear." He moved back to the table and offered her another crumpet.

She shook her head and sighed. In the pantry Beatrice could be heard humming while tins rattled.

"Tell me now, what's wrong, beyond lost brothers and no home? Though this is your home for as long as you need. But Beatrice will toss me out in the cold if you don't talk."

At that Aileen smiled and looked up at his friendly bespeckled face, blond curls still damp from the rain. Aileen was certain he would blush if she so much as reminded him of the night he'd brought her here wrapped in nothing but ' is cloak.

"Do tell," he coaxed.

"You'll think I don't trust anyone."

"I'm quite certain, my dear Aileen, that you don't. After what you've been through, I see little reason for you to trust even the friendliest lapdog here in Londontown."

She swallowed hard. "So many people have offered help, but it's only been to capture the Fian."

Nodding, Marcus reached over and removed the newspaper from the table. "Yes, so it sounds. But you can trust us, you know."

"Yes, I do," she reassured him, then stared down at her

teacup. "Of course, I wonder why you'd bother to help me. I mean, after all, you're Tyson Winslow's friend."

Marcus buttered his crumpet with the same neat efficiency she'd seen him use to apply quill to paper at his desk. After a short silence he replied, "Acquaintances might be a better way to style it, but *trusted* acquaintances. Tyson has never slowed down long enough to form a lot of close friendships. However you style it—acquaintance, friend—I don't exactly approve of the scandalous way he dragged you around London. I'm not speaking for Beatrice now because she only knows what she's read and what you've told her, but as for me, I—and forgive me if my words offend—I rather thought he was using you and your Irishness."

Aileen felt warm at his blunter than usual words. She worried as well that Marcus the reporter might be putting two and two together regarding the Fian and Tyson.

"Whisht," she said, deliberately lapsing into a simple brogue. "What have I got that Tyson could use?"

Marcus looked at her a moment, thoughtful, as if measuring his words. "Tyson always had a wild streak in him when it came to things Irish. Let's just say I suspect he may have his finger in the pie a bit deeper than he should—about the Fian and all."

"Supposing he did," she countered, "and with you being a reporter, why don't you write the full story?"

"Some things are worth more than a story," he said obliquely, looking up as Beatrice returned.

"Ah, here's our tea." He busied himself moving plates to make room for the teapot. "Besides," he added quickly, "as a story the Fian is more useful alive. Not that we're speaking of Tyson Winslow, mind you, but that same type—someone prone to flaunting society I mean. Both Tyson and the Fian sell newspapers. They provide ongoing serials. Let's just say that I don't want to write his—I mean, their—last chapters yet. . . . Beatrice," he said, changing subjects abruptly, "shall I toast you a crumpet?"

"If you promise not to burn it," his sister murmured, smiling at Aileen. "And what is my ambitious brother thinking of writing now?"

"We were speaking of newspaper work."

"Well, I know what you should write, brother."

"What?" He pierced a crumpet onto the tongs of the toasting fork.

"Instead of those radical pamphlets you spend time on, you should write Aileen's story and tell about her two wee brothers. Describe them. If enough people read the pamphlet, someone might recognize them."

Both Marcus and Aileen stared in astonishment at sweet, sensible Beatrice. "I could," offered Marcus at last. "Alderman is a discreet enough printer."

"But I couldn't possibly afford a pamphlet," objected Aileen, though the idea instantly intrigued her; already her mind worked with ways she could earn the money, unless, of course, the printer would take a draught against arrears. From an Irish? She doubted it. "I could find a job—something discreet."

"I can pay for it," Beatrice said in a tone of voice that would brook no objection. "I have my dowry money." At the shake of Aileen's head, Beatrice added emphatically, "No, don't object over a few guineas or whatever it costs. I shall spend my dowry as I choose, and it would be well worth it to meet your brothers someday. Already they feel like my own. We'll begin tonight. Aileen will tell the story again. You, Marcus, will take dictation, and I shall do revisions. And Alderman shall print it, all as you suggested, Marcus—mind the crumpet now. . . ."

Moments later, while Aileen and Marcus looked on, Beatrice scraped the burned surface off her crumpet and smiled lovingly up at her brother. "You may burn toast, but you've such good ideas, brother, and the project is just the thing to keep Aileen occupied."

When the knock came, Marcus had already left for his newspaper office and Beatrice had gone to market. With candle in one hand to ward off the gloomy day, Aileen opened the door and stared in bewilderment. Before her stood a wizened woman, dressed totally in black, rheumatic hands clutching an old shawl about her shoulders.

"Nora's me name, but that's not important. I come 'bout this pamphlet." The woman pulled a tattered sheaf of papers out of her cloak and flashed the dog-eared cover. Without looking, Aileen knew the title: *The True Story of the Lady in Blue Who Attended Vauxhall Last Month and Did Drown Same Night, Including A Plea for the Return of Two Stolen Boys of Irish Nationality.*

Aileen literally held her breath before finding words. "Why have you come?"

"It might be I know where these boys are."

"Where?" A breathless syllable of hope.

In answer the woman thrust a scrap of paper at Aileen. "I can't write. Had me brother write down the name of the factory. They talk about the Fian so much, they've been caned, so me brother says." She turned as if to vanish in the night.

"Wait," Aileen said, suddenly panicked. Emotion filled her words. "Won't you tell me how to find the place?"

Turning back, the old woman pointed a gnarled finger south and gave her directions for finding the factory on the other side of the Thames. "Make glue they do, but no one's supposed to know. A slave factory, it be, workin' little ones."

Aileen winced. "Are you certain?"

The woman nodded. "Me brother was diggin' a grave for the uncle of that fancy chap in Parliament—Nicholas Seymour—and he heard him talkin' and told me. It's Mr. Seymour owns the place, near as I can make out. But if you're wantin' the boys, be wise to look soon. They don't come out of there—except dead." She looked at Aileen. "There now, I've scared the wits out of you. . . . Lost me own son to a fever long ago, and so I'm a sentimental fool. I hope you're reunited then, and tell no one, not even the good Lord himself, that I tattled."

"Thank you." Aileen pressed her hand to the old woman's gnarled one. The woman slipped away, and the busy street swallowed her up.

Numb with joy, Aileen shut the door and leaned back on it. Could it really be them? Aileen wanted to race out into the streets, but caution held her back. There'd been so many false leads, so much heartache and pain. Was the Lord going to make up for it after all?

Immediately she wondered if she should wait and take Marcus with her. But Marcus wouldn't be home until late tonight. And Beatrice, who was at market in any case, seemed far too delicate to go on such a mission.

So who would help her? Kit, if she could find him, though Kate Reilly would give them the very devil for going to another factory and risking harm. As Aileen reached for her cloak, the solution came.

Maeve. Certainly Aileen needed to tell Maeve what she'd learned about the owner of the factory. Maeve had been so sympathetic about Aileen's brothers. If she were lucky, this might even be Maeve's free afternoon.

She left a hurried note for Marcus and Beatrice, pulled a shawl on over her head, and set off. Already she planned what she'd do with her brothers—buy them ginger cakes and take them to the Punch-and-Judy shows and the hurdy-gurdies.

It wasn't Maeve's afternoon off, but with little effort loyal Maeve arranged to trade times with another maid who had no family to visit. And at last, three omnibuses later, Aileen and her friend entered the street named by the old woman—Watley Street. Immediately Aileen spotted the building.

The Whitcomb Glue Factory stood crumbling and shuttered as if defying prying eyes to see inside. Upstairs, even in the attic, wood barred the windows. All in all, the place looked like the sort small children would avoid on a windswept night in case ghosties lurked around the corner. Nearby, an overfed rat slunk away from the stoop to hide in a gutter.

Aileen told Maeve her plan, and somewhat reluctantly the girl agreed to masquerade as her sister, while Aileen tried to deliver a message to the boys. The only entrance, however, might have fortified a Norman castle. In answer to her knock a tiny slit in the barred door opened. Aileen trembled and drew Maeve close. A guard with matted hair peered out at them. After bloodshot eyes perused Aileen and Maeve, a rusty voice rasped, "What you be wantin'?"

Aileen's heart beat fast. "We—we've come with a message from Mr. Seymour, the owner. I'm his maid, and a pair of Irish boys here are to be released," she said with more bravado than she felt. "Their mother is on her deathbed—"

"You're lying. Whoever we got in here's an orphan. Me orders are not to release anyone, and not to let anyone in, no matter what lies they tell."

"It doesn't matter. I need to deliver a message to the Connolly boys."

"Who from—'er Majesty, the queen?" came the sarcastic rejoinder. "Go on, get out of 'ere, afore I get my pistol."

Like a cold slap in the face, the tiny hole in the door slammed shut.

"We'd best go," said Maeve, trembling.

"No, I can't. Not yet."

Maeve suddenly slumped against the brick wall. Aileen moved to her. "Oh, Maeve, I'm sorry, this has upset you."

Maeve pressed a hand to her temple. "I'm a wee bit dizzy—the excitement and all."

Aileen felt torn over what to do—take her friend back home or stay and watch for her brothers. In her heart she knew. "I can't leave, Maeve," she said. "I'll help find you a coach for hire, but I have to stay."

Maeve nodded. "It's all right. Just so I know where you are. People might be askin' after you."

"I'll be fine. I can't give up now, not when I've gotten this close. I only need to know for certain they're in there."

"You'll never get past that foreman."

"I only need to prove they're here." She flagged down a dusty hack for Maeve and wished her friend Godspeed. For hours Aileen stood in the doorway of the building across the street, watching the Whitcomb Glue Factory for any signs of life. For a long time only the smoke wafting up from the chimney of the place provided evidence of life. A few pigeons ventured near the place, and occasionally the brave robin.

At last dusk fell, the plume of smoke from the stack dwindled to a few puffs, and then nothing. A light appeared in the tiny attic window, and Aileen leaned closer from her secluded vantage point. Someone was opening the window. She ran across the street, stopped directly below, and craned her neck to see.

The boy leaning his head out the window was a redhead, but she couldn't see his features. "Patrick?" she called. "Patrick, is it you?"

"Aileen." Her name came from far above, like a wish upon the wind.

At once someone jerked the boy away, and she heard the unmistakable crack of a whip, followed by shrieks of pain.

"Fian ain't gonna rescue you, and neither's anyone named Aileen." Again the whip cracked, and Aileen had to cover her ears to block out the terrible sound. She ran to the door and banged. When that brought no results, she spotted a loose brick, pulled it from the building, and began to hammer the door with it.

The door opened so unexpectedly that she nearly fell down, and a bald-headed vulture of a man stalked out. In his hand he held a whip curled like a snake, which with one swift motion he lashed at Aileen's feet. She jumped back just in time to avoid the sting. Undeterred, the man advanced, his grin evil. "Are you sellin' any interestin' goods, lassie?"

Picking up her skirts, Aileen turned and ran, down twisting lanes and alleys, past dogs and cats and people and carts. She never stopped running till her lungs burned from the effort. Eventually a kind vegetable peddler offered her a ride.

After climbing on, she fell back to catch her breath and considered her options. It was a miracle Patrick was alive at all, and what of Seamus? She'd never seen him and probably never would unless he had help—help of the sort that, unlike Maeve, could look on the place without falling into vapors. A man. And she knew which man. The man who thought her dead. The Fian.

She had to reconsider her vow to stay away from Tyson. Surely she could see him once and not endanger him. After all, her brothers' lives might be at stake. She had no choices. But where to find the elusive Fian? Somehow she made her way to the Parliament buildings, to the visitors' gallery to find Marcus, but he was nowhere to be seen. Nor was Tyson Winslow anywhere in sight. Intimidated by all the hustle and bustle of the politicians and the construction in progress, she left.

She recalled the exotic barge where Tyson had taken her to transform her into the Lady in Blue, but had no idea where in London she'd been, save somewhere on the Thames.

Her eyes teared at the irony. At long last she'd found her brothers—but now she had no idea where to find Tyson Winslow, let alone his hideout as the Fian.

All of a sudden she brightened. There was one person in her acquaintance who knew every secret hideout in London and who never got the vapors. Kit. Surely *he'd* be able to lead her to the Fian's secret hideout, and Kate Reilly would never be the wiser.

Sixteen

WITH HIS USUAL bravado, Kit hailed a wagon to the waterfront. "Don't know if Tyson Winslow's at the Dog's Paw, but I've heard it whispered as a hangout. It's a fearsome place, so stay close." Despite the warning, pride edged his voice.

At the sound of Tyson's name Aileen's pulse jumped. She missed him so, but this was no time for sentimental thoughts. She had Kit and herself to look out for. Finally they approached the mullioned window of the Dog's Paw, a place which even in broad daylight looked rough. By now Aileen's heart pounded in her ears. Inside, in the main room of the tavern, raucous voices raised a pitch. A barmaid squealed, and across the room a loud argument between two seamen turned into a contest in profanity.

In response to their query about Tyson Winslow, a serving wench led them to a back room. The girl knocked once, then opened the door, all the time keeping an appraising watch on Aileen.

Grateful to escape the scrutiny, Aileen slipped inside, and stopped in her tracks, her heart in her throat. On the plank table, a lone candle chased away the shadows of the dimly lit room. And there, with his back to her, poring over a large map, stood Tyson.

Propped up on one elbow, Digby leaned over the map, too. The older man growled, "What is it?" and looked up. At first sight of Aileen, he dropped his magnifying glass.

"Blimy," he whispered. He stood there, looking as if he'd seen a ghost, which Aileen supposed might be a fair assumption, considering.

"What the devil is it?" Tyson grumbled, shoving the glass away and rolling up the map. He glanced at Digby and then pivoted, his expression of curiosity instantly changing to one of disbelief. He didn't say a word, just stood and stared, his face turning as white as Aileen's felt. The map slid out of his hands and rattled to the floor.

She swallowed hard under his scrutiny, wondering how he'd react—would he be mad first, or a bit glad to see her again?

But his eyes held neither emotion. Rather he looked quite haunted, gaunt as if from lack of sleep, leaner than when she'd seen him last, the white open-necked shirt and dark trousers fitting him looser. He made a sudden move toward her, as if to touch her, but checked himself and instead grasped a chair back. His knuckles gripped it so tightly they showed white.

As a misty rain ran slowly down the single window, the candle flickered from the draft of the half-open door. The room smelled of coal burning in the grate, and the only sounds were the crackle of the fire and the echo of tavern noises.

Tyson's gaze moved from Aileen's bonnet to her dress, frowning at the unfamiliar style, until, still without a word, his gaze slid up to her face, and at last he looked into her eyes. His own shone green and full of pain, as if bruised deep inside.

Still none of them spoke till Kit's words broke the mood. "You said the Fian's cohorts met here," he whispered. "We come to find him. You won't be angry at me for bringing Aileen, too? She came back, you see, and she's an urgent message for the Fian."

Tyson dragged his gaze off of Aileen long enough to look down at Kit, frowning as if wondering how a small boy had gotten in here.

Kit frowned back. "You're not angry are you . . . that we came?"

"No, lad, I'm not angry." Even when he finally answered Kit, he never stopped staring at Aileen. "What did you say you wanted?" His voice sounded distant, faraway, and Kit moved closer so that he stood bravely between Tyson and Aileen, as if protecting her.

"I've found my brothers," Aileen said.

Kit sensed her emotion and apparently interpreted it as fear. "We told no one," he offered gamely, but received no response. "It'll take one of the Fian's riots to crack this place. It's wicked, with bars on the windows. Aileen told me. Do you know how we get a message to the Fian?"

"Yes, Digby here can get a message to the Fian," Tyson said in a vague way and took a step toward Aileen.

Kit looked from one to the other, obviously puzzled, as if wondering at the taut mood of the room. At last Digby, who'd been watching Tyson all this time, moved around the table and clasped Kit on the shoulder. "Boy, if you've got a message for the Fian, you'll have to come with me to my room where we can talk in privacy." He steered Kit out the door, saying as they went, "Wait till we get there, then tell me the message, leaving nothing out. . . . Are you certain you weren't followed here, now?"

The door clicked shut, and Aileen's heart flickered with the same gentle tremor as the candle flame.

"Why?" Tyson's question was a choked syllable. "Why did you disappear? I thought you'd died."

She flinched. If she could she'd have taken his pain.

"Why did you do it?"

"To protect you." Her voice sounded small, especially as she explained about Leedes. "He said they were going to arrest you and make me give evidence against you."

The expression on Tyson's face shifted from agony to speculation. "It was you who wrote that pamphlet, wasn't it?" he guessed.

"Marcus wrote it." She blushed.

"Marcus Owen hid you? By God, I'll have his job." At his sides his hands tensed into fists.

"No, he was kind. . . . I'm sorry if you worried."

"Worried?" The word could have been underlined with either a half laugh or a half moan. "You don't know the half of it, Aileen. I'd sooner be arrested than live through these last weeks. You were one of my cohorts, and you vanished without a word of explanation to me. Not even a note. You let me think, along with the rest of London, that the Lady in Blue was—"

"I'm sorry," she said softly, fumbling with the door latch. "I only came now because I need you, but that was a mistake. I'll take Kit and leave—"

"Wait."

Suddenly she felt him close, his hand covering hers. She turned. His other hand came up to touch her hair, the lock that spilled out of the bonnet and brushed her cheek. Ever so long they stood like that while he looked at her—as if he were afraid to touch her, afraid she would vanish again.

"And after you're done needing me this time, then what?" he asked.

"I'm not certain."

She thought the noises outside in the main room were

growing louder, more raucous, but put it down to her wildly spinning imagination.

"You'll vanish again?" he asked with a calm that unnerved her. "Have Marcus Owen write another pamphlet to taunt me?"

"No—I mean, I haven't thought that far. Truly," she added when she saw the skeptical arch of his brows. In fact, she couldn't think past his hand warm on hers. She'd forgotten how his eyes could be the color of an Irish meadow, how they could alter the tempo of her pulse. She'd missed him so. . . .

Abruptly she realized the banging on the door was not the echo of her heart, but real. Already Tyson was pushing her away to the safety of a secluded corner. He opened the door a crack, and while Aileen flattened herself against the wall and listened wide-eyed, Digby's voice came through. "Take cover. It's Leedes and his thugs."

Leedes. That could only mean . . . he'd followed her and Kit.

"Take the boy and get out the other way," came Tyson's terse command to Digby. After slamming the door shut, he pushed a chair under the latch. Seconds later he grabbed Aileen to him. "Stay by me. Don't say a word. Can you swim?"

When she shook her head, he cursed and mumbled something about how it would probably be his luck to find a mermaid when he had to flee across the desert. Already he was pushing open the tiny window that opened onto the Thames. In the main room of the tavern, a pistol shot rang out and patrons shrieked.

Someone banged on the door. "Open up, Winslow. You're for the gallows."

"Leedes seems determined to escort me everywhere," Aileen said, angrily tugging at the ribbons under her chin then tossing off her bonnet. She felt her hair spill down over her shoulders.

Tyson blew out the candle and reached for her. "Take off your skirt, lass. You're going to do a repeat performance of the Lady in Blue—only this time you won't drown."

She fumbled with the buttons of the long bodice, and all the time the banging on the door increased in ferocity. Tyson pulled her toward him and lifted up her skirt and swiftly tied the billowing fabric about her waist. "You'll swim easier in pantalettes."

She tried not to think about the swirling mass of dark river outside the window of the Dog's Paw; the murky depths of the Thames were not appealing even by daylight. "There's nothing but water out there," she reminded him.

"And nothing but pistols behind us," he informed her with cool logic. After hoisting himself through the window, Tyson reached for Aileen and, hands tight on her waist, pulled her out after him. She steadied her balance on a ledge of old timbers. Directly below, the dark waters of the Thames waited. "Whatever I do, don't let go," he ordered.

Instinctively Aileen clutched Tyson's hand for balance while he inched them along to the edge of the building. They stopped. The next step would be a free fall into the Thames. Aileen looked back. The muzzle of a pistol was nudged out of the window she'd just crawled through, then aimed—at her.

"Tyson," she whispered, crossing herself as she whispered a quick Hail Mary.

"Hold your breath."

"I can't."

He pulled her close. "Of course you can. Let me show you a little trick I know. . . ." And then he was kissing her so quick and sudden she forgot to breathe, and giving her a tug, he pulled her with him over the ledge. She was underwater, sinking, sinking, until with a strange buoyancy she rose. She reached for something to hold on to and realized she'd lost her sense of direction. Up was down, and down was up. Strong arms enfolded her, and she entwined herself around Tyson.

When her head broke water, she choked and then took great gasping breaths and clung to his shirt. "We'll drown," she managed between panicked breaths.

He gasped for air as well. "Nonsense." Before she could panic again, he rolled her over onto her back and, tucking a secure arm under her shoulders, swam her toward a cluster of little boats. A shot split the air, and Tyson hid them behind the stern of a rowboat.

When the shooting ceased, he moved on through the water, pulling her with him past boat after boat. They stopped. Oblivious to splinters in her hands, she clung to the bow of a boat while he climbed aboard. Seconds later he tossed a rope over to her and reeled her in.

"Come on up, Lady in Blue," he said with an engaging leer. "This time you don't run away from me."

She clambered over the deck and fell soaking wet into Tyson's arms. Gradually she caught her breath, and finally she was able to stand and look around. Coughing, brushing wet strands of hair out of her face, she blinked with a sense of familiarity. He'd brought her here before, to change into the Lady in Blue gown. "This is Digby's barge," she said, then, alarmed. "They'll follow us here."

"Nay, Digby's barge isn't that well known. I'm only surprised he hasn't brought the boy here to hide."

"Give them more time. They'll be safe," Aileen reassured him. Kit could escape anything.

Tyson reached for her then. "Come here. The swimming lesson's over." He took her into the warmth of Digby's exotic little cabin, where they stood looking at each other.

Tyson stared at her tangled hair and her dripping dress and his breathing didn't improve at all. Her clothes clung to her, as did his own trousers and shirt. Reaching behind her, he pulled the blanket off Digby's bed and wrapped her in it, his hands lingering on her.

After adding coal to the tiny stove and lighting it, he stripped off his wet shirt and hung it over a chair. Aileen sat down to undo her shoes and then fumbled with the formidable row of buttons which lined the bodice of her dress. Through the wet fabric the outline of her breasts was only too clear. Against his better intentions, he gave in to his yearning to touch her.

He pulled her close to him and began to undo each button, until he reached her waist. He paused, feeling her flesh warm beneath his touch, then he reached up and helped her slip off the dress, one shoulder at a time until she stood before him in only a wringing wet chemise. Before he lost control completely, he handed her Digby's nightshirt. "This should do," he said tersely.

After reaching for a pair of Digby's trousers for himself, he suddenly left her in privacy and went below deck to change. The earlier rain had let up, but now dusk was coming and with it the fog. He tossed an old greatcoat of Digby's around his shoulders. Like the barge, it smelled of oil and coal, but he was glad of the warmth. For a long while he stood on deck watching for signs of Digby, but by the time the light faded, he'd concluded the old man must have taken the boy elsewhere to hide.

He knew he was only avoiding the inevitable. Sooner or later he'd have to go back inside and see her. He'd be in there now, but he didn't trust himself. He felt taut all over, and should he walk in there he wasn't sure what he'd do. He still couldn't take in the fact that she was alive after all and had merely been hiding from him under some grand pretense of protecting him.

He was, he reminded himself, the Fian, and there was no room in his life for a woman. Yet that easy denial didn't explain away his instantaneous reaction when she'd walked into the Dog's Paw—when he'd seen her face again. It had taken all his willpower to maintain some righteous anger rather than gather her into his arms and feel her softness. And when he'd heard her voice again—he'd nearly forgotten the Fian existed. . . .

Behind him the latch turned and he held his breath. He could feel her behind him, but he didn't turn. He had a good imagination and could well picture how she'd look. Already his body had hardened in response to the image.

"It's cold out here," she said, looking up at him.

He slanted a look at her. "The deck is wet and you forgot to put on shoes," he observed. "Has the fire gone out?"

"No, I've made it brighter. Warmer." She moved to stand beside him at the railing of the barge and rested her hands near his. She had small hands, he noticed.

"What will you do after you find your brothers?" he asked abruptly.

"First I have to rescue them."

"And how did you propose we rescue them? A simple riot for no more reason than two more lost boys working in a factory?"

He felt her crumble and hated himself. He'd wished for a second chance to help her and here she was, standing beside him, dressed in Digby's nightshirt, pink little toes peeking out of the garment, sleeves ridiculously long.

"They've been caned for telling stories about the Fian."

He felt as if someone had taken the cane to him, not them, and immediately regretted his sardonic words. He had no right to hurt her because of his own pain. Emotions bleak, he stared out at the Thames, but he didn't attempt to focus on all the bustle of boats. The fog surrounded them.

"I'll help you get them out. I know that's what you want."

She was silent a moment, and he felt her shiver. "And afterward, I shall take them far away from here. I'm tired of hiding and running."

Her words were like a knife cutting through him.

When she reached up to touch his hand, her gesture felt like an apology. He didn't want that from her, he admitted, though God knew he wasn't sure what he did want.

He looked at her and caught his breath. She looked so small and vulnerable in that ridiculous nightshirt. Reaching over, he rolled up first one sleeve, then the other for her.

She reached up to touch his forelock. "Your hair's wet. You should come in the cabin now, else you'll catch your death."

"I may catch my death soon anyway."

"I wouldn't recommend it."

"What? Catching my death?"

"Yes. I've been 'dead' these last few weeks, and it's terrible being so anonymous, hiding—"

"I agree, it was quite terrible."

"You're angry that I duped you. I was only trying to save your life."

"I'm angry that you left without a word. And now you tell me you're going to leave again."

"I'm still hoping to receive a letter from my brother. I saw Kate Reilly earlier today, but nothing's come. Still, I know he'll write."

He felt something painful twist his heart, but didn't want to examine it too closely or give it a name. "You'll follow your brother, then?"

She stared out at the gray Thames. "Sure and I won't stay in England to see the Fian hang. I couldn't bear that."

"The Fian's too clever to hang."

"And too aristocratic and fine for the likes of an Irish maid?" she asked.

He shut his eyes, trying to hang on to the last vestiges of self-control, which was fast slipping. His body was begging for release, his soul begging for an end to this banter. "That's not so. You gave me ample reasons why you wouldn't dally, as you like to term it."

"I've reconsidered."

"Have you, then?" The bow inside him had never been more taut. Her voice tugged at him.

"Yes," she said quite matter-of-factly. "I don't know what ordinary is anymore. Since I left you at Vauxhall, I've lived day to day, and this day I'm with you. If tomorrow, I'm gone, it needn't be a loss to you—"

He turned on her, unstrung. "How do you know what's a loss to me? You're not a servant to Lady Pamela any longer. To me you're Aileen Connolly, brave Irish lass, nothing less." He saw her flinch at his harsh words. In a softer tone of voice he said, "I'm taking you inside. You're freezing." With that he swept her up into his arms and with his back pushed open the door, then with one bare foot kicked it shut again. The room was blessedly warm, especially with her in his arms, and he wanted to go on holding her, to make up for the hours of agony when he thought he'd lost her forever.

Nevertheless, he deposited her on the bunk, marveling over the way her hair spread over the pillow, the way her body warmed that nightshirt. If he didn't pull away now. . . .

She'd wrapped her arms about his neck and kept them locked there even while he lowered her to the bed. So tightly did she hold him that their faces nearly touched. "Stay with me, Fian," she whispered. "Don't leave me yet. Three times now you've saved my life. Superstition has it that after the third time I owe you a favor."

"I don't need any favors." His voice sounded hoarse.

"Is sharing warmth too much to take? As you said the night we slept in the haystack, we had to keep warm, and after all, we almost died together, then as now. . . ."

Her eyes were like the Irish sky pulling him down, and so he knelt there still.

He reached up to disentangle her from him. "The problem this time, colleen, is with the sleeping arrangements. Unlike our night in the haystack, this time I should be unable to hold you in such innocence, and I recall quite well last winter you sat in my coach arguing the dangers of dallying."

"I did that, didn't I?"

He nodded. "I counted myself quite fortunate to have a kiss from you."

She looked at him with guilelessness. "Nevertheless, we created quite a scandal. But since I've been 'dead,' I've reconsidered, and I realize that I don't ever want to die again with my innocence intact."

A half smile curved his mouth. "Is that so?" He found words difficult. The blood raced in his head, and he watched the light of a single candle near the bed throw shadows off her face—light and dark, teasing her face the way her words teased him. He wanted very badly to lay his head between her breasts.

She reached out and shyly began to unbutton the shirt he wore. "Yes, it's so. Why should other women have the Fian and not me?"

"What if I told you no woman has ever had the Fian?"

"Tyson Winslow would suffice, I suppose, according to what I've heard in Vauxhall gossip."

"How would you know what suffices?"

She bit her lip. "It would suffice to have you lay with me."

Innocent girl. He lay down beside her, thinking she might cease taunting him, and he might gain control, but then with scant warning, she pressed herself against him, the full length of him, the way she had the night in the haystack— except of course, his blood was roiling this time.

With her soft pliancy folding around him, he was lost. Truth be told, the instant he'd seen her alive and trembling in the Dog's Paw, he'd been lost. With a groan of longing for the inevitable, he reached for the hem of the ridiculous nightshirt she wore, and his only endearment was a litany of sorrow that he couldn't slow down her first experience with passion.

They came together like a flash storm of lightning. Intense, like when he'd kissed her in the park, but more urgent. His taunting kisses then had but foreshadowed this mingling of the wild Fian and her purity. The combination created instant riot in his soul. She never cried out, though he knew there must be pain. She clasped him to her, breathless while he defined passion for her. It was he who cried out at the release of ardor too long suppressed, and he molded her to him more completely than he'd been able to at the haystack.

This time, though, he not only forsook gallantry, but lost himself in her. Indeed, no sooner had their passion climaxed than he returned to the beginning of ardor again, as quickly as one scans back to the first line of a poem. Dissatisfied at having denied her any prelude, he took his time now, gently pulling the nightshirt over her head, then burying his face in her hair, just long enough to feel the silk of those wild black tresses, to remind himself she was real and here and not a mere memory. Then with his hands he caressed her body with the velvet touch he'd longed to give her the first time. His lips moving down her body built to a crescendo, the passion of the warrior claiming his own. She touched him back in an ageless poetry that comes by instinct.

To him, because it was with Aileen, the experience was instinctive as well—all unexplored—as if he'd never in his life touched a woman. And indeed, he could vaguely recall having women, easing his flesh . . . but he'd never in his life wanted as he did now to take a woman by turns wild and tender to the state of grace he found with Aileen this night.

He held her fast, not wanting to ever let her go, losing himself in the climactic moments of the poem. He stayed with her after all. To let go of her was loneliness. Utter loneliness such as he'd never known. Dark closed over the little barge, and the candle burned down forgotten.

It was first dawn of the next morning when the knock came on the door. Aileen stirred and heard Kit's voice calling them. Tyson slipped out the door, and Aileen lay there still languid from lovemaking.

She heard the sound of Tyson's voice, Kit's voice, then silence—the longest silence, and she fell asleep again. When she woke up again, Tyson was gone. While she dressed, her head began to throb from the worry. Where was Tyson?

Barefoot, she pulled open the door of the cabin. Kit sat there on the plank deck, hands in the pockets of his navy seaman's coat, looking for all the world as if guarding the door. He looked up at her with grave dark eyes, the streetwise glimmer all but faded. Gulls lounged on the stern as if they hadn't a care in the world.

"Did you have a very close call last night? How did

Digby get you away?" she asked. Kit looked so shaken, so pale, that she knelt down by him. "What happened?"

"The old man—"

"Digby," supplied Aileen, her voice rising in alarm. "What happened?"

"He shoved me through a trapdoor, and I climbed down and went out along the water, but Digby couldn't get out. . . ." Kit's voice cracked, and tears filled his eyes.

"Do you mean they caught him?"

Kit shook his head. "He got shot tryin' to follow me out the trapdoor."

"But he'll mend?" She felt a band tightening her chest.

A shadow passed over the sun. Kit was still shaking his head, eyes solemn, and she pressed her hand to her mouth, fighting the nausea of horror.

"He's dead, Aileen. I saw the blood and heard 'em say he was dead. One of 'em would 'ave got me if I hadn't took my knife to 'im."

"Kit, stop." She put her arms about Kit's shoulders and realized he was shaking. Beneath the streetwise boy was just a scared youngster. Back in the cabin she found one of Digby's old sea jackets and draped it around the boy for extra warmth.

"I'm all right," Kit said with a quavering chin. "I've seen men die before . . . just not so much blood."

"Kit," prodded Aileen gently, "where's Mr. Winslow?"

The boy looked up, as if trying to remember. "Mr. Winslow took the news awful grievesome. He told me not to let you leave."

At that Aileen panicked. "But where'd he go?" She stood up and grasped the railing, scanning the horizon. "Don't you see, Kit? If he returned to the Dog's Paw, they might still be waiting for him."

"Why would they want Mr. Winslow? It's the Fian they was after."

Tears blurred Aileen's vision, and she reached down to hug Kit. "Those men are evil. Anyone who even knows the Fian could be killed. Didn't he say anything else?"

"Digby was a good man."

"What?"

"That's what he said."

"Yes, yes, Digby was a good man. . . . Kit, listen to me," Aileen said. "You sit in the cabin where it's warmer. Now that I'm awake I don't need a guard. I promise to come right back." She crossed her heart.

Kit looked up in alarm. "But I said I'd—"

"You guarded me just fine, but now I'm awake and I don't need watching over. Kit, which way did he go?"

Reluctantly, Kit finally pointed. It was the direction of the Dog's Paw.

Aileen was already hoisting herself over the side of the barge, then she headed barefoot across the sand of low tide toward the bend in the shore up ahead.

As she ran, she wept guilty tears. Because of her Tyson had lost his best friend. She'd give up hope of ever seeing Roddy again if she could give Tyson back Digby. She'd give up most everything if she could give him back Digby.

Weak from crying so hard, her legs nearly buckled beneath her. She struggled up and forced herself to walk up from the narrow beach that was coming to an end. With an effort she walked up a flight of stone steps to the embankment and immediately headed for the Dog's Paw, which crouched quietly in the distance, looking with one shutter askew as if it had suffered a black eye last night.

She found Tyson walking back down the twisting street that led to the front entrance of the Dog's Paw, and her heart went out to him. "Tyson," she called out, her throat dry from crying. She couldn't move another step and clutched a lamppost till she caught her breath. Early morning peddlers wove around and about each of them. A mongrel insisted on barking at a gin wagon, and two ladies of dubious reputation sauntered by.

Expressionless, Tyson walked toward her, stopping some feet from her, face grim. "This neighborhood isn't a safe place for a morning stroll," he advised, his emotions hidden.

"I know about Digby . . . I'm so sorry." She wept.

"I had to see to some things in his room." He held a key, apparently to Digby's room, which he jammed down the pocket of his trousers. "You were supposed to stay on the barge." It was an accusation. He might as well have come right out and blamed her for Digby, especially when he stood there looking at her weep and offered no comfort.

"Did you stop to think when you rushed to the Dog's Paw yesterday that you might be followed?" His words were measured, deadly calm.

"I know it's my fault. All I was thinking about was my brothers. If I could change things—"

"You don't know what you're saying." He advanced, his face gaunt. "It's my fault as well. I should have stayed with him instead of—" He broke off, his voice ragged, and looked away from her.

"Instead of rescuing me." Aileen's voice was tiny. Instead of making love to her. . . .

Briefly he caught her close to him in a wordless embrace and whispered softly against her hair. "My last promise to Digby was to help find your brothers, and I mean to keep my word."

It was a silent walk back to the barge.

Seventeen

"YOU TOLD KIT what?" At the mention of the name Fian, Tyson looked up from an old trunk of Digby's and nearly dropped the Oriental flask he'd been lifting out. Last night, after Digby had been laid to rest, he'd begun to talk about how to rescue Aileen's brothers, and they'd disagreed on the means. Like the tide, the subject had risen again.

After settling the flask down, Tyson tested the flexibility of an old saber Digby had saved—a souvenir of some long-ago voyage to the Far East. When he realized Aileen hadn't answered his query, he looked up at her and nearly closed the trunk for the rest of the afternoon. Clad in rather fetching seamen's breeches, she was sitting cross-legged on the deck, polishing the glass of a telescope.

He opened Digby's ditty bag and emptied the contents onto the deck. The paraphernalia of a sea captain fell at his feet—logbooks, shaving kit, jackknife, and mementos of foreign travels—American books, an ivory letter opener from China, and even a length of India cotton—faded now. Digby had had no relatives and, in a brief handwritten will, had given everything to Tyson. With Aileen's help Tyson had spent a long day putting the little barge into shipshape condition—a fitting tribute to Digby's memory. As Tyson sorted things back into the ditty bag, he looked up at Aileen. She had the telescope trained on the rows of brick buildings on shore. He wouldn't be able to put off rescuing her brothers much longer, nor did he want to. What he did want was safety.

"Tell me again," he asked gently. "What were your exact words to Kit?"

"I told him the Fian would ride again." Aileen stood up and walked to the deck railing, telescope now lifted up to a pair of high-flying gulls. "It's true, isn't it?" she said, her voice hopeful. "You told me that tonight you'd get Seymour's factory exposed. Remember?"

"You don't have to ask if I remember, lass . . . and for God's sake don't cry. They're still alive, but we won't be alive if we rush into that factory."

Aileen said nothing, but her eyes darkened with worry. At last she trained the telescope on him. "You know, you vaguely resemble someone I know—someone named the Fian."

He tried not to smile. With silent movements Tyson continued to alternate between his work and watching her. The sun glistened in her black hair and gave her skin the luster of a pearl. The roses bloomed in her cheeks, and he had to concentrate to keep desire from stirring in his loins. Now wasn't the time. Now was the time to convince her of the need for caution. What irony, he thought. The Fian— Ireland's hero—convincing a fresh-faced Irish lass in a pair of breeches of the need for caution.

Even Aileen once upon a time had chastised him for taking chances, and the Lord knew, Digby had. But Tyson was feeling cautious since finding Aileen again. He owed it to her—and to Digby's memory—to conduct himself more safely. And he had a safe plan for tonight.

But he knew how worried she was and for the hundredth time explained that plan. "I'm going out tonight as Tyson Winslow, Member of Parliament, not as the Fian." A search through property records by Tyson's solicitor had revealed that Nicholas Seymour owned the factory in which the Connolly boys languished. With that scrap of information Tyson knew he could rescue the boys without another dangerous riot. He'd been intending to cancel out of tonight's dinner party, but had decided the occasion provided an excellent opportunity to publicly ruin Seymour—and thus force a release of the boys. It would be his revenge.

Tyson glanced up. Aileen was watching him, frowning, and he wished he could give her what she wanted that instant. "Tonight—at the dinner—is best," he finished.

"But later tonight—after the dinner . . . you are going to ride tonight as the Fian, aren't you?" she asked.

He looked down, pretending to be absorbed with a stubborn knot in the ditty bag. He didn't want to spar with words.

"Aileen, I almost lost you, and that changed me. And now I've lost Digby. I'm not ready to ride as the Fian again. Not yet. My plan for tonight is more cautious."

"Whisht," Aileen said softly, defiance at the ready. "If the Fian won't ride, then I'll go back and find a way past that ugly doorman." She tossed her head and turned away.

He felt a war waging within him between the taut desire of his body and anger at her stubbornness. The sparks of conflict, he admitted, had been there from the night he'd met her, but had been fanned higher. He lived with constant frustration. Because of her, he'd been slackening control over what was best for the cause. Today, at last, he was pulling in the reins and thinking as the Fian should.

"You'll not go there without me," he said in a quiet command. "You're talking remarkably brave for a woman who once cursed my cause with a pox."

She cast a sideways look at him, and her eyes shone with pent-up temper. "A pox on it still. You'd use it for glory while I only want the Fian to rescue Seamus and Patrick."

She was pulling the bowstring taut within him again. He tossed the logbook he'd been flipping through into the trunk along with a coil of rope. "The cause involves a lot more people than merely me. I have every Irishman whose life depends on me to think about."

"Then where are these Irishmen you're working for now?" she taunted. "I'm the one here now, the one who knows your identity. Don't you owe me something?"

"By God, I promised you your brothers on Digby's death. I only want to try legal means."

She turned and faced him, eyes flashing. "But everyone in Irishtown is waiting for the Fian to ride. They need you. I need you. Sure and I can do the part that Digby did. Raise a pistol and, when Scotland Yard comes, warn you."

Fear knifed through him, and he felt a muscle move near his jaw. "Don't even think it." She wouldn't dare. "Had you not known how to use a pistol, I might never have brought you here to London. But you take its danger for granted."

"Are you sorry I forced you to bring me here?"

"Sometimes," he said, deliberately noncommittal. He recognized Aileen's expression—petulance that preceded every woman's demand to know how a man felt about her. Tyson had a stock answer for all the other women he'd known—*No woman forces me to do anything.* Easy flattery usually helped him exit gracefully. But he didn't want to exit from this situation.

"Are you sorry now, this very moment?" she probed and looked up at him from under her lashes, ready to use feminine wiles.

He took a deep breath for control. "What about you? Are you sorry you came with me?" he parried.

She shook her head. Unpinned, her black tresses quivered upon her slim shoulders.

What he wanted at this moment, he decided, was the feel of her against him, and so he dropped the gear he was sorting and walked over to her and gathered her into his arms. Her own arms came up about him, and he pressed his face to her hair.

"Banshee, believe me, when I'm through with Nicholas Seymour tonight, all London will know him for what he is, and every illegal factory he owns will be shut down."

His words, he knew, sounded calculated rather than passionate. What he didn't reveal was how hard he fought the urge to carry her over the threshold of the cabin and have her again, an urge that magnified when she rested her forehead against his chest. He stroked her hair, losing himself to that one sensation, until her words broke the spell.

"I only want—" Her voice thickened with emotion, and he felt her breath against his shirt warm right through to his skin. "I only want Seamus and Patrick. Everything I've done has been to help me find them."

"Everything?" he questioned, one eyebrow raised, voice taut. He took her gently by the forearm and held her back just far enough so he could look into her eyes.

They were swimming with tears. "I don't care what happens to Nicholas Seymour," she said.

"But I do. That's partly what's made me the Fian."

"Then take your revenge later."

"I'll do both."

"At some fine dinner with the Seymours and the Grenvilles and—and—"

"Trust me, Aileen."

"I've trusted you all winter. Trust won't unlock the factory. You wait and see." Anger flashing in her eyes, she suddenly flung herself from him.

"Aileen—" He took a step toward her, wanting to take all her passion and kiss some sense into her.

She ran into the cabin and turned the lock. Three times he pounded on the door, but there was no reasoning with her. "Go to your fine dinner," she called out. "I'll unlock this door when you bring my brothers to me."

"You little vixen. You're behaving like a spoiled society brat." She made no reply. The last time a woman had locked him out, he'd turned on his heel and lost all interest forever. Now he felt compelled to have his say. "Stay in there, then. There's nothing you can do to help tonight in any case."

He stalked away to Digby's chest and dumped in helterskelter the remains of the old man's possessions. One thing about having Digby as a cohort, he mused—the old man might have been a pack rat and talked back, but at least he never locked himself in the bedroom. With a savage thrust, Tyson slammed down the lid.

Kit returned then, and Tyson gave the boy a set of keys and instructions to take some maps to Digby's room at the Dog's Paw. After a pause he added a few terse directions about hurrying back to guard Aileen on the barge and this time not to let her wander off to places unknown. If he was going to the dinner party, he might as well leave for his townhouse—which Kit assured him was no longer being watched—and change.

Pulling an old seaman's coat up over his ears and a Scotch cap over his forehead, he walked away from the

barge then and hailed a hackney. Yes, in other days, long
before he'd met Aileen Connolly, he'd always walked away
from women when they became a nuisance, walked away
without a backward thought. He set his jaw tight, remembering everything she'd done to him. It had been a mistake
bringing her to London. Hadn't he tried to tell her that—the
night he met her?

All during the ride he thought about her, the feel of her
body against his. He should have taken an ax to the damn
door and now cursed himself for growing soft.

Later, for a fleeting second while he was tying his
uncooperative cravat, he almost ripped it off, let Seymour
and the dinner be damned, and went back to her.

But that would be a mistake. Never had the Fian
permitted a woman to alter his plans, and he didn't want to
make any exceptions now—particularly not for tears or
attacks of the vapors.

The barge felt suddenly too quiet. Sensing Tyson was
gone, Aileen sat up. Instead of his footsteps on the deck,
she heard only the keening of sea gulls, and she knew with
a certainty that he had left. He probably thought she was a
silly female having an attack of the vapors and that he'd find
more elegant company at his fancy dinner.

Well, let him go. She dried her tears, but lay back down,
burying her face in his pillow, miserable. How could she
have let herself fall in love with that man? She was the
daughter of a poor potato farmer, and he was a member of
London's finest society set. Why, they were so unsuited she
could never appear with him at the dinner he was attending
tonight.

And then she became angry all over again. How dare he
care more about his own revenge on Nicholas Seymour than

her brothers? How dare he abandon his promise to rescue her brothers? All at once she heard her name called.

"Aileen, where are you?" Kit's voice came through the door, muffled, but exuberant.

She rushed out ready to question Kit, but stopped in her tracks at the sight of keys dangling in Kit's hand. "Whose are those?" Aileen asked, her mind already racing with possibilities.

"Digby's. They're the keys to his room at the Dog's Paw."

Exactly what she'd hoped. Aileen held out her hand. "Mr. Winslow's gone on an errand. I'll keep the keys for him," she said casually, and dutifully Kit handed them over.

"Kit, did you tell Martin Kelly that the Fian would ride tonight?"

"Aye, just like you told me. Wasn't I supposed to?"

"Yes, you were. . . . now I need to spread the word further. Mr. Winslow's gone on an errand involving the factory owner—a society dinner. He'll decoy the owner, in fact, so the Fian will have little interference. It's an ideal night. You know who to tell, don't you? Tell them all to be ready."

"But I'm supposed to guard you here on the barge. Mr. Winslow said you weren't to wander off."

"Did he?" Aileen thought quickly. "And so I won't—he only meant that the barge needs guarding so no ruffians steal any of our things."

Kit's gaze widened, as if he were remembering the riot at Percy's Whip Factory. "You're not going to the factory?"

"The Fian rides tonight. It's the factory where my own brothers are enslaved. Sure and wouldn't I be nearby to help them out?"

"Wouldn't you rather wait here, Aileen, while the Fian

and his men storm the place? Mrs. Reilly will be frightful
mad at me if she finds out you're going to a riot."

"I never said I was going to be throwing bricks or
carrying torches, Kit. I'll simply be—around the corner.
Now run and pass the word around Irishtown, then return
and secure this boat. . . . And Kit, if Mr. Winslow or I
don't return tonight, go to Mrs. Reilly's. That may be where
I have to take my brothers for safekeeping. Do you
understand all that?"

"Aye, I understand, but I think you're getting into
danger, and Tyson's going to be madder at me than Kate
will."

"Nothing's as dangerous as where my poor brothers are,
Kit. You have faith in the Fian, don't you? Has he ever
failed?"

Kit shook his head. "If anyone can get them out, he can."

"Yes, he can. And now you hurry and do as I said. The
Fian's counting on you."

She watched him scamper over the side of the barge.

"Kit," she called on an impulse and waited until his
blond head reappeared. "As soon as I find Seamus and
Patrick, I'll be leaving London, and I was wondering . . .
would you like to come with us?"

"You mean out in the country?" The boy hoisted himself
back up and sat on the railing, straddling it with one foot
dangling on each side.

"I'm not sure where we'd go, Kit. It would be an
adventure. Perhaps America even."

"But Mr. Winslow's staying here?"

"Mr. Winslow has his duties in Parliament."

The boy looked thoughtful. "Kate Reilly would miss
me."

"Yes, but she means to stay. . . . Kit, if you say yes,

have your good-byes to Mrs. Reilly said. I may have to take you quickly."

She watched the boy trot off, hated deceiving him—not over wanting to take him out of London—she meant that—but about her plans for tonight. Yet, she couldn't lead that boy into a riot—if she did indeed create one.

And why shouldn't she? After the latest killing, the Irish were as ready to explode as dry kindling. All they lacked was the spark of the Fian. The fleeting sight of the disguise would set them off. She'd heard Tyson say so.

With Tyson at a public dinner party, officials and thugs like Leedes would be caught off guard . . . Oh, she could do it. She had to. Patrick and Seamus weren't going to spend another night in that vile place. Nor was Tyson Winslow the only one who could call himself the Fian. . . .

Later, alone, wearing one of Digby's seaman coats, Aileen made her way to the Dog's Paw and asked a serving wench for directions to both Digby Trigg's room and the mews where she knew Tyson kept the Fian's horse.

"Tyson Winslow sent me," she explained when the girl balked.

The tavern wench looked interested at the name and stared Aileen up and down as thoroughly as she would a rival before relenting. "I'll take ye to his room. Mr. Winslow's already packed most," she added on a sullen note. "He was goin' to divide up the rest of it with us."

"I'm only after one thing, and it wasn't Digby's."

The girl turned friendlier at this news. "Aye, well, then, I s'pose it'll be all right."

Locking the door from inside, Aileen groped for the dark shadow that was the washstand and lit a single candle. Then she moved to the battered trunk that sat at the foot of the bed and dropped to her knees. This trunk was locked. Of course it would be. Tyson Winslow would have made certain of that. She pulled out the keys Kit had given her and tried one after another. The last one fit. It turned. She heard the latch give and with a squeak of the hinges lifted up the lid.

Reaching down past a pile of Digby's clothes, she felt for the coarse fabric of one well-known garment and moments later pulled out the dark hooded robe of the Fian.

After finding a scarf as well, she bundled them inside the seaman's coat for hiding. She pinned her hair up into a knot, blew out the candle, and made her way out to the tavern stables. With a bottle of spirits lifted from Digby's room she dickered herself into the loan of a black horse. Not Cormac, for he was too big for her, but another one similar in coloring.

On foot still, she guided the horse out into the dark lane where in a hidden recess she stopped long enough to discard the seaman's coat. With trembling hands she pulled on the robe, and with coal dust from the lane she blackened her face. Finally, she tied on the scarf and pulled up the hood. Then she climbed up on the horse.

Undaunted by the possibility of arrest, Aileen grasped the reins tightly, dug her feet into the stirrups, and guided the black horse through the streets of London. Out in the open country the horse might have proved unwieldy with her limited riding skills, but here, on the twisting London lanes, she was forced to ride more slowly and looked over her shoulder frequently, on guard for any law official.

As she rode, Aileen occasionally leaned over and in a hoarse whisper passed the news to the familiar-looking Irishmen who looked up and, thanks to Kit's forewarning, recognized her dark shape as the Fian. "Revenge for the killing of Digby Trigg . . . Revenge for the Fian's accomplice . . . Watley Street . . . Pass the word for Ireland's sake."

And the word did spread like a fire alarm moving steadily

across the streets. The Fian. She had only to appear in the mask and robe, speak the name Fian, and to her gratification, men took up the hue and cry. Men replied with a call to ready pistols or, lacking that, rocks. As some people feel it in their bones when a storm is brewing, she knew a riot was in the air.

The dinner party took place in the heart of Marylebone at the sumptuous new townhouse of Lord and Lady Grenville, and Tyson sat impatiently through the courses. Nicholas Seymour sat across the table from him, pointedly glaring. Tyson ignored the man, which only seemed to deepen Seymour's frown.

As was customary, the ladies remained for the toasts, and as the last murmurings of private conversations died down, a servant moved around the table, refilling the crystal stemware with port.

At last Lord Grenville stood up, wineglass in hand, and began a long-winded speech. Tyson's attention wandered to thoughts of Aileen and where she was. He felt uneasy about leaving her. No, more than uneasy. Worried.

". . . and so may this evening's pleasure yield a bright morrow . . ." Lord Grenville lifted his glass in the first toast. "To a lady long departed who once graced this table fair . . ."

"Your sister," someone correctly guessed.

Tyson leaned back and relaxed. Perfect, he thought. If they had to play a game, it was the one he'd have chosen. The one where each lady or gentleman in turn had to name an absent gentleman or lady. He would have his opening. Around the table the toasts continued, and the guesses—right or wrong—became the source of merriment.

Cornelia, the Lady Grenville, surprised a few with her

mystery person. "To the Lady in Blue, whoever she may be," she proposed, her bejeweled hands expressive.

Tyson felt himself blanch.

"Cornelia, you're not playing fair," somebody complained. "Nobody knows. Besides, the woman's dead and no one cares, not even the scandal wags."

"I know. She's an Angel in Blue," another female guessed, and Lady Grenville with hand on heart downed half her port to laughter and cries of "Huzzah."

Though Tyson lifted his glass, he did not drink and for a fleeting moment his thoughts wandered back to Aileen. He still felt uneasy that she was alone with no one to watch over her but Kit.

When at last Tyson stood, all eyes riveted on him, the men with grudging admiration, the women with frank appreciation. Posed casually, one hand in trouser pocket, with his free hand he lifted his glass. "I echo the toast to the Lady in Blue," he said, immediately sensing the sparks of displeasure from his uncle. Quickly he continued. "And to the owner of a factory on Watley Street, who, I believe, is not absent from this table, but one of us."

A shocked intake of breath swept around the table.

Nicholas Seymour jumped to his feet. "What the devil do you mean?"

"An Irish workhouse, it is," Tyson taunted. "You ought to know who owns it, Seymour."

Now Lord Weston jumped to his feet as well. "Tyson, you're disgracing us."

But Tyson ignored his uncle. "Bought you a lot of cravat pins and walking sticks, I'd wager, didn't it?" Tyson lifted his glass in the toast and tossed off the wine.

"Your vulgarity is not amusing," Seymour said.

"Well . . . well," Lady Grenville stammered, for once

at a seeming loss for words, "but isn't anybody ever going to guess who the Lady in Blue is?"

"Or guess the fate of her brothers? Which slave factory?" added Tyson.

"A ribald lie." Seymour stood and glared.

"Gentlemen!" The host pulled himself to his feet. "The ladies," he reminded both men.

"Hear, hear," chimed in another.

Lord Weston stood abruptly. "Good night, I shan't stay to witness my nephew's social suicide. Thank you, Lord Grenville. Lady Grenville," said Lord Weston, heading for the door.

Lady Pamela, her face a frigid mask, turned on her husband. "I knew you were engaged in trade," she said in scathing tones, "but I thought it was honest. You could have warned me, my dear, before you allowed me to be so publicly humiliated." The rest of the ladies, as Tyson had expected, adjourned, amidst a buzz of titters and a flutter of fans, from dining room to drawing room, and left the men poised like jungle animals.

Face flushed, Seymour adjusted his jacket and puffed out his chest in feigned injury. "I'll have satisfaction for this slur."

"Dueling is illegal," Tyson said calmly.

"Then do you suggest we have it out with a pot of glue?"

"Oh, is it glue that you produce there? I wasn't certain."

Oh, yes, he'd brought out the wary animal in him, observed Tyson. Stalking Seymour with reckless words was infinitely easier than fighting as the Fian.

As if on cue, someone banged on the door—so loudly the sound echoed right through to the dining room. From the number of bangs it could have been royalty arriving, and all the men, as if anxious for a distraction, pushed their way to the dining room door. Across the hall the ladies were peering out of the drawing room door.

A red-faced butler stood in the hallway, talking to a messenger. "The ladies and gentlemen here are advised to take care riding back into London tonight." The messenger cleared his throat, as if nervous with so many aristocratic faces staring at him. When queried, he managed to reply, "The Irish are rioting again. Word is the Fian's riding again and it's a bad one. I'm stopping at houses with carriages outside to pass a word of caution."

Now silence held the room in its spell.

Tyson and Nicholas Seymour each stared at the messenger, then Tyson looked back at Seymour, waiting for his reaction.

Nicholas Seymour's eyes reflected disbelief.

As for Tyson—he stepped back so abruptly a delicate Queen Anne chair fell down with a crash. Startled further, he knocked over a crystal goblet, and immediately red port stained the tablecloth like slowly pooling blood. Conversations went on about him, but he might as well have been struck mute.

"What did the messenger say?" a hard-of-hearing guest asked.

"The Fian is leading a riot!" his host shouted.

Seconds later Tyson had strode to the hallway calling for the butler. "Fetch a groom. I need a horse."

"But, sir, which one is yours—?"

"It doesn't matter which one is mine. Get me any horse in the bloody mews. I have to leave at once." His voice rose with untamed fury, and servants scurried off.

Within moments Tyson was riding at a gallop across London, cursing himself. It was Aileen, of course. As sure as his mother was Irish, Aileen had pilfered his disguise from Digby's trunk and harbored some foolish notion that she could rescue her brothers herself. Thought she could lead a riot, the foolish creature. He should never have left her alone. She had no idea of the pent-up passion she could unleash in the Irish.

He laid the crop to his horse and cursed himself. Why hadn't he thought she'd defy him and try this? Why hadn't she trusted him? The beautiful impulsive little fool. She could die. She was young. She had brothers who wanted her back. She had—had him who wanted her back. And that finally was what made him push the horse to the animal's limit.

As he saw Aileen's face beckoning him to hurry, he finally faced the truth he'd avoided for so long.

He loved her—and he'd take her place this moment if he could get close enough to tell her so.

He loved her, and he faced at last on that dark ride another truth he'd been ignoring—that someday he might have to choose between her and his cause.

Eighteen

WITH AN UNCANNY knack for scenting out the dangerous, Tyson managed to locate the riot almost at once.

Of course, he recognized the familiar sounds of the mob—shattering glass and screaming voices. Reining in, he slowed his mount and rode right into the melee, not bothering to look at the factory, but scanning the mob for any sign of Aileen. The little banshee had no right to do this, to drive him to this state of desperation.

The riot exceeded even his expectations, and he was surprised she'd been able to organize this mob. But then all she'd had to do was dress like him and spread the name Fian, and the mob took over. Anyone could have done the same. Starting a riot, however, wasn't as dangerous as getting caught in one.

Flamed out of control, the din had exploded into an angry rage, punctuated by chants of freedom for Ireland. Someone threw a torch into a broken window. By all that was safe the Fian should now be riding off to seclusion, leaving before authorities arrived. At this stage of violence Digby would be signaling them to leave.

But Digby was dead. No one had been named to take his

place. If Tyson could find Aileen, catch her eye, he'd signal her, better yet, he'd haul her up onto his horse and take her away from here, brothers or no.

At that moment he saw her—across the mob, so far from him she might as well have been in legendary Tara. She made a small figure in an oversize black robe, sitting astride a black horse. Her hood had fallen down, and despite the mask, he could tell by the heavy black hair that it was Aileen. Oh, yes, as surely as he could tell his own hands held the reins.

Too late he saw blue-uniformed authorities move in and grab her horse, and he felt the blood rush from his face. More men moved in surrounding her, men in frock coats— plainclothes Scotland Yard men, he'd wager his own life on it.

He pushed his horse through the mob as far as he could, then abandoned the beast. On foot he began to make his way through the rioters, elbowing, shoving his own Irish friends out of the way with scarcely an apology. Some noticed him and opened a space for him, but most were too busy beating in the door of the factory.

Unable to see her, he panicked. "Aileen!" he yelled so loudly that his voice tore. "Don't take her. That's not the Fian," he bit out to those around him, until Martin Kelly caught him by the arm and held him fast.

"Easy, Mr. Winslow. Whether it's the Fian or not, they've not hanged him yet. You've got to stay back. We can't be lettin' you get arrested now as well. We can storm the prison."

"Prison?" At the words *hanged* and *prison*, Tyson felt as weak as if he'd contracted fever. Aileen was going to prison—the prison about which Digby had so often warned him. For a minute the mob buffeted him, and he provided no resistance. Gradually, with more and more voices joining in, the news rippled back through the mob.

"They're takin' the Fian." Repeated over and over again, it resembled the chorus from some macabre nightmare. As the words passed deeper and deeper into the crowd, some rioters rushed the authorities, yelling, "Free Ireland!" and received a clubbing for their sympathies.

Desperate, Tyson pushed near the front. He could only stare at Aileen, yards out of his reach, while a Scotland Yard man held a pistol to her side and another bound her wrists with rope. With an unexpected ferocity he suddenly rushed her captors. Uniformed officers moved in to haul him back and threatened him with a charge of disruptive behavior. He laughed in their faces.

A keen-eyed Scotland Yard man, dressed in the ordinary plain clothes of topcoat and trousers, apparently recognized Tyson. "Mr. Winslow, you belong back in Parliament. It'd be awful compromisin' should you be arrested along with the others."

Tyson scoffed. "I'm the nephew of Lord Weston. Do you think I'm afraid of being arrested?"

"On charges of sedition? I should think so. Now go home and leave this mess to the authorities."

"You idiot. You don't understand what a mistake they're making. That's not the Fian."

"Let the authorities decide that, sir," the young Scotland Yard man said. "We've waited a long time to capture the Fian, and we'll have our interrogation. Besides, who else could it be? Looks like the Fian to me, plain as day."

"Anybody could wear that disguise," Tyson said, his voice growing ever hoarser. "You could take me instead and—"

"Easy, Mr. Winslow," said another of his Irish friends, muscles straining visibly from the physical effort of holding

Tyson back. "Calm down, man. It's a loss. A bitter loss, but with luck, it may be only a jail term, and then we'll have our Fian back again."

Held back as he was, Tyson slumped with the bitter realization of failure. He'd come too late . . . too late to do anything but see Aileen hauled off in a prison wagon. Before she'd ridden out of sight, he'd seen her gaze fastened on the upper windows of the factory. She hadn't noticed him.

"Go on home with you, Mr. Winslow, before you're arrested yourself," they kept telling him.

Go home, they told him. . . . Where was home? Lately, it had been the barge in a single room on a narrow bed with Aileen in his arms.

Still he stood there, half-formed ideas coming and going as his mind worked with ways to rescue her. He had many avenues open to him as a member of the Commons. If there was a trial, he'd find a way to delay it. If it came to a hanging, he'd take his pistol and shoot down the rope.

Dragging his gaze from the direction of the departed wagon, he headed for the factory, back straight, stride long, blazing eyes defying anyone to order him out. The riot was dying down of its own accord. Already the factory door hung open, and a crew of burly Irish—men who hadn't been arrested—hauled out a kicking and flailing ruffian—a foreman, Tyson guessed. Others followed in a steady stream, in their arms holding emaciated children whom they carefully placed in wagons.

At one glance Tyson could see it was a sorry sight, and what his eyes didn't tell him, his ears did.

"Slave conditions, Mr. Winslow. Working hours past what the law allows, and no sign of food."

"Yes."

"A cane as tall as a man in there—and rats."

"I see." Tyson could form no more than terse replies. He had only two goals—find Aileen's brothers and then throw himself into rescuing her.

Like an automaton, Tyson scanned the faces of the children lined up in the hallway of the factory. Girls. Blond boys. Boys with two good arms. None resembled the description of Aileen's two brothers.

Outside the doorway he found an official who was supervising the removal of children. "Where are they taking them?" Tyson demanded. "I want to help search the place. I'm looking for a pair of lost brothers."

"Aye, well, we've got them all out what was locked in the place," said the officious young man. "You'd have to search the hallway or else the Foundling Home where we took some already. Don't worry, sir. We've got the situation under control."

"Do you?" Tyson said, voice tight. "What's to stop the owner from filling this place with another batch of orphans?"

"Nothing, as long as we don't know who the owner is."

"Well, I do know his name. I want him strung up."

"Who, then?"

"Nicholas Seymour."

The young official shook his head with disbelief. "Go on with ye. Highly unlikely. You won't sell that to Parliament or to the newspapers."

"With proof of ownership I will. When London finds out how the ambitious Nicholas Seymour kept his wife in gowns and ribbons, I'll distract the newspapers from the arrest of the Fian."

"No Irish sympathizer can make London believe a story as farfetched as that. Besides, 'tain't my place to close factories, sir. The Fian's been taken off in ropes, and all that's left to do is see to the wee children."

Suddenly unstrung by the thought of Aileen's hands bound with rope, Tyson pulled the priggish fellow toward him, his grip stretching the man's collar until Tyson raised him onto his toes.

"I've got documented proof of ownership. I'll send it to your headquarters in the morning." Abruptly he set the man back down and stalked off, vaguely aware his cravat had come untied and his left coat pocket was torn and dangling. He ran a hand across his face in frustration, and when he brought his hand down, stared at the blood on his fingers. Reaching for a handkerchief, he pressed it to the scratches.

As he walked toward the door of the factory, an Irishman walked out, a skinny urchin in his arms. "This is the last one," the fellow said.

Grabbing the stump of a candle from the man, Tyson lifted the blanket. The child had tangled blond ringlets. A girl. He could bear no more and, turning on his heel, abruptly left.

Exhausted, he rode away into the fog—keeping company with such lonely sorts as stray cats and dogs and with the street crier who rang his bell to mark the small hours. . . . He didn't care much where he went until somehow in the middle of the night he found himself on Marcus Owen's doorstep.

When the cart jerked into motion, Aileen fell to her knees but quickly stood back up, only to have a pistol put to her ribs. The rope binding her hands cut into her wrists. If she hadn't left her home in Ireland this way, bound and shoved about, the rough treatment would have shocked her more. As it was, she was more humiliated. Had she really thought she could play this game of Fian and get away with it? Of course, as soon as they discovered who she was—a woman—they'd release her. They'd *have* to.

Behind her the mob still shouted and broke glass. It began to chant the name, "Fian . . . Fian . . . Fian . . ." Someone laid a whip to a horse, and the cart picked up speed, knocking her down to her knees again. Heartsick, she concentrated on thoughts of Tyson. Where was he? Did he know what had happened? Would he even care? She rode like that for miles, the bumpy cart pushing slivers through the robe and breeches both, right into her knees until at last, mercifully, the cart stopped.

And now more rough-handed men yanked her out. A bald-headed brute dragged her up a steep flight of steps and into a building. Numb with shock, she let herself be led into a large room lit with candles. The light shone so hot and bright in her eyes that she blinked. Someone pushed her into the center of the room, and when her eyes adjusted to the light, she saw herself encircled by men—some uniformed and some in frock coats.

A knife sliced off the ropes. She brought her hands forward and rubbed first one wrist and then the other. Finally the bald-headed man jerked off her scarf, and she felt her hair come out of its pins and tumble down her back.

"What the deuce—!" a male voice exclaimed.

Once again her bald tormentor moved up and with a swift pull ripped off the Fian's dark robe. The savage gesture tore the front of the shirt she wore as well, and Aileen clutched her hands to its bodice. Terrified, she held her chin high and felt the flush of mortification steal up her cheeks.

"It's a woman," someone said needlessly.

A louder, more authoritative voice barked out, "You fools. This isn't the real Fian." Someone moved close and lifted her hair and, as if to verify it was real, tugged it by its roots, so hard her chin arched up. "Obviously an imposter."

Her eyes teared from the pain, but she didn't cry out, only bit her lip, until finally, blessedly, her interrogator let go.

Everyone stood in silence examining her as if she were a stone from a Druid monument. In the flickering light, shadows floated, obscuring faces. The bald man receded into the shadows.

"I know who that is," a uniformed bystander burst out. "It's that Irish maid—the Seymours' maid. The one who created such a scandal last winter with Lord Weston's nephew."

Someone picked up a candle and, holding it close to her face, circled her from all angles, as if he were a vulture assessing her chances of survival. "True?" A pock-faced interrogator had replaced the bald man.

Aileen didn't want to bring the Seymours into this—not with their murdering plans. She felt safer with Scotland Yard than with Lady Pamela. Nor did she want to implicate Tyson.

"Answer me." Harsh words hissed near her ear. "Answer, maid."

"Sure and I'm Irish, but I'm no one's maid."

"You mean you quit your post. That's what I heard from the Seymours."

"Perhaps I did. I've two lost brothers to—"

"Shut up. You'll only answer when spoke to."

Aileen finally steeled herself to look at her interrogator. With a sarcastic smile he turned to his colleagues and began to lecture them, coolly ignoring her state of dishabille. "Gentlemen," he began, "this simply goes to show how little you can trust the Irish."

Eyes downcast as protection from the glare of the roving candle, Aileen clutched the robe to her so tightly her nails dug into her palms.

Her interrogator continued. "The final rule with the Irish is simple—bed 'em, but never trust 'em. That devil in Parliament, Tyson Winslow, courted this one. Handsome taste he has, but you don't suppose he'll take her farther than his bed—even with his political sympathies."

Crude laughter broke out, and Aileen felt tears sting. The ribald comment hit too close to her own fears. And still the cruel comments continued. "I'm even guessing this mysterious female who enjoys dressing in disguise might be the same Lady in Blue who had all London in a tempest over naught. What do you say, Irish?" He turned and stared at Aileen, and when he smiled the pockmarks only deepened.

Mercifully she found her voice. "It's not a crime to dress in a blue gown, leastways, not in Ireland."

Her interrogator set down the candle and moved close to Aileen. "Decided to speak, have you? Well, it is a crime to dress as the Fian, except I know of course you're just pretending. What do you know about the activities of the *real* Fian?"

"Nothing," she whispered.

"Surely you talked when you borrowed his disguise?"

Truly frightened now, she shook her head.

The interrogator slapped her so hard she tasted blood. She could feel a welt rising on her cheek, and the tears coursed down, slow and hot.

"Take her to a cell. Solitary cell," her interrogator spat out. "We'll see what she's got to say when she appears before a magistrate."

"Charged with what, sir?" spoke up a naive-voiced young officer. "She's not the real Fian."

"You fool. London doesn't know that. We can use her as a scapegoat."

"But what charge? Sedition?"

"Treason."

First light had broken into a gray dawn when Tyson opened his eyes. Blinking, he saw wadded in his hand the pamphlet Marcus Owen had written. By his elbow he found a cup of cold tea. Disoriented, he stared at the cup, at the way pink roses wove round the saucer. Roses. The color of a dress Aileen had once worn. Instantly his mind cleared. He leapt to his feet.

"Owen," he called, glancing at a clock, panicking at the time lost. He thrust off his torn frock coat and his vest, so that he wore only trousers and shirt. He ripped off his cravat and sent it flying into the fire.

Owen, in breeches and still tossing a shirt over his head, came on the run from bed. Beatrice, hastily dressed in a wrapper, brought Tyson the farewell note Aileen had left, and though the note wouldn't help a wit, Tyson eagerly took it, devouring Aileen's handwriting. Wringing her hands, Beatrice fluttered about making fresh tea for them.

"Someday," Tyson said, "I'll want to know how you came to acquire Aileen's story and write the pamphlet. You put me through weeks of hell. I'll never forgive you for that."

"I'm a soft touch for a woman in need of help."

"Obviously. . . ." agreed Tyson, adding in a dry tone, "So what ideas do you have for helping her now?"

Marcus thought for a moment. "Perhaps as a reporter I can find out when she's being transferred from jail to Old Bailey for trial. Would that help you forgive?"

Tyson considered the notion and finally nodded. They sat down again. While Marcus dutifully took notes, Tyson told Marcus about Nicholas Seymour's illegal factory holdings.

"That's all? I thought you were going to give me the connection between Seymour and the Lady in Blue."

"You wrote the pamphlet, Owen. You can put the rest of the story together yourself." He stared out the window at the quickening dawn. "I'm going back to that factory for one more look in daylight for Aileen's brothers. Do you

want to see it so you can add that authentic note to your
editorial?"

Marcus, Tyson noted with a rueful smile, didn't need a
second invitation. Tyson led the way to the scarred building. In the morning light the place on Watley Street looked
like a battle scene, and with Marcus following, Tyson
walked in the open doorway, picked up a forgotten candle
from the floor, and lit it.

Overhead he heard a scurrying sound. Tyson looked up at
the ceiling. It could be rats, but then again, perhaps a child
or two had been overlooked here last night.

With soft footsteps he climbed the stairs to the next floor.
All was silent. Again from overhead came a scurry of tiny
feet. As noiselessly as possible, Tyson climbed up the last
flight of stairs until he stood outside the attic door waiting
for Marcus to catch up with him. When Tyson pushed open
the door, it creaked slightly, and Tyson stood still. Eerie
shadows danced off the raw timber of the inner roof
structure, and he blew out the candle. The air smelled of
mildewed straw and fetid confinement.

With a restraining hand on Marcus's arm, Tyson signaled
for silence. Had a floorboard creaked? Or a door? The room
itself rustled with energy, as if someone were hiding there.
If he just waited long enough and was lucky, two stow-
aways might reveal themselves. Behind him Marcus's
breathing ticked away the minutes.

At last, ever so gradually, voices—barely audible—
floated across the darkness to Tyson.

"Shh." With a signal to Marcus to wait and guard the
door, Tyson moved on cat feet a little farther into the room.
He listened again and voices, whispered, and childish,
rewarded him.

"Seamus, are they gone yet?"

"I think so," came the return whisper.

Tyson swung in the direction of the voices. He saw a decrepit piece of furniture, a wardrobe, but ample enough in size for a pair of boys. The voices continued to carry out to him.

"Seamus, it's hot in here."

"Be quiet a little longer."

"You promised to tell me a story if I was quiet."

After a pause someone began talking in the singsong voice of a storyteller. An Irish brogue accented the words.

"So Princess Aileen brought the Fian, but the bad fairies found out, and they took Aileen off to the dark caves in the seven hills."

"But how will she get out of the cave to find us? Seamus, you're only telling me a story to keep me from crying. . . ."

Shaken by what he'd heard, Tyson relit the candle and, making no effort to conceal the sound of his footsteps, crossed the rest of the way to the wardrobe. The storytelling voice gave way to a flurry of "Shhs."

Tyson reached for the doorknob and flung open the wardrobe. Reflected in the candlelight were two pair of eyes. A dark-haired boy—face pinched thin—pulled his arms about a younger, sickly-looking boy with red hair. Tears coursed down the cheeks of the younger one, leaving white trails in the dirt on his face. Both boys huddled back in the wardrobe.

Tyson knelt down and stared kindly at the older one. "Why, you're the spitting image of Aileen, aren't you?"

"How do you know?" The boy kicked out a foot as if to push Tyson away. "Go away. We aren't letting any strangers cart us off."

"Ah, and you have her same spirit." Tyson smiled and reached out.

Both boys shrank back from his touch, and he supposed

he looked frightening, unshaven and haggard from lack of sleep.

"I'm Aileen's friend. She told me to fetch you and keep you safe. You needn't worry. The factory's been closed down."

"We aren't going to an orphanage. Aileen knows we're here. Patrick saw her from the window. We're waiting here."

"Aileen won't be able to come for a while, but I'm going to take you to her."

"Why didn't Aileen come get us? She was here, once before."

Tyson swallowed hard. "She planned to, only I found you first."

"Who are you?"

Conscious of Marcus Owen standing within hearing distance, Tyson nevertheless gave the only answer they'd believe. "I'm the Fian, come to rescue you like your sister asked of me."

The little redheaded boy rubbed his eyes and blinked several times. "The Fian? Is it him, Seamus? Is it?"

The older boy, Seamus, kept a protective arm about his little brother and eyed Tyson skeptically. "You don't look much like the Fian," he said.

Startled, Tyson replied, "Well, then, lad, what should the Fian look like?"

"I don't know," Seamus admitted. "That's because they say he rides in disguise."

"Your sister has—my disguise. It's a very long story, and one I'm sure she'll want to tell you herself." He reached for them. "Now come out. How could I know Aileen was your sister if I weren't acquainted with her?"

"Tell us something more, so we know you're really her friend," Seamus demanded.

"First of all, you're both from Devintown. This little chap with the red hair is Patrick. And you, Seamus, well, Aileen never told me how much you look like her. You've a big brother, Roddy, who's in America . . . and Aileen has told me she'll never stop searching London till she finds you two. That's why I'm helping her now, because she's helped me with the Fian's work."

"She has?" Seamus stared openmouthed.

Tyson nodded. "And brave she is."

"It's him, Seamus," Patrick declared, and when his big brother didn't dispute the statement, the boy climbed out and allowed Tyson to pick him up into his arms.

Slowly Seamus's skepticism evaporated, and he, too, climbed out of the wardrobe. Tyson could hardly keep his eyes off Seamus, partly because of his frailty, but mostly because of the startling resemblance to Aileen.

"He came, Seamus," sang Patrick, tears still coursing down his cheeks. "You didn't make it up. Aileen found the Fian, and he rescued us." His voice rang with a singsong chant of delight. Behind his unscrubbed face and dirty clothes and tangled hair two big blue eyes stared in happiness at Tyson.

"Well, sure and didn't I tell you all along?" said Seamus with an I-told-you-so ring to his voice.

"Patrick," Tyson said, "can you keep a secret?"

"About the Fian?"

Tyson nodded. "Tell no one."

From behind them Marcus Owen cleared his throat. The boys started, as if wary of whips and other painful punishments.

"It's all right, Mr. Owen is a friend of mine and of Aileen's. He hid her for a while to keep her out of danger."

He looked at Marcus Owen, notebook in hand, waiting

for him to ask the obvious question: *Are you the Fian, truly?*

Instead, Marcus stood there in mute astonishment.

"Aileen will be a very happy lady, *Mr. Winslow*," he said, slipping his notebook into his coat pocket.

"Who's Mr. Winslow?" asked Patrick, confused.

"Merely an acquaintance of the Fian's," supplied Marcus, who moved across the room to help lead Seamus out. "Someone I used to know as a schoolboy."

The men's eyes met and held, then without a word, they led the boys downstairs.

Nineteen

UNEXPECTEDLY, AILEEN HEARD the guards coming, heavy
boots echoing on the stone corridor that led to her cell, and
the horror of her dank, dark world was complete.

It wasn't a meal they were bringing, for she'd already
choked down a breakfast of stale bread. Abominable, but at
least it staved her hunger. Not knowing if guards were
returning to taunt her some more, she pressed back into the
corner of the cell, tucked her prison dress about her, and
laid her head on her knees, waiting. When the footsteps
stopped, she could hear their voices and the rattling of a key
ring.

Closing her eyes, she tried to block out the terror, but
couldn't. Last night she'd had another nightmare, a dream
that began with her brothers coming closer and closer to her,
and when they were almost within reach of her embrace,
their faces merged into one—Tyson's face.

With a cold clang the key turned in the metal lock of her
cell door, and she felt herself tense, wondering if she'd have
to kick and claw this guard away like the last time he'd
come in, "wanting a favor from the Fian's doxy," as he'd so
crudely put it. She decided to give herself the advantage and

stood up, hands clenched into fists, body poised to kick out.

Two guards entered, both clean-shaven, and neatly uniformed, a clear contrast to the crude lout who'd tried to rape her a few days ago. Watching these men advance, she guessed they'd come to take her to her trial. Involuntarily Aileen touched her throat, as if feeling the hemp of the gallows rope already.

"C'mon then, girlie," one of them lisped, reaching for her arm and tugging at her.

Rather than fight and end up shackled, she obeyed and, flanked by the guards, began the walk down the long stone corridor of Newgate. The only sound—the offbeat rhythm of three different people's footsteps on the stone—Aileen's and the two guards'.

Cold, she wrapped herself briefly in the comfort of memories—memories of Ireland and her brothers. If it weren't for never seeing her brothers again, she could accept her fate. She could even accept dying in Tyson's place if it came to that. But she'd dearly have loved to see Seamus and Patrick once more.

Now, it seemed, time had run out. She had no idea what to expect in an English court of law. She only knew what the Fian had told her on the night they'd met—that if caught he'd hang. She expected no less for herself.

She walked past cell after cell where other women extended their hands through the bars in a sign of support. At least, if convicted and hung, she'd probably die a heroine—the Fian's accomplice. Eventually perhaps Seamus and Patrick would hear about her fate. Perhaps, too, they'd tell her story and add it to the legends of the Fian.

Suddenly the guards turned a corner and headed for a door that led outside Newgate. Relieved, she realized she wasn't going into the courtroom—not yet. Hope soared and dipped like an uncertain bird.

The number of blue-uniformed guards tripled. Their debate—whether or not to handcuff her. The decision was affirmative, and, upon command, she held out her hands, curled into fists, while the cold metal clamped round her wrists. Someone held open the door, and with the escort of prison guards, she exited the prison.

It was raining, and the cobblestones were slick beneath her soles, while heavy drops immediately splotched her gown and washed through her tangled hair. Aileen lifted her face to feel the clean rain. She breathed in fresh air as well—just a gulp or two before someone thrust her into a coach, and once more she knew dark confinement.

The vehicle could most charitably be described as serviceable. Instead of plush seats a wooden bench awaited her. The window in the single door was high, grimy, and barred. Even though movement caused the handcuffs to bite into her flesh, she shifted on the bench just enough so she could see the raindrops through the window bars, steady and rhythmic like soldiers marching down from the sky.

One guard, complaining about the rain, climbed inside and, pushing Aileen back down, sat on the bench opposite her. He'd barely warmed it before a superior official opened the door and hauled the fellow out.

"Are you daft? This prisoner is going before the bar of the Commons today, and I don't want to lose her between here and there. Even if it snows, you ride outside and stay alert."

With a slam of the door Aileen was locked inside, alone, her heart beating a tattoo.

The Commons. Parliament was going to question her. Would Tyson Winslow be there? Would he ask her questions to which he knew only too well the answers? Would he do something foolish like take the blame for her? No matter what happened, she'd never give him away. Till this moment she hadn't admitted to herself how memories of him had sustained her through the days in Newgate. And now—she was on her way to Parliament.

They'd traveled perhaps ten minutes when unexpectedly, daringly, thunder vibrated through the coach. At once she recognized the sound as a pistol report and ducked her head. Though she couldn't see a thing outside, she heard the men surround the coach, recognized their Irish brogues, felt the heavy impact on the coach where an Irish and a guard scuffled.

Outside someone shouted. "Send for reinforcements and . . ." A gunshot muffled his last word.

Someone else, someone with an Irish brogue, gave the next command. "Sure and 'tis the Fianna, the Fian's army. Rein in the horses or the Fianna will do it for you."

Immediately the coach lurched to a stop, nearly throwing Aileen off the bench. When she regained her balance, she raised up her handcuffed wrists to the door latch and peered out into the street. As she watched through the rain-streaked window, men moved toward the coach from out of nowhere until she couldn't see a thing but Irishmen.

Oh, yes, the Fianna. The soldiers of the Fian, just as Seamus liked to talk about them. She could hear them chanting a Gaelic song in rhyme, and an army of horses' hooves clopped against the wet cobblestones. Warriors they were and poets they were, and most of all, her rescuers. Silent tears fell.

Another pistol shot rang out, and she ducked. Someone thrust the butt of a pistol against the glass of the window. Cold air rushed in, followed by a reassuring voice. "Aileen Connolly, you're a wanted woman. Now, duck your head against the far side of this lousy excuse for a coach while we show it what Irishmen think of English prisons."

It was Martin Kelly's voice, she was sure of it, but she

had no time to be guessing. She pushed herself as far across the coach as she could, and a split second later an angry ax began to destroy the coach door.

With each ear-shattering fell of the blade, wood splintered and metal crunched. Had she not been handcuffed, she'd have covered her head. As it was, she squeezed shut her eyes. Splinters of wood flew in toward her, showering her dress and hair.

"Hurry up, Kelly," someone called nervously.

"I *am* hurrying. Aileen," Martin warned, "one more blow. Duck your head again."

She dropped her head to her lap, listening to the rhythmic Gaelic chant of the Fian's army, and next thing she knew, men were pulling her out of the coach and lifting her up onto a horse.

"Martin'll take you out of here," someone said reassuringly.

And he did, mounting swiftly, and clutching her as he might a sack of grain. In the distance she heard a policeman's rattle, but because the Fianna, the army of Irish, far outweighed the strength of any English on the scene yet, Martin easily swept her away. Behind them the Gaelic chanting grew dimmer and dimmer, replaced by the staccato clip of horses' hooves on wet pavement. Numb, she let Martin take her where he would, and soon he turned into a dark courtyard between two buildings.

"Well done, Martin," said a too dear and familiar masculine voice. "You're a good man. May God bless the years ahead."

Martin lifted her from his horse and transferred her to another man's arms, to an embrace that cradled her against a familiar heartbeat. Tyson. Like her, he was soaking wet, but she knew at once the familiar feel of his arms about her. Closing her eyes while the rain poured down on her, she

said a prayer of thanks to the Almighty for little blessings—
the touch of Tyson's hand to her face, her hair, his arms
about her again, words of forgiveness.

"There'll be no time for tender reunions," said Martin
brusquely. "Best head out of London before the Yard knows
what's happened."

She felt Tyson's nod. Gently, never letting go of her, he
tried to rearrange her into an easy riding position and saw
her handcuffs. "I want these off," he said, his voice
dangerous. She hadn't heard that tone since the night he'd
taken a knife to her and accused her of being an assassin.

"Easy, man. We thought of everything," said Martin,
tossing a ring of keys to Tyson. "These were in the guard's
coat."

When Tyson fumbled with the keys, it was Martin who
reached over and unlocked the handcuffs. But it was Tyson
who ripped them off and flung them onto the cobblestones.
His hands flew to Aileen's wrists, soothing the red welts.

"Be gone," warned Martin. "You've no time to spare."

Tyson positioned Aileen close against him and spurred
Cormac forward. "Hang on, little banshee. You're safe
now. Don't cry. I won't let any of them have you, not
Scotland Yard, especially not Parliament."

"They'll know you took me."

"Shh, love, it's over. . . ." His words were muffled by
the sound of Cormac's hooves.

Had he called her love or was that her overwrought
imagination? Had he pressed his face into her soaking wet
hair for just a second, or were her senses playing tricks?

There was no time for questions. She could only let him
carry her away to safety. As Martin had said, reunions
would have to come later.

The rain poured down still, running off her hair, molding
her dress to her. Tyson's clothes were equally drenched, as

was brave Cormac, who carried them north out of London.

When she thought she'd drop off from exhaustion, Tyson slowed the horse at last, and Aileen looked around. They were in a tiny village that Londoners had probably forgotten existed.

One weary-looking inn, the Red Goose, sat by the roadside. Few travelers came this way, Tyson told her at once, as if to allay her fears. The railway had bypassed this somnolent village, and even the mail coach had ceased its stop here. As a result the inn was bereft of business. There'd be few if any other guests to bother them.

While she stood dripping wet inside the door, Tyson asked the innkeeper for a back room and dropped down many coins. They wanted privacy, Tyson said, insinuating they were a couple eloping to Scotland. If anyone asked after them, they'd come and gone already. More coins dropped into the hungry-looking innkeeper's hands, enough to pay for silence.

With a lover's gentleness Tyson swept Aileen up into his arms and carried her, drenched, to the room. He stood her in front of the hearth, absorbing her shivers with his arms while the obsequious innkeeper's wife, who doubled as maid, lit the fire.

The room was small. Looking around, Aileen counted one bed, a washstand, and whitewashed walls, like in her cottage at home. But that was enough—warm, dry, and filled with Tyson's presence. As soon as the grate gave off warmth, the maid handed Tyson a candle as well. He gave the woman—a plain thing of homely proportions—a coin and ordered a bath for the room. When she scurried off, he gave her an admonition to hurry and slammed the door shut.

Turning at once to Aileen, he one by one unfastened the buttons on the wretched dress she'd worn throughout her days in prison. "This is becoming a familiar task—peeling wet clothes off of you, love." With single-minded attention, he undid her from her soaked dress and wrapped her in a blanket.

Briefly he warmed her trembling lips with his, not a kiss so much as a communion with her. He did the same with her wrists, placing his lips on the chafe marks left by the handcuffs. When a knock came on the door, Aileen jumped. But it was only the innkeeper and his wife with the tub. Aileen sat wrapped in a blanket while the old woman made a dozen trips up and down the stairs hauling buckets of hot water.

At last Aileen relaxed in the water, and Tyson retrieved a change of clothes for them from his saddlebags—a blue muslin dress for Aileen that Kate Reilly had given him, and trousers and a plain white shirt for himself.

When he returned, he pushed open the door without knocking, and Aileen again jumped, nerves still raw from the taunting prison guards.

After dropping the clothes onto the bed, Tyson knelt down by the tub and lifted her hands into his. "How bad did they hurt you in Newgate?"

She shook her head. "I want to forget it."

He looked skeptical. "Did they touch you?"

She flinched. "It's over, and I lived through it. I won't tell you any more. You'll only get angry."

He let go of her hands and cupped her face in both of his hands. "Aileen, I couldn't ever be that angry with you."

"Were you going to question me if I was taken to Parliament?"

"I was going to kill whichever man tried. That's why I thought it best to have you rescued before you got there. I'm wanted for enough other crimes."

He lifted her hands again, and she winced.

"What is it?"

"I—don't know. A sliver I think."

He examined her left palm and found a tiny bit of wood embedded in her skin. For the first time in his life he realized rage over something as trivial as a sliver.

He called the innkeeper's wife to administer to the hand, and he heard Aileen ask if there was a nightgown she might borrow. Her voice trembled, and he cursed himself for forgetting the details that a woman needed. "Bring a brush as well," he ordered and gave the woman more coins, then left only long enough to see to Cormac and change out of his own wet clothes.

When he returned, his gaze went at once to the wooden bathtub that sat by the fire. It was empty, and he pivoted toward the bed. Aileen lay there, changed now into a high-necked gown resembling stiff cream, threadbare in places, but warm. Her eyes looked large and frightened, and she was staring at him.

"If you're going to ask again what are the sleeping arrangements, you must know you have no choice. I'm not leaving you."

"What did you think I'd want?"

"You just came out of Newgate because of my crimes. Perhaps you want me to sleep out in the rain. If so, I'd—"

"Please stay with me."

He felt something elemental relax. That was all he wanted—not to touch her, not now, but just to stay with her.

He moved toward her.

"Was the dinner party a success?"

He stopped and bent over her, brushing back a damp lock of her hair. Had that really been the last time he'd seen her? It seemed an eternity had passed since that night on the barge.

"Was it?" she asked, her voice all innocence.

"Yes, in fact, I was in the process of verbally lashing

Seymour—when a messenger interrupted with the most
alarming news. The Fian rode and led a riot." With a gentle
touch he tipped her chin up and looked at her.

"I'm not as good at it as you are," she said, wide-eyed.

"The trick, lass, is not to get caught."

The blue of her eyes deepened, tempting him to drown.
He'd sworn he wouldn't touch her tonight, and he'd not
break that promise.

"You're angry I locked you out of the barge, aren't you?"

He wanted to laugh. He couldn't be angry at this moment
even if someone put a pistol to his head.

"I'm not angry, but I blame myself I left you there . . .
What made you think you could get away with it?"

"I had no choice. . . ." then, after the merest pause she
changed the subject. "What happened to my brothers? They
were in the factory, weren't they?"

He turned away so she couldn't read the frustration that
he knew must show in his face. He kept his voice carefully
neutral. "Most ended up in a Foundling Home—except for
Seamus and Patrick. They're all right, Aileen. You're going
to be with them soon. They're waiting for you now."

He turned around to see tears welling in her eyes, and he
was ashamed of himself for the envy he felt toward her
brothers. Him. Tyson Winslow. Envious of a pair of
helpless little boys. But he knew why. As soon as she and
those boys were reunited, she'd take them to America. He
didn't have to ask, and he didn't really want to face her
answer—not yet.

Someone slammed a door in the inn, and she visibly
tensed. Immediately he bent to her. At that moment he
wanted to personally kill every guard in Newgate who'd
come near her.

She wrapped herself against his chest, body pliant but
hands closed into fists. He pulled her back off the pillow,

and they lay entwined. The beat of her heart against his was like a clock ticking away the time he had left with her.

"You won't leave me tonight?" she whispered.

He shook his head, taken aback that she had doubts. There was nothing to say, nothing to ask, and he knew it. All that had to be said could be said with a pair of arms and the pressing of his lips against her hair, which was still damp from the bath. He combed his fingers through it over and over. She moved against him, and he nearly stopped breathing, wanting her, but not letting himself. Finally her hands uncurled, and he caught them in both of his, linked his fingers through hers, and pressed his palms to hers. For the longest time they lay together until the innkeeper's wife knocked on the door to remove the bathwater.

Aileen sat up, eyes wide, looking as if she expected a guard from Newgate to accost her. With a muffled curse Tyson quickly untangled himself and hauled the water out in the hall himself, giving the woman a coin to be gone. He threw the bolt and picked up his pistol, loaded it, and took it back to the bed and laid it by his pillow.

His shirtsleeves were wet where water had splashed down them, and he rolled them up. Aileen lay on the bed, hands curled into fists again. He knelt over the bed and stroked her wrists until he could lock hands with her again. He lay down beside her and pulled her head to his chest until at last she slept. When she was asleep, he reached for his pistol.

He held her all night, his pistol poised upon his stomach, pointed at the door to the little room. He felt the steady rise and fall of her breathing, but never took his eyes off the door, ready to shoot, to kill anyone who touched that door. Even a poor woman come to fetch ashes from the grate would have been at risk.

The silken feel of Aileen's hair tangled in his hands.

Here and now—that's all he wanted, and he'd kill anyone who opened that door and took this night from him.

Above all he dreaded giving her up tomorrow. . . . It was clearly what she wanted, though—to have her brothers more than anything. More than him. At least he'd get to see her face light up when she saw them. He'd take that much more from her.

Twenty

WHEN AILEEN AWOKE, a gray dawn filtered through the window. To give her privacy Tyson left just long enough to order breakfast. When he returned, however, he carried not just food, but a letter from America. Kate Reilly had given it to him when he'd brought Seamus and Patrick to her for temporary shelter. He should have handed Aileen the letter last night, but something had held him back. As long as she didn't know it existed, she was still vulnerable, still dependent on him.

He looked at her, dressed in the blue gown Kate Reilly had given him, and he noted the color exactly matched the blue of her eyes. The letter burned a hole in his pocket.

"Why won't you speak to me?" she asked.

"There's nothing to say."

"You're angry about me riding as the Fian."

"Why should I be angry?" She'd only risked her life. A mere trifle.

"Is it because I'm a woman and no woman can be the Fian?"

"Actually, many people have called themselves Fian." How could he tell her he was so grateful to have rescued her that words eluded him? "You get into far too much trouble when I leave you, it seems," he observed.

"I'm sorry." She fumbled for the brush.

She was sitting on the bed, trying to pull the tangles out of her hair. It hung long about her shoulders, and she attempted—with disastrous results—to pin it up. The Lord knew he'd spent enough time in idle repose watching London women pin their hair up or take it down before him that he could at least improvise in this situation. Feeling like an awkward substitute for a lady's maid, nevertheless, he pushed in a last pin and with fingers that seemed too large fastened the back of her gown.

And then he spread currant jam on a slice of bread and gave it to her to eat.

"Where are we?" she asked at last in between hungry bites.

"We're in a tiny village on the way to Yorkshire. I'm taking you farther out into the country. You're as wanted as I am now, and I'm going to hide you away with a gypsy band."

"Gypsies?" Her gaze flew to his face.

"Friendly. Your brothers are with them now." He paused, watching her face relax, then poured hot chocolate into a cup and handed it to her. "Marcus Owen promised to write a scathing denunciation of Scotland Yard's inept handling of your case, so they'll be too embarrassed to hunt you down too far. Still, you need to lay low."

"For how long?" She'd been stirring the chocolate but now looked up, alarmed.

"That all depends." He couldn't put it off any longer. At last he handed her the letter from America. "Kate Reilly's been saving this for you," he said.

For the first time since he'd rescued her, her face melted

with emotion, and she pushed aside her food. "Roddy. Oh, Roddy. I knew he'd answer me."

Watching her tear the seal, he saw the money that fell out with the letter and knew it was enough for passage to America—barely. If he'd felt jealous of her little brothers, it was nothing compared to what he felt toward this older brother.

She glanced up once from reading, and her eyes held nothing but happiness—a shining look she'd never once bestowed on him. He turned to stare out the window, counting the dewdrops that fell down the panes. She would do what she wanted. He knew her well enough. But suddenly he couldn't stand the uncertainty.

"Will you go to America, then?"

At her pause he turned around.

She had folded the letter and was looking at him.

"Yes . . . eventually. I won't stay in England to see the Fian strung from the gallows. I couldn't bear that, but I'll stay as long as—" Her voice caught.

"As long as you haven't found your brothers."

She swallowed and seemed to force a smile for him. "Aye, until we're reunited. . . ."

"Then we should continue on before it gets any lighter," he said, turning away to gather their few possessions. He felt as if an anchor weighed him down.

Wasn't it a lifetime ago that he'd put her up on a horse and rode with her into London? Now he was taking her away, reversing their movements. The only thing he couldn't reverse was the loneliness he felt already. He held her fast, and they rode in silence until at last he caught up with the gypsy caravan.

Like a gaily painted train, it meandered through the English countryside, bound for Scotland. When he found it, the wagons were winding across a meadow laced with daisies. He pulled up Cormac in a wooded area, so they could wait for the caravan to stop, and so he could have a last moment with her.

"Aileen Connolly, can I trust you to stay put with these gypsies? Until the caravan reaches Liverpool, you're never too safe."

"You're leaving?" She sounded alarmed, as if the possibility had just occurred to her.

He nodded.

"Where are you going?" she asked. "Back to London?"

Again a nod. She took a deep breath. "It's all right. I won't be afraid."

He couldn't help the tiny smile that lurked in his eyes. "Your problem, banshee, is that you aren't afraid enough. Beware now. If Scotland Yard found you a second time, not even the Fianna could rescue you again."

Pulling her close against him briefly, he memorized the way she melted into him, and just as abruptly, set her away from him. If he didn't look into her eyes, it was deliberate. Better to avoid tears and questions. Worse, he feared that if he caught her glance, he'd beg her to stay awhile, and he had no right to ask that of her.

He walked her to the edge of the meadow, his hand in hers for courage. At the last possible moment he let go of her.

Lingering at the meadow's edge, he watched her, wondering when he'd started to love her, knowing that he'd love her till the day he died.

He only wanted to witness the reunion, after which he would return to London and talk with Martin Kelly about the Irish situation. Utterly drained as he was, the prospect failed to stir up much fervor within his soul. Why, he asked himself, was he so devoted to the cause? At the moment he had no answers, but he supposed they'd come. All he knew was that he couldn't have both a life as a wanted man and a life with a woman.

Aileen didn't dare look back, or she'd be on her knees begging Tyson to stay. She knew he'd be returning to his cause, and to his aristocratic life. Roddy had told her in her letter that he dearly wanted to meet the Fian, that the Irish cause needed a man of his abilities in America. But she'd not tempt Tyson with the cause. She was tired of the fighting and subterfuge.

The caravan had stopped near the shade of an isolated stand of oak trees, and the gypsies were setting up camp. Dark-haired women moved into the meadow searching for herbs. One by one Aileen studied the wagons. Her glance settled on a red and yellow one.

She walked past a cheerful cluster of wildflowers springing up amongst the grasses. She felt as bleak as a wintry heath. She'd sacrificed love for this moment of reunion with her brothers. Small wonder tears stung.

Moving closer, she saw two boys playing with a dog near the back step of the wagon—dark-skinned boys. With only instinct to guide her Aileen moved in their direction, steadily closer until one of the boys looked up and noticed her. He stood up in surprise and with a nudge to his little companion pulled him to his feet.

One held a deformed arm close to his body. Seamus?

"Aileen!" It was Patrick's voice, and he was running toward her, followed by his older brother.

And then she, too, was running and at last scooping up little Patrick into her arms. Though his hair might be dyed gypsy black, it was nevertheless her dear Patrick, and the little boy wrapped his legs around her and crushed himself to her while she swirled round and round with him.

Seamus ran up behind him, and kneeling down, Aileen hugged them both. She set Patrick on his feet, and he

squirmed so he fairly danced for joy. "Aileen, Aileen," he
said, as if he were bursting with a secret. "You'll never
guess who rescued us and brought us here!"

Wide-eyed with feigned ignorance, Aileen asked, "And
who might it be?"

Patrick jumped with joy. "The Fian, Aileen. He's real.
We told you. We tried to tell you he'd help us. He's real,
and he found us. . . ."

"London is very big," Seamus said in a more somber
tone, as if the ordeal had taken him a step closer to maturity.
"Of course the Fian found us," he told his younger brother.
"The Fian knows everything there is to know about London, including how to riot."

Aileen felt her smile fade. She tried to break away from
the boys so she could run after Tyson. She didn't want him
to go back to London. She was afraid for him.

But Patrick was tugging on her hand. "What took you so
long?" he demanded.

She turned back, eyes glistening with tears. "Well, as
Seamus said, London is very large, and . . . a couple of
times I got lost."

"And who found you?"

"Mr. Winslow."

"I know who that is," began Seamus.

"Mind your tongue, Seamus, you know-it-all. That's a
secret."

Aileen smiled wanly. It was so good to hear them fight
again—like brothers.

Wordlessly she handed Seamus the letter from America.
The boys fell to examining the seal and the handwriting.

"Read it, Aileen, read it to us."

And so she did, though her voice wavered.

"Are we going to America?" Patrick asked excitedly.

Nodding, she caught the pair of them to her and wept. It

was Seamus who awkwardly patted her back. "It's all right, Aileen. I took good care of Patrick, and now we're together again. That's all that matters."

Aileen stood up and glanced back to the wooded space where Tyson had left her. He was already gone.

Tea tray in hand, Sally scurried out of the drawing room, face flushed from the tongue-lashing she'd just received. The butler snapped shut the door, and still Lady Pamela continued her tirade. Once started she'd never been able to stop herself from a tantrum. And she was very angry, angrier than she'd been since she found out that her father had lost the family inheritance and left her impoverished. She'd wanted to kill her father for that, and now she felt the murderous rage rising within her, like aged wine ready to be uncorked and spill over, staining everyone around her.

She directed her immediate venom at her husband, who sat in a wing chair, staring at the contents of his half-empty liqueur glass. After folding the copy of the *Times* into narrower and narrower columns so that only Marcus Owen's editorial was visible, she slapped the fireplace mantel with it.

Turning to her husband, she glared at him. "Stop sulking and talk to me. I'm facing social ruin, and all you can do is sit there. Even I, daughter of a man nearly your equal in stupidity when it comes to money, would have known better than to buy into a slave factory. How could you think to get away with this?"

He looked up, expression bland. "Perhaps I would have gotten away with it had you not brought that Irish girl here."

"You can't blame me, Nicholas Seymour. You're the fool, the political corpse. And because of you I'll never have social prominence, which was such a simple thing to acquire. Adulation comes quite cheap, you know. Fool everyone with flattery and easy charm, and you've got it. Do something stupid like you've done with this factory, and it's gone, like this." She set the newspaper over a candelabra and, watching the flames consume it, continued to lash out. "Why, of all the factories those jackanapes could have sent that girl's brothers to, did they choose yours? If I'd only known you owned such a place, I'd have counseled you to sell it."

"Calm down, my dear," came her husband's languid response. "People forget what they read in the papers. Next week some young swain will be occupying the editorials with his amorous adventures, and our scandal will be old news."

"You make it all sound so easy." She stood there holding the flaming newspaper, consumed with the urge to torch her husband's handsome face. Instead, she threw the thing onto the grate of the fireplace. Even Cornelia had cut her dead at Hyde Park yesterday. Cornelia. The spiteful bitch.

Turning, she saw her husband looking at her as if she were a whip he wanted to flog against the floor. Standing up and advancing on her, he spat out sentences in the same snapping cadence with which he flogged his horse. "You're a silly woman, Lady Pamela," he said with sarcasm.

He paused in his tracks, mouth twisted, breath heavy with alcohol, and backed her into the portrait of herself, the portrait for which she'd paid a precious fortune of his money. Now the gilt frame tilted crookedly and tore the wallpaper.

"I know more than you give me credit for, my dear. Much more than your society friends could bear. Did you know, for example, I killed a woman when I was but a lad?"

"No." She'd thought she'd known everything there was to know about her husband. Pressing back against the wall, she felt her eyes go wide with fear, and her hand flew to her throat.

"How?"

"An accident. You know I married you because the idea of your title and blueblood connections appealed to me. If that's of no use to me anymore, who knows but you might meet with an accident, which would allow me to find another woman to help me with my aspirations?"

Her gaze narrowed on him. "You wouldn't dare do away with me. You're nothing but a second son, and you'll always need my family name and its influence."

"Are you going to help me still like a dutiful wife, or not?"

She pulled away. "Of course," she said a trifle nervously. She wasn't defeated yet—not totally. But she had to keep her husband calm a while longer. "I have another plan," she said quickly. "Why do you doubt me?"

"Tell me about it," he said in an even voice.

Trembling, she did and felt herself flush at his slow mocking smile.

"Leaving London again for this plan?"

"This time it won't fail."

"Perhaps, but remember—be careful lest you end up in an accident yourself," he said with a cruel smile. He sank down heavily into his chair.

Shaken by his threat, Lady Pamela flounced out of the drawing room, leaving instructions to fetch her husband's valet to minister to him. Confident of her latest plan, she walked upstairs with the regality of a lady to the manor born. She deserved better than Nicholas Seymour. Far better.

Nesbitt fluttered about finding the dress she requested, and Lady Pamela stared at herself in the mirror, smiling for the benefit of the servants.

She knew, of course, that she'd never be received at court now—for if Cornelia could cut her dead, then the queen would never accept her. The best she could hope for would be Victoria's death in childbed, and in her favor was Albert's too easy ability to get Victoria with child. Yes, if the queen died, then Lady Pamela could start charming another court. But that was for fate to determine— and Albert. . . . Briefly she smiled, then abruptly her thoughts returned to that stupid editorial.

She felt her murderous rage focusing on one object—that Irish girl, who'd been consumed with finding her brothers, who had ruined her plot to murder the Fian months ago. Though she'd never admit it to her husband, in a way, Lady Pamela did hold herself at fault. After all, had she not hired on Mary Aileen, and practically thrown her at the feet of Tyson Winslow, matters would not have gotten this far out of control.

Gown changed, she called for her bonnet and cape and coach. When Edmund Leedes came calling as arranged, she was waiting out front and bade him get into the coach with her.

"You should have killed Tyson Winslow when you had your chance at that tavern," she admonished.

"We did in his cohort, Digby Trigg," Leedes blustered.

"That wasn't good enough," Lady Pamela said, as if biting off the words. "Now, you've one more chance to redeem yourself, Mr. Leedes. I've no doubt Mr. Winslow is the Fian, but it's getting more and more difficult to catch him off guard, especially since the Irish girl and her brothers left London. Now I've one last idea. Understand that exposing the Fian now doesn't matter to me. My husband's ruined all that. But I'll take my revenge, have my satisfaction in the way a man would, Mr. Leedes."

Leedes's double chins waggled, and he ran a nervous

finger down his tartan vest, while with his other hand he reached for his flask.

"Kindly put away that flask while in my presence, Mr. Leedes, and listen closely. I want Tyson Winslow to suffer."

"You said yourself he's hard to trap."

"But there's someone else still in England who's much easier to lure, and killing her would be as good—perhaps more effective—than killing him. Now, it will take three people to carry out this plan—not counting myself of course, but as far as you know I'll have merely left London to visit friends in the country. Is that clear?"

Leedes nodded, gaze narrowing in shock as he listened. The coach stopped in a dark alley, and the Albino climbed in, filling the coach with the smell of the teeming London streets. Pockmarks dotted his stark white skin, and in the dim light of the coach the whites of his eyes glowed red and malicious. Lady Pamela always cringed a bit when she had to do business with the man. She pressed back against her seat while explaining what she wanted from him now.

"I'll do anything if it pays good English coin," he rasped, looking with arrogance at the fat man next to him.

"Good. You'll be paid in full after the deed," Lady Pamela said.

The Albino put a hand on the door latch, but she held him back, rapping his knuckles with her reticule. "Don't leave without my invitation, kind sir. In my social circle, that's only polite behavior."

"I've naught to do with your social circles, ma'am," he said, tone surly.

Lady Pamela sucked in her breath. Barring her husband when he'd been drinking, this notorious highwayman was the only person she'd met who could drive a stake of fear through her ambitious core. She swallowed and tried to regain the upper hand.

"Quite understood, sir. Nevertheless, a third person is involved in this plan. And without her neither of you can perform your deeds. Do I make sense?"

She looked from one man to the other. Leedes looked typically confused. He never could see the scope of a plan, nor did she want him to. The Albino on the other hand looked skeptical, mocking, and filthy. She made a mental note to have the groom wash down the coach later—inside and out.

They rode along, Lady Pamela and her two hirelings staring at each other until at last with the handle of her parasol, she tapped the roof and signaled the driver to stop.

The door opened, and a fourth person climbed up the step and got into the coach beside Lady Pamela.

"What's this?" said the Albino belligerently. "I don't work with no amateurs."

Leedes blustered in his boorish way and fluttered a handkerchief in the air. "But it—it's—"

"Kindly don't splutter so, Mr. Leedes," Lady Pamela snapped before turning to the Albino, drawing a deep breath, and facing down his surliness. "Without this *amateur*, you'll likely not catch your prey, sir. Do you think even a stupid Irish girl would willingly go off with a man who looks like you?"

The Albino tensed and rammed his fist against the coach door. "You wouldn't be bothered by my lily white skin, now, would you?"

Lady Pamela swallowed nervously. "Of course not. That was tactless phrasing on my part," she said quickly. "I only meant a man as obviously dangerous as yourself needs a—shall we say—a lure. If you'll listen just a moment, all will be clear."

She smiled ingratiatingly and with deliberate flattery welcomed her fourth passenger. "How good of you to join us, dear. You're so very loyal to me."

Her voice turning icy, she added, "I was just telling these—uh—gentlemen, how much we're counting on your help."

Twenty-One

KNEELING IN THE grass, Aileen looked up from the patch of dandelions she was clipping and pulled a hand across her forehead, searching for Seamus and Patrick. It was still difficult to let them far from her sight, and she didn't breathe easy until she saw them playing across the meadow. They were near a stand of trees, not far from the London road along which a donkey cart plodded.

Seamus had been letting Patrick play the Fian, much to the little boy's delight. Already they looked healthier. A few days of sunshine and fresh air had brought a glow to their eyes and spirit to their play.

Oh, life wasn't easy yet. Aileen still felt jumpy when strangers approached the gypsy camp. She watched until the donkey cart passed safely by before bending to her work again, and it was some time later, at the unmistakable sound of horses' hooves trotting along the road, that she looked up, instantly alert again for Seamus and Patrick's safety.

The horse and rider had stopped. Nervous, she stood up, ready to run to her brothers, who jumped up and down around the intruder. Dropping her basket, she started forward at once, opened her mouth to warn them away, then stopped.

The horse was black. The rider, a man dressed in dark riding trousers and open-necked white shirt, looked heart-breakingly familiar. Windblown brown hair whipped about his brow. If she were close enough, she was certain he'd have hazel eyes, a cleft in his chin, an aristocratic profile. He might even call her banshee and say he was glad to see her.

"Tyson," she said softly, so quietly that only her heart could hear.

As if he'd heard her, he immediately turned to where she stood in the field of dandelions. He smiled and began to dismount. She was running then as fast as she could, barefoot, across the field, smiling, biting her lip to hide her childish joy. Her only thought was that he cared for her. He'd come back because he cared.

When she was a few yards away, she slowed down and walked, ladylike, to where he stood flanked by her exultant brothers.

Patrick jumped up and down. "The Fian's come to see us, and I'm going to show him our vardo." Already he tugged at Tyson's arm.

Seamus stood looking rather manly, as if anticipating more adult conversation with the Fian. Tyson didn't take his eyes off of Aileen, and finally Patrick stopped talking and waited, smiling, to see what his sister would say.

"Hello," she said, feeling flushed, tousled, not certain whether she should call him Fian or Tyson.

"Hello, Aileen," he said, his gaze steady on her.

The silence stretched, palpable, between them.

"You've come back." She said the obvious.

With a word of caution he handed Cormac's reins to Seamus and Patrick and took a step toward her. "I brought you passage to America. Roddy sent enough for third class, but I think, considering you were my—accomplice—I could at least help you travel more safely."

"I see." She felt as if the breath had been knocked out of her. He'd come all this way only to make certain she left for America. Fighting disappointment, she looked at the ground. She was barefoot. Barefoot and an Irish peasant lass. What had she expected? That he'd come and say he couldn't live without her? Tears blurred the ground where she stared at the unlikely combination of her bare toes and his fine leather boots—the boots of a gentleman.

When she fought the storm away, she saw that he'd moved closer. He took her arm, gently, but his words were directed at her brothers.

"Take the horse over to the vardos for me, will you boys? I want to talk with your sister alone, and after dinner we'll talk—man to man. Is that a satisfactory arrangement?"

"You'll tell us what London's saying about the Fian then, won't you?" asked Seamus.

Patrick jumped up and down. "And you'll give us a ride on Cormac?"

"Yes."

"Now?" Patrick asked.

"No, not now. Now run and tell the Romanies that they've a friendly guest for supper and finish your sister's chores for her. Will you do that for the Fian?"

"Faster than you can talk to Aileen," Seamus said.

Tyson's eyebrows shot up in surprise. "That fast? If your sister and I talk longer, you mind me and stay close to the camp—Fian's orders. You're not to stray so far off. It's the Romanies who look out for you, not the passing villagers. Do you promise that to the Fian?"

In quick agreement they nodded and led the horse off. Standing side by side with Tyson, Aileen watched them go.

"Where can we be alone?" he asked, staring after them.

"By the pond," she said, dreading the coming conversation.

By turns they were silent or talking about the boys until deep within the canopy of the forest, he stopped her in her tracks.

"Aileen—" he began, his voice very quiet.

"Why did you come?" she asked, studying the leaves on a particularly young elm.

"Aileen, I want to talk to you." He turned her by her shoulders.

She sighed. "You shouldn't have come, you know. You could have been followed, and as you can see, we're doing fine here. In any case, I can't accept money from you. You found my brothers for me, and that's all you ever owed me in exchange for my—work."

"You ask too little of me, then," he said, his fingers on her bare shoulders, rubbing little circles into the silk of her skin.

"There's nothing I need." She looked up, unable to see the rest of him for the green of his eyes. Behind them in the woods a lone bird trilled.

"It's true. The village is full of kind people who've wanted many fortunes told, and there's a music teacher who wants to copy some of the gypsy music. The boys are eating well. They're growing strong again before the voyage, which we haven't even set because of course it all depends when the gypsies get us to Liverpool, but I don't mind the wandering life. You see," she said a bit breathlessly, "I wandered around London so much—from Kate Reilly's to the Seymours' house to Marcus Owen's to Newgate—"

He flinched as if she'd hit him. She changed the direction of her words, striving to make her life here sound idyllic.

"We're happy here. There's nothing we need."

"When you chronicled your wanderings in London, you left out the time on the barge with me."

"Did I?" She looked away just a second. "I—I forgot."

"Aileen, I don't believe that," he said, his gaze so close her senses swirled. He looked entirely too serious to suit her.

Afraid of revealing her emotions, Aileen broke away and ran deeper into the woods, not stopping until she stood barefoot beside a sun-drenched open spot, ankle deep in the pond.

She knew of course he'd follow, and she stood there waiting for him to catch up. "I said I was going to show you the pond, didn't I?" she said with a bright smile.

He stopped a few yards from her and looked at her while she ran her fingers down the folds of the skirt, scarlet colored and in the gypsy style. His gaze followed the movements of her hands, then wandered up taking in her loose blouse, her flowing black hair. "Why do you keep running away from me?"

"Why did you come back?" she countered, chin up. "I told you—I—I don't need your help anymore."

He had kicked off his boots and moved toward her. "I don't want you to leave at all, banshee."

She felt a million emotions play across her face. They were all mirrored in his eyes. She didn't want to ask what he meant, so she decided herself on his meaning. "You should want me to leave. You're quite right to accuse me of being a banshee—from the night we met, I've brought very bad luck to you. I've brought you social ruin. I've caused Digby's death, and practically had you killed, and—"

He pressed a finger to her lips. "All those awful things would have happened without you. You've not brought the bad luck at all. You've brought me the good. Do you hear me?" Gently he let his hand slide down her chin and throat.

She swallowed hard. So perhaps he did care. . . . But they weren't suited. "We discussed this once before. There must be dozens of ladies back in London who suit you better."

"I don't want any of those ladies."

"Why not?"

She saw the smile play about his eyes, as if he were amused. Now she wasn't sure what he wanted, but it couldn't be healthy for his life and safety. She backed up deeper in the pond.

Oblivious of the effects of pond water on his trousers, he closed the distance between them and, reaching for her, looked into her eyes.

"Does the fact that I've aristocratic ties to London bother you then very much?" he asked softly.

"Very much."

"Why?"

"Because it makes us different."

A smile twitched at the corner of his mouth.

"I mean, of course, that you're meant for a lady of society."

"I disagree. I'm not at all meant for such a lady."

"We have nothing in common," Aileen whispered, her reasoning nearly gone, intoxicated as she was by his touch.

"We have much in common," he countered, looking at her lips as if he were going to kiss her.

She swallowed hard. "Such as Ireland, you mean."

"That's one rather obvious area of agreement."

"I've ridden as the Fian," she said.

His eyes momentarily darkened. "Unfortunately, yes."

"We've kissed?" she said, unable to hide her blush.

He smiled. "Indeed. You're coming closer to the answer."

"Many London aristocrats have attractions to Irish maids—

with . . . with unexpected consequences, I imagine. If you've come to soothe your conscience, you can rest easier. I'm not carrying your child." She'd actually been disappointed to learn so and saw the flicker of disappointment cross his face. Before he could recover from her words, she continued. "So, you see, there was really no reason for you to come . . . or stay."

"Aileen, I didn't come for so cross a reason. We have more in common than that."

She turned a stubborn back to him. "Sure and you've the wisdom of the Fian. So where is this good luck I've brought?"

"Love," he said quite simply, "is usually kept in the heart."

"Love?" Stunned, she whirled toward him. She wasn't surprised for herself. She'd known for so long how much she loved him. It was hearing him say the word that startled her so.

"Love," he repeated quite calmly, and then, pulling her into his arms, he began to do the most delicious things with his lips—all the things she'd come to know during their short time on the barge, and against her better judgment, she found herself responding.

But once again this was a different kiss—this one was complicated. It had to with . . . with—

"You can't love me," she said, abruptly backing away, moving deeper into the pond.

For a split second he looked stunned, then, with passion blazing in his eyes, he waded in after her. Waist-deep in pond water, he fought off lily pads to get to her. "Lass, peeling you out of wet clothes is continuing to be a habit between us."

He didn't have to remind her what would happen next. Aileen moved behind a fallen log, hanging on for balance.

With an exasperated sound, he suddenly dived under the water and came up on the other side of the log, next to her. With no warning, he grabbed her, and with easy movements pulled her closer, locking their bodies together.

"Let me go," she said, laughing. "You impudent Englishman!"

"I told you long ago—I'm not an Englishman. I'm as Irish as you are. How do I get you to believe me?" He pulled them both down so only from the chin up were they out of water. "Seymour's spy, Lady in Blue, banshee, Irish lass—why do you get to play at all these roles and not me?"

"Are you aware that we'll soon be in over our heads?" she said.

"You, my love, have been in over your head since you met me . . . now, why aren't I supposed to love you? Tell me, banshee." Grabbing her wrists, he began to slide her underwater. His hands slid from her wrists down her arms to her torso where he held her just beneath her breasts.

She reached for his hands.

"An answer, if you please." His hands moved up to tease her gypsy blouse from her shoulders while at the same time he began kissing her throat.

"No."

"No, what? No, you'd rather I didn't peel off what's already wet, or no, you refuse to answer?" he asked, continuing his sensual exploration.

"Both."

He grinned. "Do you realize that because of you, I've lost my social standing in London?" He reached behind her neck and lifted her wet hair up and over her shoulder.

"I've made you a social outcast?"

"Forever."

"I'm sorry."

"I'm not," he said, arranging her hair with more care

than he'd ever given a cravat. "I've never had the desire to live the life of the London aristocrat. To me, it was a mere convenience, one I'd gladly give up."

"And what of the Fian? Would you give that up?"

His hand stopped where it was, near her cheek. The only movement was the water dripping off his forehead. For a long moment he looked at her, disbelief filling his eyes. "You jest. That's as much of me as the banshee is you."

"You have to understand, Tyson—aristocratic men don't love Irish servant girls. They're supposed to love—"

"I've never been impressed, my love, with what I'm supposed to do."

He touched his lips to the hollow between her breasts and the sensation jackknifed her. Delicious pleasure sluiced through her, and when he pulled her up, she wrapped her legs about his torso. He carried her out to the edge of the pond and set her down, ankle-high in water. Even though the afternoon sun burned down, she shivered.

He pulled her close. "In fact," he continued, "if I want to love an Irish servant girl, I'll do that, too, over all your objections." His lips lingered against hers, tasting her. "I'll kiss her, too," he added, "and there'll be nothing you can do about it."

No, there wasn't. This kiss held no proprieties, no correct behavior. It was abandoned, flagrantly shocking in its forwardness. When he stopped kissing her, he was as breathless as if he'd taken her underwater again.

"You never kiss me the same way twice."

"Don't I?" A teasing gleam appeared in his eyes. "But, Aileen, you must understand about us aristocrats. We never kiss a maid the same way twice. Maids, for some peculiar reason, are much more critical of mere aristocrats."

"And why would that be?"

"Perhaps because their feelings keep changing. . . ."

"And could the Fian, then, change his feelings about the cause?" She felt him go as utterly still as if he'd been shot.

"I can't give up the cause," he said. "It's my life."

She watched the water drip off his clothes, sun glinting in his hair, molding his shirt and trousers to his body, leaving little of his masculinity to her imagination. "Then what would I be if I stayed with you? When you're the Fian, you're wild . . . dangerous. You—you have no place for a woman. Digby said so."

"For you there's always been a place."

"And where will that place be when the Fian is hanged for treason?"

He stared at her. "Lass, I can't stop loving because there's a price on my head."

"In America the Fian would not have a price on his head."

"In America the Fian would not exist. Stay here with me," he asked. Pensive, he looked at her, by turns so tender and frustrated that she felt as if she'd snapped in two.

She reached up and touched his cheek. "I've loved you longer than you know," she admitted, "so much that I can't stay and see you die. Digby would have understood. Why can't you?"

He pulled her hand into his, his voice intense. "I don't want to understand anything anymore. I want to love you. Nothing more. Why can't you accept that?"

She brushed a drop of water from his lashes. "You haven't lost me—not my love. I'd gladly have born your child—me, a good Catholic girl—just to take a part of you with me. . . ." He stood still watching her. "Don't you understand?" she pleaded. "I'm the one who spent the days in Newgate, who nearly faced the court. I understand the intrigues of London now, and I believe what Digby said— that death waits for the Fian."

"Have you turned coward on me?"

Nodding, Aileen watched one particularly wet droplet course its way down his jaw, then angle itself toward his neck.

Unable to resist, she leaned over, balancing herself with a grasp on his shirt, and boldly licked the errant drop of water from his neck. He groaned, backed up, and pulled her down into the water's edge.

They fell over into waist-deep water, wrapped in each other's arms while he began one by one to kiss the drops of water from her face, after which he captured one straggling drop that had fallen to her throat. "Temptor," she accused.

Imprisoned by his suddenly kindled desire, she tipped her head back and felt her hair sweep against the water's surface. All that escaped her lips now was a sound of pleasure.

At her moan he swept her up into his arms and carried her to a grassy knoll dotted by wild primroses. There, while the sun warmed them, he plucked off her wet blouse and skirt, and she followed suit, unbuttoning his shirt and placing her hand over his pounding heart.

He pulled her under him on a bed of grass, and by the time the sun had arched a quarter span in the sky, his hands once again knew every part of her.

Again his touch plied her with poetry. Like a new moon following the sun, Aileen, too, learned him in ways she never had during their few days on the barge. When a sudden cloud skidded over the sun, he completely covered her. She opened to his strength and his warmth, arching upward with him, moving inexorably toward fulfillment. The cloud dissolved into a thousand pieces, the sun burst again, and they lay spent, warmed by the afterglow of passion's ultimate duel.

He stared up at the sky, thinking, supreme weariness on

his face as if he were spent, defeated, and wondered when the stars might fall from the sky.

She lay propped up on one elbow, studying his chiseled face, touching the tempting cleft in his chin, giving in to temptations she'd denied herself in the haystack and even on the barge. She wished they were alone in the fields of Ireland and had no greater worries than the next crop, the next whitewash of the cottage, the next birthing of a child.

She realized on the barge she'd been the protected, he the protector, the teacher of tenderness. But in today's lovemaking something had changed. She understood her ability to hurt; she understood her desire to have his soul and felt infinitely selfish.

Coyness vanished, her hand strayed down the silken line of his stomach, his reflexes came alive as quickly as it took to grab her hand in his. He kissed the palm, then rolled her onto her back, buried his head in the hollow of her throat before calling out her name and thrusting deep within her, tenderly taking her to release. They were one, and she wept silent tears, dreading the pain of losing him.

They lay entwined until the sun ebbed, then slowly dressed. Seamus and Patrick called for Aileen somewhere off in the distance. She felt as bereft as Tyson looked. Across the meadow, the routine of the gypsy camp went on as if nothing had changed. Dogs barked. Children played. The aroma of herbs mingled with the profusion of wildflowers scenting the air. Her brothers were fighting— playing the game of English against Irish. Aileen smiled and leaned against Tyson. His arms came around her, and they stood listening together.

"Seamus lets Patrick take the role of the Fian once in a while now," she said softly.

"But I wager, Aileen, that as Seamus becomes a man, and such games turn into reality, he'll not give it up for good—not the Fian." Even though he held her so close that his words were soft in her ear, she still shivered.

"No man has ever given up the Fian," he said sadly.

"Not even for love?" she asked.

He shook his head. "Only for death."

Twenty-Two

EVENING CLOSED IN, and Tyson fulfilled his promise to spend time with the boys. Aileen watched them now, far across the meadow, taking turns riding Cormac. She helped the Romany women crush herbs but couldn't force herself to join in their chatter about the villagers.

She felt too torn over Tyson. Over America. Tyson loved her and had dropped that announcement in her lap like one would an unexpected gift. Did she have the right to fling such a gift back in his face? She felt as well the pressures of time. When Tyson had gone off to play with the boys, he'd given her no inkling of how long he was staying. The next time he left, she knew it would be forever, as America would be forever for her. She felt utterly torn and shaken by his declaration of love.

The sudden sound of a wagon on the road from London caught her off guard. As was her habit lately, she looked up to see who it was, and what she saw made her catch her breath. Riding high in the wagon was a young girl with brown coils above each ear. Dressed in mauve dress and black shawl, the visitor looked so much like Maeve that Aileen could scarcely believe her eyes.

After a brief word to the other gypsies, she walked closer to the wagon, certain that her eyes were playing tricks. They weren't, and she felt immense surprise and pleasure. "Maeve. It *is* you!" Maeve's face was mottled red from crying, her skirt dusty from the long ride, and at once Aileen said, "What's wrong?"

"You were going to leave England without me?"

Aileen frowned and reached up to touch Maeve's hand. "Why, no," she said reassuringly. "That is, I didn't mean to leave so suddenly. I had no choice. . . . How did you find me?"

"Tyson Winslow told me. . . . I—I waited outside the Parliament buildings for him."

"Truly?" Aileen frowned. It seemed so out of character for Tyson to tell anyone where he'd hidden her. On the other hand, Tyson did know Maeve was her friend.

"That's not all I found out, Aileen," said Maeve, climbing out of the wagon, shoulders shaking with grief. Her eyes were red-rimmed.

"What is it?" Aileen felt uneasy.

"It's about Mr. Winslow. You have to know something."

"Do you know he's here now, Maeve?"

Maeve seemed surprised. "Is he? Then he mustn't see me. Please, Aileen, you've got to know something." Maeve began walking away from the wagon, toward a stand of trees by the road.

Aileen still felt Tyson's arms about her, his words of endearment, the way he'd made them one. Despite her own misgivings about staying with him, she found it hard to believe he'd done anything very terrible. Now, Maeve had her curious. Even so, Aileen felt certain she could explain away whatever Tyson had said or done to upset Maeve.

"Maeve, Mr. Winslow leads a very complicated life. You're probably exaggerating what you heard."

"I heard it from one of Lady Grenville's friends—when I was fitting a dress for her." Maeve's eyes darted back and forth, as if nervous. "He won't hear me, will he?"

Aileen reassured her that Tyson was away across the meadow with her brothers and couldn't possibly overhear whatever dreadful news she had. If only the girl would stop moving so.

"Maeve, stand still and talk to me." What could be so dreadful? Had Tyson become engaged to a London beauty and merely come to Aileen for easy love before marrying some fine lady?

As Maeve, sobbing, backed up farther into the trees, Aileen followed. "Please tell me."

"I can't talk to you here, Aileen. If Mr. Winslow even sees me, he'll know I'm going to tell on him." Eyes red, she continued to back deeper into the wooded area.

Listening, Aileen felt jealousy race through her, ending in a knot in the pit of her stomach. There were so many fine London ladies who would want Tyson. She followed the sobbing Maeve, half running to catch up with her.

"Please, try to stop crying, Maeve, and tell me what it is about Tyson that I need to know. . . . Maeve, please."

She reached out for Maeve's sleeve, but all at once someone reached out from behind and clamped a rag to her mouth. The cloth scratched and, worse, smelled vile. The scent made her head spin in intoxicating circles. She tried to call out and warn Maeve, but couldn't utter a word. She saw Maeve's face, strangely close, eyes glittering with satisfaction. Strong arms and dizzying fumes threatened to overpower Aileen. Desperate for fresh air, she reached up to drag the cloth from her mouth and nose. As the world about her spun and grew gradually darker, she heard Maeve call as if from down a long tunnel.

"No, don't touch me. You know I'm part of the plan. You can't do this to me. It's Tyson Winslow they want. . . ."

*   *   *

All the time he played with the boys, Tyson's thoughts were never far from Aileen, wondering how he could convince the stubborn little beauty of his love. He'd never felt happier and more miserable at once in his life. Above all, he didn't want to leave her, and in the back of his mind constantly wondered how he could convince her he meant what he said.

Finally, when she never came to check on the boys, he grew worried. If she was avoiding him this long, perhaps she meant it when she said she wouldn't stay with him. But then, what had he offered her? "Stay with me," he'd said. As what? His mistress? He'd never, he realized, said the word marriage. Perhaps that would change her mind.

"Seamus, we need to give Cormac a rest now. Take him over by the other horses and brush him. Patrick, where's your sister? Go look in the vardo, would you?"

Tyson himself prowled the camp, and just in case his imagination was playing tricks, he returned to the pond where that afternoon he and Aileen had made love. He stood there at the water's edge, alone. He'd nearly lost her twice before. It couldn't happen a third time. He wouldn't let it.

Those Romanies who were willing to involve themselves in the troubles of the gorgio checked inside every vardo, then fanned out to comb the woods and meadow. A pair of Romanies visited the village, returning to report that it was shuttered and asleep. Most shrugged. One old gypsy woman smiled slyly. "A visitor came."

Tyson smiled. "I know." He was the visitor. Who else would find her here?

But when Patrick came running back, saying, "Aileen's not there. I can't find her," Tyson felt a knot tie itself around him.

Feeling fear now, he quickly found the sly old woman again. "Who was the visitor?"

"A girl. A gorgio girl. A friend, she said." With a nod of her head she indicated the stand of trees near the winding road to London.

In quick long strides he was there, searching, seeing at once the signs of struggle—the branches broken off a young elm tree, the flattened saplings, and—caught in a pine tree—a torn piece of fabric, red, the color of the skirt Aileen had been wearing.

Something more ominous troubled him, too. Instead of the loamy scent of spring earth, instead of the woodsy scent of newly burst leaves, the air was overladen with the noxious, still nauseating scent of ether. Chloroform. If Aileen had vanished without a sound, that could explain it, and for a moment he felt sick with disbelief and stared down at the tiny scrap of red that was all he had left of her.

Once again she was gone, and the truth struck him in the gut when he returned to camp and found little Patrick sobbing on the steps of their vardo.

Stroking the little boy's head, Tyson picked up Patrick in his arms and carried him toward his horse, cursing himself for all kinds of a fool. Why had he left her? Just because she'd been safe this long didn't mean she still wasn't at risk—all the more so today because he'd come and run the risk of being followed.

Seamus came bolting toward him from the woods. Tears glistened in the boy's eyes. "What could have happened to her? She can't have been stolen . . . can she? We were supposed to be safe here. We're going to America . . ." he said, a note of doubt in his voice.

"It's my fault," Tyson said woodenly. "I didn't take enough care against being followed." His features were

stark, shocked, but he forced a lighter tone into his voice.
"I'll find her. She can't have gone far."

Already the Romanies were readying a horse for the boys
to use, while Tyson saddled Cormac.

"Where are we going?" asked a tight-faced Seamus, who
clutched Patrick in front of him.

"London—to find Nicholas Seymour."

"Does he know where Aileen's been taken?"

"If he doesn't, I'll make him find out." He held no
illusions about the abduction. Lady Pamela would have her
revenge. Well, so would Tyson. He'd fling the Fian at their
feet and let them kill the great legend. But he'd also kill the
man or woman who touched Aileen before he got to her.

The day's proceedings in the Commons had just gotten
underway when Tyson burst into the assemblage. Tyson
himself was still dressed in the clothes he'd worn at the
gypsy camp and cared not a fig what anyone thought of his
casual attire. He stood there surveying the scene—dismissing at once the few ladies and friends and reporters who
sat in the gallery area. From the corner of his eye he thought
he saw Marcus Owen stand up and come toward him, but he
ignored him, too.

A pair of bewigged clerks in black robes stared slack-
jawed at the sight of Tyson Winslow's less than genteel
appearance. The Speaker of the Commons was standing,
facing a table full of bills to be confirmed and appeared to
have just crackled open a sheet of parchment and taken a
deep breath in preparation for reading. Pausing, he looked
down his pince-nez at the latecomer who had so brashly
disturbed the solemnities. Nearby, frowning, stood the
sergeant-at-arms and the chaplain. Tyson spared them all an
impatient glance and noted with a rather detached interest
that the prime minister had turned quite white.

Then ignoring them all, their holier-than-thou stares and disdain, Tyson stood there, scanning the assemblage, looking for one person and one person only—Nicholas Seymour.

At last Tyson spotted the man he'd come for—smiling with arrogant conceit as if daring Tyson to interrupt.

While the Speaker began reading some officious speech about the proposed Corn-laws, his words were punctuated by the staccato clip of Tyson's boots on the floor of the chamber. The Speaker kept reading and Tyson kept walking across the room until Tyson tapped Nicholas Seymour on the shoulder.

Seymour turned, by now red-faced, expression bordering on apoplectic, frowning at what he obviously considered a shocking breach of propriety.

"I want to talk with you," Tyson demanded.

Seymour glared. "You've a bloody awful sense of timing. I can't walk out now. It'll have to wait, Winslow."

Oblivious to the shocked gasps around him, Tyson grabbed Seymour by the lapels of his fawn frock coat and lifted him up from his place on the bench. "It can't wait."

The Speaker nervously droned on. Nicholas Seymour cast a quick look in the direction of the prime minister, bowed his apologies, as did Tyson, and the two men backed out until protocol allowed them to turn and walk frontward toward an exit.

Tyson and Nicholas Seymour got as far as a cloakroom where workers had abandoned piles of stones and boards, work on reconstruction at a temporary halt. Tyson placed a hand on Seymour's shoulder and swung the man around, pushing him against a pile of oblong stone.

"Where is she?" Stone rasped against stone, and fine dust flew up around the men.

A humorless smile creased Seymour's smooth features,

and his eyes might have been cold marble. He brushed some of the dust off his cravat.

"Where?" shouted Tyson.

"Who are you talking about?" Seymour asked. He had recovered his usual expression of studied boredom.

"You know damn well who I mean—Aileen." His hands curled into fists at his sides, and he yearned to pound Seymour's sanguine features into the bricks. "She worked in your house at one time, Seymour."

"Ah, yes, of course. Lucy's maid, if I recall." His voice held nothing but deprecation, and he smiled. "Really, Winslow, didn't you get enough of her in your bed?"

At that Tyson reached for the elegant new walking stick Seymour sported, a cherrywood piece with an ivory duck carved onto the handle. He snapped it in two and tossed the pieces onto the construction workers' debris. "You pompous bastard."

Seymour sneered. "I told you—you could at least have restrained yourself until Parliament adjourned for the day. When the queen hears about this, she is going to be annoyed."

"Which will set back your ambitions to gain her favor, won't it?"

Seymour looked from the broken walking stick as if this interview were no more than a boring nuisance.

"Where is she?" For Tyson self-control was becoming more and more elusive.

"The queen? In her palace, I imagine."

"You know I'm speaking of Aileen Connolly."

"My wife handles the servants in our house."

"Including using them to trap the Fian."

Seymour smiled, a thin-lipped imitation of amusement.

"I always knew the Fian was you. I only lacked the proof," he said regretfully.

Tyson stood exposed and didn't care. "And you—you've broken every law of child and man, and on top of that you're a murderer. Unlike you, I don't lack proof."

Nicholas Seymour's face paled, the smooth marble features wrinkling in bewilderment.

"On what authority do you have that?" he asked, obviously shaken.

Tyson allowed a pause, during which only the sound of voices from the Commons chamber filtered out to them.

"I asked you . . . on what grounds do you dare impugn my reputation?"

"The dockside accident," Tyson said quietly. "Years ago you ran down a woman with your coach—an Irishwoman."

Seymour's attention was riveted, his face pale. "How could you know—" he blurted out, then paused, staring off in the distance, as if remembering. "The boy. That was you." He looked at Tyson with vague amusement. "If I recall, I lashed out at you with my whip, didn't I?"

Tyson didn't care to relive the details. "That was my mother you ran down, Seymour. For years I've waited, biding my time to expose you as the murdering lout that you are. Exposing your slave factory was a fair start, but kidnapping and murder are so much more. Whatever I do, know this, Seymour—your political ambitions are as good as finished. I hardly think the queen will tolerate a prime minister who's a murderer, do you?"

Tyson watched while the Honorable Nicholas Seymour loosened his cravat, as if the room were suddenly too warm.

"You can't totally ruin me, Winslow. That was an accident. The court records say so."

"And Aileen's abduction? That's no accident. Who took her—the Albino?"

Seymour turned pale. "You still can't prove anything.

Who'd believe a highwayman against me, Nicholas Seymour, adviser to the queen?"

"Nor can you prove I'm the Fian."

Seymour smiled again. "Then it appears we're at a stalemate—one which I gather neither of us is willing to break."

He started to walk away. "I'm prepared to break it, Seymour."

Seymour turned. "Oh?"

"I'm willing to trade information. You can keep all your murderous secrets, except one—the whereabouts of Aileen at this moment."

Nicholas Seymour frowned ever so slightly. "And what are you willing to trade? Some of your smuggling secrets?"

"A signed confession that I'm the Fian, that I've committed treason against this country."

The other man stood quite still, disbelief and temptation flickering across his features.

Tyson stalked across the hall to a lone desk, pulled a piece of parchment out of a drawer, and dipped a quill into an inkwell. He wrote a confession, then signed and blotted it.

When he stood up, Nicholas Seymour advanced and held out his hand for it, his gaze greedily devouring the parchment.

Tyson held it back, watching Seymour practically lick his lips. "It only needs a witness."

"May I?" Seymour reached for it.

"Where's Aileen?"

Obviously weighing his options, Nicholas Seymour looked with longing from Tyson's confession to the chamber where the prime minister sat. He turned back. "At an inn north of here on the road to Liverpool."

"Name it."

"The Briar Rose."

"If you've lied to me, I'll come back and kill you."

Tyson dipped the pen into the inkwell, shook off the excess, and offered it to Seymour, who smiled patronizingly, then bent to witness the document. "It matters little if you find her, Winslow. Enjoy one last toss in the bed with her. You'll be hanging by a length of hemp before the week's out."

Tyson shoved the piece of parchment at Seymour's waistcoat, already turning on his heel. Long strides carried him back outside to Cormac, calling over his shoulder, "That remains to be seen, Seymour. If I were you, I'd walk in there now and stop the proceedings so you can hurry and collect your bets on the identity of the Fian."

When Tyson looked back one final time, Nicholas Seymour stood staring at the parchment as if he didn't believe his eyes.

Satisfied that he'd done all he could, Tyson strode out of the cobblestoned yard of Parliament and left London.

Twenty-Three

WHEN AILEEN, GROGGY and nauseated, regained consciousness, the Albino dragged her out of a wagon and to the front door of a crumbling inn. For a few moments she held out hope that a caring keeper or an eventual mail coach might provide a means of escape, a hope that proved as fleeting as a snowflake on a maypole.

Even through her grogginess she saw that the walls of the place needed a new whitewash, the shutters needed nailing, the thatched roof needed patchwork. No innkeeper claimed this place, no traveler would stop here to seek shelter. And if the Fian came, he'd find death. It was up to her to help herself—and to protect Tyson.

Unexpectedly the Albino tightened his grip on her arm, and his voice in her ear came as a snarl, low and menacing. "Move on in so's I can collect my coins." With a last shove he pushed her toward the door.

On rusty hinges it swung open, and there stood Edmund Leedes, looking as satisfied as an ugly toad who'd just swallowed the entire lily pond. "Don't get up any hopes of rescue now," he said. "The railroad's bypassed this village and near to closed it down, so don't be expectin' ghosts of the past like mail coaches."

Behind him, trembling with the anticipation of a society hostess about to receive royalty, stood Lady Pamela, regal in velvet, yet somehow childish with her hair hanging loose and beribboned. She cast a nervous look at the pistol before turning to grace Aileen with a smile.

"Good evening, Mary Aileen. I missed saying farewell when you left my employment in London. For your admirable work I'd have given you something extra, a guinea, say—had you bade me farewell." Her eyes narrowed, a cat about to pounce. "And had you not spied on my household."

Aileen stood there, chin up, not replying, but Maeve, sprawled prone on the ground, filled in the silence with retching caused, no doubt, by the effects of the drug. Finally she lifted up her head to complain.

"You deceived me. I was supposed to help you get Aileen. I've been loyal."

Aileen felt her heart stop. Once again the Fian's words of long ago came back to haunt her. *Trust no one, not even me.* Not even Maeve. Maeve. How could she?

"Pull yourself together, Maeve," Lady Pamela ordered, her gaze shifting back and forth from the women to Leedes and his pistol.

"That—that ugly man had no business giving me the chloroform, too." Maeve sniffled.

"The Albino had to get you out of the gypsy camp."

"Maybe we don't need you anymore, lassie," said Leedes.

White-faced, Maeve dragged herself to her knees and finally stood. "But that's not fair," she whined. "You haven't paid me yet. I risked having the Fian catch me by going to that gypsy camp."

Faint suddenly, Aileen leaned her head against the outer wall of the inn, swallowing back her own sickness, breathing in deeply to clear her head. Orrisroot. Lady Pamela's scent. She felt her knees buckle.

Leedes pulled from his coat a sack of coins, which he tossed in the Albino's direction. Jangling the contents of the sack, the Albino turned to Aileen. "Have heart, luv," he said with a tweak of her cheek. "If you lure your man here, they may spare you." Laughing, he sauntered out, stuffing the sack of coins down his shirt and vanishing into the English netherworld.

Still unable to fathom Maeve's treachery, Aileen looked around, thinking of ways to escape. Could she run? Not if Leedes was determined to use that pistol, which he poked against her rib cage. He nudged her toward the staircase leading upstairs.

On the way a pair of swords over the fireplace of the inn's abandoned taproom caught her eye. Such weapons held infinite possibilities for defending herself, except that Leedes and his pistol blocked the way to them. The pistol was a grievous nuisance.

As she walked upstairs, she thought about that long-ago night in the church—the night she'd met the Fian. Somehow the Fian had knocked a pistol out of Leedes's hand, but she had no idea how he'd done it, and hated her incompetence. There had to be a way to escape.

Lady Pamela had preceded them and at the top of the stairs stood waiting. She took the pistol from Leedes and held it with as much enthusiasm as she might a snake.

"Leave us now so I may escort the ladies to their room. It's rude of me to keep guests waiting in the hallway, and besides, Mary Aileen needs to change into something prettier." She cast a disparaging look at the soiled gypsy garb and handed Aileen a white gown.

Deciding her best option would be to assess the escape routes from this "guest room," Aileen followed Maeve. They crossed the threshold of a dark attic room, a small place in which Aileen immediately spotted a window. She felt a ray of hope.

Leedes vanished and Lady Pamela invited the two women to use the pitcher and basin to wash away the dust from their hasty journey. Aileen stood still, wondering if she could overpower Lady Pamela.

"Do it, or I'll shoot this pistol," her former employer said. "My aim with weapons is not perfect, but the room is small. Turning the wavering pistol directly at Aileen, she added, "I've worked so hard to have the Fian captured, and you've been in my way constantly. If it weren't for him and then you, I could be much more socially prominent by now, you see. But you've one more chance to help me. I've even arranged for you to have your own personal maid. You've only to tell Maeve what you need, and she'll assist you. I shall make up another room in case the Fian comes. And Mr. Leedes shall repair the lock to this door." Before Aileen could respond, her captor was gone.

Dear God in Heaven, Lady Pamela was insane, living in a child's world where she was still some impoverished earl's little girl. Lady Pamela—a child both in the title she insisted on clinging to and in her world of pretend. It was more imperative than ever that Aileen escape.

Aileen lit a candle on the washstand, and gradually she was able to examine her surroundings in more detail—a damask-covered tester bed, a gilt chair, a Queen Anne table complete with tea service and fine china—all quite similar to the furnishings in Lady Pamela's London townhouse— except in miniature. Beneath her feet Aileen felt the luxury of a Persian carpet, the pattern sliced down the middle so that it would fit in the tiny room. Ignoring Maeve's sniffling, Aileen walked the perimeter of the little room, feeling for other doorways. There were none. That left the main door and the tiny window.

She looked up. Above her she saw the rough outline of an attic framework and the thin thatch of the roof. She noticed again the occasional bird land on the roof and peck away at the thatch. She wondered briefly how worn it was. Thatched roofs grew thin with age, and a possible source of escape began to form in her mind. But perhaps the window would be simpler.

She longed for the quiet to think, but the incessant sound of Maeve's sniveling precluded such luxury. In any case, she needed to time an escape. The Fian had taught her that. For a moment she stood still listening for the outdoor sounds of a horse on the road, most of all for Tyson.

Meanwhile, it was imperative she act normal. She decided to talk to Maeve, but what could she say to the girl after Maeve's deception? Through a haze, Aileen recalled the day Maeve had all too anxiously convinced her she should try for a post as maid at the grand Seymour townhouse, and suddenly the riddle of Maeve's strange behavior fit, like a glove going onto a hand.

"Maeve, how could you?" Aileen managed.

Maeve sobbed. "They tricked me. They used me."

"We're Irish, Maeve. Where do you think their loyalties lie?" She changed quickly into the new gown.

Maeve only sniffled again, a pathetic and weak sound.

"How long have you been spying for her?" Aileen asked, brushing her hair over her shoulders.

"Not all along," said Maeve, sitting nearby in a chair. "Not when we came over on the boat. But after, in the coach. She offered me work. She offered to pay me money. I needed money to buy pretty things. Dresses and capes. I wanted to attract a young man, but you being pretty wouldn't know the worry about that. . . . And now even they've double-crossed me. They told me they'd pay me to trick you out of that gypsy camp. They never said they were going to lock me up, too."

"You deserve to be locked up," Aileen said with uncharacteristic anger.

"A fine thing to say," Maeve pouted, beginning to cry. "At least you were my friend."

"Yes, I was your friend, Maeve. Was money worth that much to you, then, that you'd help capture Ireland's greatest hero?"

Maeve hiccupped. "I'm scared."

Aileen had no words of comfort and lapsed into silence.

When Lady Pamela returned awhile later, she smiled approvingly. "We'll have tea now," she said, seating herself in a gilt chair by the Queen Anne table.

Aileen shivered. Over by the door, Leedes, huffing and puffing, sat on the floor like a sausage stuffed in tweed. He made annoying tapping noises near the door. When Aileen, curious, glanced over at him, Lady Pamela's voice pulled her back.

"You'll never escape."

"We were free, like the gypsies."

"You'll never be free, either. And when your lover comes for you, we'll be waiting. . . ."

Beside her on another chair, Maeve whined over and over. "I'm scared. I'm so scared."

Aileen felt a dark cloud pass over her heart. If Tyson came to find her, she'd know he loved her beyond a shadow of a doubt . . . but there was the irony. The bitterest irony of all. If he came, she'd see him die. She saw the candle flicker into a double image and realized tears filled her eyes.

Leedes opened the door. "I'm going to fix this latch

now," he said. "Neither of you move. When the Fian comes to rescue you, he'll find it easy to open."

With the sudden realization of Leedes's intentions, Aileen stood up. "You're tying one of your exploding devices to the door, aren't you?" Her words held more anger than panic. If that exploding device went off, she'd never escape. Worse, she could never warn Tyson.

With a hysterical scream, Maeve rushed to the door, but Leedes blocked her exit. "Where do you think you're going?" he asked with a cold leer.

"You're not locking me in, too? I don't want to die. I helped you." Maeve sobbed.

Lady Pamela droned on, trying to calm Maeve. "Of course you have to stay with Aileen. She's my guest, and you're her maid. Besides, you don't think I'd trust an Irish girl to run around loose knowing the secrets you do?"

Maeve ducked around Lady Pamela and ran out into the hallway. "No . . . I'm leaving."

With one easy reach Leedes pulled her back.

Maeve ran to Aileen and fell at her knees, sobbing on Aileen's lap. "Aileen, I'm sorry . . . truly, I'm sorry. I only did it because I wanted pretty things."

"I know. You told me."

"Forgive me, say you'll forgive me before I die."

But it was because of Maeve that Tyson's life was at stake now, and for the first time in her life Aileen felt sorely short of forgiveness. Her reply came in a trembling voice. "I wish I could. May God forgive me, but I can't pardon you, Maeve."

"Then help me. Make them let me go. I don't want to die."

Aileen reached out a hand to Maeve's head. The girl was so pathetic. "I can't get myself out of here, Maeve. If you just wait with me, perhaps we'll be rescued." Aileen doubted that very much, but lying seemed to be the only hope of calming Maeve.

"No, no," Maeve pleaded, looking up with stricken eyes, her face wet with tears. "Don't you understand what Mr. Leedes is doing to the door? We'll die if anyone—"

Lady Pamela jumped up. "Shut her up."

Leedes was there, dragging a crying Maeve away out into the tiny hallway of the attic, and seconds later a muffled shot stopped Aileen from any thought of movement. Maeve's crying shut off as abruptly as the slamming of a door on a noisy room.

Aileen's heart stood still. She shut her eyes tight and leaned her head down, faint. Maeve. Oh, Maeve. Poor naive little Maeve. She wished now her last words to her had been kinder.

"Now, don't you move off that chair, Irish princess, or your fate will be the same." It was Leedes's voice.

Aileen tried to spit on his hand then, but her throat was so dry she couldn't.

"Leave off, you meddling doxy."

"Mr. Leedes, don't speak to my guest that way," Lady Pamela said. "Dispose of Maeve's body and then complete your work on the door . . . else the Fian will arrive and find us unprepared."

"We could stay and see him, have the satisfaction of knowing he's met his fate."

"Do you think I want to blow up with them?"

"I'll not fail this time."

"See that you don't, but as for staying, I'm really far too well bred to watch any more. . . . Too much blood for my taste, Mr. Leedes. I'm going for my horse."

"Leave, then," he told her, his froggish face gloating more than ever. "I'll stay with the Irish princess while she waits for the Fian."

Aileen heard Lady Pamela's footsteps recede down the stairs. She turned her head to try and see what Leedes was doing with the door. He shut it, but that didn't disguise the horrifyingly familiar scent of sulphur. The chloroform had made her ill and dizzy. The orrisroot reminded her of Lady Pamela's scheming. But sulphur. That reminded her of the Fian, of the night he'd first taken her in his arms and carried her away from death.

She crossed herself and said an Ave Maria for Maeve. But the time for grief was short.

She dragged over the gilt chair and stood up on it, watching Lady Pamela ride away. Crawling through this window, she realized, wouldn't do. Below the hard dirt of the innyard waited to break her into little pieces as surely as if she were a china vase. She looked up at her last option.

One piece of thatch was so bare it looked like a yellowed sheet in need of mending. One could practically see the sun shining through the bald spots. Here and there birds—nasty starlings—pecked away, and had Aileen been the heavenly mother, she'd have given all those dear little black pests an immediate cloud in paradise.

Positioning her chair so she could occasionally keep one eye on the road, she reached up and began pulling tiny handfuls of thatch from the inside of the roof. Bits of thatch fell onto her hair, her face, in her eyes. Blindly she kept on ripping.

Twenty-Four

As HE APPROACHED the inn from far down the road, Tyson heard the pistol shot crack through the window of the place. He spurred Cormac into a gallop, promising the beast a sweet pasture if he'd get him there while Aileen was still alive.

He moved his hand to within easy reach of his loaded pistol and was nearly there when another horse and rider came bounding down the road from the inn. He reined in and none too soon pulled to one side. A scruffy man on foot—a man of white skin and white hair—ran out in front of the retreating horse. At once Tyson saw it was Lady Pamela who rode, and the man on foot—the man with white skin could be none other than the infamous Albino.

"You cheated me on my coins!" the Albino was shouting, jangling a sack in front of Lady Pamela's horse.

"Get out of my way, you grotesque simpleton," she said, whipping the horse, her auburn hair flying about her face.

With swift reflexes Tyson detoured Cormac around a stand of trees. As he did so, the Albino reached up to take the whip from Lady Pamela. Without warning, Lady Pamela's horse, eyes wild, reared up. Before Tyson could react, Lady Pamela flew off, landing crookedly on the other side of the road.

Tyson had no time to stop, even when the Albino spotted him and rushed at Cormac, coming so close Tyson could see the reds of his eyes. With one swift movement of his leg Tyson kicked him in the groin and leveling his pistol, pulled the trigger, aiming not to kill but wound. Immediately after the shot cracked through the air, the Albino crawled up onto his knees, and then as blood began to stain his pants leg, he fell to the dirt.

Tyson dismounted at the door to the inn and strode through, calling Aileen's name.

Leedes was coming down the stairs, but as soon as he caught sight of Tyson, he stopped and with a smile acknowledged him.

"We knew you'd come."

"Where is she?"

"Your Irish princess? You'll have to search through every room in the inn, try every single door yourself."

Tyson wanted to unload his pistol into Leedes then and there, and cursed himself for wasting his shot on the Albino. Tossing down the useless pistol, he scanned the room until his glance fell on the antique sabers hanging in crossed position over the fireplace of the inn.

Grabbing one, he turned. At the foot of the stairs stood Leedes, a pistol pointed at him. Leedes pulled the trigger, but only a hollow click registered in the room. In disgust at his own apparent neglect, Leedes threw down the weapon.

Tyson teased the man's stomach with the tip of the saber and Leedes backed away. Again, Tyson moved close and taunted Leedes's stomach.

"Tell me she's still alive," Tyson said with icy calm.

Leedes blustered, backing away from the top of the saber. "Of course she's alive. What do you think I am?"

"Loathsome, Leedes. Utterly loathsome." He backed Leedes into the dining area of the inn.

Leedes picked up a stool and tossed it at Tyson, who immediately ducked.

When he stood again, Leedes, expression triumphant, had picked up the other saber.

Heavy of foot, Leedes could only jab at Tyson, who feinted first one way then another. He'd not held a sword since fencing class with Marcus Owen, but with Leedes as his opponent, he didn't need an expert's skill—quick mental reflexes sufficed.

Like a buffoon, Leedes jabbed, while Tyson easily moved this way and that, avoiding the fat man's thrusts until he had him out the door in the courtyard of the inn.

"Tyson," someone called from high up in the sky. "Tyson!"

When he heard his name float down from the sky, he recognized Aileen's voice. The sound was so sweet to his ears that he looked up, and Leedes's next jab skimmed the sleeve of his shirt, drawing blood from a skin wound.

"Tyson," called Aileen, a note of desperation in her voice. "Stay away . . ." The rest of her warning mingled with the sky and the birds, floating down so faintly he could scarcely believe what he heard. Had he heard her say the word *bomb*? When Leedes missed his footing, Tyson saw his opportunity. With one swift riposte, his sword blade sliced through the layers of fat that made up Leedes's paunch. Just as swiftly he pulled the sword back out and left Leedes staring down at the blood spilling out of his abdomen.

Leedes's eyes bulged in shock and horror. Dropping his sword, he lifted his vest gingerly, touched the wound, and brought his fingers up to see the blood.

Dropping to his knees, he felt his head go fuzzy. He

hadn't expected to face death, not yet, but he saw it coming toward him, like a raven, ready to carry him off.

It was too soon. He had his mark to make in society. He had places to travel, women to seduce, more exploding devices to invent. He had yet to see his name bandied about the London papers and in the London coffee houses. He was supposed to die of old age, in his bed, with admirers clustered round, telling him what a worthy life he'd led.

He looked up, the inn wavering in front of him. He saw darkness and light, saw the mediocre events of his life exit out of that inn, beckoning him to follow. No. Not yet. Not this way. Not like a dog lying in a pool of his own blood.

The solution to his dilemma came to him in a flash of clarity. Still lucid, thank God, he knew how he wanted to die—taking the Fian with him. There'd be more glory in that feat than all the plotting he'd done for the Seymours.

Tyson Winslow—the Fian—had already run into the inn, and the Irish girl's screams rang from the attic. Leedes only needed time—time enough to crawl up those stairs and pull open the door himself, triggering the latch that connected to the detonator on his primitive bomb.

On hands and knees he began crawling across the dirt toward the inn and though it required enormous gulps of air, he made it to the stairs and began dragging himself up, one step at a time. He heard his desperate inhaling and knew he sounded like a beached fish, gasping his last. One step after another, each slick with his blood, he crawled closer and closer to the door that imprisoned the girl.

From the attic Aileen could hear the grotesque grunting of Leedes, the sound coming ever nearer, and it didn't take but a single guess to know what the man intended. Leaning out the window, she called, "Tyson . . . On the stairs . . . Help me . . . The roof." She fell against the sill, exhausted.

Leedes's grunting increased in volume as did the *flop-flop* sound of his boots dragging their way up the stairs.

Her only hope lay in getting herself out that roof. Climbing back up on the gilt chair, she tore frantically at the thatch. She tore until her fingers bled from the tiny bits, but finally succeeded in pulling away enough thatch to expose a piece of sky the size of a bottle top. Then thatch fell in on her head, and she realized someone was up on the roof tearing from the outside.

"Tyson, is it you?" Her voice was hoarse from yelling, and she wasn't sure he'd heard her.

She reached up to tear away some more until one of his hands touched hers and grasped her tight, as if he'd never let her go. "Hang on, banshee," Tyson said, but the teasing endearment sounded more like "darling."

He pulled more away and then both her hands could touch his. Gripping her wrists, he pulled her up until her feet left the chair. It toppled over and her feet dangled. With a swift tug he pulled her through the roof, and when she came out, they toppled over into each other's arms.

Without wasting time he grabbed her hand and together they shimmied to the edge of the roof. She looked down onto a haystack, and the next thing she knew he was pulling her and she was falling free, falling, falling, until she landed in the hay, her gown tangled about her waist. Tyson held her tightly, then slid on down, and when she did the same, he caught her in his arms and ran for the far side of the yard.

Moments later an explosion rent the inn.

Aileen pressed her face to Tyson's chest and clutched his shirt.

"Don't leave me," she whispered against him. "I never meant what I said. I love you because you're the Fian."

"Would you love me were I not the Fian?"

"Of course, but—" She pulled away to look into his eyes. There'd been a cautionary note to his question.

He explained. "I've had to give up my identity, so there's an end to me as the Fian. . . ."

"You did it to find out where I was," she guessed.

At his silent nod she couldn't help frowning. "But you can't stop being the Fian. No one can take your place."

His elegant kiss to her hand told her of the infinite tenderness his words would hold.

"You've got it backwards, love," he said. "Many can take the role of the Fian, but no one can take *your* place. . . . Now are you coming with me and your brothers to this place called Boston in America. . . . or did you decide once again on returning me to London at pistol point?"

Smiling, she shook her head and moved into his embrace.

Epilogue

"BY THE AUTHORITY vested in me as captain of this ship, I now pronounce you man and wife." The captain snapped shut his Bible and peered from under bushy gray eyebrows first at Tyson and next Aileen, who with a tremulous smile looked up into her husband's face. She felt at once gloriously radiant and shy . . . and the moment was surprisingly bittersweet.

In brisk tones the captain said, "Well, you'd best kiss your bride, Mr. Winslow, and be quick about it before this ship heels again."

At the mention of the word *kiss*, Kit and Seamus both stifled giggles. Stern-faced, the captain turned to the three boys who were lined up like stairsteps.

"I wager these boys have never seen the bridge of a ship before, have you? Take my word for it, laddies, when I was your age, I found the bridge of a ship more interesting than kisses." Smiling at Aileen's blush, the captain herded Seamus, Patrick, and Kit out of the doorway and left the newlyweds alone amidst the mahogany sanctuary of the captain's cabin.

Gently capturing her face in his hands, Tyson leaned

down and touched Aileen's lips, gently as a mist lingering over her, until she felt the tides of passion deepening the kiss.

The sudden swaying of the ship broke the kiss and pulled both of them off balance and against the porthole where Tyson captured her between outstretched arms that braced the wall.

Aileen stared at him once more, resplendent in dark frock coat and trousers, and a cravat, which was so perfectly tied she couldn't resist reaching up to loosen it for him. As she did so, she felt his gaze rove over her, admiring her gown of blue, thinking of the attendant memories blue gowns held for them. It was a froth of blue—taffeta and lace—and she felt overdressed. But then, one didn't marry at sea every day of one's life. Nor even embark for America every day for that matter.

"Aren't you the least bit afraid?" she said in a whisper.

"Of my wedding night?" he replied with rich irony, a smile playing about the corners of his mouth, as with one hand he reached down to pull her to him.

She caught his hand and stayed it. "You know what I mean. Of leaving Ireland . . . leaving home . . . ?" Turning in his arms, she stared out the porthole. Land was still in sight, barely there, but visible, if one peered hard enough—misty, green, and growing smaller by the minute. She felt the keening pain of leaving, but as if he'd read her mood, one hand came down to link fingers with hers.

"Did I marry the right lass, the one who once declared she wasn't afraid of me or London or anything?" he reminded her gently.

"Aye, it's just . . . just that I'll never see Devintown again, never put flowers on the graves of my parents, never . . ." Her voice caught.

"Aileen—"

"We're leaving with nothing . . ."

She felt the comforting pressure of his arms circling her waist. "You're leaving with my love," he reminded her.

"Aye, I can go anywhere with that." She reminded herself he was giving up as much as she was.

"And if it would be enough, my arms would be your shelter, my lips your sustenance, my heart your home—"

"Whisht, your poetry is the Fian talking, and you promised the Fian would not go to America, that there'd be no more politics—"

"*Irish* politics."

"What of your promise?"

"You ask too many questions for a bride who should be anticipating instead her wedding night," he whispered close to her. After picking up her posy of roses from where it had fallen on the floor when the ship had heeled, he led her out onto the deck. There for a few more miles still they could look at the receding shore of Ireland.

She tossed the posy overboard, and together they watched the flowers land in the ship's wake.

The salt spray reached up and kissed her cheeks, and so again did Tyson, devastatingly gentle, genteel, aristocratic. Taking her hand, he tugged her away from the crowded railing and back downstairs to their cabin.

Wistfully Aileen wondered if the Fian was really gone. After all, a man didn't simply change overnight. But then, she reassured herself, if he was at all regretful at what he'd given up, she had an entire sea voyage alone with him—a long voyage—to put all thoughts of the Fian to rest. It would be as Tyson said. The Fian would live on in legend, in the stories of Seamus.

They entered the cabin, and she gave in to her curiosity. "Is the Fian truly gone forever?" She heard the bolt catch and looked up into the passion of his gaze. She caught her breath.

He closed the space between them, and she forgot that any other world existed but this man's embrace.

Was this Tyson? No. Even before his lips came on hers, she knew the answer.

It was the wild and dangerous kiss of the Fian—for her and her alone.

HISTORICAL ROMANCE —

—send in the coupon below—

To get your FREE historical romance and start saving, fill out the coupon below and mail it today. As soon as we receive it we'll send you your FREE book along with your first month's selections.